THE QUEEN'S TOURNAMENT

S. ANNE

To all who love a Hero, but know the Villain fucks better.

PRONUNCIATION GUIDE

Searaphina Satagra	Sarah-phin-a	Sa-tar-gra
Alathieria Satagra	Al-athi-eria	Sa-tar-gra
King Amard Satagra	Am-ard	Sa-tar-gra
Velasilio Vesariah	Vel-ah-sli-io	Ves-ar-iah
Arekin Lesana	Ar-ek-in	Le-sa-na
Kadance Zadieria	Ka-dance	Za-dier-ia
Datriminish	Da-tri-min-ish	
The kingdom of Neraphiana	Ner-phi-ana	
The kingdom of Vixeruas	Vix-er-aus	
The kingdom of Tarpidora	Tar-pi-dora	

CONTENT WARNINGS

This book includes themes of explicit sexual content, death of parents, blood, gore, death of mythical creatures, and explicit language.

Recommended for readers 18+ only.

TROPES:

Feisty FMC, Possessive MMC, Golden retriever MMC, Twin flames, Magical creatures, Slow burn, Spice, Deadly trials, Fantasy High Fae.

CHAPTER 1

WHERE IT ALL BEGAN

Searaphina

Startling awake, I sit up in a daze, my eyes heavy with sleep as I search my empty chamber for what has woken me. Muffled yelling and heavy footsteps come from my door. I slide from my silk sheets, a shiver wracking my body. Standing I move to my wardrobe, taking my over-gown and throwing it on. The icy floors numb my feet with each step towards the door; my hand shakes as I reach out.

My hand hovers over the door just as it is pushed towards me. The sudden movement has me stepping backward so quickly that I almost land on my ass. As I catch myself, my hands fly to my chest and I prepare to scold whoever dares to enter my chambers with such disrespect.

"How dare you..." The words die on my tongue as I am met with Velasilio's dark purple eyes, only they are red-rimmed and lined with unshed tears. Her silver hair looks like a Quartier's nest. My gaze searches her face; she looks ill and her mouth is slightly parted.

My heart begins to beat wildly as my breath catches at the sight of her. "Velasilio, what is wrong?" The noise around us is nothing but a buzzing as I reach out, placing my hands on her arms, moving them up and down to see if she is injured.

My search is halted as she places her own hands on mine. My eyes look back to hers and she sniffs before dropping my stare. Her voice is so quiet I almost get her to speak again. "I am not hurt but, Phina, it is..." A hiccup stops her from speaking.

I wait to see if she will continue, but she just sobs. I look over her shoulder to see what is going on. The noise hits me as the whole castle seems to be awake. All of the staff fill the corridor and I hear sobbing. I look at the entry to my room. Usually two guards stand at attention, but they seem to be more alert tonight with their hands resting atop their swords.

I look down once more at Velasilio. I do not mean for my words to be so harsh but my patience is wearing thin.

"It is *who*? What has happened!?" The demand seems to shake her from her sorrow. As she looks at me, her eyes search mine for the briefest moment before she opens and closes her mouth. And then she says it.

"It is the King and Queen." Dropping my gaze, she starts to toy with her overgown. My breath catches before I pull her further into my chambers.

"You need to wait here. I need answers."

I can see that only the guards seem to be moving around, possibly searching for some fae. All of the other staff are huddled in small groups, crying and speaking in hushed tones.

All murmurs stop as I enter the corridor, and they all turn to look at me. Then they bow deeply. Deeper than usual for a crowned princess. They seem to look at me with a different respect: the kind only given to a Queen.

The word is in my head now. *'But if they are treating me as a Queen...'* I turn down the corridor and begin walking.

My pace increases as the reasoning for their behaviour shines in my mind. The King and Queen must be dead.

I stumble a step and strong hands catch me. I look up into the eyes of a new guard, one who does not normally serve me. Turning in place, I notice there are four new guards behind me. They bow their heads but I see the sorrow on their faces.

The need to know the truth spurs me on and I walk with a brisk pace as I head towards the King and Queen's chambers.

Reaching the darkened stone corridor, I rapidly ascend the stairs. The sound of the guards' armor and their heavy steps follow me. The closer I get to the landing the less I hear, the world around me now a distant buzzing. My lungs begin to burn and my limbs grow heavy; when I crest the last step I am met with a stoney face that only softens when he realises who I am.

Galindor, one of my father's personal guards. His large arms are crossed over his broad chest as he bows his head. I wait for him to look me in the eyes.

Keeping his head down, Galindor stands strong and proud but the waver in his voice betrays him. "Princess... This is not something your father would want you to see. For his sake I cannot allow you to enter."

His words surprise me for a moment. Standing tall, I step up to him and demand. "You will step aside as your Queen commands it."

I notice the slightest flinch in his face before he steps to the side and bows. With a much softer voice he says, "You have my apologies, my Queen."

I take a deep breath to steady my nerves for what I am about to see. All I know is that they are dead.

As the door swings open, the pungent scent of decay and the metallic tinge of blood rush me. But there is something else in the air, something almost sweet. The odor is so strong I have to breathe through my nose or the taste will linger on my tongue.

The gruesome scene before me is more than anything my mind could have conjured. King Armard and Queen Althieria lay on the bed. It looks like they had been preparing for sleep. Their hands are joined in the centre of the bed and their legs hang from the sides. The Queen faces away from me so I am unable to see anything but the King is turned towards me. His skin is tinged blue and dried blood coats what I can see of his mouth. There are lines of ruby from his ears and eyes.

His stomach looks like it has been melted from the inside out. The flesh is gone and only a pool of guts remains. From what is still intact I can see part of what I believe are his intestines; they are now a deep green that seems almost black. I am unable to tear my eyes off of the pit of gurgling guts and blood that should be the King.

I am in such a trance that I almost jump when a soft hand gently takes my own. My gaze shifts from their bodies to Velasilio.

She dares not to look, her face is now green; the stench is powerful and would turn even the strongest of stomachs.

Her voice is quiet and full of sincerity as she suggests: "Come now, let the guards take care of them." I do not want to leave but, as she pulls me, I follow reluctantly.

Several guards, the council males and a healer are outside of the chambers. Each offers their apologies before moving into the room to assess the situation.

Velasilio begins to pull me along. My mind is in a frenzy as I begin to think of everything thatI will need to do.

I am Queen. I have been preparing for it all my life.

I am so in my own head that I do not even realise that we are almost to my chambers. The guards rush forward and open it for me.

Velasilio requests privacy, closing the doors. I know they will be on high alert and not leave their posts. I walk with numb feet to my bed and sit.

'It is all going to work out.' I am torn from my thoughts as Veal-silio speaks.

"Phina I am so sorry. We will find who has done this, I vow to you!" Her voice wavers as she tries to find strength after her loss. She steps towards me, and takes a seat beside me.

Shaking my head, I stand and snap at her: "Vow to me! What good are words? They are nothing but empty promises. All in this castle vowed to my mother and father and look what happened to them! Poisoned at their own daughter's birthday feast!" Moving towards my window, I look out to the moon, only just hitting its apex on a night that promised such joy that has now been tainted.

Velasilio follows me; she reaches out but stops before she touches me.

Turning from the view of my kingdom, I face her.

She seems so frightened—is it of me or what has happened tonight? She does not look at me, instead her gaze lingers out of the window, so I continue. "I do not mean to scare you, you have been the only one I can count on. Our bond is like no other…" Before I go on, her face perks up as if an idea has just come to her.

Turning on her heel, she all but runs from my room. I sigh before taking a seat at my vanity. Taking out a piece of parchment and an ink pen, I start to list all that will need to be done. Funeral. Inquest. Coronation. Before I can go on, Velasilio comes back in. Placing my pen down, I turn to her.

Raising an eyebrow, I cross my arms. "Would you care to explain why you rushed from my rooms, leaving me at my darkest hour?"

Her small smile falls before she straightens. Her voice is just above a whisper. "What you said about trust and our bond, it made me remember something I found." She looks to the scroll she holds.

She passes it to me. I untie the green, silk tie and unfurl the page, then read it over.

I feel the nervous energy coming from Velasilio. When I finish, I look at her, but she stares at the floor and picks at her nails.

"A blood tie?" The question lingers in the air.

Stepping forward, she explains. "I was in the library with your father." She flinches before she continues. "It was tucked into another book, one that had been hollowed out. It was about fevers and twin flames, so I thought best we read it knowing that both will soon be part of our lives."

I interrupt her. "Silio, get to the point."

Nodding her head once, she swallows. "Of course, I found it interesting but never expected we would need to use it. I thought that, since you are now so unsure, we could perform this ritual. We have everything needed and the moon is almost at its peak, so we must hurry." There is strength and determination in her eyes. She knows this is the only way I will be able to fully entrust her with my life.

There is an overwhelming optimism in the air. Being able to complete a blood tie with Velasilio feels right. An oath will be spoken to seal the tie around our hearts, souls and minds. This is the only way to ensure we never lose one another.

"If this is something you wish, I can think of no other I would bind myself to, not even a twin flame. What do we need to do?"

CHAPTER 2

BLOOD TIE

Velasilio

Rushing through the castle, I find what we will need: eight tall, taper candles, a sharp, silver dagger and a single strand of red twine. Searaphina awaits me in her chambers while I collect what is needed. My cheeks feel stiff and dry from the tracks my tears have left. The castle is in a frenzy and when I was stopped by several guards asking where the princess was I told them that she has found refuge in her chambers. They were quick to turn and stride in that direction.

I find the last item needed before rushing back to her room. Eight guards now stand at the doors, hands on the hilts of their swords, ready to defend their Queen. As I approach, they look ready to kill; a single hand comes out as a deep baritone voice speaks.

"Halt. What is your business with the Queen?" Dezmond's voice is stern and shows no hint of a jest. He knows who I am and that I would never harm Searaphina, though I understand why he has requested me to answer. Still, how dare they think I am of any threat to my Queen.

I am ready to yell and curse his stupidity. My cheeks heat and my heart picks up at his arrogance. I watch as the corner of his lip lifts, as if he knows exactly what he is doing.

Before I answer, I stop myself: this is not how a lady behaves. I cannot scream at a royal guard who is just doing their duty, no matter how much of a twatnuckle they are being. Inhaling through my nose and out of my mouth, I speak calmly.

"Dezmond, I am here to aid and offer the *Queen*." I make a point to emphasise that she is now the Queen.

His slight smirk drops and he narrows his eyes at my attitude before they go to the items in my hands.

"And what aid and comfort, will a bunch of candles and string be for our *Queen*?" He shoves her title back at me as he eyes me with suspicion. I thank Datriminish that I had the forethought to place the dagger in my boot.

"The candles are to light the room as she is feeling quite distressed and distrustful of the dark and the twine is so she may work on embroidery to soothe her nerves." Not at all what you would use for embroidery but I hope that he will not know this.

We stand still, staring at one another. Dezmond is one of the younger guards and has been a consistent rock in my shoe, always getting in my way and making excuses to stop me.

When he does not answer, another guard steps forward, scoffing at Dezmond, before pushing the door open. My smirk is nothing if not pure evil delight that he has been outranked; I fight the immature urge to stick my tongue out as I pass.

As soon as I enter the chambers I search for Searaphina. Then I see movement at the small window. Sitting on a stool as she watches the moon, it almost looks like she is speaking to it. Unable to take my eyes from her, I begin walking forward. I catch the upturned corner of the worn rug and stumble, causing a few candles to go flying. Searaphina turns quickly and it feels as though a heavy weight has settled over the room.

A shiver runs down my spine as her eyes appear to be glowing. I hold her stare for a moment before ducking down to collect the fallen items. "My apologies Phina, I was distracted, I did not mean to frighten you."

She stands and makes her way over to me. "That is quite alright, I am just shaken from the events of this evening, but we must hurry; if the moon leaves its peak before the ritual is finished we will have lost our only chance."

Now on her knees with me, she takes the candles and begins to place them into a circle around us. She seems to be in quite a rush. The moon must have moved quickly while I was out. Removing the parchment from the pocket of my gown, I re-read the instructions.

"The candles must be in a perfect circle, somewhere that catches the moon's light." Shuffling over on hands and knees, we move into the moon's rays and sit facing one another on our knees.

"Now we must light the candles." I stand and walk to the small fire, choosing two long, thin pieces of wood to light the ends. Sitting back in the circle, I face Searaphina and hand her one.

"We must start with the candle directly behind us, then we will move around the circle to our right. They must be lit at the exact same time. Ready?" She nods, and we begin.

With all of the candles lit, we face one another, and I offer Searaphina my flame. "Hold these while I tie the twine into a single knot." Placing the red twine between us, I take it at both ends and tie them at the base, creating a circle, signifying our lives tying together as one.

Placing the knot between us, I have to move quickly so that the flames do not burn out. I lay the blade and the parchment next to the knot before taking my flame back from Searaphina. I take a moment to look at her. She seems calm. There is an eerie, uncomfortable weight in the air and she does not seem to feel it.

"Phina? Are you okay?" My voice shakes slightly at the end even though I try to calm it.

"Oh, yes, very well." Her tone is flat; I wonder if she has frozen out all feelings.

I need to complete this ritual. I need to make her feel safe.

"We must burn the ends of the knot strings, one for you and one for me." I offer the tie to Searaphina. Taking one of the hanging strings, she burns the tip; I do the same to the opposite one.

"Blow out your flame." We gently extinguish the flames.

Picking up the dagger, I go to ask for her left hand but she already has it outstretched; I guess she read the paper between us.

"I am sorry for the pain I am about to cause you." I offer the apology as I take the blade and slice a thin line through her palm. The blood wells immediately but she does not make a sound, just keeps her hand open and flat. Moving quickly, I repeat this step on my right hand. I whimper at the sting.

I hold the twine between us. "You must rise on your knees for this part." She does, and I stay low on my own.

"Take part of the loop in your hand and hold it tight; the blood must flow to the knot." With a nod she takes the left side of the loop holding it tight.

I release my hold before I take the opposite side in my right hand. The frayed edges of the twine send small jolts of pain into my flesh as it feels like it digs into my skin, embedding itself there. The temperature plummets and a shiver wracks my body; my hand clenches tighter on the rope and my blood drips down. My gaze is caught on the sight as I watch it flow down the rope and meet Searaphina's at the knot, dripping to the floor as one.

The voice that leaves Searaphina is harsh and demenading. "Speak."

My eyes shoot to hers. She looks right through me, her eyes cold and distant, and I know I must finish this for her. I recite the words that must be spoken.

"I willingly bind my blood to yours, in trust, loyalty and love. I will never harm you through words, action or mind. We will be as one. If you are to lose your life, I will follow you into the dark. None will take your place. I vow that my life, soul and body are yours to protect and serve always."

With the last word the world plunges into darkness.

CHAPTER 3

COUNCIL MEETING

Searaphina

I am Queen.

The morning feels different. I feel different.

After Velasilio passed out last night. I quickly hid the blade and wrapped my palm before I called the guards in to place her on her bed and clean up the mess.

I convinced them we were praying to Datriminish, our one true god.

It is said there were three gods, one of light, one of dark and one of neutral magic, but now we only have Datriminish. We assume he is the neutral god, as magic has all but vanished, with only slivers of it to be found here and there, such as the binding we completed last night: rare and only to be used when it is truly life or death.

We have a minimal understanding of most magic. My teachers always wished for me to understand our dark past, so I have read many books to truly understand our history. I know what I need to do for my kingdom.

Over a thousand years ago, my great-grandfather fought a war against the Vixeruas kingdom. Emperor Kraetek ruled over all lands with an iron fist, not allowing any others to rise into power, and killing any magic users. He was afraid that, one day, another, more powerful fae would overthrow him, so he banned the use of magic unless it was under his instruction.

Many magic users were killed. Others were kept prisoner, not allowed to reproduce unless under his command; this is why we do not have any fae with more than a smidgen of lesser magic today.

Laying in my bed, I stare at the ceiling as my thoughts continue to swim about the past and what we could have been, what *I* could have been if magic was allowed to be free.

There will be a council meeting this morning. We need to discuss the funeral and my coronation. We will need to begin an inquest into the King and Queen's murder. King Baritus is the one with the most motivation to want them dead. It was *his* great-grandfather who kept us all under his thumb; surely he wishes to reign in the same way.

I am only two hundred and nineteen. I am not yet of age to marry, as my fevers will not begin for another two years. Unable to produce an heir and marry puts me in a dangerous position.

I think back to last night, to the vow that was made, and I am thankful to have a loyal fae like Velasilio by my side.

My spinning thoughts are interrupted by a gentle knock at the door. Sitting up, I call out, "Enter."

Velasilio steps in, two buckets in hand. Her eyes look puffy and her face is red.

"Morning Searaphina, I have warm water for your bath. May we enter?" Her voice is timid, not her normal tone at all. I wrack my brain to find out why she may be feeling off today.

"Please." I gesture with one hand to the bathing chamber doors. Shuffling in with two heavy buckets each, she and three other maids make their way across my room.

Standing slowly, I stretch out my tired muscles and pull on an overgown to shield my body from the cool breeze of the morning.

Once the sounds of sloshing water have finished and the other three maids have left, I make my way to the bathing chambers, where Velasilio waits for me. The scent of jasmine fills my nose; it is my signature scent, no others in the castle wear it or bathe with it.

"A warm bath to wash away the horrors of last evening." I try to add a bit of pep to my voice. The castle is sure to be in a gloomy mood today, I will need to lift spirits and remind them that, while this is a time of great sorrow, they do have a new Queen and we will need to celebrate.

Velasilio moves towards me and twirls her finger for me to spin, I give her my back and slip off my overgown, so that she may untie my sleep gown. Shrugging my shoulders I let the dress fall to the floor and step into the tub. She pours a few other liquids into the bath that clouds the water in a shimmery purple hue. I lift an arm out for Velasilio to help me wash. I bathe in silence and it is honestly needed as I make a list of everything that I will need to do in the coming days. There will be the funeral, coronation, investigation and the royal tour in hopes that I may begin to feel the first pull towards another.

Most twin flames do not reveal themselves until after the fae has reached their two hundred and twenty first birthday and are able to breed. Some *may* begin to experience the call to another before then, usually the males; when two males are fated they often know before their heats begin.

Males experience a heat whereas females experience a fever. Both end with you fucking the closest fae if you do not have a fated. This is a problem for royals: though a child may be hard to conceive, if one is out of wedlock they are illegitimate, and you are seen as unworthy to wear the crown. Others may then take the chance to challenge you and take the throne.

This is not something I will ever allow to happen.

he space of the council chambers is small, only just fitting the large, dark mahogany table and twelve chairs in it. My seat takes up the majority of the space at the head of the table, as it closely resembles a throne. It is times such as these I am glad I am able to retract my wings; trying to sit or sleep with them out is most uncomfortable.

Rows of small windows provide little light. I sit at the head of the room furthest from the door. To my right is a smaller chair yet no less grand for my consort, but is currently filled by Velasilio, showing her position within my court. Filling the other ten chairs are the council males. Each one shows signs of their age, from graying hair to long beards that would take more than one lifetime to grow.

Some of these males have been a part of the council since before my father took the throne. I will be the first Queen to have taken the throne by birth and not by marriage.

These males have never given the wrong advice and, as such, have held to their positions for far too long; times have changed and so has how the fae think. When the kingdom is settled I will request that they all step down and allow a new age of council males and females to step up.

Time moves so slowly down here, or at least it feels that way. My throne-like seat is becoming more uncomfortable by the minute. I am glad that Velasilio is here, she has a parchment and quill and is taking notes for me so that we can go through it all later if we need to.

"Majesty, how would you like to proceed?" Daterrit asks me in a calm voice. None of the others have spoken directly to me, only having quiet conversations about what to do next, how to go about finding the killers.

I have always wanted this, was raised for this, and now it is my turn to step up.

"We need to first hold a funeral. Any inquiry into their deaths must be kept private, we do not know who may have been a part of the assasination." A course of nods occurs as they wait for me to continue.

While their ideas may be outdated, I can see their loyalty is strong, maybe I will not need to be rid of them so quickly. "Next, we will need a show of strength. The funeral will be tomorrow morning and, in the evening, my coronation." I pause to see their reactions. Some try to hide their reactions while others raise a hand in the air to ask a question.

With a nod, I allow Jisip to speak. "I believe this to be a fine idea, to give the kingdom a bit of joy on an otherwise sad day. We will also then be able to announce an engagement soon after, as you will need to officially be Queen for us to begin to entertain suitors."

Frustration bubbles inside of me, I hold back the scream that gets stuck in my throat. I had thought that with my age I would be able to wait at least a year before they tried to push marriage on me. I may not be a virgin but I have not shown any signs of my fever or even an inkling to a twin flame.

More hands fly up and I continue to give them a chance to speak, something I soon regret. Being Queen is a challenge, but one I will rise to. Soon they are taking turns offering their opinions and arguments.

"No, the funeral is sacred and must be the entire day!"

"A new Queen is more important than the dead, if war comes to our door we need unity!"

"She is young and has not yet had a fever, there is no chance for offspring so we have time to let her find love, if not her twin flame."

"A twin flame is not an easy thing to find, what if she never does?"

Knowing I can at least answer these questions I clap once to quiet the room; to my surprise they listen. "I hear your thoughts and questions and now I will answer them."

Taking a deep breath through my nose, I exhale and continue to explain what we will do. They may be my advisers but in the end I am Queen and they will listen to me.

CHAPTER 4

RULES OF COURT

Velasilio

I had no idea how Searaphina was going to be this morning, with her parents' gruesome murders last night. I thought she may need time to come to terms with their death and being crowned at a young age. Many royals are wed by their two hundred and twenty first birthdays but not crowned until they have produced at least one heir. The chances to fall pregnant are slim as we only have a fever three times a year. Being unwed, without a child and the crowned ruler of Neraphina is unheard of.

The royal funeral will be held tomorrow as will the coronation. We have had correspondence from nearby islands that have spoken of Vixeruas warriors entering their land. There have not been any acts of aggression yet. The council is scared that they are preparing to invade so they wish to rush the funeral and the marriage.

Luckily, our land is separated by a large area of sea; it seems as though they are using these smaller islands as hopping stones to get closer to us. The kingdom of Vixeruas sits in the high north while Neraphina is to the south. There is one other large island to the east. That kingdom was destroyed with the fall of the gods, war broke out and not a single fae was left alive, now wild beasts roam the land freely.

"So it is decided then. The funeral is tomorrow morning, my coronation will be in the evening and the following day myself and Velasilio will leave for the royal tour. I will entertain any suitors who ask for an invitation to the castle or for a meal and if I feel a pull I will alert you all." Searaphina sounds so regal and leaves no room for argument. Looking around the table, I take in the many stunned faces of the males who seem to have expected their new Queen to be a little less sure of herself.

I feel an overwhelming sense of pride in her, she will be the Queen we need.

With everything planned right down to the tour that we will be leaving on in two days time, come the evening I am exhausted, and so is Searaphina.

I am bringing her food that the chef has prepared, the new royal taster has tried each item and cleared it of poison. Walking towards her chambers, I am greeted by the most annoying guard, Dezmond. His perfect white teeth shine at me as he tosses me a smile before he stops me with a hand up.

Rolling my tongue over my teeth, I bite my cheek before I say something rude to him. Instead I smile sweetly, "Yes Dezmond? Is there any particular reason that you have decided to stop me?" Okay, maybe I add a little sass to my tone. Unfortunately this only makes him smile wider.

"Oh I'm afraid I have to pat you down before you enter our Queen's chambers, new regulation." Standing in front of me, I have to look up into his dark amber eyes as they run down the length of my body before coming to meet my gaze once more. He is easily one of the more attractive guards, his hair is kept short and out of the way, his face clean shaven, his height is easily over six feet. Not especially tall but still much taller than I am.

Raising an eyebrow, I repeat. "New regulation?"

Nodding his head, he copies me. "Yes Miss, new regulation."

I cannot be bothered to deal with him this evening, it has been a long day. So I decided to toy with him. "Well if the Queen's dinner gets cold because you wish to throw your weight around and you do not mind dealing with her being angry that she must wait, then by all means *please* pat me down." I step forward, holding the tray to the side to offer him access to my body.

He stares at me, unsure of what to say, and then I hear a chuckle behind him. Cassidie has her hand over her mouth as her shoulders rise and fall. Smiling, I stroll right past Dezmond and stop to pat his shoulder. "Better luck next time." Before I move on, Cassidie opens the door and allows me through. As the door closes I hear a slap and, "You're an idiot".

Searaphina exits her bathing chambers as I make my way to her sitting area. "Oh good, dinner, I was about ready to eat Cassidie." She laughs to herself as she takes a seat in front of the fire.

"My apologies for my tardiness, I was held up by new regulations."

Uncovering her dinner, she looks up at me with a questionable look.

"Dezmond," is all she says.

I give her a curt nod before taking the seat opposite hers. "He is so infuriating, ever since he joined your royal guard last year he seems to be determined to annoy me at each step. With his perfectly chiselled face and his stupid big arms and thick thighs." What is even more frustrating is the giggling coming from Searaphina.

"Are you laughing at my misery?" I question, crossing my arms.

Raising her hand to her mouth, she tries to stop the laughter, clearing her throat before speaking. "Oh Silio, do you not see that he likes you? He is annoying you to get your attention."

I refuse to believe her so I shake my head. "That is just what mothers tell their daughters when a young male is nasty."

This only seems to amuse her further as she snorts a laugh and says, "If you say so."

When she has finished eating I collect her plate and head to the door, stopping at the entrance. "Phina, tomorrow will be a hard and exhausting day, get some rest. I will be here bright and early to help prepare you."

The fire's glow lights her face and I see that she is thinking about something quite hard. "That will be all, Silio."

I nod once and leave, wondering what is going through her head and if I will be able to help her.

Searaphina

When I wake, the sun is shining. It feels like a dark cloud has begun to lift, we have sent out spies to Vixeruas to find out who had the King and Queen assassinated and why. My kingdom wants answers; just today we had two more letters from outlying islands that they had been attacked by the dark fae. I shared this news with the council and they have now discussed a new husband for me immediately. I understand their fear and I will do what is needed, but first we need to get through today and then my royal tour. Velasilio is excited as she will get to see her family again after two years of missing them.

It does not take long for Velasilio and the others to fill my bath, bring me food and help me dress. My first gown for today is black, with a large skirt, a corset bodice, and a sweetheart neckline. A sheer shawl covers my shoulders. My long hair is pinned back so that my face is clear for all to see. My tiara is small and silver, showing respect to the late royals.

Velasilio is in a similar gown, only hers has a blouse underneath to hide any flesh; her skirt is the same as my own. Her hair is pinned into a bun. She hands me a black handkerchief that I tuck into the small, lined pocket in my gown. Today I must appear regal and the sorrow of my bereavement true. This evening, joy will be on my face as I experience the moment I become their Queen. The moment that everything I have done in my life has led to.

Leaving the castle, we head north to the largest temple of Datriminish and the royal tombs. Moving the curtain of the carriage, I take in the large structure.

I have not been here for many years. The structure is tall and wide with two large, dark, wood pillars one either side of the door. Stain glass windows line each side of the building. Sconces burn bright at the front to symbolise that Datriminish is here. The whole castle and most of the villagers are waiting outside with flowers, food, coins and small beasts in hand: offerings to our god to allow their King and Queen safe passage into their eternal slumber. They were loved and ruled their kingdom with wisdom, care and the support of those around them. I know that my rule will be different but I hope that I can make this kingdom great.

As the carriage comes to a stop at the walkway to the front doors, all eyes turn to look at us. A foot-male races to open the door. My four Queen's guards line the exit. Dezmond and Cassidie keep to my left, Onree and Gregor to my right. Ever since my parents' death they have been stuck to me like glue—not that I hate it, at least three of them are good to look at.

Gregor is older and was one of my father's favourite guards. He served him well and now he watches over me with the same loyalty. He steps forward and offers me his hand as I hold my gown to the side and descend the small steps, be careful not to fall.

There are slight murmurs of sorrow and sending of well wishes sent my way, but most remain silent with their heads bowed. I see Velasilio follow me from the corner of my eye and watch as Dezmond makes a point to step up before Onree can. If I did not find such joy in her anger with him I would have requested he stop and stay on task to protect his Queen.

The two, large doors open and the priest emerges. He is five foot eight at most, his older age seems to have shrunk him down. No fae knows exactly how old he is, only that he has been around for almost the entire life span of my family's reign. His white and wiry beard reaches to his legs. The top of his head bald with a swipe of red down the centre signifying his place.

His voice is loud but calm as he calls to me. "Searaphina Satraga, a sorrowful day as we say goodbye to your parents and our King and Queen. Please come forth and we will begin." With a bow he turns and heads inside a signal for me to follow.

Walking along the path, I take in the many sorrowful faces with silent tears dripping down their cheeks. Flowers are offered to me, but I do not take them myself, instead gesturing for Velasilio to take them. She steps forward and accepts the offerings with a polite smile and places her hand on their shoulder as a sign of respect.

A basket appears on her arm and I know that one of the many fae here would have given it to her. They will all have the chance to present their offerings once the funeral is complete, but only the fae of the court are allowed inside while I am here. Usually all are allowed in but with the assassination the council has urged me to close the doors and surround myself with more guards than usual. I have heard their warning and ensured that my four chosen guards will be with me at all times and take turns guarding my doors at night in shifts of two.

Dezmond, an orange fae with a strong build and short, dark orange hair has worked alongside me for many years now. Onree is a young, light red fae and still learning. He is the grandchild of Gregor a green fae, his frame is similar to Onree in that they have square shoulders, they do not appear to be strong but have a hidden strength that does not need to look bulky. And then there is Cassidie, a powder blue fae. Her long hair is always tied high into a single point that then cascades down her back. She is new to the guard, only having joined a few months ago, but she has more than proven herself on the training fields but appears to be closed off and not as talkative as the others. I may have to offer her a private ordinance to find out the reason for this.

I have ordered that the doors stay open during the service, while the village fae may not be allowed to enter they are at least able to listen. Continuing our path, we enter the large building and move to the front to take our seats. Along the single pew sits myself, Velasilio and my four guards, two on either side of us. As the other members of the court file in, they leave the pew behind me empty and fill the rest.

The temple ceilings rise high. The stained glass window to the front of the room has an image of the great Datriminish. His one shoulder robe reveals his muscular peak and thick arms. His long, silver hair is tied into a bun at the top of his head, darker skin the perfect contrast to the white as he stands with his hands by his sides, his chiselled jaw and perfect nose similar to many of the fae males today. His eyes are glowing a beautiful gold as shades of blue, red, yellow and green flow around him as if they float on the wind and obey his command.

If Datriminish was a male alive today, I would definitely be enjoying his strength and stamina.

"Phina? Are you okay?" Velasilio's voice is full of concern and kindness and yet I cannot understand why it frustrates me so.

"Yes Silio, I am as well as can be expected," I snap back, only as soon as the words leave my mouth, I know that it was not the correct thing to say. Her eyes search mine for a moment before she nods once and leans back into her seat.

Heaving out a sigh, I try to get my emotions under control. I do not miss the subtle movement of Dezmond's hand, it looks as if he wants to take Velasilio's hand in his own to comfort her.

The priest begins his sermon.

"Welcome one and all on this mournful day. We will begin with a prayer to Datriminish and then you will stand and offer your blessings to our dearly departed King Amard and Queen Alathieria." Holding out his arms, he begins the prayer. Bowing my head, I pretend to speak along with the others, only my eyes are glued to Dezmond; he also is only moving his lips for his attention is squarely on Velasilio. This could be a fun new development.

Shuffling down in my bath, I enjoy the new, bubbling mixture that Velasilio has added. She said it has some form of calming properties. I was a bit sceptical at first but the longer I sit the more I am enjoying it. The slight popping noise is calming and my chalice of wine is only helping me to relax before my coronation. The funeral felt as though it went all day: after the lengthy prayers we then made our offerings before moving outside and watching as the King and Queen were given a final bow and carried into the family crypt to be sealed away for eternity. Once this was complete we left. Many of the villagers stayed behind to pay their respects.

After my coronation, the royal tour will be an excellent way for me to meet many of the villagers who know what is needed to keep the kingdom alive and well. I will have the chance to thank them personally and make them feel important. It will also serve as a good opportunity to try and find even the slightest hint as to who my twin flame may be, if I even have one.

Many fae feel the first flutter in their heart and soul upon their first meeting. Depending on your age, it can be more than a smaller flutter, if the fae is close to or past their two hundred and twenty first birthday they will feel a deep connection and pull towards the other. If they are younger then it is a gently guiding tug. Most males will feel this first, and that is why there are many male pairs more so than two females, or female and male pairings. There is only one other thing that could bring your twin flame to you and that is to go through a fever or heat.

Females will enter a fever as their two hundred and twenty first birthday approaches or just after, this is the time they are fertile, and, as such, become emotional and quick to pounce on the nearest fae to fuck over and over until the fever is finished. This basic need to breed can last for over a week.

Males will enter a heat: they find a fae to fuck over and over and sometimes try to impregnate as many fertile and ready fae as possible —if they do not have their mate that is. If they have found their mate they will only have a burning desire for them.

In both cases, the chance to find a mate is higher as your scent changes and strengthens. If a same sex fated pair finds one another after their first fevers or heats, one chooses to be able to carry the child and the other will produce the seed, and their bodies will change accordingly. While there are a few fated pairs throughout the kingdom there are also many who are not fated but enjoy each other's company enough to marry; they are also able to reproduce during fevers and heats, it is just harder to do so.

My musings of the world around me are interrupted by a tap at the bathing chamber door. Shaking off the thoughts of fevers and children I call out.

"Enter."

Velasilio enters with a towel in hand. "Phina, it is time to dress."

Grumbling, I stand as she looks away, passing me the towel. Wrapping it around my body, I take her outstretched hand and step out, making sure to give her a deadly look as I do so: she simply rolls her eyes at me.

Her words are full of sass as she reprimands my attitude. "I see the new bubbles are a hit, I apologise for interrupting but your royal subjects are waiting to crown their grumpy new Queen."

Rolling my eyes back at her, I hold the towel tight before I turn to face her and offer her my own sass. "Well then what are you waiting for? Dress me or we shall be late, I do not wish to have Dezmond whip you for your tardiness!"

Placing her hands on her hips she purses her lips at me and shakes her head so I continue, placing my left finger to my lip and tapping in thought. "Well, I suppose you may enjoy having his hand on your ass, maybe I should order it, he may even fuck the attitude right out of you."

As the last word leaves my lips her face drops and goes completely red before she turns to storm out of the doors, only to run straight into Dezmond's chest.

CHAPTER 6

MORTIFIED

Velasilio

From my position on the floor, I look up and into the smoldering orange eyes of Dezmond as he has a boyish grin on his face.

'What is he doing here? He was waiting outside her chamber doors not two moments ago and now he is here... Why? Oh Datriminish please say he did not hear Searaphina!' I hear the slight giggle behind me and I turn to see Searaphina holding back laughter.

A strong hand takes my own and starts to pull me up. "My apologies my Queen, Velasilio," Dezmond says. "I heard shouting and was coming to investigate. I was not going to enter your bathing chambers without permission." My gaze swings back to him as he rights me.

Searaphina speaks before I can. "That is quite alright Dezmond, I am lucky to have you here to protect me. Silio and I were merely having a jest." She eyes me and I have to bite back my snarky response. It is one thing to sass my Queen when alone and another to do it in front of her subjects.

So instead I bite my tongue and nod once with a small, "Indeed."

Dezmond's gaze jumps from me to Searaphina before he bows

low. When he does he speaks softly to me so she will not hear him. "I would be honoured to rid you of that attitude." I almost choke as he speaks, and he offers me a wink before turning and leaving us alone.

I know that my cheeks must be red as I turn to Searaphina who bursts out laughing. "So, did he hear me?"

Anger surges with embarrassment as I try to whisper-yell at her. "PHINA! I have to see him each day. If I were to enjoy him in such a way and things ended badly, what would happen?"

That stops her laughter, "I would dismiss him and get a new guard for you to... How did you put it? 'Enjoy'." She raises her eyebrows at me and my anger recedes. I shake my head before speaking.

"That will not be happening, now let us get you ready to be officially crowned our Queen." I see the way Searaphina's eyes light up and, though my heart still weeps for our lost royals, I know that I must be strong for Searaphina, I will not let her down.

Several hours later, as the sun has begun to set, Searaphina is ready, as am I. Her coronation gown is a masterpiece. The ballgown has a low cut back allowing her wings to be on full display; the three individual parts move together as one, the vibrant green webbing matching her eyes. I have tied her hair up at the back and curled it, the deep red waves bounce with each step she takes. Her makeup is simple, pink and brown tones to complement her ivory complexion. Her ballgown has a sheer over sleeve that hangs from her shoulder and a low but tasteful dip at the front. The design is simple enough, though each dazzling thread works its way over the gown like growing vines.

My own gown is more extravagant than usual with a similar cut at the back so my own wings can be on show. Their dark purple edging with matching swirling patterns on the web shows my heritage and the close relationship with the royals. My silver hair is half up and half down, the low front of my gown is more than I would usually allow but Searaphina argued that if her breasts cannot be out then mine must be for balance. As my Queen, I am not allowed to fight her, plus Dezmond has been struggling to keep his eyes off me so maybe she has the right idea. I should scold him and remind him of his duty, but with so many other guards here this evening I know that Searaphina is well cared for.

I walk slowly behind Searaphina in the same temple we were in this morning, only now the walls are lined with flaming torches to light our way. With the royal crown resting on a cushion in my arms, I focus on each step to make sure I do not fall. The delicate thing is well over a thousand years old and the three large emeralds in each of the pointed tips are worth more than my life.

Finally, we make it to the top of the aisle; we have been taught how this all happens so many times that it almost feels like muscle memory at this point: kneeling before Searaphina. I extended the crown to the priest and wait for him to take it. Once it is removed, I bow to my Queen and move to her left side as she moves to her knees.

"On this most sacred of days when we have buried the dead and sent King Amard and Queen Alathieria to meet Datriminish in the afterlife, we now crown our new Queen." Turning his back to us all, he takes the crown and holds it over a burning fire pit.

"I call upon Datriminish to bless this symbol of our rulers, cleanse this crown of any negative energy that may hold on to it, and grant it a fresh beginning while allowing the wisdom of those who came before to hold tight and bless the next ruler. May her rule be long and full of love and happiness. If she happens upon troubled times, may you guide her through. On this evening we crown your chosen to reign over Neraphina and take care of the fae who reside here."

I am completely in awe of how his hands have not burnt off: he stands still, holding the crown as it begins to glow red from the heat, and yet he holds it, calm as anything. Once he finishes the blessing and bows to the glass depiction of Datriminish on the window, he turns to his right and places the crown into a cold bath of water. The metal hisses as it sinks below, leaving bubbles in its wake.

After a moment, he picks it up and places it in a new cloth to dry it. I have been taught this ceremony many times but to actually see it is another thing. How the priest remains untouched is unfathomable to me.

When all is said and done, he turns back to Searaphina and places the crown atop her head. "Rise, Queen Searaphina of Neraphina, and greet your royal subjects. Long may she reign."

The whole room erupts as we all mimic his words, followed by a round of applause before the court lines the aisles, ready to offer their blessing and well wishes to their new Queen before our feast this evening.

Once all have finished and taken their seats once more, Searaphina moves to stand in the centre of the chamber.

"I am honoured to be standing here today, where my parents once stood. I promise to be a fair and just ruler, to care for you all and protect you from the ones who seek to harm us. I vow to find out who killed King Amard and Queen Alathieria. I will not rest until we know the truth." The room erupts in applause. She raises a single hand and they all quiet.

"The time for sorrow is over, for now we must move forward. Please return with me to the castle for a feast before I leave in the morning for my royal tour." As she stops speaking she moves down the aisle and I quickly follow her outside before we step into the carriage. We fold our wings against our backs so that we can sit comfortably.

As soon as the door closes I turn to her, my voice full of excitement. "Phina, you are Queen!"

Smiling sweetly she places the back of her hand under her chin and tilts her head. "I sure am, and a cute one at that."

We laugh. It has been a long and exhausting day but it is not over yet.

When we arrive back at the castle, it is a flurry of motion as we are swept into the throne room and food is placed in front of us. We eat, drink and are merry. Come tomorrow we leave for the royal tour and I get to see my family. After two years, I wonder if anything will have changed.

CHAPTER 7

REGRETS

Velasilio

'*I refuse to open my eyes, I refuse to acknowledge that stupid bird that sings like the day is bright and full of happiness, it can go die.*' My violent thoughts are interrupted as a knock comes from my door.

Rolling over, my stomach goes with me, and I have to fight back the nausea. Once I finally swallow it back down, I try to pry my eyes open. But with each blink feels as though a thousand tiny daggers are stabbing at them. With one eye slightly open and the other still shut, I call out: "Yes? Who is there?"

A deep chuckle comes before they answer. "It's Dezy, you asked me to wake you this morning. You were afraid last evening that you would not wake in time."

Groaning at the voice, I roll back over and try to think about what he just said.

'*Dezy, who is Dezy? And why does my mind feel fuzzy and my teeth hurt, wait the other way around. Wait! Wake me?*' Sitting up straight, I remember: we leave today for the royal tour.

Rolling out of bed with absolutely no grace I call back to him. "Dezmond?" Again with that annoyingly sexy chuckle.

"Well if you wish to go back to our formal names I suppose we can." I try to make sense of what he is saying—what happened last evening? I remember the feast and then Searaphina offered me a drink and then another saying that it was the last chance to relax and not have any responsibilities, and then we danced I think. Oh my, we got drunk, very very drunk, I must have made such a fool of myself. This is why I try not to drink at royal events. It is unbecoming of a Queen's lady to be wasted on wine like a harlot.

As my mind catches up, I quickly stand and throw my overrobe on. I run to the door and wretch it open, nearly hitting my toe in the process. "Oh Dezmond, I apologise for anything foolish I may have done last evening."

Standing barefoot, I look up into his smug and stupidly handsome face, he looks perfect and edible. But I still want to smack him as his eyes run the length of me. I know I must look a mess, my hair is everywhere and I am only in a thin overgown and nothing else, clenching the front closed so that I do not offer him a free show.

"Well Miss Velasilio, you look ravishing this morning, are you ready to help prepare our Queen for her royal tour?" His tone is full of sarcasm as his eyes roam the length of me again.

My short temper gets the best of me as I swiftly turn and shut the door in his face, I know that my own must be beet red now from his lustful gaze. His gruff laugh comes from under the door and I find that I do not find it all that annoying, rather it has my mind wandering to all the sensual acts we could enjoy together.

Shaking off my sexual desire, I rush around to ready for the day. I am already late to help Searaphina. I send a silent prayer to Datriminish that she will not be cross with me.

The cart is stuffy and hot. We have only been travelling for an hour and, lucky for me, Searaphina was more interested in mocking me for my drunken mistakes than being late to prepare her this morning. Sitting across from her, I mope as she continues.

"So then you asked Dezmond to dance but he had to decline as he needed to stay at his post. Well you did not like that answer and proceeded to find an available male and dance with them, making sure to stick your tongue out at him each time you swirled past him." Her laughter fills the cart as she holds her stomach, only just able to finish her story.

Placing my head in my hands, I try to hide my shame. "Phina, I apologise for my behaviour. I must have embarrassed you, I promise that I will not have much wine ever again." Lifting my head, I look straight at her, hoping that she can see how sincere I am.

I watch as her face changes: gone is her laughter, now a small frown rests on her lips as her eyes soften before she shuffles forward and takes my hands in her own. "Silio, it is okay. You may have had a few too many drinks but it is nothing the court has not seen before, just do not make a habit of such behaviour."

I hear the slight warning in her tone along with the understanding: I am her handmaid and as such my actions and behaviour reflect on her. It is not frowned upon in court to have a night of inebriation and more reckless behaviour, but do not become the court drunk.

With my face set in a straight line, I nod. "Of course my Queen, I promise to only become befuddled with liquor on the odd occasion." At my choice of words we both break into a fit of laughter.

As we settle in for the rest of the journey I am thankful that our first stop is the furthest and then we will stop at each village on the way back to the castle. Tonight we will sleep in the Duke and Duchess's home before heading into town. Tomorrow we will leave at midday to travel the hour's journey to my parents' estate.

I have not seen them in two years. As a young child, I visited often and stayed with the royal family for weeks at a time, but my training was still ongoing and I needed to finish it before I could step into the role of a Queen's maid. As my family lands are quite far away from the castle, the fae of our village are known for being a bit more rugged and do not always speak with the necessary decorum. I find that these old habits have a tendency to slip out from time to time, and my parents insist they do not know where my horrendously short temper came from.

A gentle nudge on my shoulder has my eyes blinking open as I hear Searaphina speaking to me. "Silio, wake up."

Rubbing at my eyes, I sit up straight. "Apologies Phina, I must have dozed off." Pulling back the curtain, I look out to the dark sky. We are travelling on a dirt path surrounded by large trees. If I angle my head I can just see the Duke and Duchess of Desinta's home, the flaming touches out front offering light in the sea of darkness.

"No need to apologise. I, too, fell asleep, the journey has been long and we had a very busy day yesterday." Looking back to Searaphina I take in her appearance: she looks as tired as she sounds, her hair sits flat and her usually ivory skin seems more pale than usual. There are two dark, sunken circles under her eyes.

Sitting up a bit taller and putting on my most motherly voice, I say, "Well when we arrive it is supper and straight to bed for you."

Searaphina's mouth pops open in surprise with a slight giggle before she clears her throat. "As my moth... I mean maid commands." She bows her head with both arms outstretched in mockery.

When her eyes meet mine again we both lose it. Travelling by carriage may be the nicest way to get around but being stuck inside with only a small number of breaks to stretch one's legs and use the privy is not enough to keep the cabin fever at bay.

A small knock comes from the roof, sliding over to the left side. I pull back the curtain and unlatch the small window. As it swings open, Cassidie's beautiful face appears as she leans down from her horse. As she sees my face her smile drops slightly, she catches it just.

"Miss Velasilio I was just going to alert our Queen that we will be arriving shortly and to prepare, the Duke and Duchess have the entire household ready to meet her." I hear Searaphina's unimpressed grumble at the news.

Hiding my own smirk, I thank Cassidie, closing the window and repeating the news to Searaphina who then insists that we stop so that I can retrieve her perfume and make up from one of her many bags that rest inside the second carriage behind ours. Moving quickly, I collect what is needed and prepare our Queen to greet some of her royal subjects.

CHAPTER 8

THE FIRST OF MANY

Searaphina

Thank Datriminish that it was so late when we arrived last night; I was exhausted from the journey and the previous evening.

I had a lovely visit last night from Cassidie who ensured I returned safely to my chambers. Unfortunately she was on first watch and, even with my offer of a most enjoyable night, she declined as it would not be fair on the others. She also worries about what others may say—she of course did not actually tell me this, but I could tell by the way she left the door open and did a quick sweep of the room with Onree standing just outside. I will need to speak with her and let her know that my sexual appetite is well known to the kingdom. It is not frowned upon for young fae to enjoy the company of others before they reach breeding age. Once you are able to conceive it becomes different, especially for royals. No matter if you are male or female a child conceived out of wedlock is not fit to rule.

Under the rules of Datriminish a child born to unwed parents is a child born of lust and their soul is tainted by such. This of course *only* applies to the royal lineage, others are free to do as they please though many have adapted this into their own lives and once they begin their fevers and heats will settle down. This is why many hundreds of years ago the royal decree of marriage by two hundred and twenty one was put into place.

To ensure no others may contest the royal line and it will live on, once you are wed with a child a blind eye is turned to any affairs you might have. As long as at least one legitimate child is born. I find this to be idiotic and that is why, once I am wed and no longer at risk to lose my throne, I will be challenging and changing some of our more archaic laws. How are we to find our twin flames if the best time to do so is once we have reached two hundred and twenty one?

Anger surges inside me at the pure idiocies of my predecessors to allow such ridiculous laws to continue. I know that they were raised to believe in such things but the new generation are beginning to question and I for one am ready for changes. I just wish I did not need to be obliged by them to keep my crown and my head before changes can be made.

Not wanting to lose my fire, I sit up in my bed. It is smaller then my one at home, only just big enough for three. The entire chamber is on the more quaint size but, I must admit, they have furnished it well: I have a small writing desk and cupboards for if I was to stay longer than a single night. Slipping from the bed, I put on an over-gown that hangs from the bed's end. Sitting at the desk, I begin to make a list of the things I will change when my rule is solidified.

1. Replace some of the council males and add females.
2. Change laws on children out of wedlock. It is so hard to produce a child. Why have a law against more of them?
3. Possible marriage of multiple partners?
4. Increase training and begin higher intake of soldiers for the possible war.

5. *Find and punish those responsible for death of King Amard and Queen Alathieria.*

6.

My list is interrupted by a far too chipper Velasilio. "Good morning my Queen, it is a beautiful day to visit the town." Turning on the stool, I watch as she ducks under Desmond's hand and offers him a nod of thanks. Her arms are filled with, I am not actually sure what, until four other maids follow her in with large, steaming buckets in their arms.

After directing the others into the bathing chambers, she strolls up to me and smiles like she has had far too many sugar snaps today. "Well, what is it that you are doing my Queen?" Peering down, she mouths the words as she reads.

"You are very noisy, Silio." Her eyes leave the page to look at me with a smug smile before going back to her task.

When she is finished and stands, she looks at me, still with that unnerving smile. "What have you eaten today that has you looking like you are but a moment away from stabbing me and laughing about it?"

Her laugh is just as unhinged and I find myself holding back my own, especially when the other maids scurry out of my chambers without a single word. They must have heard our exchange, I wonder if they see our relationship as uncouth. The thought makes me laugh as I think back to my own kingdom and what they must think of us, though I would assume that they have a better understanding as they watched us grow together and become the females we are today.

"I fear we may have scared off the others." Looking towards the door where the others have left, Velasilio follows my eyes and when we meet each other's gaze again we both burst out laughing.

After a few moments, we take a few deep breaths and regain our ability to speak. Velasilio wipes away a single tear from her cheek.

"Okay enough of this. I am simply excited for the day and to be able to see my family tomorrow."

"Yes, that is definitely very exciting. Now please tell me what is on this tray?" Looking down, I see a multitude of colours and fragrances hit my nose at the same time.

"Gifts from the Duke and Duchess, they are known here for producing all of the tonics for our baths." Turning, she begins to walk to the bathing chamber.

"We should begin your preparation, the villagers will be waiting for you." I follow her, ready to bathe, dress and begin the tour by meeting the fae I will rule.

Today was just as long as yesterday and now we find ourselves back in this stuffy carriage and on our way to the Vesariah estate, where Velasilio was raised. Her family lands are vast; the second largest in the kingdom, they are known for producing our livestock and, as such, need a lot of room for the creatures to roam.

Our meat comes from the Callidon: a two-headed beast that has four hooves and a large body. Its pelt is thick with fur and is used for bedding. The fae there are known for having the best understanding of all beasts as they interact with so many, even some of our more deadly creatures that live on the island of Tarpidora, a forgotten kingdom where many fae once thrived. Their magic was at one with the land and brought harmony to their island but, when the last one perished in a war against Vixeruas, the deadly beasts took over and now roam the island.

Even the dark fae could not kill the beasts faster than they breed; nothing but ruins lay there and if any enter there is a high chance you will never see them again. Only fae with wisdom, strength and courage are able to escape with their lives. Most who travel there are in search of rare items, some of which can be used in spells and magic rituals.

There has not been a fae born with the ability to use magic freely in Neraphina for over two thousand years. We are only able to manipulate the smallest amount with rare items and the correct words.

There is no true magic here.

Though there are rumours that dark shadow fae have been born in Vixeruas.

Shadow fae were known to go insane from the shadows that plague them. The last dark fae with a link to magic was Queen Genivie. From what we know, neither of her sons have shown signs of magic and her daughter died in the womb when she was killed.

Stuck in my own mind, I do not notice that we have already arrived. I want to do some more research into my enemies, perhaps it will help me in future. Velasilio's leg is bouncing. She must be nervous. It has been a while since she has seen her family, I know that they write often but that is not the same.

Velasilio

Night has fallen once again. When I look at Searaphina she seems lost in thought.

Today was busy: we took the carriage into town and walked among the people. A festival had been set up to honour their new Queen. Many stalls offered her goods as tokens of respect, but Searaphina would not accept these and ensured they were all paid for. We left with many fine-smelling perfumes and washes for our baths, including more of the fancy bubbling solution. We are still stuffed from the amount of bread, sweet pastries and wine we were given, so I do not believe that we will be needing any supper.

The carriage begins to slow and I look out the window to see my parents' sprawling estate up ahead. Each window is lit from the inside and I see the rough shadows of the entire household waiting outside. In the centre are four large shapes: my mother, father and two younger twin brothers. A gentle hand moves over my leg. Turning from the window, I see Searaphina leaning forward, her hand resting over my knee.

"You were bouncing your leg again."

"My apologies if I disturbed you, you were so deep in your

thoughts that I did not wish to take you from them." Shaking off the nervousness, I sit up and place my hands on my knees. My gaze catches on the hem of my gown and the thin layer of mud that coats it. My mind moves in a frenzy: will they think I am dirty? Will they think I do not care for my appearance?

I am shocked from my thoughts when Searaphina's voice calls to me and her hands take mine. "Silio, Silio."

My voice is small and distant as I answer. "Yes, Phina."

"You are worrying too much, they will love you as they always have and if they do not I will behead them for you." There is a finality to her voice that almost has me believing that she would have them killed. It must be a jest, so I offer a nervous laugh.

"Of course." Just as we sit back in our chairs the carriage comes to a stop and the door is opened. I stay in my seat and wait for Searaphina to exit. Shuffling from her seat, she pats my hands and offers a smile before leaving me alone. I listen as her name is called out by the herald and her feet crunch on the stone.

A gloved hand waits for me just at the exit. Taking a steady breath, I step forward and take the hand, leaving the safety of the carriage.

With as much grace as I can muster I descend the steps and stand next to my Queen. Looking up I see my family, my friends and the fae I was raised around each one with a large smile. This could just be to see the Queen or because I have come home after such a long time away.

My mother, Kaylin, stands in a simple, high neck, deep blue gown with her matching hair tied into a high bun. Her wings are gently against her back but still visible: their vibrant blue stands out against her dark choice of outfit. My father Veincent's wings are in a similar position only his have a slight mixture of blue and purple throughout—the tips are a light purple and then darken into a deep, ocean blue at the base. His suit is tailored to fit him like a glove, the lighter purples complement his darker complexion.

Both of their faces are still sharp but show signs of aging with small smile lines around their eyes and lips. Father's hair is still thick and he now has a manicured beard to match the dark blue colour.

Both of my parents have ocean blue eyes and I find my own welling with tears at seeing them.

My little brothers are no longer little. They both tower over me at well over six feet, matching my father's height. Their bodies are now built with muscle, wide shoulders and large arms. They are identical twins but Aeztrian has long, light blue hair with purple at the tips and Kestrain has short hair of a darker blue. They both sport the same mischievous grins and matching eyes to mother and father.

Once the royal procession is complete and my parents turn and begin to walk with Searaphina ahead of me with her four guards, my brothers stand still, watching me, waiting for the perfect moment.

Stopping their stroll, Searaphina turns to me. "Velasilio I will meet you inside."

Bowing low I reply, "Thank you my Queen, I will ensure all of your things are taken to your rooms." Without another word, they continue on their way. My parents made sure that all of their children would behave with the appropriate decorum around any visitors which is precisely why both of my brothers are staring at me looking like completely unstable lunatics as they stand completely still. When I see the large doors close and we are left outside all alone, I run.

My lungs are burning and my dress is now ripped at the ends as I run through the trees and low bushes, but I do not care I will not let them win. This is a game we have played every single time I return home. I have to reach the tree of whispers before them.

In the woods at the edge of our estate on the east side is a large white tree. Its low-hanging branches often sounds like whispers as the wind moves through them. It is our special place away from everything proper and formal, where we can just be us.

A stabbing pain begins in my left side and I stop to lean against a tree. I have not run like this in far too long, too many days sitting eating sugar snaps and drinking tea.

Just as I feel like I might be lost I hear the low whispering and I know I must be close, it is like my body remembers where to go even if my mind feels lost.

"This is too easy," I say to myself as I run. And then I hear it, another voice.

"Let's make it harder!" Before I can react, the world spins and I am on the cold, damp forest floor with my oaf of a brother on top of me. He laughs at me before jumping up and running off.

"Kes, you little shite!" Screaming at him, I quickly stand and rush after him.

Shocking myself, I gain on him. He turns his head to look back and I watch as his eyes widen when he realises I am on his tail. "Not so fast now are you!"

Uncurling my wings, I use them to give me an extra bit of power as I jump onto his back, swinging my body at the same time and taking us both down. Luckily, I tuck my wings back away before we hit the ground. Rolling onto his side, Kes makes sure not to hurt me with his massive body as we go down.

Rolling off my brother, we both sit on our bottoms and look at each other, his face marred by surprise and pride as he asks, "What the fuck was that Sil? All the tea and biscuits have not slowed you down."

We both break out in laughter as we take in our appearances: both of our clean outfits are now caked in mud and ripped from the fall. Our laughter stops abruptly when a completely clean Aez stands in front of us.

"Thanks for taking out my competition, think I'll go win now!" Turning on his heel, he takes off. Kes and I look at one another before we are both scrambling to get up and chase him down.

As we run through the dark forest, Kes shouts to me, "You take left, I take right." I give him a curt nod before we split off.

It does not take long for us to catch up to Aez. He is running slowly with a cocky grin I cannot wait to swipe off his face and then I see Kes on his other side mouthing, 'three, two, one.' We both rush in, slamming into Aez and taking him down, only I do not go all the way with them.

While the two meatheads wrestle, I stand and walk the last couple of feet to the whisper tree. As I stand in front of it, I look back at the two still in a pretzel of limbs as they swear at one another. I whistle loudly to get their attention. They both stop and stand quickly, eyes locked on me. My hand is raised and, just as I place it on the tree I state. "I win." They both shove each other one more time before yelling at me.

Throwing his hands up Kes says, "You used us against each other."

While Aez just complains, "That's not fair!"

I know the smug smile on my face will only serve to infuriate them further as I laugh. "Oldest trick in the book, I have been using that against you two dolts for years."

My mistake was turning my back on them to walk home. The two, now muscular males rush me, picking me up before we all drop to the floor in a mess of mud, laughter and swinging arms.

*S*tretching out in my old bed, I feel like I have had the best sleep of my life. My parents have kept my chambers the same as when I left; while they may be a little young for me now I appreciate that I always have a place to come back to. Every time I leave I know that I am leaving a piece of my heart here with the ones who raised me.

After our game last night, my brothers and I snuck in through a servant's entrance as we have many times before. The whole evening brought up so many old memories and my heart feels fuller just being here. Searaphina was understanding of me taking time to be with my siblings as she had another maid fill her bath and unpack her sleeping gown and something for her to wear today. I, like my brothers, quickly ran to our own chambers to bathe and dress for dinner, to ensure our parents did not see the mess we had made of ourselves. When we were younger such antics were seen as adorable and loving. Now they are seen as childish and something they wish for us to grow out of, though I do not believe that will ever happen.

Dressing for the day I chose a gown more to my mother's taste: the square neckline covers my breasts completely and the long sleeves are sheer to provide some comfort from heat of the day; the deep purple gown sits just above my ankles to protect from the mud and muck when we stroll through the village today. The friendly creatures both great and small roam all around the area. The ones that bite are usually kept in their paddocks.

Once I am dressed, I leave my chambers and head to Searaphina's. Across the castle because my parents ensured she was in the best rooms besides their own. They have increased the guards in their own home after the assassination as many of the court have. With no new news about who or what killed them, all of the fae are scared.

As I walk though the halls, I see Gregor speaking with Onree just outside the Queen's chambers. From the slight hand manoeuvres I can only assume they are talking of battle and how to defend or kill one's opponent. They must hear my footsteps as they stop speaking and turn to face me.

"Good morning, Miss Velasilio." Gregor is the only fae to call me this besides Dezmond, though in his case it is more to flirt and annoy. Gregor is a male of honour and respect.

"Good morrow." Onree is a male of few words but still remains polite.

"A good morning to you both." I offer a small curtsy before closing the distance between us so that I may raise Searaphina.

I knock three times and wait until she tells me to enter.

Walking in, I see why my parents have placed her in these chambers. They are far larger than my own, with fancy decorations and furniture, they have recently changed these rooms as I do not recall them ever looking so feminine. The bed spread is silk, with sage green and bright florals covering it, there is a writing desk that is plain and a vanity with a matching silk chair to the bed spread.

"You look well rested," Searaphina calls to me from her bed, still wrapped in the covers.

"Thank you, it is nice to be home again." I sit at the edge of her bed. "Are you ready to begin the day?"

Huffing out a breath, she frowns at me. "Are you okay?"

"No I am not. I do not understand how Cassidie is able to resist me." Sinking deeper into her sheets, I try not to laugh at the childlike pout on her face.

Seeing the corners of my lips tilting up, she bolts upright to scold me. "Do not laugh at your Queen! I need your help." Her voice goes from stern to whiny so quickly I cannot stop the laughter that bubbles from me.

Giving me a stern look, she points her finger like she may yell at me again. Raising my own hands in surrender, I answer. "Maybe Cassidie needs more of a connection before she sleeps with others? Have you tried having a conversation first?"

She chews on her bottom lip before she eyes me with a suspicious look. "No I do not believe that I have, maybe I should give that a go."

"I do not like that look," I quip. What she says next tells me I was right.

"How do you feel about riding a unicorn?"

CHAPTER 10

GETTING TO KNOW HER

Searaphina

Velasilio's parents were absent from breakfast, their herald told us they had an urgent matter to deal with and would be back in time to see us off but apologise that they will miss the festivities. It did not sour my mood as I had spoken with them last evening but I could see that it hurt Velasilio that she would not get a lot of time with her parents.

After breakfast, I told her that we can invite her whole family to the castle soon and that seemed to perk her up at least until she found out about my brilliant plan.

"You want me to ride Cassidie's unicorn?" Her eyes scan the beast from top to bottom like it may bite her.

"Yes." Her angry gaze shot to me. I loved seeing if I could hit the spot where her temper got the best of her, she was always so in control. To add a little fuel to her fire I continue. "As your *Queen* it would give me great pleasure to see you ride this unicorn." Reaching a hand out, I gently pat the dapple-grey beast's bottom.

As it snickered and kicked a foot we both stepped back, much to Dezmond's amusement. I had forgotten he was here. "I don't completely understand why our Queen has requested that you ride beside me today or why Cassidie must replace you in the carriage."

Cutting him off, I give him the answer. "It is because your Queen wishes it."

Closing his mouth he quickly nods. "Yes, Your Majesty. Come, Velasilio, I will help you up." Kneeling down, he cups his hands.

Velasilio takes one last look at me. I swear that if looks could kill I would be dead. I give her a sweet smile and wander back to the carriage. Cassidie stands by the door, her face puzzled as her eyes watch the disaster that is Dezmond trying to help a very uncoordinated Velasilio on a unicorn. A few curses leave her mouth, some that have even Dezmond blushing. When she is finally atop the beast, she is as red as a smacked bottom and apologises to him for her language. He nods once before moving to straddle his own steed.

Cassidie makes a noise that is something between a laugh and clearing her throat and I see why: to my left are Velasilio's twin brothers mocking her by attempting to get onto an imaginary unicorn and falling off. When I look back to Velasilio she searches around her to make sure that no others can see and she lifts the back of her hand to under her chin and quickly moves it out again. Quite the vulgar gesture.

Shaking my head, I finally climb into my carriage with Cassidie behind me. Sitting on the right side as I always do, as my delicate stomach can not handle moving backwards, Cassidie takes the opposite seat. As the carriage begins to move she looks most uncomfortable and then I notice she is not watching the windows.

"Do you also get sick if moving backwards?" As I ask, closing the curtains so that she can no longer see outside. She does not speak but nods slowly, seeming to concentrate very hard.

Sliding across, I pat the seat. "Please join me." Before I finish speaking she moves. Her frame is not too much larger than mine so we fit comfortably next to one another.

Her sweet scent of fresh rain is strong when she sits so close to me.

What I would give to see those powder blue locks flow freely, my hand tangled in them as I push her head down so that her mouth closes over my...

A bump in the road has me shaking off my raw thoughts and change to what Velasilio said to get to know her.

"Cassidie, why did you join the guards?" My question must catch her off guard as she turns swiftly to look at me.

"That is an interesting question to ask, my Queen."

"I just wish to get to know my guards. I already have known Dezmond for some time and Gregor was in my father's royal guard; his nephew Onree does not seem as though he enjoys conversation. You are next in line for me to understand why you want to protect the crown." Her face changes as if my response has upset her, as if she wanted more, and I bite my tongue from changing my answer.

"If that is what my Queen wishes, then I suppose I have no choice. I am afraid it is not a happy story." Her face drops.

"When I was only a hundred, my family were farmers in one of the outlying villages. Bandits came and took everything we had, and when my father tried to fight back they drove a blade through his heart. My mother was quick to hide me. Told me to be quiet lest they find me and take me to sell in Vixeruas." Cassidie pauses, taking a deep breath before she continues.

"I was hidden under a rotted floorboard as my mother spilt a bag of grain over the floor, to hide any evidence that I was there, but they had found my doll so they knew a young fae lived there, and when they demanded to know where I was my mother refused to tell them, so they ran her through as well. I still remember the cramped space where my legs fell asleep as I held them to my chest. I tried to keep my breathing even and shallow so they didn't hear me. My mother's body fell just above where I was and every time I smell the scent of blood I am taken back to the sound of hers dripping down the boards and onto the dirt below me. I waited a day and a half to make sure that they were gone, in that time I vowed to myself that I would never let that happen again. That I would train with the royal guard and protect the innocent."

A single tear drops down her cheek as she sits up straight. I feel that I need to comfort her in some way but I do not know how. I reach my hand out to take hers but she speaks again, causing me to halt my movement. "I am sorry if I have upset you, that was not my intention. I have no problem with telling my story as it is one that I hope you hear and as Queen ensure that these things do not happen under your rule."

Turning in her seat, she faces me, and her eyes search mine for an answer I am not sure that I have. As Queen, I can put many things in place to stop these bandits from stealing, killing and taking young fae, but even I know I cannot stop them all.

So I do the one thing I can: placing my hand on her cheek, I lean in and kiss her softly. As I pull back I feel her hand take mine, holding it in place before, her tongue runs the seam of my lips and I open for her. Our tongues meet in a moment of raw emotion, I feel, as she slowly moves so that her body is pressed against my own. Just as my back hits the soft bench seat, the carriage stops. Jarring us both, we break apart quickly and then Cassidie is up and outside. I sit with my hand on the smile that tugs at my lips.

"Searaphina!" Snapping from my thoughts I look to the purple eyes that are glaring at me.

"You made me ride a unicorn with Dezmond so you could fondle Cassidie with sexual passion?" I go to tell her off but her words catch me off guard.

"Fondle with sexual passion?" I wait for her to elaborate, instead she bursts into a fit of giggles.

"I do not know, my mother said it once when she caught me in the stables with a young male experiencing my first kiss." I, too, laugh when she explains it.

"I would have said that we were sharing a private moment." I begin to straighten my dress as she rolls her eyes at me.

"I am sure it was, but now we have arrived. Are you ready to greet your subjects? They are eager to meet you." I shoo her with my hands and manoeuvre to leave the carriage.

She did not lie, they are very excited to meet me; it would seem the entire village and more have come to the festival.

The street is coated in straw to keep me clean, and lined with stalls with various goods and food. There are a great deal of small creatures roaming; I even catch sight of a group of Antipores floating by, their four little paws hanging down as their delicate wings carry them across the breeze, their long necks extended and looking for danger.

It does not take long before Velasilio takes my arm and we begin to experience the many stalls great and small. I can feel my guards' presence around me but I can tell exactly where Cassidie is as her hand brushes mine in a silent gesture.

As the day and festivities nears their end there are only four stalls left. These house living beasts, some to be bought as pets and others to be shown off. There are four attractive males standing at each of the pens, only one catches my eye more than the others. A handsome male with dark blue hair cut short at the sides with a longer section in the middle. His chest is broad without being too large and his muscles look as though they have come from hard work. The only thing that stops my approach is the snarling coming from behind him, which he seems completely unfazed by.

Pulling Velasilio close, I whisper, "Who is that?"

Her own gaze, which has been stuck on Dezmond for most of this trip no matter how long she refuses to admit she likes him, follows my line of sight. "Hmm? Oh him, that is, ahh, I think his name is Arek?"

"You think or you know?" I whisper again even though she is speaking at full volume.

"I think. I have seen him around, his family runs a farm just outside of the village, they usually handle the Xanvitors." Screwing up my nose, I look at her.

"Why would any sane fae go near such beasts?"

"Well we eat the meat, use the pelts, and they are good to pull farming equipment if you have a docile one." She shrugs her shoulders as if the six-foot-three, horned beasts are just a daily occurrence to her.

"I know what we use them for but are they not extremely vicious?"

"They can be, but his family, the Lensana, are used to handling such beasts and have bred out most of the aggressive behaviours." Again she shrugs and I shake my head at her. Then I realise that we have both been staring at this male who is now staring back.

Something inside me rolls over and I feel the need to run. I do not know if it is to or away from him but I take Velasilio's arm, turning her in the other direction, and we leave.

Velasilio

As I place the final bag on the carriage with Onree's help, I feel like I am being watched, but when I turn around I see no others. Strange. Searaphina exits the front door with my mother and father following behind her. They are speaking as if they are good friends and I am happy to see them all getting along.

Moving to stand beside the carriage, my heart hurts that I have not had time to spend with my parents and come to think of it, I have not seen my brothers since this morning, they would never miss a market, far too much food and tomfoolery to be had.

As my parents make their way down the path, they bow to Searaphina before she turns to me. "They have asked for a private word with you before we depart." She smiles at me before taking my hand as she passes and squeezes it.

I wait until she is inside the carriage. The guards have all mounted besides Dezmond who disregards my words that I am safe and stands beside his steed and waits for me. Rolling my eyes at him, I turn and walk toward my parents. As I reach them, I go to offer them both a hug but my father holds out his hand, stopping me. My heart hurts with his rejection, but I understand that it may be seen as improper.

"Father, I know that I am the Queen's handmaid but I assure you she would never request that you do not hug your child." I smile at him with a slight jest in my tone as I wait for his response.

When he says nothing but shares a pained look with my mother, I wonder what has happened. As I look around, I see that my brothers are not here. "Please do not say that something has happened to Kes and Aez?" I rush out, feeling tears already welling in my eyes. I cannot lose them.

My mother rushes forwards, hugging me tightly. My hands automatically go around her as I sob into her chest.

My father's voice is stern, but his face falters, betraying him. "No, they are unharmed."

I blow out a breath but my relief is short-lived as my mother is pulled away by my father. Her arms go around his waist as he swallows before he speaks again.

"They did not wish to be here for this." I watch as he moves, my mother off him and stands tall. Be here for what?

The air around me drops and a chill works its way over my spine. What were they called away for today? What could have happened? "You, Velasilio Vesariah, are hereby disowned by the Vesariah line."

Coldness cuts through my heart, splintering it into a thousand pieces and sucking all of my air from my lungs. The words that leave me are raw and bleeding as I beg for answers. "What? Father, why?"

His eyes dart to mine and I see the sorrow there. To sever a family line is to cut through the blood that binds us. It is an ancient and archaic tradition only used for those who have dishonoured their families.

"You have disgraced your family and tainted your soul, you will never truly be whole and for that we can no longer accept you as part of this family." His voice cracks and the pain becomes unbearable.

I drop to my knees, the dirt and stone biting into my skin, the pain in my chest overwhelming me and I feel numb to everything else. The wind picks up and the world around me blurs and becomes nothing. All I can see is my mother now, on her knees reaching out for me, tears coating her cheeks. My father looks to the sky and I watch as his own tears fall to the ground below him.

"When you leave here, you are never to return, you are disowned and we will never speak of you again." As the final word is spoken my heart shatters and a white hot pain sears through me. Screaming out in agony, I let the tears fall. The salty taste fills my mouth as I crumple into a ball, only just aware of my father dragging my mother back into the house. I just see my two younger brothers stand at the edge of the forest, holding hands as they kneel in pain with me, feeling our father's words tearing our souls apart, never to run through the woods again, never to joke or care for each other. I will never be allowed home and I have no idea why.

*S*unlight blinds me as I stir. My entire body hurts; it feels like I was thrown from a moving carriage and trampled by a herd of unicorns. Groaning, I roll over.

'Oh this is nice and soft, hmm smells like jasmine, wait jasmine?' That scent and a hand on my head jars me awake and I sit up quickly.

Searaphina looks startled but calm as she speaks to me. "Silio, it is okay, you are safe."

My heart is racing and I feel a phantom pain lingering in my chest. Then I remember: that searing pain, the look of regret on my father's face as he dragged my hysterical mother away, my brothers watching from the trees, falling to their knees and clutching their chests and then darkness.

It feels like all the air is sucked from my chest as the tears begin to build, blurring my sight as my nose stings. Fighting the urge to roll into a ball, I ask, "W-What happened?" There is no strength in my voice, only pain.

Shuffling forward, Searaphina wraps her arms around me. "Your father severed your connection to the family line." With each word, a new tear falls.

"I am homeless with no family. What will I do?" I do not mean to speak the words outloud. Searaphina pulls away before turning me to face her.

"Do not ever say that, you have me. We are all that we need. I no longer have a family. I am an orphan and, now, so are you." Her words are meant to help to calm me but they only make it worse.

While the tears fall, my heart beats harder than ever before as I ask the one thing I need to know. "Why?"

Sucking in slow breaths through my mouth, I focus on Searaphina. I know that she has the answer I need. I can see it on her face. "Please Phina, I need to know, you cannot hide this from me."

She swallows. "Silio, I overheard something once they returned from their urgent matter." She stops, reaching for my hands and taking them in her own.

"I think it is because of the blood tie. I do not know how they found out but I promise you I will investigate until I have answers. They seemed to think the blood tie is some type of dark magic." Searaphina keeps speaking but her words become a distant buzzing as my mind races.

'I was doing what I was told, I was sent here to protect the future Queen to be her friend, advisor, a fae she could trust and now I am being punished for doing what was asked of me. I HAVE LOST EVERYTHING. They do not understand it, if I take the parchment back to them, show them, they will understand, they will see it is a good thing. It will protect Searaphina and the Neraphina kingdom!'

"I have to go back!" Standing, I run towards the chamber doors. Searaphina races after me, calling my name but it does not reach me, the only thing I can hear is the beat of my broken and shattered heart. Opening the door, I run straight into a wall of muscle. Dezmond's hands wrap around my arms, pinning them in place as I begin to yell and scream, trying to hit him, kick him, anything to let me go.

"I have to go back, they need to understand!" I hear the distant sound of some fae calling for the healer but I pay them no mind as I struggle against Dezmond; he holds me to his chest as he sits down, wrapping his tree trunk legs around my own, holding me in place so I cannot hurt him or anyone else.

He whispers to me, "Sil, it's going to be okay, you will be okay." It is the last thing I hear before the world goes black.

CHAPTER 12

A SHADOW

Searaphina

Her face ashen and her hair limp, Velasilio offers me my gown. I do not know when she last took the time to care for her appearance or slept a full night. I often hear her wake screaming, calling out to her family, asking them to stay and not to leave her all alone. Dezmond has requested to be able to support her, I have allowed him to do so as long as he continues his duties with me at the same time. I know Gregor, Onree and Cassidie are more than capable, but with everything going on and being away from the castle I do not wish to be at risk.

Velasilio spends her days following me like a ghost, only doing her duties. I have prayed to Datriminish that she snaps out of it soon. I need her back. With the royal tour coming to an end and no twin flame in sight I know the council will be filling the halls with eligible males they see fit for me to wed. Their breeding will be impeccable and their families wealthy so they are seen as appropriate males. I have requested that they also send out invitations to some of the more desirable females as well to see if they wish to come to court and try their luck for my hand.

Once the lace of my corset is done, I turn to Velasilio and take her hands in my own. "Silio, please take the day to rest. We will be here for two more days before we return home."

Her head is down as she looks to her feet. Placing my hands on her face, I gently tip her head up. Her large eyes meet mine: they are sunken and have begun to redden around the edges. Her lip trembles as she closes her eyes and a single tear drips down her cheek as she agrees with me. With her hands in mine, I lead her out of my chambers and into her own. I take her straight to the bed and she sits at the edge, her eyes downcast.

"You will sleep, then when you wake, bathe and dress, you will attend the ball this evening and we will have fun." My voice is stern and leaves no room for argument. She just nods once before laying down.

I need to stop indulging her sadness and try to bring her out of it with some lighthearted fun. It has been five days since her father disowned her and it is time to step up, she is the Queen's maid and has duties that require her attention.

As I leave her room I turn to Dezmond. "Stay with her today, wake her in four hours and assist her if she needs it."

I continue past him and wave at Onree, Cassidie and Gregor to follow me.

"Of course, my Queen."

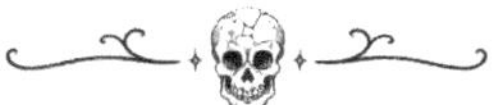

'Datriminish *above, that was a long and boring day!'*

I stroll into Velasilio's chambers. She stands before a long, dirty mirror dressed in a dark blue, sweetheart neckline gown that is fitted tight to her body. When she moves, purple hues shimmer along the gown and the sheer, thick straps. I cannot make out her face but she must notice me as she turns and offers a gentle bow.

"Phina, I did not hear you come in." Her eyes meet mine. I notice a small amount of light has come back to them.

"That is quite alright, I did not wish to disturb you. I was unsure if you were still sleeping." Her soft smile drops as her eyes go to the bed before she looks back at me.

"I understand that I have let you down and have not been myself recently. Today Dez and I had a conversation or two and he helped me to focus on the small, positive things happening around me. My grief will never stop or shrink but I will grow around it." She looks at her hands as they rub together, her cheeks turning pink.

Stepping forward, I take her hands in my own. Her gaze lifts and our eyes lock onto one another's. She offers me a sweet smile but I can see that she is only moments from tears once more. I need to distract her.

"So it is Dez now?" I raise my eyebrows suggestively. She laughs.

"Phina none of that, we simply spoke."

"I am sure that is all that happened, did you happen to be naked when you spoke, perhaps in bed or with you still riding his dick?" Her eyes widen and her mouth pops open in an 'O' as she reprimands me.

"Must you speak so brazenly? I was definitely not naked nor was I on his member." Her cheeks turn pink as she pulls her hands from mine. Throwing my head back, I laugh. She has always used more appropriate language, even if it is just the two of us.

I often find I allow my royal decorum to drop and just be a young female when no others are around. Velasilio does not unless she is angry or drunk. Then, she often loses all inhibitions and allows her fun nature to be revealed. I have many fond memories of her as a drunken mess and the court not being able to say a single thing as they knew I have my own temper if Velasilio is disrespected. She may be my maid but she is also a part of me; what is said of her is said of me. We are two halves that create a whole.

"Very well, perhaps this evening we will find you a male that you can..." Placing her hands on her hips, she waits for me to continue. Biting my tongue, I think of the best way to say this.

"A male that you can have a respectful conversation with." Her hands drop and she blows out a breath before she can speak. I talk over her.

"And then you may sit your petite bottom upon his face." Her eyes almost bulge at me before she places her hands to her lips and I know she is holding back a laugh.

With an evil smile I ask, "Was that not the most graceful way of me telling you to let a male devour your pussy?" I am unable to finish my sentence without bursting into laughter which pushes Velasilio over the edge as well.

Once we have calmed ourselves, we straighten our gowns and leave her chambers to enjoy the evening's festivities. As we stroll through the manor house to the ballroom, my four guards follow us. When we enter they will ensure my safety with two of them at my back and the others will remain at a distance to be looking out for any danger.

"Cassidie and Dezmond will stay with me this evening, Onree and Gregor you can be on the lookout." A course of agreements can be heard as we arrive at the large doors.

The harold standing to the side quickly moves in front of us knocking twice to have the other servants open the doors. As they slowly move inwards, gold light and warmth hits us; the delicious scents of roasted meat and fresh wine are next, and last is the sweet sound of music. A string quartet is playing a lively melody for couples to dance.

"Introducing Queen Searaphina and her maid, Velasilio." Trumpets sound from somewhere and a path is cleared for us. As I enter, each court member bows or curtsies to show their respect. I offer them a polite smile as I stroll to the cleared space, which I can see has been used for the evening's dancing.

As we stand at the edge, the music becomes louder and the others go back to their prior activities. The many couples dancing ensure to put on a display for me as I watch them. As my eyes track them, my mind wanders to a different pair, one that stands next to me. The entire walk here I had kept an eye on Dezmond and Velasilio. It would seem that their joking and teasing flirtations have settled into a more intimate game now, in fact they have not spoken once. It is easy to see that they clearly like one another. It has been this entire tour and I believe that over time they may come to voice these emotions, though I am bored of waiting, I may need to help push this along.

Lifting my hands, I clap once. The music stops, and all dancers still. With a smile, I project my voice. "I am looking for a male who would enjoy a dance with their Queen and another for my dear friend Velasilio."

With haste, two males stride forward. From their clothing—fine pants with tight, fitted blouses that are tucked in, and waist coats—I can tell they are from good households. When they speak their names, I know exactly who they are.

"Good evening, my Queen. My name is Lans Onti and this is my cousin, Cullen Onti." They bow deeply before holding their hands out for us to take. They are the sons of Dukes in the neighbouring town and are both highly respected males. Perfect for a Queen to dance with. I take Lans's hand and allow him to sweep me onto the floor.

His hands are large and soft, a male who lives a cushioned life, most likely has been handed everything. His blonde locks are curly and stay close to his head, his green eyes meet mine and his smile is straight, his teeth white. As we twirl, I get a glimpse of Velasilio and Cullen. His dark hair is tied back, his ocean blue eyes focused on only her, whereas her own seem to wander to a certain male each time they pass. My gaze darts to Dezmond, his own track each step they take while they also move to me from time to time. I should correct this behaviour and remind him that I am his sole responsibility here but this is far more enjoyable. His hands begin to ball into fists as Cullen leans in and whispers something to Velasilio that has her laughing.

It is good to have her coming back to her old self; she was of no use to me if she was unable to break the confines of her grief. Not that I would let her go, but having to get another maid to learn everything would have been quite annoying. I am thankful that Dezmond was able to help her.

As the music slows and Lans bows once and thanks me for the dance, I keep my eyes on Velasilio. Cullen does the same, only he takes her hand and places a soft kiss to the back of it. My gaze immediately goes to Dezmond who watches the exchange with fire in his eyes. Next to him, Cassidie has eyes only for me as she should.

When the music begins again, a new fae steps forward. This one is a bright pink fae her hair is cut short to her ears and styled at the top, her gown has a cut out in the front and I see she wears pants under. Introducing herself as Madonna, I accept her invitation to dance.

This is the way of things for the reminder of the night. As we dance, Dezmond watches Velasilio, I watch them both, and Cassidie watches me. I do notice that she looks to grow increasingly annoyed with each fae I dance with, often more towards the females, interesting.

Velasilio

Using all the strength I can find, I pull the corset tighter, cinching Searaphina's waist. The gown she has chosen today is new, the skirt is cut short and she wears trousers underneath. I did notice a few fae wearing this style last evening. It is definitely one I like, all the joys of a nice gown with the ease of pants. This would make riding a unicorn easier, no longer needing to sit sidesaddle or have your thighs becoming chaffed from sweat. I may need to look into purchasing one myself.

"Is that as tight as it goes?" Even as she asks I can hear that she struggles to breathe.

"If I was to pull this any tighter you would not be able to breathe." Tying off the ends, I stand back to take in her attire. The pants are black while the skirt is a deep emerald green that stops just above the ground at her back and to the sides. The corset is a separate piece that matches the skirt and has a low cut front that stops at the centre of her breasts.

The entire ensemble is stunning. While I stand in a more simple, lilac gown that has a sweetheart neckline and long sheer sleeves that hang from my shoulder but reach my fingertips. Today we are to enjoy that last day of the royal tour and tomorrow we will return to the castle.

Today, the Duke and Duchess of Onti are hosting a tournament in the Queen's name. I am interested to see this as we have not attended one in a few years as they are often seen as frivolous and a waste of coin. They are only to be completed on a special occasion or if there is a matter to be settled that requires a battle but they do not wish for the bloodshed that comes with a war.

Brushing her hands down her body once again, Searaphina takes in her own look before turning to me with a smile. "Well let us be off, it is a short ride to where the tournament is being held." With that, she turns and strides from the room with me following behind.

Sitting in the carriage, I try to ignore Searaphina as her eyes stare holes into my head. I know what she will say and I am not in the mood to hear it. I slept terribly last evening. I felt horrible dancing with each of the males, in front of Dezmond. He did not look as though he was concerned, as each time I swept my gaze over him, his eyes were on his Queen. Even if I was hoping for him to care, he has not said anything to me of his intentions, but I know that there is more there than a possible friend.

Of course I had seen him around the castle before she became Queen, but he never made much conversation, only an odd comment or two.

Turning, I lock eyes with Searaphina, unable to take it any longer. "What would you like?" My tone has more bite than I mean but I have little control today. My mind has been in a mess for the last few days and I am unable to contain my true behaviours.

To no surprise, Searaphina matches it with her own bite. "I would like you to put on your big female trousers and go fuck Dezmond instead of sitting here and sulking."

"Phina! Why must you be so vulgar about it?" Refusing to answer me, she only shrugs and continues on.

"Silio, I do not see why you are waiting. Being in your position comes with special abilities. Not a soul will speak ill of you for *fucking* any fae you wish." Squinting my eyes, I place the back of my hand under my chin and flick it out at her. This only causes her to cackle a laugh at me.

"Fine, I can see when my helpful advice is unwanted, I shall leave you be... for now." She rubs her hands together as if she is an evil, dark fae.

Shaking my head, I settle back into my seat. I lift the curtain to see that particular male riding his unicorn; the way his thighs press inwards to keep the beast moving, his left arms relaxing on his leg, the way his large hand is resting on his thick thigh. Biting my lower lip, I start to think about where those hands can go and what they may be able to do. Hearing a slight giggle, I close the curtain and sit back, crossing my arms, and stare daggers at Searaphina, but this just causes her to laugh louder.

Before long, we arrive at the tournament.

Leaving the carriage, we are led up large, wooden steps and onto a platform with a row of cushioned seats.

Luckily, the day passes quickly. Seeing that many warriors fighting for a title seems silly to me, but they all battle with such ferocity and strength it is hard not to marvel at them. Many use strength to win and others use wisdom to outwit their opponents, there is hand to hand combat, a joust where I feel sick for the unicorns' potential of injury, and many more challenges. When they are complete, each of the winners are offered a prize in gold, and an invitation to tonight's ball. I have a feeling that it will pass just as last evening, with so many dances that my feet will tire and I shall need to soak them once more. There is also a possibility that, if I ask Seara-phina nicely, I could dance with Dezmond.

*L*ast evening was horrible. I danced and danced with so many eligible males that I lost track of each name, and the one male I *wanted* to dance with refused me. I understand why he needed to care for our Queen's safety and yet I find that I am frustrated by the twatnuckle. He stood there all evening with a face that looked as though he was ready to kill and averting his eyes when I looked over. Of course I noticed this and, still, when I asked him to dance he turned me away. Now I sit in this stupid carriage on our way back to the castle with no royal consort for Searaphina and no plan as to what we will do next.

The council will be expecting answers and if we do not have them they will have a plan and a son or nephew to offer as a suitor for Searaphina. Many of which I am sure want nothing more than her title. I just wish for her to find a male or female who will love her and enjoy her company, not just the things her title offers. She deserves so much more than this. If she must marry, let it be her twin flame or at least a fae she may learn to love. I need to come up with a plan to help her to ensure that the fae she marries is honourable, has a strong wit and will be able to protect her.

I begin to chew on my fingernails while I think of what to do.

"Silio are you alright?" Searaphina's voice snaps me from my thoughts.

"Hmm?"

"You are lost in that head of yours again, what is going on in there?" Leaning forward, she taps a finger to my forehead and I cannot help but laugh softly at the action.

Swatting her hand away, I answer, "When we return, the council will want a meeting."

"Yes, they will."

"They will want to know if you have chosen a fae to wed and when you say you do not know they will thrust their kin upon you."

"Thrust their kin? Silio you sound as if you are going mad?" Her head tilts to the left as she surveys me.

"I am not mad, I mean they will be throwing their eligible males into court to gain your attention." Searaphina nods her head along with me.

"This is true, but I am Queen. I have the final say and, yes, I do plan to marry around my two hundred and twenty first birthday but I will ensure whoever I choose is the right fit for the crown." Her hand rests on my leg as she offers me a gentle and reassuring pat.

"I understand this but with royal duties taking over you will not have time outside of balls and feasts to meet new fae, and what if your fated is a commoner? You will never meet."

"We just went on the royal tour, there was not a single male or female who...gave me any reason to believe that there could be a connection."

Her slight pause offers a glimmer of hope: she was trying to choose her words carefully. Did a fae actually gain her attention or did she truly not feel anything?

CHAPTER 14

WHAT FUN

Kadance

"Big K!" His shrill voice pierces my ears and I have to hold in the urge to slaughter him where he stands.

"Oh K look, your bestie is here!" Ray perks up with a mix of joy and sarcasm as she speaks. She has been in a foul mood this week and I know why, I just refuse to confirm my suspicions.

Through gritted teeth, I demand, "Don't encourage this vapid parasite, Ray."

Picking up my beer I take a large swig.

With a shiteating grin, Ray drinks her own before Zeck, the local 'attraction' as he likes to call himself, walks towards us. I rather call him a flea under my boot and not worth a single speck of my attention. Though I can't understand why, if only the old god would listen to me and smite this stain from our kingdom. He is nothing but a bottom feeder who thrives off the misfortunes of others.

Standing at the end of our booth, his eyes run over me, and my skin crawls. The stench of flowers causes me to scrunch my nose and take shallow breaths, as to not ingest his overpowering perfumes. I never trust a fae who hides their scent using this stuff. My sense of smell is more powerful than most and yet if these fake aromas are used even I am unable to tell if the fae is a dirty fucking cheat or honest.

"Oh Big K, why the sad face?" Leaning over the table, he reaches out to touch my hand that rests next to my glass. As his hand moves close to mine I can see that he is testing me to see if I will pull away.

With my right hand on the table and my left resting on my thigh I unsheathe a dagger and bring it down, embedding it, along with some fabric from his stupid outfit, into the table. His pathetic yelp is music to my ears as he freezes in place. Ray picks up her drink and downs it before calling for two more across the crowded inn. Even with so many fae cramped into the space, Robert hears her; he offers a nod as he begins to pour our drinks that Lil will bring over. They are a well-oiled machine: a father and daughter team that work well together is a rare thing.

With my left hand on the blade I let go to down the rest of my drink all while ignoring the now-shaking Zeck bent forward over the table. My mug hits the table and causes the now-pale male to flinch. His eyes stay locked on my face as he swallows and goes to speak but I cut him off, my voice low and monotone.

"You really fucked up tonight. My day has been well shit and you coming over to me and bringing your foul, fake stench just irritates me further. If you don't wish for this dagger to be in your gut next, I suggest you get the fuck away from me." With that, I pluck my dagger from the table. The second he is free, Zeck pulls his arm to his chest and runs, and I watch as he goes.

An amused chuckle comes from Ray and I turn my head to look at her instead. Dagger in hand, I point it at her. "Yes?"

Shaking her head, she sits back in her chair and crosses her arms. "You really are an asshole, you know?"

"I have heard that once or twice." The corner of my lip tilts as she chuckles again.

"Here we are, two more mugs of ale. Can I get y'all somthin else?" Lil asks.

"All good here, thanks darl." I offer her a small smile that has a blush working its way over her cheeks. She does a quick nod and rushes away.

Watching as she walks away I take in the sway of her hips and her perky ass. *'Maybe I should get to know her better.'* My thoughts don't make it far before a hand comes down on my own and I turn to see Ray staring at me with her, 'don't you think about it' look.

"Absoulutey not, I like this place and I won't allow your second head to get us banned from here too." She makes a point to look downwards but the table is in the way so she just looks stupid.

Lifting my glass, I take a long sip and let her stew as she crosses her arms again, waiting for me to agree. Making a few exaggerated sounds about swallowing my drink, I place the mug down and open my mouth to tell her exactly where she can shove her 'rule' and that I will stick my cock wherever I wish, when a set of four King's guards come in and the entire tavern stops. From our booth in the far left corner closest to the bar I watch as they search for some fae. I always sit with my back to a wall, facing the exit, for this exact reason.

Ray sits up straight as the room goes quiet. When she spots them, she quickly hides her head and looks at me. "So are we running or..." She doesn't get a chance to finish as they spot us and my name is called for all to hear.

"Kadance!" The King calls.

Strolling into the throne room, I make sure to take my time. He has disturbed my night and I am in no rush to be given my marching orders, though, if it involves bloodshed, I could be swayed.

The large space begins to darken as night falls, the few lights that are lit emit a low light. The King sits on his throne, the three step dais elevating him above the others. The high ceilings and dark wood floors make everything echo, including my name, the six times he has yelled it.

As I reach the foot of his dais I make sure to give a quick nod and then hold his gaze. "Yes, my King." My tone could be taken as sarcasm and I am lucky he has need of me or I would find myself in the dungeon. That thought has my lip tilt at the corner. He could try.

When I actually focus on his face it is set in a frown as he gives a disappointed shake of his head. "Your special talents are needed. You are to go to Neraphina..."

I cut him off before he continues. "Neraphina? What use are those light fae to us?"

His nose scrunches and his eyes narrow as anger coats each word. "If you would shut your mouth and allow your *King* to finish I would tell you." Wanting this over sooner rather than later I hold up my hands in surrender.

"We have news that King Armard and Queen Alathieria are dead. Before you ask, it does not matter how, only that they are and now their daughter Searaphina has taken the throne. We do not know enough about her."

"You want me to go all the way to Neraphina to fuck their Queen?"

I swear, if it could, steam would be coming from his ears. Standing quickly, his wings snap out; their dark leather with spiked tips similar to many of the dark fae, only his are far larger than most, (yet still I know mine are bigger). Standing still, I cross my arms over my chest with a small smirk. I don't even flinch at his attempt to intimidate me.

Taking a deep breath, he balls his fist before his wings settle against his back again. "You are not to lay a hand on the Queen. Your task is to use your shadows to infiltrate her court and be a spy for your King. We need to know everything about her and what she may already know of us." My mouth opens to offer a remark but he continues to speak loudly.

"You are not to fuck a single light fae in that court! You leave tomorrow morning. They are not to know of your presence, is that clear!"

Rolling my shoulders, I inhale deeply and reply like the good little soldier. 'Yes."

"Good, now get out of my sight." With a flick of his hand, he dismisses me.

CHAPTER 15

A COUNCIL MEETING

Searaphina

After two days in a carriage, only stopping overnight at an inn for rest, I am exhausted and ready to lay in bed for a week. But I am Queen now and that is unacceptable, especially when my future is being discussed.

So now we sit in the council chambers ready to discuss what will happen next. My two hundred and twenty first birthday is just over two years away. The council would prefer I marry before than to ensure all children conceived are seen as legitimate, this would mean I would marry for the crown and not love. I know Velasilio wishes I could wait like her to find my twin flame, all she wants is the more rare and true of all relationships.

My royal tour was my opportunity to see if I had an internal pull towards any other, my fated will not reveal themselves until my two hundred and twenty first birthday, or just before, as the need to be with them would increase. There was one male I thought could have sparked something but it quickly faded away when Velasilio joined me. I assume it was a moment of lust as it had been a few days since I enjoyed the company of another. I may need to find a moment alone with Cassidie this evening: we have grown rather close and have shared a moment here and there on our travels, but she would not allow anything further to happen while I was not *'appropriately protected'*. I told her that, with her in my bed I was more protected than with her at my door.

"Don't you agree, your Highness?" Alabaster's stoney voice asks, his gray eyes staring at me. One of his aging hands strokes his long, white beard while the other drums impatiently along the table, waiting for my answer.

'Shit!' I had not been paying attention. I was lost in my own thoughts of lust.

Clearing my throat and sitting up straighter, I reply, "I believe this idea has merit, but I would like to gather some more information prior to making my decision."

Looking at each other, they have quiet murmured conversations before all turning back to me and nodding their agreements. I will need to speak with Velasilio and hear what I have just agreed to think about, hopefully it will not bite me in the ass. My gaze sweeps over to her as she sits to my right, scribbling down her notes to ensure I never miss a thing. I have only been head of these meetings a few times now and each time they cover so many items I am unable to retain it all. I try to peek at what she is writing and I see the words *feasts* and *court*, safe to assume they wish to hold a feast for the court soon.

That might explain why, when I asked to gain more information, they all took a moment to understand why.

I try to focus on what is next on our list and, as expected, it is the one thing I have just spent the last week focused on and would rather not speak of. Clearing his throat, Alabaster speaks again.

"Was there any success with the royal tour?" I want to roll my eyes—can they see a consort next to me?

Pushing the words aside, I decide instead to be the Queen I am. "Unfortunately I did not feel a spark towards any fae." I watch them all carefully to see how they may react, to my surprise they do not even flinch, just nod once and then Alabaster continues.

"As to be expected, as a twin flame is rare indeed. We must move forward and look to the security of our kingdom. Just this morning, we received two more letters from islands closer to the north speaking of dark fae entering their lands." This gets them all speaking and of course they all agree.

Holding a hand out, he quiets them all. "We have compiled a list of all the eligible males in the land whose families have prominent places among the court..."

Holding my hand up, I stop him. "You must add all eligible females to that list as well."

Pursing his lips, he says, "We will add them to the list, we only hope that you chose a male for your consort as it will be easier for you to produce an heir then with a female."

"Very well, I will take your advice under consideration." I understand their concerns, but I will allow my body to tell me who is right for me to marry and have a child with. After at least one royal heir is conceived I will be able to sleep with any fae I wish and it will not matter as we have what is needed.

After another fifteen minutes of back and forth over a ball in my name to be held in a few weeks time to introduce me to the eligible fae of court, the meeting finally comes to an end. Onree, who has been quietly standing behind me for the duration of this meeting, steps forward and pulls my chair back so that I may move away from the table. At the same moment there is a collective screech as wooden chair legs are scraped across the stone floor. The way they move in perfect unison standing from their chairs and bowing their heads is extremely creepy.

Shaking off the uneasy feeling I take a handful of my skirt and pick it up, careful not to stand on it as I leave the table.

As I make my way out of the chambers, Dezmond moves to stand in front of me and opens the door. The scurry of soft footsteps follows me.

Looking over my shoulder at Velasilio, her gown is simple lilac;

she often uses different shades of purple in her gowns as they complement her tawny skin, silver hair, and darker wings. Unlike most, her wings have an almost black lining. When we stand beside one another you would not think we were cousins.

She usually smiles, but not today. Instead, her brow is furrowed and her eyes set in concentration while her mouth moves as if she is whispering to herself. Shrugging to myself, I keep moving out of the chambers, ready to be in the fresh air again.

Cassidie and Gregor offer me a small bow before they begin to walk ahead of me. Onree and Dezmond will follow behind. Just as I take the third step, I hear a quiet curse before I turn and see Velasilio, her face inches from the stone stair as Onree holds her waist, having caught her just in time. Her face is now slack with shock and she looks over her shoulder to him.

"Thank you Onree, that would have been unpleasant." He offers her a small smile.

"It was not a problem Velasilio, I would hate to see you harmed." He quickly pulls her upright and she stumbles a step and presses against his chest; if I am not mistaken I see a slight blush work over his pale features. From the corner of my eye, I take in Dezmond who is looking rather displeased.

Bending, he quickly collects the papers she had dropped in the fall, standing he extends them to her. "Here Vel." He makes a point of using a nickname and his eyes focus on Onree, not on her; both males seem to size one another up.

Her gaze darts from Onree to Dezmond. "Thank you, I was so focused on these that I misjudged where the step was." She speaks quickly and it feels as though she may be trying to settle them down.

Rolling my eyes at the stupid alpha males, I say, "Well, take your nose from those and let us move outside. I am in desperate need of fresh air." All three sets of eyes move to me now and I hold in my laugh at the way they all look as if they are children who have been caught doing something naughty.

Finally the moment breaks and she thanks them both before racing up the stairs to my side. She leans in to whisper, "Thank you, I do not know what just happened."

I quickly look back before I shrug. "You, Miss Silio, seem to have caught the eye of not one of my guards but two. If they keep this up I may need to dismiss them."

CHAPTER 16

Velasilio

As we move through the many corridors and staircases to get to the south garden, I cannot help but feel eyes on me as I move. The tension from the males a moment ago was not something I had expected. Dezmond and I are not together, he helped me through a particularly rough patch after my father disowned me and helped me to write a letter to him which should have arrived by now.

I wish to hear from my family and have answers. I have been trying to find the answer myself but I see no reason in sight. I have tried to keep myself busy with helping Searaphina though her own grief, and to find a solution to her problems within court.

The largest at present being the influx of suitors trying to get to her through me. I have sworn never to allow another male who had visited court to leave me heart broken when they proved their true intentions. A few succeeded in sleeping with her, too, only because we kept our connection quiet and Searaphina did not know. I often try to be with others who *visit* court rather than the ones who live here. Most of the fae around our age who live at court have already been with Searaphina and I am not interested in sleeping with her discarded partners.

I am thankful that, while Dezmond has been in the guard for some time, I have not seen him chasing Searaphina and that she has taken an interest in Cassidie.

We finally step out of the castle and into the lush garden. There is such a magical quality to the flowers that grow here, as they are not seen in any of the other castle gardens. It is one of my favourite places to think.

With the last frost of winter fading faster with each sunrise, we are seeing the new blooms begin to break through. Many of the court members are out this morning enjoying the sunshine.

All of the noise fades away as I close my eyes and inhale the fresh air, filling my lungs and helping to clear my mind. I need to find a way to help Searaphina. She will not accept any fae who is pushed upon her by the council; she will want to make her own choice. Opening my eyes, I step forward and place my arm in hers as we begin our stroll.

With the new season, more of the royal court will flock to the castle. There will be high teas, balls and feasts to be held over the coming months. Many of the females we pass stop and curtsy to their Queen before they continue on their own leisurely strolls. The gravel crunches underfoot as we move, the sounds of birds chirping and the buzzing of insects as they fly from flower to flower feeding. I watch as a feathertail lands on a tree branch next to a nest, another pops its head up and they share a moment nuzzling one another.

I cannot stop the sigh that leaves me as I watch the exchange and then I feel a gentle tug on my arm. "What is frustrating you, Silio?"

My stare leaves the two love birds and I look forward, taking a breath in before I speak. "What will you do?"

When Searaphina responds, I try not to let my annoyance show. "I am unsure of what you mean? I will continue to be Queen." Her flat tone and complete lack of understanding rubs me the wrong way.

"Phina, you know exactly what I mean. The council will be

throwing their own family members at you soon and they will expect you to pick a fae, not to mention we are no closer to finding your parents' killer. If it was King Baritus, the dark fae are a threat and one that may attack again" I rush to get all of it out in one go and to keep my anger from showing at how little she seems to care.

She stops moving and turns to face me, her hands come to either side of my head. "Oh sweet Silio, you worry too much. We have the guards on high alert, no fae is getting near me unless I allow it. I will marry when I need to and they will secure our kingdom, it is all the more reason to just accept the fact I will find a consort here at court and settle."

I go to speak again but she stops me with her hand over my mouth. I am sure to an outsider this may seem inappropriate, but the court are well used to our relationship now and not a single fae blinks an eye at us. "You must stop. We have just returned, you are searching for a distraction from what happened with your family. We need to take a few days to calm ourselves before we throw ourselves to the fires and allow ourselves to burn."

Her hand leaves my face and I just stare at her, I do not think I even understand what she has just said. I fight everything in me not to keep arguing with her and instead I just nod at her and we both turn and continue on our way. Though my mind does not: there are options as Queen. She can try to have them change the law that a child out of wedlock is legitimate, but then what makes a royal line? It would mean that any fae could be crowned and there is no care for lineage, chaos would soon follow, no that is not an option.

As we keep moving though the gardens, the sun starts to drop behind the clouds and night will soon fall. Looking over my shoulder, I take in Dezmond, the way that his shirt sits tight to his biceps and how his amber eyes stare back at me before looking away. I move from him to Onree, his blue hair is cut short and I want to run my hands through it.

My thoughts are interrupted with a quick tug on my arm, forcing me to look forward again. "So have you decided which one you will ride? Or will you take them both?"

My face heats and I quickly go from calm to embarrassment. Glancing over my shoulder, both males look anywhere but me; they clearly hear the remark.

And now I have to kill my best friend and Queen. "Oh Phina you are just..." Without finishing my sentence, I go to give her a little nudge.

But of course she anticipates this and steps backwards just in time, so instead of bumping into her I trip over my own feet and go spinning towards the bushes. Unluckily for her, I am still holding her arm and taking her down with me.

Twigs snapping and our combined shrieking is all I hear as we tumble into the shrubbery. I do not know what hurts more, the hard and unforgiving dirt beneath me or Searaphina's elbow as she lands on top of me and takes away any remaining breath I had. The world is dark and I cannot see anything from underneath my Queen; her hair is in my mouth and the sweet scent of jasmine is in my nose. Before long, I hear and feel the slight vibration of others running to their Queen's aid. I cannot for the life of me work out how none of the guards caught us. It was perfect timing to take my Queen out apparently, I do hope none of them get into trouble because of me.

When Searaphina starts to laugh, I join her. "Well that was not your finest moment," she teases while she struggles to move.

Just then, many voices sound in a panic, "Your Majesty", "Are you alright?" and "Quickly, help the Queen to stand."

My voice is strained as I cannot breathe properly. "Absolutely not, and, while I am happy to cushion your fall, I would appreciate being able to breathe again."

She manages to move just off of my stomach and we lay almost face-to-face, our legs tangled. "Well I guess that will teach you from trying to harm your Queeeee—." She does not finish as she is pulled from the bush.

I do not see who it is as the last rays of sunlight blind me when I look up; it all looks like a large and quick shadow. I blink, and it is gone.

"Now that the Queen has been rescued, a little help please." I call out to any fae who might be listening, and then a hand appears from the bushes. Taking it, I allow them to pull me free. When the spots dancing in my vision leave, Dezmond stands in front of me with a goofy smile on his face.

When I look past him, I see Searaphina with Cassidie, whose hands move gently over her Queen's body all to ensure that she is unharmed in her fall. They are cute together and they look like they are happy, even more so when Searaphina takes her hands, leans forward and kisses her cheek. Cassidie's ivory skin goes bright pink as she asks a final time if the Queen is okay before moving to stand at the back this time, swapping with Onree, who is now at the front looking sheepishly over at me; he was closest to the Queen and probably feels terrible that he did not catch her.

"Vel? Vel, are you okay?" I did not realise I had been staring off at everything else and a worried Dezmond was trying to speak to me. Shaking my head, I make eye contact and smile.

"Dezmond, I am fine," He reaches up and pulls twigs, leaves and even flower petals from my hair. He chuckles as he continues to pull out all the plant life I have picked up. I laugh with him.

CHAPTER 17

Kadance

The flight to Neraphina was long and boring. After I arrived, I kept a low profile with the locals. Many are out in the sun today and I was able to listen in as they wasted their day strolling and talking. I spent the better part of the day listening to them yabber about how beautiful their new Queen is, how generous and kind she seems, much like her father and mother who were well-liked, from what I have gathered. Some of the servants spoke to one another of instances where they had seen a more violent and aggressive side, of Queen Searaphina, though most seem to believe that her strength will help her to deal with the dark fae issue. Now *this* got me interested: Baritus has not spoken of his own fae causing issues for the light fae and I wonder if this is a dirty little secret of his. I will need to investigate further. They spoke of the dark fae presence in the outer territories, small islands where the main source of trade is fishing.

After dark, I make my way towards the slums to find an inn to stay in. Well, Neraphina's idea of a slum, I suppose: the place is nothing like the slums in Vixeruas, but most of the fae here are wearing clothing far less fine than the others. This area is darker the scent is of mud and shit, no torches line the walk way as the night falls.

There's an inn with crumbling bricks, a frayed thatched room, and iron bars filling gaps in the door where wood has slipped away. Perfect. With a few gold nerphi in my hand, I push open the door, ducking as I enter. My nose is accosted by the stale ale. The room is small, only three booths to the far left side and four standing bar tables with stools in the middle. The far left is a stand for musicians and at the back is a small bar. To its left, a set of stairs leads above to where the chambers are.

Pulling the hood around my face, I make sure that my wings are flat against my back. I often enjoy having them out and on show, scaring the shit out of some and causing the scent of lust to perfume from others. The thought has my lips tilting up; I know that I would get a hearty mix of fear and lust here, many other fae wouldn't know if they should fight or fuck me, I would enjoy both.

I stride past the few who stand around drinking and make my way to the bar where a small, blue fae stands, polishing glasses. "What can I get ya?"

"One chamber and no questions." That has her looking up but before she can argue I place four gold nerphi on the bench. Her eyes go from the coins— probably more than she sees in a week—and then back to me.

Placing the glass down, she calmly reaches under the bench and removes a large, iron key. Placing it in front of me, her hand sweeps out and takes the coins. "Chamber four." With that she goes back to her task.

Taking the key, I turn and make my way to the room. Before I am out of ear shot she adds, "I hope you ain't going to be any trouble." That almost makes me smile: if only she knew who she just gave a key to.

I spent the morning exploring the castle. It was far easier than it should have been to get inside; these guards have to be some of the most useless I have ever seen. Not one noticed me or tried to stop me. Shame, as I would have enjoyed their pitiful attempts to do so.

It's not all down to their stupidity. I am excellent at my job, it helps I can use the shadows to my advantage, and adding a small image into their minds also helps; if they happen to notice that there is a large shadow, I request they move along and they do. Lesser magic may not be as powerful but I find that when the locals have no idea how to protect themselves from a simple mind spell that is their problem, not mine.

Today is all about gaining information. I have sent a letter to my King with the address where I will be staying while I am here. It will not take me long to get what I need and leave.

I detest the light fae, they are all fake smiles and hiding the most delicious and fun parts of themselves. Denying their true nature. They may seem to be open about their sex but I can see through that. It's in their laws about offspring, if an illegitimate child is born to royalty they can't take the crown. If you don't care about sex, why give two shits about what it produces?

In Vixeruas there are many children born of lust and they are celebrated, that is probably why our fae are thriving while theirs are dying off, another reason why my King wants to reunite our lands as one. He will take Neraphina by force if needed. Honestly, I would prefer it but he might want to take a more diplomatic approach and offer a marriage treaty for one of his three children.

Yet he has me here spying instead of engaging in peace talks. It would be easy as the whole castle is buzzing about the many upcoming balls and their hopes that the Queen will find a match soon. If she is so eager to be wed and breed then why not force her hand and push that she marry one of his children? I am sure at least two of them might be interested. I know that the third would absolutely refuse.

Each chamber I enter increased my hatred for how cherry and bright this place is: all of the rooms are white and filled with bright-coloured furniture. Screwing up my nose at the third yellow-decorated chamber in a row, I yet again find nothing of use. I am still looking for the council meeting room and the Queen's chambers. I found the throne room it was full of a flutter of fae preparing for a feast coming in two days. I listened in as they chatted and worked but there was nothing more to gain than I have already heard.

As I leave the throne room, I come across a group of young females: each one speaks of a dark and mysterious male they have seen roaming the halls today.

'*I need to have a little fun and they don't know it's me.*' A smirk crosses my lips as I think of a few more ways to toy with them, then one mentions feeling eyes on her and after that I can't stop myself.

On silent feet, I move towards them, using the alcoves of doors to hide in. Casting a small spell, I envision my hands gently running up and down one of their arms. She quickly jerks her arms to her chest and looks behind herself.

"What on earth was that?" she almost shrieks as she starts to turn in place, so I go for another one, blowing a light breeze over the back of her neck. It has her squealing and clutching the area.

I try not to laugh, and I allow my shadows to creep towards them, just lingering at their feet. Then the dark grey smoke starts to climb their legs. They all let out an ear-piercing scream before they turn and run, one even falls over her dress. I am smiling ear to ear now.

When the noise of chainmail clinking reaches me, I see the four guards round the corner and start searching for whatever has made the females so upset. Under the King's orders, I am not to be seen, and that means keeping a low profile, so no killing... yet.

Moving further down the hall, I continue to look for the meeting chambers. As I pass an open window to the north keep, I see that the sun is starting to lower; it won't be long until dark, and then I will have a harder time to find what I seek. The halls will become crowded as they seek the warmth and safety of indoors. Moving faster, I head towards where I believe the Queen's chambers are. When I round the corner I see just how useless the information is. Two guards stand at the Queen's door.

Just as I turn my back and begin to walk away, I pick up on a faint, sweet scent. My cock twitches as I think of the delectable creature that the sweet smell comes from. I try to inhale deeper but what the exact scent is alludes me. With my frustration growing, I decide it's time to take a trip to the dungeon to see if there are any traitors who might be willing to give me information. I track down the many staircases and halls to find the entrance. The pungent odor of rot and damp air comes from a large, dark, wooden door. When I push it open I am met with a set of deep, stone stairs. Descending them quickly, I pass a few closed doors. Just as I am about to walk past the last one, I stop, the same sweet scent is on the air, only stronger. Stepping up to the door, I listen. When I don't hear anything, I push it open. The empty space is small, a large table takes up the majority of the room, then chairs sit along either side and at the top is a large, wingback throne with a small version to the right.

This must be the meeting chamber. A rather interesting spot for it, but I can understand the logic: dark, secluded and with the thick walls surrounding it there is no chance for a spy to listen in. They believe it's safe because of these things and yet here I am.

There are papers over the large dark wood, some are scattered while others are in neat piles. I pick up one of the many parchments to see names, birthdates and portraits. As I shuffle through them I almost laugh at how pompous and ridiculous each one sounds.

Del Ambrouch. 'If I am chosen to be King I will bring peace, love and prosperity to the kingdom. I will provide the Queen with many strapping male heirs.'

That last one comes on strong, he really is just after her beauty. As I shuffle through, I find it is more of the same, each male offering their hand and what they will bring to the castle. I find it impossible not to scoff at each one. Then I see a list written by an Alabaster.

1. Who will the Queen marry?
2. How to handle the dark fae incursions?
3. Speak with King Baritus about peace.

Why do they need to speak with my King about peace? As far as I know, we have not given cause for them to believe we mean violence. A few incursions for some advantageous trade deals is hardly the work of a violent conquer.

Moving around the room, I see there is no other information here and that tantalising scent is growing on me the more I am in this chamber. Shaking off the odd sensation, I turn and leave. I now know the Queen seeks a husband; this is no surprise given their rules of succession.

As I head up the stairs, that faint scent still lingers. I try to ignore it but it almost calls to me.

'Fuck it.' Trudging up the stairs with a new energy, I chase down the scent, turning down corridors and stairs until it grows stronger, and then, just as I think I have found the source, I step outside and into a garden full to the brim with new flowers. The breeze washes away the scent I was looking for and now the strong florals are all I can smell.

I crinkle my nose before I snarl. "Fucking flowers!" I hate the way their perfume covers everything else, their overwhelming sickly sweetness hides a fae's true scent.

Looking out of the alcove I stand under, I take in the large gardens. There are a few small trees with one large willow tree toward the end of the area, a pathway winds in and out of the garden beds, they are brimming with all varieties of new life. Surrounding the gardens are high walls; a few alcoves line the walls, providing the perfect spot for me to hide in. With the sunlight fading it will be easier to be outside then inside soon.

I pull my hood up and move to the first alcove. As I do, I notice one female turn in my direction. She is bent at the knees, plucking a few roses, as she looks behind herself for whatever made the sound. I find the need to torment arising, and I need her far away from me so that I may find the Queen. Her eyes scan the area and just as she goes to turn back to her task I send out a small wave of shadows to circle her feet, dropping the temperature and whispering, "Better run."

Her eyes go wide before she swivels around so fast that she falls on her ass, then scrambles back to escape me. My lips tilt at the sight. I could have a lot of fun here, I just need a small amount of information to send home so that my King leaves me be.

I continue to survey the area, moving within the shadows. Just as I begin to believe the Queen is not here, a set of voices catch my attention from behind a large row of bushes. One voice sings to me, causing me to step forward, trying to see her, and sending a shiver straight down my spine to my balls.

I don't stop myself. Instead, I follow the sound. When I round the bushes, the most exotic female comes into view.

I take in her figure: the way her dress clings to her body, the slight jiggle of her breasts with each step, the sway of her hips. Her skin looks soft and smooth. I take in her luscious lips and imagine pushing my cock past them as she wraps her tongue around me and takes me deep.

I feel a strange pull inside my chest. I rub at it, my breakfast must be revolting against me. I watch, gathering any information I can about this pretty little fae. I don't understand the pull they say a twin flame or love has but I do know what the urge to bury my cock deep within a female is, and, right now, that's all I want to do. My mind is made up: no matter the mission my King has given me, it now comes second to my new obsession and I cannot wait to play with her. I hope that she will make it a challenge.

As the pair continue their stroll, I take in the four guards surrounding them: an older male and a female in front, two males behind.

I have found their Queen. Her beauty was not a lie and she holds herself in that way all royalty do. Ensuring I keep my distance, I watch the pair as they walk and talk. Others stop to curtsy before they continue on their way. Listening, I hear them speaking of marriage and an heir. There are also quiet murmurs of a looming war.

While the four guards stick close to the two of them, there are many other stations throughout the garden, most at the exits and entries. I count twelve guards in total. Even with their Queen here they don't do their jobs well; their eyes are often wandering to the closest female and they don't even try to hide it. If any of them were under my command, they would be whipped and, if needed, the offending appendage would be removed.

A shriek pulls me from my thoughts. Standing in the darkness, I look for whatever made that sound. The four guards are now standing looking into a large bush and then I notice feet sticking up from the bush. I don't think, I take off, pulling my hood over my head as I do. The remaining members of court rush towards the commotion with me, creating a crowd that is too occupied to pay attention to the tall stranger in their midst. For a kingdom that lost their last King and Queen due to a recent assassination, they are extremely relaxed and unaware of their surroundings.

I reach into the bush, and her sweet scent wraps around me, I suppress a groan. With the mess of bodies and bush I just grab the first female that I can; my hands roughly pull her out of the shrub and then I fight the urge to throw her over my shoulder and take her with me.

Only, before I can do anything further, I notice that the others are catching up with me. I may be faster than all of them and they may only see a blur of motion, but if I stay here any longer I will be caught and that will ruin all my new plans.

I leave. Lucky for me they are all distracted and I am able to slip away without being seen.

Back in the sanctuary of the alcove, I remove my dagger and begin to flip; my eyes never watch as I do, instead they are glued to the fae in front of me. My entire body wants to react, the need to spill the blood of the guard who has their hands on what will be mine. She smiles and I feel something crack inside my chest. It is a strange sensation and not one that I like. Anger surges in me at that guard getting the attention I deserve. They were not fast enough to catch her and they were so slow that I was able to slip in and out undetected; all but the precious gem amongst them knew I was there, she looked to me and I knew she felt it. I follow them as they continue their stroll right under the large, hanging leaves of the willow tree.

Using the leaves to keep myself hidden, I think of only her. This could become a problem. Being this close to her and without the breeze, her scent is stronger and I can tell that she is scared, but hopeful. While I enjoy watching her, my mind begins to wander and my desire takes hold.

I see her now laying on my bed, tied by the wrists and ankles. A small black cloth covers her eyes. Taking my blade, I run the cold metal along her naked flesh, slowly gliding the blade between her breasts, over her stomach and finally over her sweet little cunt. Would she shiver or moan in pleasure? Will her skin pebble and her nipples harden as I lean down and take her nipple into my mouth, biting gently? What if I kissed up her neck and then sunk my teeth into her smooth skin, what noises would she make? Would she lift her hips and grind against me, asking for more, or would she return the pleasure and leave her mark on me?

My cock hardens and presses painfully against my pants, my plans taking shape, my promise to her that I will ring every last drop of pleasure from her and then, just when she thinks I am finished, I will sink my cock into her dripping cunt and fuck her until she can't walk or talk.

With the silent promise, I know I need to leave before I blow my cover by stepping from my hiding place and taking her against the tree while her friend watches. I will learn everything I can and then I will claim her.

CHAPTER 18

QUEEN'S TOURNAMENT

Searaphina

I cannot get that scent out of my nose. It was dark and delicious, who was it? My mind has thought of nothing but the fae who pulled me from the bush, or at least I think it was a fae. They moved so quickly that, before I knew what had happened, they had vanished. As we continued our walk, Velasilio could tell I was distracted but said nothing. Now we stroll arm in arm in silence towards the large willow tree; dusk has fallen and the others are now retiring to the warmth inside.

"Phina, should we not return with the others?"

My wandering gaze returns to her face, and she offers me her sweet smile. "Not yet, I need a little more time outside before I am once again cornered by the council to introduce me to their visiting relatives." This earns me a small laugh from Velasilio, but she does not protest again.

We stand at the entrance to the willow tree, the leaves hanging down touch the grassy floor beneath, creating lush, green curtains to offer a sense of privacy. Turning to my guards, I say, "Please wait here." They each look to me as if they may argue. I understand the risk but with the gardens almost empty and their presence just beyond the tree, I am perfectly safe.

When they all have taken their places, I pull Velasilio along with me and we walk to the wrought iron bench sitting just to the left of the large tree.

Under the canopy it feels like a different world, the raw earth is damp and that scent clears my mind, chasing away the smell of my mystery fae. Part of me is sad to see it go but the other part is thankful it is no longer clouding my mind. With the sun all but gone, it is darker under the leaves now and yet the darkness feels like a warm embrace, allowing me to relax. We sit and, as the cold from the metal creeps in, I cannot help the slight shiver that wrecks my body; I also have a strange sense of being watched, though it vanishes not long after we sit down.

With my mind finally at ease, I close my eyes, only to be interrupted a moment later by Velasilio's voice. It irritates me, but I open my eyes and look at her.

"Hmm? I did not hear you, I was enjoying the peace and quiet." I try not to sound annoyed but that is a challenge when I do not get time to relax often. My mind is always on, always thinking of what I must do next to ensure my rule and the kingdom.

Unable to hold my stare, she looks at her hands before she starts to crack each finger; the sound makes my skin crawl, even if it does comfort her, so I place my hand over hers to stop it. "Silio? If you have something you wish to tell me please go on, you know I cannot stand that sound." I push my voice to be as calm as possible but today has been trying.

When I move my hand, she stretches out her fingers before she rubs them together and looks at her feet. "I will not let you lose hope. A partner is more than a breeding tool, you are more than that and you deserve happiness just as any other fae, it is so... so, utterly unjust!"

I can tell she was close to actually swearing just then. Watching her stumble over her words, all irritation washes away. I know that, out of every fae in this kingdom, she would do anything for me.

Her face hardens as her rage begins to simmer, I see a single tear roll down her cheek before she quickly swipes it away.

"You are the only one to make the choice, you should get a chance at love even if it is not your fated. You deserve someone worthy of you and the crown."

I give her hand a gentle squeeze. "You are right Silio, if I were a common fae I would have that chance, but you know as well as I that with our family titles come obligations and expectations. We are of noble birth. The only reason you have not had the same situation forced upon you is because you are no longer owned by your father, as I am by the kingdom." As the words leave my lips I watch her face fall. She takes a shaky breath in and another tear leaves her eye.

With a sigh I continue on. "With my parents dead I do not have a choice. I wish I could take the time to find some fae who was worthy or that I could love but I am not allowed the chance, unlike you. You are able to find what you truly seek, a true love, fated romance, something many fae would give anything to have. Without the family title hanging over your head."

My words seem to jar her from the sadness as she sits up straight, wiping at her eyes, quickly sniffing in and exhaling a harsh breath. "You are right, I am being insensitive. Your family is gone and I am moping though mine are still alive. I have choices that you do not, I should be grateful." Her words are strained. I do not believe any of them. I understand that she feels guilty and I can see that my words have made her remember that parents who banish you are still better than dead ones.

"That is what I wanted to hear! Now, let us think, how do you find a partner who is worthy?" I raise a hand to my chin and tap at my lower lip.

"What makes them worthy?" Velasilio muses. "They must be brave." I nod along with her. "Smart." Nod. "Kind and gentle."

"I suppose that would be a desirable trait for a royal consort. They must be strong and have a decent hand with a blade." Velasilio nods along. "They should hold wisdom and patience."

"Ohh, they must have decorum and know the appropriate etiquette," Velasilio adds.

"And, above all, they must be trustworthy and able to keep royal secrets."

We are both sitting at the edge of the bench now. "They must have good genetics." Velasilio is always trying to keep things respectable.

"They must be well endowed, do you mean?" Her head jerks around to look at me so quickly I almost jump back.

"Phina, They must have strong genes to pass to the child."

I cannot help but snicker at her words. "Phina, that is enough with your raunchy humour. We will need to put each interested party through a few trials to ensure that they are the right fit."

An idea starts to take shape.

"Phina? What is going around in that mind of yours?"

The words leaves my lips as barely a whisper: "A tournament for the Queen."

Velasilio

When we arrive in the council chamber, the males are already standing by their seats, murmuring quietly. Probably wondering why they were called back with such haste. Searaphina enters the room with commanding presence and the room goes silent. In unison, they bow and speak, "Your Majesty."

I cannot help the uneasiness that fills me as they address her; the harmony always sends an odd shiver down my spine. Moving with fluid grace, Searaphina strides to her seat. Onree is there waiting for her with the seat pulled back. Cassidie and Gregor are again given the task to watch the door and I wonder if the reason for this is their field training is more extensive than Dezmond's and Onree's meaning that they are the best first defence to stop any fae getting close to the Queen.

I am slow to follow her as I am confused as to what we are doing here. I also worry that the Council males may think she is crazy as I do right now.

I am thankful for Dezmond as he gently raises a hand to my shoulder and nudges me forwards, shaking away the fog of my mind.

I look over my shoulder at him; his auburn hair is short but still long enough to run your fingers through, his jaw is rounded and there is a distinct shadow of his stubble growing back, I wonder if it would tickle my thighs. Honey-coloured eyes meet mine briefly before I quickly look away, my cheeks heating. With haste I move to my own chair to the Queen's right.

Dezmond beats me to it, his long arms reaching out and pulling the chair back for me. I see a cocky grin on his face, as if he knew I may have been ogling him before. Part of me wishes to glare at him, the other is swooning at his chivalry.

Quickly, I take my seat and try to ignore the heat of his stare and then, by Datriminish mercy, Searaphina begins.

"I believe I may have a plan that will please us all." I watch the males to see their reactions.

"To find a potential royal that the fae will accept, love, trust, that this council approves of and, most importantly, I approve of..." Taking a breath, She prepares to offer her solution.

"We will hold a tournament." There is a collective murmur that goes out, Searaphina waits and does not continue until it quiets.

I stare at her. She looks to me, offers a wink and when she turns back to the males, Jisip has his elbow on the table, hand raised.

He is one of the younger males, in his mid five hundreds, throughout his hair are silver flashes that show he is entering his elder years soon. Searaphina addresses him. "Yes, Jisip?"

"What is the reason for a tournament? How does it help you find a husband? They are frivolous expenses that the crown can not afford at this time." A murmur of agreement rises from the others. My eyes dart from Searaphina to the other males as I wait to see what will happen.

"Any fae can prove that they are worthy of such a title by competing in trials that show the kingdom that they are the right fae for the position."

More murmurs as they whisper to one another and then I am shocked by what Jisip asks. "What will the tournament consist of? How long will it take?"

"These are details we are here to discuss." Searaphina is so relaxed I am beginning to think she has had one of her special teas or at least a small dose, if she had it all she would be asleep and we would be unable to wake her for several hours.

"Give us a moment please. Your Highness." Searaphina dips her head to them and they turn inward, murmuring to one another about the idea.

The males all clear their throats, we turn back to face them. "Have you reached a decision?" Searaphina holds herself tall and her face is hard. I know that even if they try to refuse the tournament she will overrule them, as is her right as Queen. They are her advisers and here to ensure that she listens to the laws set forth by her great-grand-father and his council when Neraphina broke off from Vixeruas to become its one kingdom.

Jisip speaks for them all, standing as he does. "We agree that a tournament will be the best course of action to ensure that all parties are happy."

With a gesture, she asks him to sit again. "I am glad that you see the merit of this idea, now we must discuss the details." With a nod of her head, the others all begin to speak over one another.

"Yes I agree, it mustn't be too long."

"What of a week?"

"Why not make it ten trials to test them!"

"No, that is too many trials."

Searaphina looks at me, rolling her eyes, as they argue about the details. We both know that she will make the ultimate decisions. Her gaze sweeps over the males as their conversation becomes a bit too aggressive.

Holding out her hand, she waits. When they notice her, they quiet down. "I propose the tournament lasts for a week, with no more than five trials." She stops for a moment to see if they will agree or disagree. When no one speaks up she continues. "We will hold an opening ceremony to introduce each of them, let us call them competitors. Then we will have the first trial, second and third trials will be completed back to back and then a feast, the fourth trial, and the fifth will signify the end and our winner. That will need to be quite the event."

Alabaster raises his hand.

"Do you not think that will work?" Searaphina questions him.

With a small shake of his head he answers, "Of course not, Your Majesty. I only wonder how you will get to know these males, if they are within the trials so often?"

He does have a good point: All eyes are on Searaphina but she does not back down, her brow creases ever so slightly as she drums her fingers on the table in thought. Then she has her answer.

"Before the first trial I will meet each competitor individually, in a line. If there is any sign of one being my fated I will stop the tournament. Then we will have a feast after the first trial, the same after the second and third trials, after the fourth trial we will throw a ball. This will allow time for not only me to get to know them but the court as well." They all nod along as she addresses them.

An overwhelming pride rushes through me for the Queen she is becoming. She has been able to create a solution that will please her kingdom and ensure her own happiness. I cannot shake the smile from my face.

Faranarit raises his hand. With a nod from his Queen he speaks. "This all sounds rather exciting, but what will these trials be?" I take in his appearance. His beard is long and still holds a tinge of a green, his eyes are a similar shade to that of the new leaves that come with spring. He is dressed in a pair of brown trousers with a white blouse and a matching brown jacket over the top.

Clearing my throat, I raise my hand.

Suddenly all eyes are on me. Causing me to fidget in my seat, chewing on my lower lip. I look into Searaphina's eyes: they are filled with kindness. "What idea are you cooking up, Silio?"

Sitting up straighter, I answer, "Well I am not an expert, but what if it were simply one on one combat? This would show their strength and kindness in how much harm they inflict." Rubbing my hands together, I wait for the idea to be rejected.

"That is perfect!" My head snaps up at the joy in her tone. "A simple way to show their strength and if they have mercy. They will choose if they end the other's life or allow them to live. The following trial should test their intelligence." The rhythmic sound of her fingers drumming on the table are all I can focus on as she thinks of the next trial.

'Did she just suggest allowing them to kill one another?' A small seed of doubt that began to grow over the last few weeks creeps into my mind again; Searaphina has been more distant and I wonder if it is simply because she is Queen and needs to step up or if the stress is taking a toll on her mental state.

"What of a labyrinth? One that will require them to answer a riddle to complete?" This draws me back into the conversation.

"That will work well, thank you Larience." He bows his head and accepts the praise of his Queen.

She continues. "If they must answer a riddle, the answer can be used for our third trial. If they succeed, their answers will lead them to a rare item, like a flower or the heart of a deadly beast."

I cannot help but scrunch my nose. The island of Tarpidora is the only other large landmass besides the two kingdoms; there are plenty of smaller islands dotted over the seas but they usually keep to themselves. There are no leaders on Tarpidora, as the creatures rule. They are all wild and most of them are deadly. Killing them is possible as they are only living their lives trying to survive just like the rest of us.

I want to fight this choice, but Searaphina soldiers on.

"The fourth trial is one of skill and survival. They will need to survive a deserted island and return to the castle within two days." A small smile spreads over her face as she speaks. The prospect of such a feat must be extremely appealing to her.

Jisip speaks without raising his hand, but his tone carries with it caution and concern. "These all sound to be quite violent and dangerous, my Queen, are we sure any of the males will even survive this?"

A few of the others murmur their agreements before Searaphina addresses the issue. "I understand your concern. If that does happen and no male or female completes these trials, well, then we will cross that bridge when we get to it." Each council male nods and agrees.

"Any further questions?" Opening the floor, she allows them to speak freely.

"How will males enter the tournament? They would usually acquire a summons from the royal house." This comes from one of the males whose name I am still yet to learn. I have been trying but it is a challenge as not all of them speak directly to us.

"There will be some summons for the families of the court but I only want males and females who wish to be a part of this tournament. No fae will be forced to compete, not with such a high chance of injury or death. Velasilio and I will work together on a letter to be taken to each village for a town square to announce at the end of the month to alert the people of their chance to be a royal consort." Looking to me, Searaphina smiles, seeing that I have noted down all of this information and what we need to do next.

Daterrit, the oldest of the Council, speaks up. "What of the riff raff that will attend the tournament in hopes to steal a crown? We cannot have just anyone becoming King." Of course he is worried about such things.

Daterrit is a legend around the kingdom, he was one of the greatest swords-males of our lands. No others have shown the same amount of skill with a blade in hundreds of years. He helped Seara-phina's grandfather to win the great war and separate us from

Vixeruas. It is almost sad that now he sits on the council helping to dictate law rather than fighting on the field. With the threat of another war I am sure he would join the fight if it comes to that.

Searaphina looks upset by this comment, I try to decipher her look but I am unsure as to what she is thinking at this moment. I wait for her to reply. "We must remember that even if you do not see the riff raff as suitable royalty, if they happened to be my twin flame, they would be accepted no matter their station. There will be both males and females in the tournament, if I wish to take another Queen I will."

The council wants their heir and that is easier with a male rather than another female. While it is possible, it often takes longer and you can never tell which of the partners will carry the child. As is the same with all same sex partnerships.

I notice the council all have very flustered expressions. I understand they just worry in such uncertain times. If war did come and Searaphina was killed without an heir, who would take the crown?

"With these matters discussed, Velasilio will organise the announcements to be written and taken to each village. There will be a parchment to sign up for the tournament and another asking for villagers to join us and watch the tournament take place." Not waiting for anyone to comment, she adjusts her dress, gathering it in one hand readying to stand. Faranarit raises his hand and asks.

"Apologies, my Queen. Only you have not informed us of the fifth trial?" His eyes meet Searaphina's before dropping to the table. Dropping her skirts, she gets comfortable in her seat again, her lips set in a hard line and her eyes narrowed slightly.

I would never question my Queen's choices but as her friend I worry about her actions, has the threat of war and the pressure of an heir become too much? Hopefully this tournament will help to settle her. I watch her carefully, it has been a few seconds and she has yet to answer, is it possible she does not have an idea for the fifth trial? Deciding I do not wish to see her embarrassed, I offer a solution.

"That is for our Queen to know and all others to find out. The last trial will be a surprise to all."

The room descends into silence, not a single muscle is moved. I am not even sure if we breathe, waiting to see how she may react.

"Velasilio is correct." With this, we all exhale. "It will remain a secret until the night before the fifth trial. Just to add a little drama to the experience." Turning to look at me, she smiles as the council agrees to this.

"Well gentle-males, this brings our meeting to a conclusion, there is still much for Velasilio and myself to do. I will send you updates." Gathering her skirt once more, she stands. The council males all stand and bow their heads.

As she is leaving, I gather my parchments up and stand, once she passes behind me I move to follow her, only my elbow catches on the back of my chair as I cannot see it past my papers. The chair falls backwards. The loud thud rings out in the otherwise silent room.

Bunching up my shoulders, I feel my cheeks heat. Thankfully, I have not dropped any papers. Dezmond is still standing against the wall, he picks the chair up and places it back at the table. Turning to look at me he goes to speak but, before he can, I rush past him to Searaphina's side. We exit the room and I know he is following along with Onree. As we exit the chambers Cassidie and Gregor are standing watch. Walking in front of them we only make it up four steps before Searaphina looks behind us and then back to me with a manic smile, her laughter burst free.

I try to keep the seriousness in my tone. "It is not that funny." When she looks up at me with tears pooling in her eyes I am unable to contain myself any longer. We both lose ourselves in laughter, stopping on the steps doubled over. After a moment we collect ourselves and keep moving. I can feel the heat of Dezmond's gaze burning into my behind. I really should not be getting feelings towards one of the Queen's personal guards. If things went wrong I would not be able to escape him. Only it is such a challenge to find a good male; he was a nuisance when we first met, but, after my disowning, he took care of me and for that I am grateful. Plus he is one of the few fae in the castle who have not slept with Searaphina, and that is a rare find.

CHAPTER 20

PREPARATIONS

Velasilio

TWO YEARS LATER

$\mathcal{N}$ausea rolls through me at the thought of the tournament beginning tomorrow. It has been two years of planning, building, capturing and setbacks. So many unexplainable setbacks: we would have everything almost complete and then part of the colosseum would fall down, or a creature would escape and kill its way through town. I am superstitious and I believe that it has all been a sign that the tournament is meant to fail. We were supposed to begin last year and now we are only two weeks from Searaphina's two hundred and twenty first birthday. If this does not work we have run out of time and she will have to marry whoever the council chooses.

To make sure that we are all set, I am here before the sun has awoken to ensure that all is running smoothly. Searaphina still sleeps. She will not wake up until closer to noon, since we were up all night rehearsing her opening speech that she will give later today.

We have had over one hundred fae put their hands up to compete, but, with such a small amount of time and the tournament already costing the crown more than they had set aside, there will only be enough positions for fifty. It was decided that names are to be pulled from a chalice and then it is fair. Once their names are chosen, that is it, they are a part of the tournament and can not swap out or change their position. The ceremony will be public and then they will be introduced as the competitors who will take part in the tournament.

Standing in front of the dirty mirror, I run my hands down the length of my gown, Searaphina requested that I wear a dress with more elegance today so that I am fit to stand with her during the viewing. The layers of tulle create a fuller skirt and the bodice is a tight corset with a sweetheart neckline. The sleeves run from off my shoulders to my wrist. I have chosen a simple amethyst necklace to match the deep purple of the material. My curled hair is half up and half down. I wear a nude lip colour and my eyes are lined black. I try to smile, yet I struggle. It has been two years since I have seen or spoken to my family. No replies to my letters, and when I attempted to return home I was turned away at the gate. When we began preparations for the tournament, my plate was so full I never had time to think, only work, care for my Queen and then fall into bed.

I am somewhat thankful for the task of organising the entire tournament—with Searaphina having the final say, of course. It distracted me and allowed me to push the grief aside, for most of the day. But, late at night when I lay in bed alone, it felt as though my heart was being cleaved in half as the darkness overwhelmed me.

The first anniversary was the hardest; it felt as though the binds that tied me to my family were severed all over again, and I was unable to leave my bed all day. Dezmond offered to care for me while another guard took his place protecting the Queen for the day.

Over the last two years, we have grown comfortable and I think soon I may invite him to stay the night.

I have waited because, with our two hundred and twenty first birthdays being so close together, I know that there is a chance with the tournament bringing so many fae to the castle me lusthat I may find my twin flame. I am born but a week before our Queen, my birthday will fall on the final day of the tournament. We are to have a grand ball and though it is not for me, Searaphina has ordered that my favourite desserts be made, and a cake as a celebration.

Exiting my chambers, I turn left to see Dezmond. He is wearing tight, black dress pants and a burnt orange blouse. His sword belt is clipped around his waist and thigh—so tightly around his thigh that the slight bulge above it is even more prominent than usual given the incredibly dark and tight pants he wears today.

My gaze stays fixated on his outline as I try to swallow, my mouth dry. He moves slightly and I quickly dart my gaze to somewhere more respectful. Only, when I do finally look up, his eyes are locked onto me lust, fills them. My own must look the same, as I take a single step towards him.

He wavers like he may leave his post to come towards me, but he does not. Instead he makes me go to him. I slowly walk forwards until I am standing in front of him, looking up into his heated gaze.

"Vel, can I help you with something?" He smiles, showing off his perfectly straight, white teeth.

I blink a few times, trying to shake off my desire. "Ah, no thank you Dez, I just seem to have lost my head."

"Perhaps I can help you find it?" He leans in slightly and I place a hand on his chest. We have not kissed yet but we have begun calling each other by nicknames.

Just as I think we may kiss, some fae clears their throat, and we separate like two naughty fae children being caught stealing baked goods. My cheeks heat as I look over at Cassidie, who stands straight, not even looking at us. Dezmond stands straight and steps aside to allow me entry into Searaphina's chambers. As I quickly make my way to her door, I offer a welcome to Cassidie.

"Good morning." I try not to look at her as I know my cheeks will show my embarrassment.

"A very good morning indeed." I can hear the humour in her voice.

I knock once and wait to hear for Searaphina to call me inside. Each moment is pure torture with them standing behind me.

"Enter." I all but trip on my own feet to get inside as quickly as possible. Searaphina stands ready and looking beautiful, a collection of maids run around her preparing her for the day. With my load of work increased with preparations, Searaphina has been getting the other lady's maids to help her more. I notice two in particular: a green and pink fae who look remarkably similar. They must be related, if not twins, a very rare thing for any fae couple. A single child is a blessing and two at once—their parents must have been fated.

"Phina, you look stunning." Walking over to her, I curtsy as I reach her. She turns to face me with a large smile.

"As do you, cousin." With a single clap she shoos the others out. "Silio will take over from here, your services will no longer be required unless requested." They all curtsy before leaving.

"I am overjoyed that your duties will be focused on me again. While I appreciate all you have done in preparing the tournament for me I have missed having you care for me. The other imbeciles do not know what they are doing: my baths are always too hot, cold or do not have enough water and there is never enough jasmine." Turning to the mirror she fluffs out her hair one last time; she has left it out in loose waves today and her gown is the picture of a Queen.

The dark green has gold embellishments and threading along each seam, the neckline dips to the base of her breasts and is a tight corset to her waist, then the skirt flares into an a-line at the base, with a high slit. Atop her head sits a gold, three-point crown with three emeralds, one in each tip. Her make up is simple and neutral with a dark lip.

"Well, we best get going. I do not wish to miss a moment of the excitement." She is glowing, and I am so happy to see it.

Only, a small voice in my mind whispers of worry. She has not been herself as of late; in moments when she believes no one is looking that there is an edge of cruelty. I wonder if the pressure has gotten to her, or if I am overthinking it all.

CHAPTER 21

FUCK CHANCE

Kadance

Two fucking years of waiting, of watching, making sure that I can get what I want and not have two kingdoms chasing me down. These last two years have been absolute torture but I needed the time, I had to make sure King Baritus thought that I was following orders, that I needed to be here longer than he wanted.

Twice he tried to call me back, but I gave him half-truths as good reasons to leave me alone.

Datriminish, he is a fool. A letter stating that I was close to the information he needed only for it to fall through. Then I made sure that each stage for their tournament had minor issues, so it would take two years instead of one. I would sit back and laugh as they tried to work out how the fuck a beast got loose or a structure 'fell down' overnight...

Even after two years, the innkeeper has no idea who I am. She's never seemed to care, since I keep her well paid. I have been watching my gem, learning all I can: what does she like to eat, drink, who she has fucked or wants to. So far there has been one fae who I particularly wish to rip the head off of. But I am patient. I have plans in the palace and this tournament will be the perfect opportunity to put them into motion. I have been inside the castle and I have gathered most of the information I need, but by joining the tournament I will be inside the castle walls and not a soul can say anything. I will have access to everything I need to get the final answers to my King's questions; mainly who killed King Amard and Queen Alathieria.

I have ensured that everything is in place for my plan to work. It might have taken two years but I am ready to finish this. Since the first day I caught her scent I knew there was something special about her. My obsession has only grown. I don't believe in fated or love, these are things that make you weak. My obsession has already been a pain in the ass and I have allowed it to control me, almost getting me caught on more than one occasion. The tournament will let me get close to her and then I can fuck her and be done with this. After I have had my fill I will be able to move on, that's all this is, an obsession, though the strange feeling in my chest seems to laugh at me for thinking it will be that easy.

Today is the viewing. Once my name is pulled, they won't be able to get rid of me. I know they will try but they can't because it's against their rules. I have no doubt there will be those opposed to me joining. I am a dark fae after all, their enemy or so they have been told.

Laughing to myself, I look out over the sandy ground. Slowly, each fae shuffles in, standing just behind the line that has been drawn in the sand. The stands are being filled as each nearby village has come to witness the choosing of their new royal.

I must applaud the fae who came up with this. To choose your next royal through blood and battle is impressive, to have them prove themselves is smart, because not a single fae of the kingdom can go against them as they have done everything requested by their Queen to prove they are the best. I know that *I* am the best. I don't need to prove it, but to get hold of my precious Gem, I need to be in this tournament.

The large, rounded structure is four stories high, with thousands of bench seats. The open top allows the sun to heat the white sand. A slight breeze comes from the underground and low-laying tunnels leading inside. The darkness is the only shelter from the heat.

One by one, more fae enter: females and males, tall, short, large and thin. Each hoping their name is pulled. If it is, they step forward and declare their names to the crowd.

Once the losers have been escorted out, we will stay put for a meeting and I can't wait to have my Gem standing in front of me. I will resist the urge to pick her up and take her now. I will prove I can play by some rules. Standing with my back against the wall, I keep my hood pulled high to hide. The line fills quickly until there are three rows of fae waiting for their names to be called.

It does not take long before the ceremony starts. A group of ten older males move into the centre of the colosseum, only three feet from where we stand. A guard follows, carrying a small box. He places it down and moves away. One of the males steps up.

"Good afternoon, my name is Alabaster. Our Queen will be arriving momentarily. Before she steps foot inside this arena you must all abide by the rules. There will be no shoving. If your name is called, step forward. Fifty names will be called in total no more, no less..." He prattles on and on about how to act and how not to act, including mentioning the fact there will be many guards to ensure the Queen's safety.

I completely zone out, ignoring everything each male says until that sweet scent finds me on the wind; I am immediately alert, looking for her. Then I see eight guards, four in front and four behind, surrounding a pair of females. And then I see her, my Gem.

She is glowing today, absolutely beautiful. My gaze is glued to her as she walks. Her hair flows down her back. I want to wrap around my hand and pull tight as she wraps those beautiful, dark lips around my cock. The sunlight stabs me in the eyes as I step forwards, causing me to blink and lose her for a second and, in that second, my heart seizes.

'The fuck was that!' My hand grabs at my chest. Whatever it was, it can't be good. Murmurs from around me having me holding a growl as I hear comments begging made about my Gem, many fae having the same thought I just had at seeing her.

Then it all stops. "Welcome every fae, to the selection and viewing ceremony." A round of applause sounds before the eerie sets in again. "I wish that you all could participate for my hand, alas we only have a short time to see this though. Only fifty names will be pulled from," —A large gold chalice is handed to her. —"this chalice, and when your name is pulled please step forward. Those who are not called, I will sadly have to say goodbye to. Without further ado, let us begin."

Her delicate hand swirls around the top as if she is casting a spell on them, then she reaches down and takes a single piece of parchment. "Fenterison Smieth!"

A large, orange fae steps forward. As he does he flares out his wings. I scoff to myself at the *size* he is trying to show off. He offers a bow. I can scent the arrogance coming from him. He will be fun to toy with.

"Buvariris Bar." This male is scrawny but his green colouring is dark and gives an edge of something deadly, like a poisonous creature, who looks meek to lure you into doing something stupid.

"Sobia Thomsan." Next is a purple fae. She is tall and has a similar build to Fenterison: strong, broad shoulders and large arms; she must work with her hands.

As the list continues, I begin to ignore the names and focus on my Gem: the way she holds herself, her careful eye assessing, watching each competitor as they step forward.

"Elanior Roberts, Frekily Tooew, Meliena Farea, Arekin Lesana." After the last name, a dark blue male steps forward and everything stops for a moment before she continues to call the final name.

"Kadance Zadieria." I made sure that my name would be last— having shadow magic does have its advantages.

Stepping from the shadows, the crowd parts for me as if they know there is a predator in their midst. I slowly remove my hood. Standing before my Gem and the entire kingdom, they all hold their breath to see what will happen next. So I flare my wings out just over my shoulders. I don't want to scare my Gem. And then every fae speaks at once and I am rushed by the guards.

CHAPTER 22

A DARK FAE!

Searaphina

Everything happens at once: two guards rush at the dark fae just as Cassidie reaches up and removes me from the podium. She tucks me behind her and I see that Dezmond has done the same to Velasilio. We now stand next to each other. We stare at each other, looking like fish with our eyes wide and our mouths in perfect 'O's, completely unsure of what just happened.

Regaining my composure, I try to see past the wall of guards now standing in front of me and, from the shuffling sounds behind me, I know we are completely surrounded. I cannot see anything past the mass of bodies. That is strange—if a dark fae were here to kill me would there not be fighting happening right now.

My curiosity outways safety. Taking a deep breath and standing tall, I call out, "Step aside for your Queen." Cassidie looks back at me and mouths 'are you sure?' I know that this is only out of respect, even if our relations have been more intimate lately; even if we have not fucked she knows better then to question me in front of others.

With my sure nod, she sighs, but tells every other soldier to move.

As they all move out of my way, I feel Cassidie still standing at my side, hand on her sword. Velasilio follows behind us. As I step out, I see my highly trained guards—apparently will need more training, as they are both on their asses breathing heavily and looking up at the dark fae who has two daggers in both hands. His very large, deep red, leathery wings reaching to the sky as he states,

"I will only show you mercy once. Try that again and meet my blade." He flips the blades in his hands once before tucking them back into his holsters.

His gaze moves over me and I feel like he is looking straight through me. His eyes are a dark red with a black outer ring, his shaggy black hair is loose and reaches past his ears. His complexion is dark brown with a perfect smile to go with it and there, poking out of his top lip, is a canine, used for marking your lover in a bonding ceremony to make you one.

I feel my core clench, thinking of those shark teeth piercing my skin, before I do the same in turn.

After my two hundred and twenty first birthday, I should start to see mine descending so that I can bind myself to another in such a permanent way. It is not part of marriage, it is a choice, though, during sex, the overwhelming urge to mark your partner can overrule any rational thought.

It is as if he can tell where my thoughts have gone as his smirk grows. All of my guards are still on high alert, though I cannot see why. Yes he is a dark fae and their presence on the local islands threatens war, but he has not tried to harm me or any of the guards other than the ones who now have a bruised ego.

"I mean no harm to you or your fae." His voice is deep and each word sounds like a sensual promise, how did I not notice it before? Possibly because it was a threat.

Lifting the parchment, I look at his name again. "Kadance, why are you here?"

He shrugs before his smirk drops. "I thought that was obvious."

That causes each guard to draw their sword and then his lip

twitches like he may give me a hint of that undergarment-dropping smile again.

"The obvious answer is that you are here to kill me. Our kind have been in a tense position for years now, made more tenuous after the death of our King and Queen."

"I can assure you I am here for only one thing." His stance is relaxed and comfortable. It is as if he knows I cannot voice my concerns of his King ordering an assassination as the entire kingdom watches and we have not confirmed who killed them. Over the past two years we have exhausted all options into finding their killer and all have turned up empty.

"And what is that?"

"To claim what is mine." His arrogance is enticing, a male who knows what he wants.

"I see, well I need to discuss with my council whether you are allowed to stay in the tournament or whether we should send you home." I try not to let him see the lust and desire growing inside of me.

"I would expect nothing less. I will remind you of your own rules and laws for the tournament. Once a fae has been chosen there are only three ways out. Forfeiting, serious injury and death. Unless you wish to go back on the rules you have set?"

Fuck! These were my own words moments ago. The point of such rules was to stop fae from stepping down and offering their family or friends in their place.

I try to think of a way out of this.

Velasilio steps forward. She looks up at me and inclines her head. I offer a smile of thanks, allowing her to speak for me, as this male has my mind in a mess.

She stands by my side and speaks in a way I do not hear often from her, she channels her inner royal. "These are unexpected circumstances and, as such, the Queen will need to speak with her counsel. You are not a fae of this kingdom and therefore may be here for nefarious reasons. Surely you can understand that our Queen is looking out for her fae."

This seems to amuse Kadance as he chuckles before he inclines his head to her. "Of course I understand. My only request is that I am given the same rules as the others. As I said, I am only here to claim what is mine." With that he steps back towards the other forty-nine contestants who all give him a wide berth as four of the guards separate and begin to lead them to the guest chambers that were built for the competitors just outside the colosseum.

*S*itting in the royal box, my council males stand around me each huffing and puffing about what they think. They talk of the uproar from the crowd at seeing him. I, too, agree that this is an outrage, how in the fuck did a dark fae get into my kingdom without me knowing about it? Is he really only here to marry me? Is this some plan from King Baritus to get my kingdom under his rule again through a marriage, or could this be for peace? What if Kadance is going against his King? With him, our child could be powerful, since the dark fae are known to still have some lesser magic running through their veins.

"The final decision is yours, Searaphina." The soft voice breaks my spiral, bringing me back to the conversation as the council males continue to bicker over what to do.

"Gentle-males, please." A hush falls over the space as they all turn to look at me.

"I understand your concerns, but as the rules put forth by all of us, our hands are tied. Besides, if he is in the tournament we can keep an eye on him. If we deny him entry, he may take it out on the kingdom and we would have no way to know where he is. We do not even know how he got here." With sullen faces they all look to one another but they know I am correct, it is better to have him underfoot then have no idea what he is doing.

With the surprise of a dark fae, we called off the one-on-one meetings and have decided to start earlier tomorrow instead. All fae have returned to their homes and guards have been posted to keep watch over the competitors' quarters.

I did receive news while we were deliberating that the others have all refused to share with Kadance so the extra bed has been moved into another room. With the decision made, we discuss a few extra precautions to keep the kingdom and myself safe. By the end of the day, I am exhausted and ready to eat and go to bed.

The competitors are allowed to visit the inn closest to the castle for food and drink each day. The short walk there is lined with shops, continuing clothing, weapons and medicines: everything they will need. The villagers are still able to access the area, though there is a higher guard presence there now to ensure that the competitors do not try to kill one another outside the tournament, which is forbidden.

Most of them will be there now, having an early supper before bed. They have a big day tomorrow.

CHAPTER 23

SPARKS

Arekin

DAY ONE, TRIAL ONE

Mug of half-finished ale in hand, I contemplate the day. What is a dark fae doing here? There is no other reason than to steal the crown. He is joking if he thinks the Queen will be stupid enough to allow him to stay. No good can come of having him around.

All the competitors feel the same: none of us want him here, there are already plans being made to get rid of him, one way or another, I don't like bloodshed unless it's completely necessary. Killing for fun makes you a murderer, not a hero, but I can't tell this lot that because they already cursed me and threw me off their table for even suggesting that we allow the Queen and her council to decide, claiming that the Queen is too soft hearted.

Buvariris leads the charge. I don't know why he is even a part of this, he acts like it's a chore. Agreeing with him are Meliena and Frekily, from their clothing and how they treat the staff here, I'd bet they are all from families of court, they think they are better and that their shit don't stink.

Sitting at my table, I look around and take in the other competitors. We are all here having a meal and a drink before bed, many are in groups, some sit alone. Sobia, like me, has her own high bar table. Her colours are similar to the Queen's maid Velasilio, only her purple is lighter, more lilac. The tavern is only just big enough for us all.

I sit facing the entry as more competitors stumble out ready to go to bed. To my left is a large fireplace keeping the space warm, to my right is a line of booths, one I was kicked out of. And behind me is the bar.

Looking down at my ale, I almost see the bottom, so sliding from my stool, I walk over to the bar to order some food. As I do, Fenterison joins me.

"Hey, Arei." He says my name with such familiarity you would think we have known each other for years.

If he is going to shorten my name I will do the same. "Ah, Fen."

"I can tell we're gonna be fast friends." He wraps his arm over my shoulder and I shrug it off.

"I am not your friend and I don't plan on making any while I am here, as we are all working against one another."

Holding his hands up in surrender, he waves to the barmaid and orders for both of us. "Two plates of food and two mugs of ale." I look at him as he hands over a silver nerphi. Deciding that I am not about to walk away from a free meal I wave him over.

"You can join me." We both grab our mugs and head back to my table.

We both get comfortable, sipping our drinks, before two plates of hot chicken and roasted vegetables come out; the fresh bread and gravy make me salivate. Digging in, I am half finished by the time Fen speaks, eating with a little more grace than me.

"So what brings ya to the tournament, Arie?" I take a large swig of my ale and swallow before I answer him.

"I saw the Queen two years ago on the royal tour." Before I go on, Fenterison shows me that all the grace was fake: pieces of food leave his mouth as he chatters on.

"You and every other fae mate, she is one good looking female. So is that little maid of hers, wondering if she would be perfect height for a blowy." I almost choke on my food as he starts to laugh.

Trying to clear my thoughts, I take a swig of my drink and realise that maybe if I break the rule of making a friend, Fenterison is not the best option. Looking at the others, I realise I might not have much of a choice, since they all have another fae with them chatting away happily.

Clearing my throat, I look at him. There is a large shit-eating grin on his face. "Fen, I would appreciate it if you didn't try to kill me before we even get on the battlefield."

This has him howling in laughter. The entire inn stops to look at him, he seems crazed.

"Oh Arie you are too funny, now go on, tell me more. You can guess why I am here, I want to stick my prick in that royal snatch."

I regret joking with him immediately. Shaking it off, I explain why I am here.

"As I said, I saw the Queen two years ago at a market in my village, which is the same as the Queen's handmaid Velasilio's village; her family own the land and my family work on it, caring for the beasts used for meat, furs and tools for the kingdom. We are not wealthy but when I saw her I felt a spark, inside me, in my heart. I think she might be my fated. When I saw her today she stopped and didn't move. I thought she might feel it too and then that dark fae stepped up and ruined it all." Looking back at my meal, I realise I am no longer hungry.

"Dark fae are the scum of our world, thinking he can walk in here and take our Queen for his own, fuck that. She should be with her own kind, perhaps a handsome orange fae." He strokes his chin in thought and I feel a chuckle work its way from me as he does.

"Ah, I knew I'd get ya to laugh eventually."

The rest of the night passes quickly as we finish our meals and drinks and walk back to our accommodation. I am in a room with Fen and he is too pleased about it.

Tomorrow, I will meet her one-on-one, face to face. She won't be able to deny the spark between us and then I will marry her and be King.

CHAPTER 24
LOOKING FOR A SPARK

Searaphina

DAY ONE, TRIAL ONE

Blinding sunlight wakes me, I hold my hand over my eyes to ease the burn. Why did I not get the curtains closed last evening? I enjoy the sun but not it waking me up.

Rolling over, I pull the sheets higher, snuggling into their warmth.

The sound of birds chirping wakes me once more, I had not meant to fall asleep. Slowly sitting up, I stretch out my arms and legs. When the pleasant sound of cracking of bones reaches my ears I smile, but my peace is quickly ruined by a gentle tapping on the door.

"Just a moment please." Rising from bed, I step over to my wardrobe where my overgown hangs from the door. Wrapping the strings around my waist, I ensure my night clothes are covered.

"Come in."

Velasilio enters. She and four more maids carry buckets of hot water in and towards the bathing chambers.

"Good morning Phina, I trust you have slept well?" The sweet scent of jasmine wraps around me in a comforting embrace.

Once Velasilio says, "Your bath is ready", I enter the chamber, now empty of other maids, and step into the bath. Stepping away and turning she offers me her back so that I may have privacy.

Velasilio moves to sit at my back, taking a cloth and gently bathing me.

"It is the perfect temperature, thank you." When she does not speak I ask,

"Silio, are you well? Did you not sleep?" I feel as her hand drops from my back.

"I have not been able to get a good night's rest for some months now. I worry about the tournament. We are only two weeks away from your birthday, what if it fails? Or what if the dark fae wins? Would you truly marry him?"

I understand her worry but I have my own plans that even she is not privy to. So I try to reassure her. "Silio, you have done so much to help me and if the tournament fails or should Kadance win then I will handle it. I am Queen and it is my responsibility, not yours, please do not fret." Turning back to her, I offer a reassuring smile. When her eyes meet mine I see the dark shadows beneath them; how have I not noticed them before.

After my bath, Velasilio dresses me in another stunning emerald with gold threading throughout. It is a bit fancier than my usual garb, but when the tournament is on I enjoy dressing up.

This particular neckline dips down quite low, almost to my belly button. The intricate design looks as though vines start at my feet and wind their way up and around my body all the way to the swell of my breasts.

With a final tug, I am only able to take shallow breaths. Reaching behind myself, I take hold of her hands, pulling her around to stand in front of me. With her bottom lip drawn into her mouth and her brow furrowed, I can see she is trying to solve a problem that is yet to arise.

Placing my hands on her forehead, I try to smooth out her brow. "Silio, if you continue to worry, you will wrinkle."

Reaching up, she swats my hands away. "Phina."

I lay a hand dramatically over my eyes and shout. "Ah no, you cannot attack your Queen this way!"

Waving hands at me frantically, her eyes dart from me to the door. "Hush! Or the guards may think you are truly being harmed."

Crossing my arms over my chest, I click my tongue; her eyes move to the floor as she does not wish to meet my gaze. "Silio we have been friends for many years, I can tell that my impending wedding is not the thing that truly upsets you. Please speak to me about it?"

When she does not reply, only chewing on her bottom lip as she thinks, I begin to inch towards the door. My own eyes dart from her to the exit now. As soon as I take one step, her eyes go to me and she shakes her head.

Making my tone as serious as I can at this time, I hold back laughter at her face. "I will call the guard, maybe..." I tap my chin in thought. "Ohh I will have you placed on the rack!"

Blowing out a breath, she rubs the spot between her brows and then places her hands on her hips. "Why must you act this way?"

One of the many reasons I keep her close is that she knows I am her Queen and will do as is required, but behind closed doors she will allow her sassy side free. It is sad that most of the time she is but a shadow of herself. I feel that, over time, with my rise to Queen, she has stepped back from our friendship. Allowed our roles in the court to define who we are to one another. The relationship we have will never be as simple as Queen and subject, since the blood tie means her life is mine and we are one. Something no fae has seen in many years and, as far as I know, only Velasilio's family knows of our bond; another reason she has not been herself.

Rolling her eyes and huffing out to me, she finally cracks. "If you must know, before the dark fae made an appearance yesterday, I was thinking of taking the next step with Dezmond."

I look her in the eyes: I need to see her reaction fully for this one. "Are you saying that you no longer wish to move forward with Dezmond because of the dark fae? Did you feel a slight fanny flutter for the male?" Her mouth opens in shock for a second before it drops and her eyes narrow as she rubs between her brows again.

Her hand moves quickly from her face, out with palm open, she asks, "Why must every conversation be about sex with you?"

"I do not know what you mean? I was simply suggesting that a male with such an impressive wingspan, may incite you to change who you wish to ride?" Raising my eyebrows at her, I cannot help the smile that spreads across my face. It should not bring me so much joy to try and fluster her.

"Of course I noticed his wingspan, how could I not. I just wonder why you always think with your *fanny*, as you called it. I still like Dezmond and have not changed my mind about him yet. I just meant that was all I could think of with the tournament not moving ahead. But now I am thinking of what would happen should a male from Vixeruas win. Our kingdom would not accept him, not when his own King had your parents killed and wants war." Stopping her actions, her hands fall to her skirt as she wipes them down the material.

"He would not make the best choice for King because of all of the reasons you just mentioned. But, if he was to win, I would honour the terms set in place. Hopefully, him going through the same trials as the others will prove his worth to the kingdom and if he wins they will accept him." Taking her hand in mine, I take in the dress she is wearing for today and screw up my face at the simple gown.

"Now that the matter is settled, you must hurry to change. You cannot wear this." Roaming my eyes up and down the dress before meeting her gaze again, I notice that she is not too happy about being asked to change. She never wishes to stand out, preferring to fade into the shadows and allow me to shine. How she dresses reflects on me as she is my lady's maid, so I expect her to meet a certain standard.

"Yes my Queen, I will meet you in the entry hall." With a curtsy, she pivots on her heel and disappears from my room.

Making my way to the entry hall, I pass each portrait of the previous monarchs. Our colouring is in similar shades of greens and blues, as royals are often these colours, which are a slightly darker shade to that of the commoners.

One of the last portraits on the wall is of myself and my parents with Velasilio's as well.

She has sent them many letters and even tried to visit but has been sent away. That night, she had cried herself to sleep.

Staring at the two of us in our youth, I ponder what will become of us, as the distance between us grows each day. I have noticed it since the day I was crowned; though we will never part fully. I will not allow it. If our friendship fades I will keep her with me, as no one will be able to serve me the way she does, with my complete trust.

I lose myself to the peaceful atmosphere: the wind as it rustles through the trees outside, the open bay windows allowing it to drift through the empty hall. I almost miss the sound of the muffled conversation to my left. Glancing over, Velasilio is speaking to Dezmond in hushed tones. His smile is almost devilish as she blushes. The other Queen's guards give them some space to talk but keep close to me.

They have been flirting back and forth for just over two years now and I have often wondered if I should tell her not to bother with him. I have had the unpleasant experience of laying flat on my back while he grunted on top of me for thirty seconds before pulling his semi-hard dick from my body and finishing on my thigh. Not something any fae enjoys. I am unsure if she will decide to sleep with him or not; she mentioned this morning that she had thought of it recently but is now distracted with my well-being again. If she is looking for a fae to enjoy once and have no emotions involved,

I can definitely organise some fae for her to meet.

I have tried many of the royal guards. One of my favorites is quickly becoming Cassidie, as she has a piercing in her tongue. She is able to make me sing a new tune each time she plays me like a fiddle.

Girlish giggles break me from my naughty thoughts; I shall invite her to my chambers this evening.

Clearing my throat, I say, "Well, we must not keep the fae waiting, let us hurry to breakfast and be on our way to the colosseum." Dezmond stands straight as he looks past her to me.

"My apologies, my Queen. I did not wish to make you late." Onree and Cassidie move to stand in front while Dezmond and Gregor line up behind me.

"All is well, Silio." I hold out my arm. "Come now." She quickly moves to my side and we stroll down the hall.

After a quick breakfast, it is time for us to leave for the first trial. Velasilio seems more unsure today than yesterday.

I study her appearance as the royal carriage comes to a halt in front of us. Today we will be taking the topless coach as the sun is shining and it allows me to wave at the villagers as we pass.

The carriage is pulled by two unicorn mares, one has a black mane and a purple hide while the other has a light blue hide with a white mane. Their iridescent horns sparkle in the sunlight. Both are stunning creatures.

One of the foot males steps forward, opening the half door, offering his hand to me. Gathering my dress in my right hand, the split allows me to step up with no fuss. I notice as he takes in the ivory skin on display; smiling to myself, I move to the side on the left, facing the road ahead. While I fluff with my dress, Velasilio follows, taking his hand next.

This foot male is young, I am yet to learn his name. He does seem taken with the gown she has chosen today. The darker violet colour complements her eyes well. There is a slight shimmer to the gown and a slight slit on her right leg. Her breasts are pushed high in the corset with a sweetheart neckline, sure to catch the eye of many.

His voice shakes slightly as he says, "My lady." His gaze lingers on her breasts and she makes an effort to look him in the eyes; he quickly averts his gaze.

Raising my hand, I catch the slight giggle that leaves my lips because he seems so nervous. Velasilio's eyes lock onto mine immediately. Her mouth is set into a hard line as her eyes tell me off.

I lift my hands in defeat as she takes her seat opposite me. The door is closed and, with a snap of the reins, we are on our way.

The journey is made slightly longer today as other fae are still moving through the village; each one steps from our path, smiling and waving to us. There seems to be such joy in the town today, since a special festival will be held this evening to celebrate the beginning of the tournament.

A heavy sigh leaves her lips. "The villagers are excited."

"Is that judgment in your tone, Silio?" Whipping her head around, our gaze locks, and we stay in that moment, waiting for the other to fail.

Breaking contact, she looks to her hands as they begin to play with the fabric of her skirt. "I do not understand their joy to see such bloodshed."

"It is not the bloodshed they wish to see." I lean forward and take her hand in mine.

Looking from her lap, our eyes meet once more. "What are they eager to see then?"

"The possibility of a new ruler, to see that they are worthy of the crown. It is not always a bad thing to enjoy a small amount of violence." I rub my thumb over her hands before I sit back in my seat.

Darkness takes the place of the sun over the colosseum as we near the entry.

"Now we are here, you must replace that frown with a smile." I point to my own face, showing off all of my teeth. Velasilio laughs.

"Yes, I will do my best." The small smile on her face does not make me believe what she says. We will need to do something about her sad spirit soon.

Standing, I move to the exit and see Cassidie waiting for me. She holds her hand out.

Smiling, I take her hand and allow her to lead me along the dark corridor into the colosseum. Behind me, Dezmond is helping Velasilio; Onree and Gregor follow me, one in front and one behind. If Dezmond continues to have his sights on Velasilio I may need to make him her private guard and find myself a new one.

CHAPTER 25

HOW TO ACT

Kadance

DAY ONE, TRIAL ONE

The day promises bloodshed and an opportunity to get up close to my little Gem. Over the past two years I have been doing as my King commanded, stay hidden and gather information. Now I have had enough. This is to be the last tournament and this means the end of 'willing' fae to keep me distracted. I do enjoy slicing skin from bone. There is a satisfaction to be gained in knowing you are all that stands between life and death for another, shame it will end. My plans for her are far more cynical than any knows. I have ensured that when I finally have her, we will not be disturbed for some time. The strange pull in my chest has only increased as the days have gone on.

Being led like beasts to the slaughter we follow in a single line. One after the other into the large stone arena. The sun is starting its climb for the day. The stands begin to fill with revellers who wish to bask in the chaos and bloodshed. There are guards nearby at all times as if waiting for one of us to launch an attack. I would not be stupid enough to do so, however my plans may cause an upheaval to the castle, once the idiot fae within its walls realises what has happened. An older fae steps out from the shadows and into the early hour sunlight. His white hair and withered robes are a similar colour to that of an old parchment stands before us.

With a spluttering cough he speaks "Pardon me good fae. I have come to inform you of how you shall address your Queen."

There is a quiet murmur as the others look around. "Now listen as I will only say this once. When Her Majesty comes out to greet you. Stand tall and proud, bow your heads and take her hand, you may place a simple chaste kiss on her hand and announce who you are and where you are from."

A snort sounds from further up the line. "Cheaste kiss? Nah I'd give 'er a taste of what she is in for." The gibberish is followed by a snickering laugh.

"If the Queen finds your behaviour disrespectful, you will be removed. Moving on, when you speak with the Queen's handmaid Velasilio, please ensure to show her the same respect. It would be unwise to lay hands on her without permission."When the wanker refuses to comment I can"t help myself.

Without moving to look in his direction I speak. "Oh I see, a flea can learn its place."

"FLEA! WHO THE FUK YA CALLIN FLEA?!" The rage feeds my soul, as I wait for this absolute wankstain to make a move. Stepping from the line and looking down to where my comment came from.

"COM 'ERE AN, SAY IT TO ME FACE!" The sheer delight I am about to receive gets my blood pumping, as I step forward making sure to expand my wings high and wide.

Ensuring the deepest voice, I am unable to hide my smirk as I look over his short frame. Not bothering to look such a low male in the eyes.

"That would be me, do we have a problem?" Crossing my arms over my chest I wait for him to speak again.

The flea just quivers and I watch as he swallows a few times before getting his words out. "Nah, I thix the flea is me." With that he steps back into line and remains silent.

Laughing to myself, I move into place at the end, I plan to make myself known to her. I will be the last one on my precious Gem's mind. Her sweet scent washes over me, calling to me like the siren, I know the moment she steps onto the sand. Waiting for her to make her way to me, is a new kind of torment that I have imposed on myself, though it will be worth it when I have her near and when she does I waste no time making my intentions known. The pair is quick with their interactions before they scurry from the field.

I don't miss how my Gem's sweet scent is slightly different after our little interaction in the sand. The little vixen might enjoy what I have planned more than I realised.

CHAPTER 26

START OF THE END

Searaphina

DAY ONE, TRIAL ONE

Stepping out of the dark, stone corridor, the sun greets us once more. I gaze upon the yellow sand that soon will be stained red.

Before we begin today's trial, I will have the individual meetings that were supposed to happen yesterday. Then I will offer an opening speech to wish them all luck. Velasilio will follow me to write down their names and, if there is a fae I find particularly interesting, she will note it down and we will look further into their families before a private invitation is offered. This will also allow me to note if I feel any kind of pull. I will only stop the tournament if I am one hundred percent sure they are my twin flame; the chances are slim but not impossible, I did feel a small spark with a fae who looked familiar, only I am not sure why.

Before we had the viewing and choosing ceremony, each competitor had their hand-to-hand combat skills tested and their history taken into consideration, so that the pairings could be fair and even, since it would be unfair to put a fae such as Sobia against Meliena. Sobia's father was once in the royal guard and has taught many of these skills, whereas Meliena comes from a family of bakers. While she may be strong she does not have the skill. With each pairing they have the choice to be merciful and only knock them out or, if they wish, they may kill their opponent. Standing beside me, Velasilio shuffles nervously, the small brown book in her hands and feather pen ready. Bending slightly, I whisper to her.

"Silio, you need not be here, you may go to the royal box now. I will have a guard take their names." Velasilio was against the option to allow them to kill one another. She has such a gentle soul, but if we were under attack, we need a King who is willing to kill for his throne. I wonder what she is most nervous about, taking the names and meeting the fae who she may watch die or to be near the dark fae?

Shaking her head, she swallows. "Thank you my Queen, the offer is kind. I must decline as I wish to show my respect as this may be the last time their name is recorded on paper and not stone."

"The kingdom is lucky to have such a kind soul looking out for it." Taking her hand in mine, we walk towards the line of males waiting to meet me.

A roar of excitement begins from the crowd; it is almost deafening. All noise slowly fades into the background as we continue our path to the line of fifty contestants.

Each fae is given the opportunity to look me in the eyes, take my hand in theirs and kiss it. I find myself searching along the line of males and females—catching sight of my prey at the end of the line. If his odd colouring did not make him stand out, his height and sheer mass would. Even from here I can see the arrogant look on his face that seems to say this whole thing is beneath him, and I could not agree more.

Moving across the sand, I reach the first contestant, a yellow fae named Frekily. His smile is supposed to be sweet but I can feel the contempt behind it. He must only be here because his family is one of court and the council has persuaded them to join. Bowing his head, he takes my hand and raises it to his lips. Dry skin tickles my flesh, I resist the urge to scratch. Smiling back, I wish him luck before moving on.

Next is a green female, her stature is tall and broad. She is not a fae of court. Her scent is like freshly turned dirt and rain, it is rather relaxing, her stoney face, on the other hand not so much; but that fades away when she drops to one knee. When she looks back to me, the dazzling smile on her face causes me to smile as well: this is a female who looks good on her knees.

"And who may you be?" I ask, fluttering my lashes.

She holds her hand out for me to place mine in it, offering a sweet kiss, her lips are soft. "I am Elanior, my Queen." She stays on one knee, until I have wished her luck and moved on. That's a hard act to beat.

The next few fae are sweet and kind, offering gentle kisses and bowing low. After over halfway, I reach a tall, green male who stands with his arms crossed over his chest, looking like he would rather be anywhere but here. He only offers a small bow and then states his name.

"Baritus, Majesty." I know his family all too well; before the loss of the previous King and Queen he was one of the males they were debating for me to marry. No decision was reached. I can see his frustration at having to prove himself. I say nothing and move on.

Velasilio has been following behind me, listening and asking her own questions. I have asked her to follow up on a few of the fae, some for more sensual acts, others to be sure they are not in this to harm me or for their families to take over the crown. Not a single competitor has touched her. They know that she is off limits, they are here for me and unless she shows them interest it is to stay that way. It is also well known that I do not take kindly to those who treat her with no respect. Velasilio made it very clear to me at the beginning that she did not wish to be with any male in the tournament, as she worries what would happen if I were to marry them.

I have no qualms about sharing a partner. I have on many occasions. She has been used as a stepping stone to get to me before and she refuses to do that again. Besides, she has a deep interest in Dezmond, for now. Perhaps I should tell her about Dezmond? It was so long ago.

But she is happy, which means I am happy. I do not wish to disturb this.

Time slowly ticks by as we near the end of the line. The next male in line is the blue fae with dark blue-lined wings. He seemed so familiar yesterday, and today is no different. I have seen his face before but I have no idea where.

I am unable to take my eyes from his; they look as deep as the ocean and match it in their colouring. I take in his stubble-covered cheeks and chin; his jaw is muscular, as is the rest of his body, toned from years of hard work and yet there is a gentleness there, and his eyes have a softness to them. His dark blue hair is cut short and those wings that are gently tucked in are a beautiful sky blue fading darker at the tips, the two points are delicate and rounded.

A rough voice pulls me from my musings. "Majesty, my name is Arekin Lesana." With a bow, he shows his lack of refinement. A strong, calloused hand wraps around my own. His breath is warm against my skin as he raises it to his mouth and places a gentle kiss on it.

My imagination runs wild with thoughts of his rough hands running over my body, would this gentleness stay or would he toss me around? Looking at his broad shoulders and strong arms I know he could with ease.

With a gentle shake of my head, I realise that Arekin's head is still down.

"You may stand, Arekin. It is a pleasure to meet you. I must ask what it is you do to gain such an impressive amount of muscles?" His head raises slowly and I feel the path his gaze leaves as he takes in my gown. Biting my bottom lip, I cannot help the lust that is surely shown in my eyes.

Standing to his full height, I tilt my head back slightly to be able to look into his eyes once more. His smile shows off his perfectly white teeth. "I am a farmer, my Queen. I tend to the livestock as my father has aged and is unable to now." Holding his head high, I can see he is proud of what he does.

I turn to Velasilio and ask that she gather more information. I do not mention the slight warmth I feel when our hands connect, as I also felt something for Elanior.

Nodding to Arekin, I begin to move to the next contestant. I pick up the slight murmur of his and Velasilio's conversation. What do they have to talk about? I file it away until later to ask her what they spoke of.

Stepping forward, I am met with yet another handsome face. This male screams *dickhead*, just my type.

"Name's Fenterison." His voice is flirty and I can just imagine the dirty things that would come from his mouth. I am surprised how soft his hands are, only my thought is lost as he leaves a sloppy kiss on my hand. I resist the urge to wipe it on my gown. I again turn to Velasilio.

The last warrior, and I do mean warrior, is Kadance from Vixeruas. His wings are by far the most intriguing. Most have held theirs out to show off the colours and unique webbing patterns, but Kadance has no need. His are out but relaxed against his shoulders. They are by far the largest and tallest. The talon-like ends give them a scene of danger. The lining is black, while the webbing is a deep red, almost the colour of blood.

I cannot take my eyes off of them, I have never seen such wings. All wings in Neraphina are the same: light and delicate in texture and style. None have a leather look or even feather, which used to be more common but has not been seen for many years, similar to the magic here.

My own wings are out today; thanks to my royal blood, they are unique. I have the three points: the usual high pointed top and bottom with a third in the middle that sits horizontal. I enjoy having them out in the sun, as the light adds a slight shimmer to them.

Velasilio's purple wings are out in a similar relaxed position to Kadance. Their light purple webbing is stunning and complements her tawny complexion, the lining is intricate and more obvious than others, so dark that it almost seems black. It is a rare trait among our kind.

Standing in front of the impossibly tall male, I look up. He nods his head before a sinfully dark voice, full of dirty promises, skitters over my skin.

"Kadance Zadieria, of Vixeruas." His eyes never meet mine as he seems to scan his surroundings at all times. My mind freezes. Did he just pretend to bow? What an absolute asshole, I have never met a fae with such conceited behaviour. The shock that rolls off of Velasilio is palpable, and her mouth is wide open on an 'O'.

It takes me a moment but I pull myself together and put as much authority into my voice as possible. "I see they have no real manners in Vixeruas?"

Shrugging his shoulders, he looks down at me, his lips tilted into a small smirk.

"I am only here to have some fun. I have no doubt that I will claim what is mine."

That statement again, claiming what is his, does he mean me or the crown? Crossing my arms over my chest I raise an eyebrow. "You must believe quite highly of your skills on the battlefield?"

Scoffing, he bends down slightly. "I know of the skill I possess." He is fully smirking now. I do not know if I want to punch him in the face or kiss him.

"I truly hope the *skills* you have will be enough!" My mood is beginning to sour with his arrogance. The fun side of this conversation is over as he continues to speak to me like a commoner.

"My skills work well on the battlefield and my massive cock more than makes up for my attitude." With a wink, he stands tall once more, still never looking directly at me. Velasilio stands stock-still next to me. In fact, the entire colosseum is silent, waiting to see what will happen.

Clearing my throat, I hold my head high as I address him. "As you are not from here, I will not punish you for your lack of respect. I am unsure how you do things in Vixeruas. But here we do not speak so brazenly." Turning on the spot, I walk towards the stairs that lead to the royal viewing box.

A small yelp has me turning around once more. Looking back, I see that Velasilio has fallen and Kadance has caught her. From where I stand, I have no clue what has been said but a few hushed words are exchanged between them. As he rights her, he gives a wink with a sinful smile on his smug face. She all but runs from his arms.

He very obviously adjusts his *massive cock*.

Well, I do hope he gets punched in the face after such behaviour.

When Velasilio catches up to me, I pull her in close. Looking down at her, I raise my brow. "What did he say to you?"

Shaking her head, she soldiers on. "It is not worth repeating."

CHAPTER 27

A CHOICE

Velasilio

DAY ONE, TRIAL ONE

As I follow Searaphina, each competitor shows me the appropriate respect with a slight bow or curtsy. I smile sweetly as I take down their names and if Searaphina wants me to look into them further, she whispers 'Yes please' and I must hold back my laughter each time. I am enjoying having a chance to see each fae who will potentially become the royal consort, though I feel this is most likely going to be the hardest part, as it makes me connect with them before they possibly die.

No, I will not allow myself to think that way. There is no way any of the fae here will want to kill each other when a simple knockout is all that is necessary.

Another challenging thing I have not anticipated is trying not to find them attractive. Each fae is more striking than the last, with their broad shoulders, strong muscles. I am not usually attracted to females but there are some here that, if they asked nicely, I would likely allow them to take me on an evening stroll. I am unsure if anything further would happen but I enjoy the idea of having them around.

But they are all here for their Queen. They wish to marry her and, if I lay with one of them and they are to win, I must see them, day after day, knowing that they are sleeping with my best friend, when I know what sounds they make and how they feel against my skin. The thought makes my stomach turn.

One positive for the day is that I will never need to do this again.

I allow my mind to empty; all information is written down as needed but nothing is held. Nearing the end of the line, I notice a familiar head of dark blue hair, wide chest and strong legs. He holds himself with power and respect: a good fit for our Queen. When he speaks, his voice is far deeper than I remembered. It has been years since I have seen him and, though we were never close, his parents cared for all of the creatures used for meat, fur and more. They were well known on our land, as almost every family had some kind of dealing with them.

Searaphina seems to pay him additional time, giving me her sign to gather more information. She has asked him more than the others as well, which is a good sign.

As she moves on, I step up to him. "Good morning, Arekin." I give a slight curtsy.

"Good morning to you as well, Velasilio." He bows slightly before we both stand.

"I heard that you have taken over for your father, I hope he is still well?"

"He is well, just his back is not what it used to be, I have taken over his duties." His lips bow into a slight frown as he speaks.

"That is both good to hear and sad, I feel for your father, as farming is his life's work. And your mother, how is she?"

He smiles as he thinks of her. "She is well. She still handles all the book work, she has a meeting with your family soon. How are they?"

He could not have known what happened, but I do my best to not let my smile slip, even if the tears begin to well in my eyes.

"They are... Well, I believe..." My voice cracks and I take a deep breath.

Arekin's face drops. "Velasilio, I apologise if I have upset you." He reaches forward, his hand gently hovering just above my arm like he does not know if he should touch me.

Shaking my head, I hold my parchment to my chest. "No you have not, it was lovely to see you again, please take care and good luck today." I move quickly to follow Searaphina, who has already moved to the next male, one who immediately has me forgetting my worries with his arrogance.

His tone is cocky as he introduces himself as Fenterison, and I am given the cue again. I know she will be very interested in this one as he is exactly her type, hot wanker. Rushing through her conversation with him, she turns and makes her way to the last male quickly.

I have not been looking forward to this.

Standing beside Searaphina, I have to tilt my head almost all the way back to look into his face: the top of my head would reach his mid-chest. If not for his height, his wings would surely see him stand above the rest, they are so different. I have never seen wings that are so dark and incredibly powerful-looking. My hand moves without me releasing it. I reach out but stop myself before either of them notice. I am so enthralled by them, I do not realise my mouth is wide open.

I am so focused that I do not hear what he says at first but, as I focus in, I am surprised at how brazen he is. "I will claim what is mine." His voice sings to my soul of the lustful promise that comes with such a statement.

Searaphina holds herself well, speaking with elegance and grace in front of such a horribly mannered male. I am so focused on his promise to claim that I am not fully listening, but there is no missing his next words.

"My skills excel on the battlefield and my massive cock more than makes up for my attitude." My eyes feel as though they may bulge from their sockets, my heart skipping a beat.

Without meaning to, I glance at his pants and notice the thick outline of what could only be his impressive package. I do not realise the conversation had ended until—

"It won't bite." Startled, my eyes dart up to his, looking from him to Searaphina's retreating form. My feet move quickly, turning to run, but it catches on Datriminish's knows what, and I head face first towards the sand. I let out a startled yelp but my mind screams, *'You idiot'*.

Just as I brace for impact —squeezing my eyes closed and my hands outstretched— when I suddenly stop. Slowly, I open my eyes one at a time only to see the sand inches from my face. I feel a warm and incredibly muscular arm wrapped around my middle. I am gently pulled to my feet. Now, standing upright, I feel a warm, solid body pressed to my back, and I notice the slight bulge that rests against my lower back. Turning slowly in his arm, I tilt my head back and look straight into dark red eyes that I swear are looking into my soul.

His smirk is that of the devil, sliding his hand from my waist and taking hold of my hip and pushing me back slightly, he bends down so that his lips meet the shell of my ear. His voice is so dark that it wraps around me, swallowing me whole as he whispers. "It's common for females to lose their ability to function around me, don't worry I will still have you screaming my name."

I stand stunned, not sure what to do. Hundreds of fae are watching this encounter unfold, so I do the only thing I can. I break free from Kadance's embrace. When his arm simply falls away, confusion fills me, as I am not strong and he could have held me longer if he wanted to. He must believe he has toyed with me enough.

With haste, I catch up to Searaphina with a red face and bruised pride that my clumsiness knows just the right moment to make me a fool.

As we walk, she pulls me in close and looks down at me with a single eyebrow raised. "What did he say to you?"

"It is not worth repeating." We climb the stairs and enter the royal suite. I take my seat as Searaphina moves to the front of the box. She holds her hands high and the colosseum goes silent.

The competitors are still standing in their line; once the opening speech is complete they will begin to pair off.

"Good morning, and welcome to the Queen's Tournament." Searaphina waits for the crowd to cheer before she continues. "Today is the first trial: hand to hand combat. Competitors may choose any weapon they wish. You have been paired according to your skill levels and training. Throughout this and all other trials you can choose to surrender before it begins. If you do not, the only ways out are disqualification, serious injury or death. This may come at the hands of another contestant or the trials themselves. Outside of the trials you may not harm one another, if you do you will be removed from the tournament. We look forward to seeing you each prove yourself and that you deserve to stand by my side."

She pauses and waits for the competitors to get set up. There are twenty-five circles drawn in the sand and each pair stands inside, weapons at the ready. "We pray that Datriminish will bless you all. Begin."

I wait on baited breath to see what Arekin will do.

CHAPTER 28

A HORRID DISPLAY

Kadance

DAY ONE, TRIAL ONE

Once the opening speech is delivered we get into our duo-s to fight. Looking at the opponent in front of me, I see it is the flea from earlier looking as though he is about to piss himself from fear. I had not thought he would be a worthy opponent but, seeing that I was not a part of the pre-tournament testing, I can only assume their best fighter has been put in front of me. He tries to look brave, standing tall as he selects a set of daggers. After seeing the ones strapped to my body and thinking I, too, would use them. I smile a large and toothy smile as he steps forward, choosing the long board sword instead.

His face drops again as he realises his mistake. The weapon racks are removed and the final words are spoken. It's time.

I move faster than most and swipe a clean slice through the flesh and bone of his neck. The force I use sends his head hurtling to the floor and it rolls away.

The body slumps into a heap at my feet. Throwing the long sword down, I look out over the others, most of whom have just begun their own battles. I simply smirk and move into the shadows. Not my most creative death by any means but the job is done. Besides, I can't let my true demons run wild as of yet. I would hate to scare off my little fae female. After all, I want her to like me, for now, anyway.

The others take care of their opponents in dramatic fashions: they slice at each other, refusing to give up until one of them is laying unconscious. Only a few actually kill their opponents. I believe they are trying to look ruthless like me, but it's all bullshit but then I see that my Gem is looking at him. That pathetic blue fae, his name is something to do with an 'A'. He and his appointment continue to dance around one another and she can't take her eyes off him. If he continues to try and take what is mine. I'll just have to take his life.

CHAPTER 29

MERCY OR DEATH

Arekin

DAY ONE, TRIAL ONE

After the events of this morning, I am sure that today will have one of the most vicious deaths ever seen. Kadance has already proven hat he is the most intimidating of us all.

Looking around the pit, I see that the unfortunate soul who is with Kadance just so happens to be the idiot from earlier. I will be against Demarit, he is a worthy match for me. I know this as our families trade livestock, his family relies on him as he now he runs the farm, his father has retired due to his older age. Because of this I can't kill him. The roar of the crowd is the only sound I can hear.

Facing Demarit I look at the weapon in his hand, we both have long swords, this will make for an even match. There are many other weapons out today, some have daggers or axes or even fight with their bare hands. I prefer an axe but for this particular battler I thought a long sword would be best. The crowd is silent as the Queen gives her final comment before clapping her hands once, telling us to begin.

The crowd surges, sounding like thunder as they cheer. Glancing over my shoulder I see Kadance made quick work of his opponent, the headless body feels like a warning to all others, that he is not only deadly but bloody quick.

The sensation of being watched washes over me as Demarit and I circle each other. Demarit announces his attack with a powerful war cry, sadly for him all that has done is given me time to react. I raise my sword to counter as he comes down over his own head in a large arch, while Demarit has a lot of strength behind him he has no skill. I side-step, sliding my sword along his, causing him to stumble forwards. I can see the anger that takes over as his attacks grow more aggressive and with less thought.

Dodging his next attack I step forward and my blade cuts into his shoulder as the sword runs through his tissue and muscle, he bellows in pain. Clutching his injured shoulder we continue our battle until the ground begins to stain red with our blood. Demarit has gotten a few good hits and if it were not for our quick healing we would be finished by now. I can see the exhaustion starting to wear on us both, I feel it in my bones, the smell of dirt, sweat and blood permeate the air. He lounges for me again, I sidestep again and shove him hard in the back, as he falls to his knees I make the choice of mercy. I know the others will see me as weak. As I look around the others are ending their fights all with a lot of blood and gore, many are still alive but they will need time to recover from their wounds, a few have killed their opponents but I refuse to be one of them.

Moving my hold to the pommel of the sword I use it to knock Demarit out before he can regain his footing and stand. He goes down and dust flies into the air. Some of the crowd yell at me to end him while others scream mercy. Throwing my Sword to the ground.

I hold up my hands and shout as loud as I can to be heard over the crowd. "I choose mercy."

Two guards come over and drag my unconscious opponent Demarit from the pit.

I don't want to become a killer to win the crown. I will show that I would make a strong and fair ruler. I know our Queen is fair and kind, I hope that I may catch her attention in showing that we may match. I have longed to set my sight upon the Queen again ever since our paths crossed at the market two years ago. Queen Searaphina visited for the royal tour, my home is on the lands that Velasilio's family own and I was at the market showing some of our finest beasts. As soon as our eyes met I felt a pull towards her, one that could mean we are fated to be together, only she turned and walked away rather quickly. Maybe I was wrong?

Taking a moment to steady my breathing as I survey the carnage that lays before me. The ground was yellow, and is now mostly a dark red. I know many eyes are on me now but the pair feel as though they are burning me. Raising my head, I lock eyes with our Queen.

CHAPTER 30

AN INTRIGUING MALE

Searaphina

DAY ONE, TRIAL ONE

My eyes catch on the way his muscles move as he stands there breathing heavily. I follow down to his broad shoulders and then to his face, set in a frown as he watches what looks like the lifeless body of his opponent be dragged away—surely to wake pissed with a pounding headache. His gaze tracks over the mess the others have made during their fights. The blood-soaked sand, drying in the sun's heat. There's a metallic scent mixed with sweat from the competitors and crowd alike.

Unable to look anywhere but at him, I track the slight shake of his head at the butchery the others have shown. Stilling for a moment, his gaze shoots to mine, and our eyes lock for a heartbeat. There is a gentle pull in my chest, a most intriguing male indeed.

A thunderous cheer comes from the crowd, jolting me from my trance. The first trial has come to an end with only a few hours of entertainment.

The crowd stands in ovation to the winning males and females, calling out to them as if they are gods.

Standing from my chair, I move to the edge of the suite, where all will be able to see me. Raising one hand, hush falls over the colosseum. "Congratulations to the twenty-three victors. You have each shown strength today."

We would have twenty-five, but, unfortunately, two competitors were in such an aggressive state they continued to hack at one another until they both collapsed and there was no saving them. This tournament is looking to be a violent one.

"We cannot wait to see what you do in the next trial. This evening you will feast with the court though there is a curfew, so you must be back before the moon hits its peak. So eat, drink and rest, for when tomorrow comes you will need all of your strength and wit."

I turn on my heel and stride towards the exit. As I pass Velasilio's chair, she stands and follows me.

By the time we reach the pit, the competitors are lined up. They will walk behind the royal carriage to receive blessings from the towns-fae. We make our way out of the pit, my four guards keeping close. Each male and female bows their head as we walk past, all but Kadance of course. His eyes track us as though we are prey, and a shiver works through me.

Shaking off the feeling, I raise my head high and keep moving, not giving him the satisfaction of affecting me. I just notice his lip tilt in a smirk. Darkness envelopes us as we enter the tunnel, I hear the many footsteps echoing around us. When we reach the carriage, I step in first, followed by Velasilio. The competitors are lined up in pairs behind us, ready to move on. With a click of his tongue, the coach-male gets the unicorns moving.

Traveling through town, some of the villages offer their prayers and well wishes, while others throw flowers. Some of the fae even toss their undergarments to make their intentions clear; during the tournament there is no rule against having such trysts, as there is the chance they may find their twin flames. If this happens, it is highly suggested they leave the tournament and follow fate's design.

The journey back takes longer today with so many lining the roads.

Once we arrive back at the castle, I move to my chambers for a bath, as the day has worn on me and the sand seems to always find a way into places it should not be. This evening there will be a feast held in one of the lower levels of the castle for the victors. Velasilio and myself will join them, but first I must prepare.

Velasilio is not far behind me and she brings the other maids carrying fresh water for my bath. Once it is prepared, I dismiss her, needing some time alone.

I step into the warm tub. Sinking down, I let the scent of jasmine wrap around me. I let myself relax, slowly washing my body and humming to myself. The room is silent around me until I think I hear a small creak. Suddenly, it feels like someone is watching me. Sitting up, I search the room. When I do not see anything, I use my most Queen-like voice.

"This is the Queen's chambers, you must leave imed—" Footsteps cause me to stop speaking. I know those soft steps and I release the breath I was holding just as Velasilio makes an entrance with towels in hand.

"My apologies Searaphina, I forgot to fetch you a fresh towel." A small frown plays on her lips.

Relaxing back into the water, I notice that my bath has cooled. "That is alright, it just felt as though I was being watched for a moment, but it must be the pressure of the tournament." Nodding along, she does not question me, but I wonder if she too has felt eyes on her.

"I understand, would you like me to stay with you?" Her offer is sweet but I can see that she is tired.

"No, we have a few hours before the feast, go wash up and have a sleep. I will be doing the same. I will see you this evening." With a curtsy, she turns and leaves.

CHAPTER 31

A FEAST

Velasilio

NIGHT ONE, TRIAL ONE

After a much needed rest and a quick wash, Searaphina and I are both dressed and ready to head to the feast. The dining hall has been done up with several smaller tables for members of the court and the competitors. There is a head table for Searaphina, myself and the council males. The atmosphere is warm and inviting with the scents of roasted meat, fresh bread and gravy. Each table is laid with various items, from cooked foods to fresh fruit and sweet delights, like cakes and biscuits. In the centre of the room is a small dance floor and a set of three musicians sit in the left corner playing a violin, a harp and a flute. The music is light and fun, needed after the day of blood and gore.

The entire room stops as the Queen is announced and the court all bow and curtsy. With a smile and wave of her hand the music begins again and so does the ample chatter; the mood is joyous as fae dance together and drink.

I find a smile on my own face. My gown is missing the corset this evening, opting for room to eat. I love a feast and a corset restricts the amount I may have.

The Queen takes her seat and I follow on her right, as always, With their Queen here, the others slowly follow, also taking their seats, as they are now allowed to eat. I scan over the fae filling the room and I notice that almost all of the competitors are here; some may have decided to have a quick meal and rest before tomorrow. The feast will only last for a few hours as Searaphina has work to do this evening and when the Queen leaves many of the court follow.

After the main feast is eaten, many get up to dance. Searaphina and I take a stroll around the room to speak with each of the competitors, to find out a little more about them and see how they are feeling after the first trial. Many sound confident that this was an easy task and they cannot wait to see what awaits them in the next four trials. Each time we talk with a new contestant, one of the servants comes to Searaphina with urgent news.

After we have spoken with each of them, we return to our seats to rest and drink.

Feeling eyes on me, I look over my shoulder at Dezmond, wishing he could ask me to dance. But I understand that this is not the safest place and that Searaphina must be his top priority. I will always come second to her and, at this moment, I start to feel a small amount of resentment towards her, though it is gone as quickly as it came.

I shake my head. I will not hate her, she has done nothing to deserve it.

I turn to look at Searaphina; she looks like she heard my thoughts and I pray she did not.

"What is the matter, Silio?" Picking up my drink, I hold it out to her.

"Just thinking of the day and what horrors we saw, wishing to drink them away." I take a sip of my wine, hoping she does not push further.

A hand gently takes my wine and I look at Searaphina, her face set in a frown. "We have a big day tomorrow, please do not drink your worries away tonight. If you need to talk, I am here."

I know it is genuine so I give her a small truth: "I wish to dance." Her brow furrows as through she does not understand why I am upset by this and then she begins to smile.

"Why did you not say so, let us find some dancing partners." Taking my hand, she stands, we walk to the closest table of competitors. Elanior, Sobia, Arekin, Fenterison and Buvariris are all sitting and talking with members of the court.

Their conversations halt when they realise who is standing before them. Sobia is the first to speak. "How may we help you, Majestie?"

Searaphina smiles wide. "Silio and I would like to dance and were wondering who will accompany us."

Sobia and Elanior are the closest two and, as such, are the quickest to stand. "We would be honoured." Elanior takes Searaphina's hand and leads her out onto the floor while Sobia smiles sweetly to me.

"Shall we?" She holds her arm out for me, and I take it. She sweeps me onto the dance floor and I am shocked at how quickly she takes the lead. She is wearing pants this evening with a dashing, loose, lavender blouse and dark plumb vest over the top, fastened tight and pushing her breasts up. I understand at that moment why males are obsessed with the things, hers are large and bursting from the shirt.

I hear a slight laugh and look up to see Sobia staring at me while I was looking directly at her breasts, though they are almost eye level for me. Sobia is a taller female, at six-foot. I feel my cheeks heat and I smile awkwardly.

"My apologies, I was admiring." She cuts me off before I can finish.

"It's perfectly fine that you were enjoying my tits, I enjoy having them out for others to see." With one hand holding mine out and the other resting on my hip, she moves it around and pulls me close, whispering in my ear, "Especially pretty little females like yourself."

I let out a nervous giggle; I have never had another female make me feel this way before. Usually I am not attracted to them, but there must be something in the air this evening because all I want to do is stay here with Sobia and dance.

We spend the next few songs just swaying and twirling together, we laugh and talk, she tells me she lost both of her parents in a small land squirmish a few years ago on one of the outlying islands—still a part of Neraphina but not watched over by the crown. Her story breaks my heart, my family may have disowned me but at least they are alive.

I do not know what possesses me but, as she shows me a vulnerable side, I step up on my tiptoes and kiss her on the cheek. She looks a bit shocked and then her face goes between a smile and a frown like she is not sure what emotion to feel.

I decide to look over and see what Searaphina and Elanior are doing: the pair are gliding across the floor looking very cosy. She seems like a nice female who wants the female more than the crown.

The fact that Sobia is hitting on me and not the one she is trying to marry hits me and I freeze, my feet physically will not move. I feel mortified for kissing her.

"Velasilio? Are you okay?" Her voice is sweet and caring. It hits something deep inside me. I look into her eyes, so similar to mine only lighter, what a matching pair we would make.

Finding my feet, I step back with a nod. "I am fine, my apologies for kissing you, Sobia."

Her own cheeks flush now, her ivory skin staining pink. "I didn't mind it."

I step towards her again and she seems surprised, but wraps her arms around me anyway. Just as we begin to lean in, a throat clears behind me and I snap out of my haze. Quickly turning in her arms, I see Dezmond standing behind me, his face a mixture of rage and jealousy as his eyes dart between us. We let each other go and my embarrassment morphs into something different: an odd anger rises in me, one I do not feel often but over the past few days have been feeling more.

Crossing my arms over my chest, I stand in front of Sobia as if I am shielding her as I run my eyes over the length of Dezmond. When I speak, there is no hiding my anger. "What do you need that is so important that you so rudely interrupt us?" I almost start to tap my foot with rage as it boils inside me when he does not have an answer.

Rubbing his hand over the back of his neck, he tries to find the words. When he cannot, I huff out. "You are wasting our time."

Turning and taking Sobia's hand in my *own*, we walk away. I am upset that he interrupted us and now has stopped what could have been. I return her to the table where she was sitting. When we reach it, she pulls me back to her and kisses me. Her hands go to either side of my face, and I wrap mine around her waist. Her tongue runs along the seam of my lips and before I open to her, it is as if my brain clicks and I realise I am kissing a competitor. I break the kiss.

Sobia's lips are glossy as she smiles down at me. "You are one sassy little female." I awkwardly stare at her, unsure of what to do now. My blood no longer boils with a mixture of anger and lust, it is like a bucket of cold water was doused over me and I see clearly that I had no clue what I was doing.

I raise my hands to hers and remove them from my face, speaking as gently as I can. "Sobia, you are beautiful and I lost myself in the moment, but I promised myself I will not be with a competitor while the tournament is on. I do not want to taint a possible relationship with the new royal consort." I sound more confident than I feel. Her response is not what I expected.

"And that is what makes you so special, Velasilio, that you are so loyal you would put your own love aside to ensure that your Queen is happy. I only hope you don't end up pushing away the real thing for some other fae's happiness." Leaning in, she quickly pecks me on the lips before she turns to leave the feast.

"I will see you tomorrow." She throws a wink over her shoulder as she goes.

Standing there utterly confused as to what just happened, I see Dezmond sulking in the corner. Part of me feels bad for being too harsh towards him, but we are not in a relationship and he had no right to do what he did. Searaphina must have seen the entire exchange, as she swiftly moves to my side.

"It is time that we both leave. I have work to do and you need to escape whatever that was." She waves her hand to the space I was dancing in. I offer a slight chuckle as we leave. She does not know it, but I do have work to do. Only mine could land me in the dungeon.

CHAPTER 32
MYTHICAL CREATURES

Searaphina

NIGHT ONE, TRIAL ONE

"Ahh, why must I insist on creating these riddles myself!" Grumbling to myself, I look down at the pages upon pages of deadly creatures and rare items I can request the competitors retrieve for the third trial. Only, my brain does not wish to work; I should not have had so many wines at the feast.

I could have given this task to the council, but I do not trust them to make it fair and even, as Alabaster's nephew is Buvariris. Though, if he did interfere with the fairness of the competition, he could be tried for treason against the crown as no fae who has knowledge of the tournament may share the information with a competitor under the penalty of death or life in the dungeon.

With twenty-three riddles needed, I am running out of ideas. In the second trial they will need to make their way through the labyrinth with dead ends, traps and miniature trials of wit, and finally to the centre. If they succeed, they need to answer whatever

riddle I have come up with, given to them by the serpent-like Ridlemensira.

If they answer correctly, they will be allowed to exit. If they fail,
they will be the Ridlemensira's lunch.

I continue to work through the list of competitors; with only
two left, there is a light rapping at the door. Raising my head, I notice
the moon, almost at its peak.

When I do not answer there is another knock, only louder.

Turning in my seat I call out, "Enter", not hiding the frustration
in my voice.

It must be Velasilio, as no other fae would be coming to me at
this time of night–well, unless Cassidie wanted to join me in bed
again, though she usually just crawls in next to me without knocking.

Velasilio is carrying a tray, and, from the scent, it has a hot tea and
something warm and sweet on it. "What have you brought me?"

"I have brought you something to help get you through." Slowly,
she comes over and settles the tray down over my work. I frown up at
her for placing it there.

"I will remove it, just give me a moment." Removing the tea and
what looks to be a hot loaf of sweet bread, she places them on the
only part of the desk that does not have parchments on it. As she
picks the tray back up, she looks down at my list.

Quickly placing my hands over the paper to hide them, I shout at
her, "Excuse me! You are not allowed to see these!"

With the tray in hand, she holds it to her hip and cocks her
head at me. "Come now, you know I can keep a secret." She holds
out her pinky to me. Laughing at the childish jester, I bat her hand
away.

"Argh! Only because I am struggling so. I have two males left."
Velasilio does a little jump, placing the tray beside the desk on the
floor before she kneels beside me.

"Who might these two be? They must be quite fantastic fighters
for you to be struggling to choose the right beast for them. Well, if

they were to succeed with their wits first." She moves the papers around to be able to see who I am so frustrated by.

"Hmm, this is troublesome, I understand why you cannot decide. Kadance is quite the threat to others and will definitely need a treacherous creature or task." Her eyes move down the parchment over the two beasts I have written down as possible assignments for him.

"Absolutely, it must be the most dreadful of creatures. Today's trial proved that his skills may be unmatched by the other competitors." Velasilio only nods along, I know she heard all the same comments today; the servants do love to talk.

I find the list of beasts that I had begun to write each contestant's name on. Passing this to Velasilio, I watch as her brow furrows and she moves her lips, saying the names softly while reading. She was taught at a young age but does struggle sometimes. Often telling me the letters jump around in the page if she reads in her head.

"The egg of a Quartier, horn of Xanvitor, golden harp of a Satyr, left shoe of a Aminaduh?" I cannot help but smile as she reads; they are strange in many ways, their bodies are odd and misshapen in that they only have a head and no torso so their arms and legs stick out from the sides. Their eyes are large and they do not have eyelids which means they are incapable of blinking, it is very creepy that they always stare. I feel that the most unnerving thing about these creatures is the smile it always wears, from side to side of their head it sits, with all of its large square teeth. And they are a most annoying little creature, always stealing shoes for their collections, and their most prized are kept on their feet, so to steal one from the small, smart little things would be quite the prize. Perhaps that last one is more of a joke.

Velasilio looks from the paper to me, her brows drawn in confusion while I only laugh. "Oh my, yes. A most challenging task indeed. Have you ever tried to acquire one? It is almost impossible!" Unable to contain myself for another moment, I burst and Velasilio does as well.

Taking a few deep breaths, she speaks once more. "Alright, I guess I can understand why you have included such a creature. It would show their wit and quick thinking, as the Aminduh have never been known to remove their shoes." Smiling sweetly at her, she just shakes her head once and continues to look through the list to the last contestant.

"Arkein is the other male?"

"Indeed, he is intriguing, because, when the others did not show mercy, he did. Knowing the others would see him as weak, I see that he must have a plan in place. I believe that he is one for us to keep an eye on." Quickly looking down, I search for the beast I had in mind. Finally I see it, taking it in my hands it feels right, this is the perfect quest for Arekin. Leaning forward, Velasilio reads over the page.

"The song of a Siren... Searaphina you cannot, no male is able to resist. He would be dead before he even knew it was there." Holding a hand in front of her mouth, her concern for his welfare seems to be genuine. Has she finally taken a liking to a male other than the guard, or does she truly believe it an impossible task?

"I understand this and that is why I am yet to assign it, perhaps it would make a worthy beast of the most vicious Kadance?" Velasilio does not seem convinced as she chews on the edge of her fingers.

"A creature of such intelligence would be wasted on such a brute, he would just slay her and move on. It would prove a fae to have wisdom and knowledge if they capture the song."

Nodding to herself once, she speaks softly. "Arekin is the right choice for the Siren."

"I agree, so that still leaves Kadance. What foul beast does he deserve to face?"

We both look through the parchments on my desk, trying to find the perfect creature for him. It must be something of strength, cunning and with the same appetite for blood.

"What of this, the Deathwhisper?" Holding the drawing up, Velasilio seems unsure. Taking it from her, I look over the howling nightmare pictured in front of me.

The dark chalk shows a large creature with four legs, there is one standing on its back legs and one on all four. Their backs are covered in razor sharp spikes and their claws are lined with talons the size of my forearm. Their cute little ears and small button noses are the only thing not terrifying on them. Elongated canines and, behind them, a row of smaller teeth made for tearing flesh, line their mouths.

"Impeccable! This is perfect, we will ask for its heart." Certain of my plan, I begin to write out the riddle. If Kadance can succeed in this, his ego will surely match his head in size.

I know the kingdom would struggle with the idea of a dark fae as their King, as we have all been told the fables of their dark magic, how it can enter one's mind and compel them to do their puppet master's bidding. A shudder works through my body at the thought of such power.

"It would be very impressive if he were able to defeat such a creature, but its heart? Could it not be a claw or spike from its back, so that it might live?" Making her eyes as big as possible, she tries to appeal to my compassion.

"Silio, who is to say it could live with such an injury, we do not wish the beast to be in pain, this will ensure that it dies quickly and the heart of a Deathwhisper is a most powerful and rare ingredient." Placing my hand over hers, I give it a pat before signing Kadance's name down.

Rolling the scroll, I take my green wax and hold it over the candle burning on the desk. As it drips, I move the parchment underneath and place my seal over the top to seal the document until tomorrow.

"If you are no longer in need of my assistance, I will take my leave." Standing from her position kneeling beside me, she rubs at her knees.

"We must get another stool in here for you. We will have a long and tiring day tomorrow, we should rest." Rising from my seat, I walk to the bed where my meal awaits me.

"Of course Phina, I will be here when the sun rises to draw you a bath." With a rushed curtsy, Velasilio turns to leave.

"Thank you for the tea. Rest well, for tomorrow is sure to bring untold excitement." With a weary smile, she leaves. Sitting on the bed, to eat while my mind wanders.

I am eager to see more of what Kadance will do like, what he would do if I invited him to my private chambers? Would he pick me up and take me against a wall, or would he simply toss me over his shoulder, before throwing me down on the bed and taking me there? What positions would he put me in? Would he fuck me hard and rough so that I would be unable to walk for days?

And what of the strong but gentle Arekin? I could tell he had the upper hand the entire trial and yet he chose not to end it. He could be a more gentle lover, making sure that I had reached the heights of my own pleasure before taking me.

The two males seem to be complete opposites... What would happen if I could enjoy both at the same time?

Both males kneel at the base of my throne, and I shiver with antici-pation. The last trial is tomorrow and they wish to indulge in a night of pleasure, how can I refuse?

Kadance moves first, standing. His chest is bare, my gaze sweeps over his broad shoulders and down his muscular stomach. His black leather pants are untied and hang low, showing the most delicious V that leads my eyes straight to his "massive cock"—from the hard outline, I am not sure that it will fit.

He places both arms on my throne, caging me in. Slowly, he leans forward until his lips graze the shell of my ear, kissing just below it, sending another shiver down my spine and straight to my core. I am unable to stop the whimper that leaves me.

Raising his head slightly, Kadance growls. "Patience is not my strong suit, keep making noises like that and I cannot promise I'll be gentle." Leaning back in, he nips and sucks down my neck, causing me to groan; as wetness pools between my thighs.

Large hands reach under me, grabbing hold of my ass and pulling me forward. The quick movement makes me yelp, and I wrap my legs around his waist as he lifts me off the chair. My core now flush against his hard length, I wish for more friction, my breasts ache, begging to be free from their confines and lavished with the attention I desperately need. My mind is in a frenzy of dirty desire. Kadance's hand wraps around my hair, pulling it tight as my head moves back. Our eyes lock: his are now almost black with lust, no red to be seen.

Moving faster than possible, our mouths crash in a heated kiss; tongues entwined, heat flushes my skin. I don't even realise he has released my hair until it is gently pushed to the side and I feel Arekin's muscular body pressing in against my back. Unable to move, I am completely at their mercy. A soft kiss is placed in the valley between my shoulder and neck, causing gooseflesh to cover my arms and then a smooth voice full of sensual promise whispers to me.

"Do you think you can take us both, our Queen?" Moving my head to the side, I allow him more access. Torturously slow, he kisses down my neck to my shoulder. His hands move to my breasts as he squeezes. Kadance has my lips locked in a heated kiss as his fingers sit so close to where I want them but still not touching.

I break our kiss as a sensual moan leaves me and I close my eyes to the overwhelming feeling of both males toying with me.

My eyes flutter open as Kadance grasps my chin with his thumb and forefinger, his gaze burns straight to my core, and I clench my thighs around him.

His voice is filled with dark, sensual pleasure as he speaks. "You will look us in the eyes when we fuck you."

Nodding my head is the only thing I can do as my brain has stopped functioning.

"Good." His final word before he puts me down. As soon as my feet hit the floor, he reaches up and rips open the bodice of my gown.

I go to protest but I am turned around as Arekin drops his head, taking my breast into his mouth, swirling his tongue around my taut nipple. I feel the cold air as my dress is lifted, exposing me to Kadance. I feel the large head of his shaft pressing against my wet heat just before he...

Suddenly, I jolt awake. Looking around, I see no fae in sight. I move to the top of my bed, shivering, and slide under the covers, hoping to find my way back to finish that dirty dream.

CHAPTER 33

A DEAL

Velasilio

NIGHT ONE, TRIAL ONE

As I leave Searaphina's chambers, my chest grows tight and it feels as though an invisible string is trying to draw me back to her. I did not lie to her about my plans for this evening, but a lie by omission is still a lie. If she were to discover the truth of where I am headed, well I do not wish to think about what would happen. The strange sensation begins to feel like a heavy stone settling into my stomach. I know what I am doing is wrong and I have in some way betrayed my Queen's trust, but I know that I am only doing this in the best interest of my friend and my home.

After today's trial I have decided that Arekin must succeed, as he has shown strength, patience and mercy, things our kingdom needs. As I pass my own chambers, I grab my cloak to shelter me from prying eyes. I move throughout the castle down the many stone corridors and staircases it takes to get to the contestants chambers. Every step I take there is an ever-present shadow that follows me; it does not seem to carry any malice, just to torment me and tell me to remember even the shadows have eyes.

Stepping out into the cool night air, I pull my cloak tight as I walk through the gardens, towards the gate that will lead me outside the walls of the castle and to the contestants' chambers. Moving down an alley, I see the two storey building before me, which holds two competitors per room. I need to find the door that belongs to Arekin.

They should all return soon from the feast or the inn. I need to find an alcove to hide in while I wait. Torches line the walls, offering a reprieve from the oppressive shadow that stalks me. I find a small arch between doorways to stand in; with my dark cloak I should be fairly hidden here.

Leaning my side against the cold stone, I watch from my hiding spot as the competitors begin to slowly stumble towards me, each one seeming to be drunker than the last. I cover all but my eyes as I wait. Unfortunately for me, one of the males decides he cannot make the three feet walk into his chambers to use the chamberpot and pulls out his manhood to urinate all over the roses that line the open side of the covered walkway. I turn my back and stare into the darkness. A deep sense of uncertainty washes over me.

'*Why did I think I could do this? It will never work, I will be discovered and then, oh!*' Shaking my head, I realise that I cannot move forward with my plan. I turn and step from my hiding place and straight into the path of another.

As I begin to fall sideways. Two arms shoot out and wrap around my side, stopping my fall. Turning slightly, I look into the deepest blue eyes I had ever seen.

Arekin stands completely still, staring down at me, his gaze roams from my face to my chest as I breathe rapidly. I feel the slight movement of his hands as they come to rest on my hips. My hands rest on his chest as I feel the weight of his gaze linger on my mouth. Nervously, I lick my lips. His eyes track the movement.

"Arekin..." My words are cut off as he dips his head and closes the distance between us. As his lips press against mine, I lose myself in the kiss for only a second before I regain my senses.

The sound of my hand slapping his face, is the only sound in the otherwise silent night. He rears back as if he only now realises who I am. He ensures I am steady before removing his hands. My face, I am sure, is also wearing a shocked expression. I watch his face as a slight red handprint begins to bloom.

He touches where my mark is now imprinted. "I beg your pardon Lady Velasilio, I had one too many ales at the feast. All of my senses seem to have run off into the night."

I raise the hood of my cloak once more. "Well, see that you find them."

When I am sure that I am once again hidden by the fabric, I look at Arekin to see a sly smirk cross his face. Huffing out a breath, I twist and begin to walk away, having seen enough of these males this evening.

I move all of three steps before a large hand lands on my shoulder. "Wait, please, I don't want you to leave angry. Allow me to explain."

Mustering my courage, I turn to face him once more. "Are you sober enough to keep your hands to yourself?" Shrugging he puts his hand away to make a point.

Turning back to him I wait. He looks at his feet and breaths deeply before he speaks. "Every time you visited your parents I caught sight of you, it might be in town or when you visited the farm with your parents to ensure we had enough food for the creatures or for ourselves. You are beautiful and I have always longed to kiss you, to know you. I am afraid I thought that is why you came here tonight because you too felt the urge to be with me. I should not have kissed you without your permission and I apologise." He sounds so sincere and I believe him only. I have absolutely no idea how to respond.

Yes, he is handsome, and yes, I had seen him around the village, but my thoughts are jumbled now. So I do the one thing I can to distract him: I blurt out my true reason for being here. "I have come to offer you a deal."

His eyes widen in shock. "A deal? If you mean to give me inside information about the trials, is it not forbidden?"

"Shhh! Keep your voice down, we do not have much time and we cannot be seen together." Grabbing his arm, I led him back into my little alcove. It does not do much to hide his large frame.

"I wish to help you win the tournament and our Queen's hand. You showed mercy when others did not, I believe that you could make a great king."

In the darkness, I am unable to see his face, so I have absolutely no idea what he must be thinking. He could take this to the Queen now and I could be killed for even talking about such ideas.

"If I agree, will you help me to gain the throne?" He sounds hesitant and I do not blame him.

"I will bring you information for the trials, things to give you a slight advantage. But you must prove your worth and succeed in the trials on your own. I can only do so much to help." Taking a deep breath, I wait.

"Alright, I will take any help you wish to give." I release my breath and my shoulders drop.

"The first thing you need to know is tomorrow in the labyrinth, there is only one beast you may face, the Zypalimore. Their sight is no good, if you stand still it will struggle to find you."

"I know of these beasts as we raised many at the farm so that information is of no assistance." Dropping my gaze, I almost step back at his sharp tone.

Maybe he is not who I thought. He takes my hand. "My apologies Velasilio, the night is late and I am tired, you only wish to help. Please continue." He places a kiss on my hand, raising his head so that our eyes meet. He does not let me go.

I feel like I am rooted in place, unable to move as I stare into the oceans of his eyes. My chest tightens as my breath catches. All he needs to do is move ever so slightly forward and our lips will touch. He stays completely still as if he is waiting for me to close the gap. My tongue moves slowly, wetting my lip as his taste still lingers from his previous attempt to kiss me.

A voice breaks through the tension, I look out and past Arekin to see shadows moving towards us. "Others are coming, I must go. I have already been here too long."

Arekin's hand wraps around my own. "Is that all?" His face is lit by the torches, his smile filled with mischief as he looks to my lips, licking his own.

I feel the corner of my mouth lift and I cannot stop myself as I sass him.

"I am glad that you have *knowledge,* maybe you will not run when you face the eight rows of razor sharp teeth as they are mere inches from your skin." I make a pointed look down his body before I continue.

"The riddle will be at the end. You must remember the answer as it is a clue for the third trial." I move to leave, only he still has my hand and pulls me back.

"Can you not tell me the riddle now, so that I know the answer?" His eyes dart quickly between my own.

"No, this is all I can say. Now I must go." Pulling my hand free, I run into the darkness, praying that I was not seen.

CHAPTER 34

KEEPING WATCH

Kadance

NIGHT ONE, TRIAL ONE

I was at the feast for no more than an hour before I became bored watching other fae drink, eat and dance, which has never been my idea of fun. The trial today offered some entertainment. While I waited for them all to stop fucking around with each other I was able to study their techniques and see which of them will actually be a threat to me. From what I could see, not a single one alone will even stand a chance against me. All but that one male Arekin, as his mercy made my Gem watch him, which I can't have.He has tried to demand that I return, but I told him I will have information he needs soon. I only need to play my part for another couple of days and then I will complete my mission and tell my King I am having a much needed break.

What he does not know is that I acquired the truth a long time ago. The only reason I have kept it to myself is so that I had time to organise everything for me and my Gem.

I think of Vixeruas and what the Neraphina fae think of us. I know that there is a selection of five guards who take turns watching me, including standing near my door at all hours. The thing they don't know is that I have magic and with it the means to do whatever I want... to a degree. If I use too much the spell is weaker.

The shadow fae are known for our ability to control the shadows and various other spells; over the years, less of us were born. We have not seen a full shadow fae born to a dark fae couple in over a century, except for me.

My mother taught me what she could before she passed but that was nothing in comparison to what I have had to teach myself as my father is useless, without any kind of magic. With the shadows came blood magic, something many dark fae who did not hold power over the darkness would turn to in order to feel powerful. The problem was greed, they always wanted more and eventually it took their lives.

We developed many advancements with their help; running hot water, a bathroom with a chamber pot that is attached to a wall and has running water to wash away everything and lights, bright glowing orbs that when touched emit an amber glow.

I can't wait for a real wash with more than a bucket. I bathe down at the river, to many of the faes' surprise, they scurry off quickly when I approach. The running water is freezing but that only helps to wake me up in the mornings.

The Neraphiana fae are seen as the good and just ones, while we are the dark and depraved-half right. They see us as evil monsters with no soul and they are the good, honest fae with poles stuck up their asses.

All but my Gem. She is caring as she looks after all in the kingdom and in many ways she reminds me of my mother, in the way she cares for others and puts their needs before her own. She was one of the most beautiful of the dark fae. I was similar to her in many ways, the same dark hair, tan skin and our eyes were the same colour, as were our wings. I was always so happy I got her colours and not my father's. His midnight blue, fluffy wings would not have suited me in the slightest, far too sweet looking.

Many of the horrible rumours of Vixeruas were made up years ago to keep the two kingdoms separate. Unlike what many of the light fae think, the sun does shine and we don't have brawls and killings in the streets... At least not before noon.

I contemplate the 'worthy opponents' I will face tomorrow, if you can even call them that. They are nothing more than farmers and glorified drunks, I know they are unworthy from the conversations I heard this evening during the feast. Many had overindulged in ale and their tongues wagged. If I had not left, I would have beat the shit out of the fucker running his mouth about my Gem. He will be the first I hunt down tomorrow. I will miss the amount of bloodshed when we leave.

With only her on my mind, I feel the need to see her, to know she is safe. By this time she should be sleeping, I find myself pushing the boundaries of how close I can get to her each night. I know that from the few times I have been in her presence that if her scent is anything to go by, she is dreaming of me.

All fae have a good sense of smell but mine surpass any of theirs, this has to do with my shadow fae abilities. I am the superior species so there is really no reason for her to fight the obvious attraction we both feel. I can see it on her face, smell it in the way her scent changes and unfortunately I feel the way my body pulls me to her.

I know that my mother and little sister would try to convince me that this is more than an obsession, but they are not here, and I don't believe in 'one true fated'. The more time I spend around her the more I want her. I do believe in obsession and that is what I feel towards her, a need to claim her in every way, to make her mine.

It takes me no time at all to travel across the castle grounds and into her chambers once again. Her soft snoring tells me she is in a deep sleep. As I approach her bed, she rolls towards me, her face is screwed up as if she has dreamt of something unpleasant. Running the back of my hand down her cheek seems to calm her as she takes a breath in and relaxes, her face smoothing out. A content hum comes from her. I can't stop my smile.

Leaning in, I leave her with a promise. "Soon, we will be together."

CHAPTER 35

TREASON

Velasilio

DAY TWO, TRIAL TWO

My heart feels like it will pound out of my chest, I worry that Searaphina will hear the thunderous beat. The entire carriage ride to the labyrinth, she was quiet, just sitting and thinking about something. Her face was stern and I wondered if she knew of my treason. I could be executed for it. I only wish for my Queen, my kingdom and my best friend to have a royal consort that can be trusted.

Even if he did kiss me last night. He spoke of seeing me back at home and always wanting to meet me but never being able to, that he admired me from afar. I woke this morning and Milly, one of the maids, brought me a letter that Arekin had sent. In it, he apologised for kissing me and that he was not himself, but he felt a pull towards me, one he did not understand. Even when we were younger he always wanted to learn more about me, his mother told him stories of my family and when they came to own that land.

My heart cracked even more at hearing how amazing he thought they all were, so I tried something different. I wrote to my brothers, maybe *they* will answer me. I called Milly back and she took my letter. I was quick to burn Arekin's as he had also thanked me for offering to help him.

As I stood over the burning embers of the letter, Searaphina entered my chambers, ready to leave. She spoke with a harsh excitement and it worried me: had she been told of my meeting last evening or was she concerned for today? This was likely to be a trial that many perished in, with moving walls, floors that fall out beneath you, traps that spring, beasts and weapons that will try to kill them.

I swallow the unease as I step out of the carriage behind my Queen. Dezmond is there in a heartbeat, taking my hand and holding me close to him, I look up into his eyes and see a touch of sadness deep within.

"Vel, what is wrong?" He takes my hand. "If I upset you at the feast I was only jealous, I thought that you and I had an understanding that I was yours and you mine?"

I stare at him, dumbfounded as to where he has gotten such an idea. I am not one to traipse around but I made no such agreement with him and there is something about the way he says *mine* that just rubs against me the wrong way. I open my mouth to tell him such but I am interrupted as Searaphina calls me to follow. Before I walk off, I narrow my eyes at him and whisper, "We can talk about it after the trial."

If he is offended by my tone he does not show it. Instead he nods once and goes back to being a good little soldier following his Queen. I too follow her like a loyal pet.

As I walk, I take a few deep breaths to calm my rising rage. Lately I have noticed that my emotions have been wreaking havoc on me and I am not sure why. I am quick to anger and to cry, Searaphina looks at me like I am crazy some days. My sexual appetite seems to have grown. When Sobia kissed me at the feast I usually would pull away as I prefer male company, but I wanted to open to her, I wished that she would take me there and then, in front of the others. It only lasted for a fleeting moment before I snapped out of it.

I was horrified by my actions, even if no fae seemed to care about the behaviour. That might have had to do with the many young fae couples enjoying a more than polite kiss. I need to find out what is wrong with me, could the blood tie be connecting us more than I thought? Am I feeling what Searaphina feels or is this something more? I will need to go to the library and see what I can find. Though it has been closed and without care for over two years, I hope that what I need is easy to find. King Amard loved books and knowledge; he always said that knowledge was power.

"It is sure to be a glorious day! Do you not think so, Silio?" Searaphina wraps her arm around my own and pulls me close. Gone is the anger from before, replaced by a smiling face as we stroll through the cold, dark corridor into the labyrinth. We need to follow a small path left for us that will lead us right to the royal box where we can over-look the entire labyrinth.

"I am sure that it will be something." I try to laugh only it comes out shaky. We stop moving as Searaphina turns me to face her. With the darkness surrounding us and only a few torches to light our way I feel at ease, knowing that she cannot fully see my expression, because I can feel my guilt like a deep, iron brand on my forehead: 'traitor'.

"Silio? Are you okay, you do not seem like yourself?" She pauses, her hands now holding my arms, keeping me in place. Her four guards stand around us, their backs turned to offer some privacy. I feel eyes on me even though when I look around I cannot see any fae. Before I can reply, Searaphina's face hardens and she leans into me. Her voice drops low and there is a hint of something darker to her; in this light, with the cold air circling me, I feel sick, and then she whis-pers, "is this because of a certain kiss last night?"

My stomach drops, how does she know of it? My hands start to sweat and I am seconds from telling her everything. I feel compelled to explain it all, maybe if I tell her now before the trial they can pull Arekin from it and then there is no harm, no cheating, no treason, no reason to execute him or me.

She pulls back just enough to stand tall again but her hands stay on my own, her pointer finger taps the back of my hand. "I am waiting."

My mouth opens and nothing comes out. I try to swallow but my mouth is dry, my throat closes up and I want to cry, and then I get out something. "It was not supposed to happen, I had not planned it, please please do not be angry with me..." Holding her hand over my face, she stops me.

"Silio, what are you on about, of course you did not plan it." My shoulders drop and I try to hold in my confusion, keeping my face as neutral as I possibly can.

Her hands move away from my mouth and I lick my lips before I speak. "You are not angry with me?"

She huffs out a small laugh. "Sobia kissed you, I saw the entire thing, you were the one to stop it. If any fae is upset it is Dezmond." She nudges her head towards the male with his broad back to us. The comment makes me smile, just. I almost told her everything. I could have ended not only my own life but Arekin's as well. We cannot continue this arrangement. I will tell him tonight after this trial.

With a squeeze of my hands, Searaphina turns and places my right arm in the crook of her left. "We must not keep the fae waiting." We begin to walk into the blinding sunlight.

CHAPTER 36

LABYRINTH

Searaphina

DAY TWO, TRIAL TWO

The sun sits high and the heat causes me to sweat more than usual. Dabbing a handkerchief over my brow, I gaze over the grueling labyrinth that is laid out before me.

It is set in a circle. A small lake sits at the center. Thick walls covered in ivy, which has been growing over the last year, create a maze that has an abandoned feeling. Debris and leaves litter the ground to hide any traps that may be hidden there.

I can see the colosseum from our seats to the north of the open field we are currently in. There are strands surrounding the labyrinth made of sturdy wood and stone.

We sit in a smaller-than-usual royal box, but we still have everything we need for the security including a private chamber and selection of cured meats, cheese and fresh fruit. Each of the remaining twenty-three contestants stand at their individual entrances. The royal suite allows us a fantastic view of the chaos soon to begin.

Each fae will need to navigate the treacherous labyrinth before they are able to reach the centre where the Ridlemensira waits for them.

With everything ready to go and the crowd quieting down, I stand and move to the front of the royal suite.

"Welcome to the second trial!" Cheers sound. Raising one hand, they quiet once more.

"Today, each of you will need all of your wisdom and tenacity. This is no ordinary maze, no, think of it like a living being. One that wants your blood. Be careful where you step as it may be your last." My smile widens as I prepare the final words.

"May Datriminish bless you!" My clap echos off the walls of the silent arena, causing each male to take off in a sprint, the walls sliding closed behind them.

Solely focused on Arekin, he slowly stops running and begins a cautious stroll, while the others continue their race to the centre. An ear piercing scream rings out—following the sound, I see the source. One of the competitors has triggered a trap, he is now lying on the stone face first as blood begins to pool underneath him, with a considerable amount of arrows protruding from his back. Some of the stones have different colours or patterns on them and it is up to each fae to find a safe path. Scanning the labyrinth, I search for Kadance. I catch the slighted glimpse of red wings, standing out against the gray stone walls. There one moment and gone the next, he moves with such speed it is difficult to keep up.

Sweeping back over the others I see many are making their way through a bit slower now after hearing the shrill scream. Watching their steps closely, each one tries to clear a path in front of them. A loud thunk and hiss sounds and I look down to see Elanior staring down at her foot and then the floor disappears in front of her. She is quick to jump and reach for the walls, her fingers just catching on a stone that is just sticking out. Hanging from the wall, she uses her other hand to get a better grip. She reaches out and her fingers graze another stone, only she slips and cuts along one of her fingers. Blood seeps from the wound and then, as she tries again, she swings her body to try and find a better hold.

As she swings towards safety, she reaches out her bloodied hand. It contacts the wall, leaving a large red mark behind as she struggles. Finally, she gets the grip she needs; letting go of the other hand, she swings her body again, and again until finally she nears the end. With one last move, she flings her body back onto the solid stone. She does not get up straight away but, eventually, she does. A wall behind her starts to move, opening up and giving her a safe path, and she looks at it for a moment before she walks towards it, heading towards her next challenge.

Freckily is running down a corridor. Their foot hits a loose stone and they fall. Their body lands on a stone that then sinks, they quickly stand, looking for the danger, and then the walls start to shake and move, slowly closing in around them. Their head swings back and forth wildly. If they turn around it is a shorter escape, but then they will be stuck with a dead end, but can they make it to the other end before they are squished? I suck in a breath as I watch, wanting to scream at them to just pick a direction and move.

Just when I think they will choose the safest path, they turn and sprint towards the other end. The walls grumble and groan as they slowly move, getting closer and closer to Fecklily. And then they trip over the debris, turning on their knees and starting to search for something. They must be mad, if they run now they will make it but they have to get up.

The crowd is screaming different things to different competitors but a selection of fae are focused on Freckily as they continue their frantic search under the leaves. And then they find it, lifting the large, thick metal pole above their head, they hold it as the walls close in; when they meet the ends of the pole they shutter and groan but then they stop. Freckily stands triumphant and begins to stroll down the remainder of the path.

I look at Velasilio. Her hands are on her mouth. "That was quite close. I do not know if I would have stopped."

Taking her hands away, she turns to look at me with a small smile on her face. "If they had not then the walls would have killed them, they were lucky to have found the pole." I nod in agreement, it was lucky indeed.

Sweeping my gaze back to Arekin, I watch as he has not made it as far into the labyrinth as some of the others. His shoulders are wound tight and his body ready to attack. There is a large battle axe in his hand as he consistently scans his surroundings for danger. He watches each footstep, making sure not to step on any blocks that look slightly raised or have a pattern.

A scream sounds and he looks up to see what it is, even if the walls hide everything from view. His foot slips and he steps straight on a raised stone. As soon as he does, his eyes shoot down and he turns to face the wall that now has begun to groan as it slides open, his axe held above his head, ready to fight whatever may come from behind the wall.

Arekin

DAY TWO, TRIAL TWO

The wall hisses and groans as it opens towards me and then I hear a whistle and move just in time to dodge the dagger that comes flying at my head. I sidestep and the blade just slices through the upper tissue of my cheek, a hot line of blood drips down my face. Hissing through my teeth, I wipe it away. I get a better grip on my axe to defend myself. Taking in the male in front of me, I remember who it is: Wes, he was the second one to finish their opponent yesterday, killing them by slicing them through the gut. He is from a family of court and he is deadly with a dagger. His deep orange eyes stare at me as his lips pull into a deadly smile just as he sends another dagger flying, this time aimed straight at my chest, I get my axe up just in time, it bounces off the metal with a clang and clatters to the ground behind me. When I look up, Wes grins at me with a dagger in each hand.

My voice drips with annoyance and sarcasm when I call out, "How many damn daggers do you have!" His only response is a haunting laugh.

Taking my defensive stance, I brace for his attack. Just as he nears me, a loud thud sounds, followed by a low hissing. Wes looks down at his foot. I follow his line of sight, watching as it slowly sinks into the ground.

A low growl sounds from behind him, drawing both our attention, just as two large paws come from behind a now-open wall, followed by a large white, fur-covered head, its maw dripping with saliva. Zypalimore. This one is quite sizable, they are terrifying enough but when it opens its mouth to reveal rows of razor sharp teeth and releases a deafening roar, I brace my hands against my ears and I drop to one knee. Unfortunately the quick movement catches its attention. It swings its enormous head towards me as it tries to detect where I am. They may not be able to see but their hearing is spine-chillingly accurate. Staying on my knee, I don't move a muscle and I try to keep my breath even and slow.

Unfortunately for me, Wes doesn't have a clue about the creature. Turning on the spot, he locks his sight on the beast before a sinister smile creeps up on his face. Looking down at me, he chuckles. "Good luck."

Speaking was his first mistake; the Zypalimore's small ears pick up as it shifts towards him, his second mistake was to run. As soon as he takes off the creature follows, the ground beneath me shakes as its powerful back legs dig into the stone, giving it the momentum it needs to catch Wes.

"NO! PLEASE NO!" Wes shouts as the beast swipes at him with its large paw, sending him flying into a wall.

Howling in pleasure, the Zypalimore extends its claws, digging into Wes's legs as he tries to crawl away. Now weeping, he calls out, "HELP ME, YOU BASTARD!"

His shrieking only seems to excite it. Holding him in place, it lifts its long tail into the air, and the sharp barbed end reveals itself, hovering over its head now. It retracts its claws, allowing Wes free. He struggles to move as his legs begin to bleed from the deep slashes on them. He kneels and begins to stand before taking off in a zig zag run. He must be on pure adrenaline at this point. The Beast only listens to the shallow breathing and heavy steps, waiting for the perfect moment.

At that moment I try to help; Wes might be able to escape if I can distract it long enough and not get myself killed. "Over here." I stand quickly and wave my hands before I turn and run as well.

The beast turns and immediately runs after me, wanting to play with its prey before it devourers it. My legs pump faster than they ever have before, my lungs begin to burn, and then I see that the entry it came from is closing. I feel the ground behind me shaking as it catches up. I just need to reach the wall, and then I slip. I go crashing down and slide in a pool of Zypalimore saliva that must have fallen from it when it first appeared. My back hits the wall and the beast catches me, but it does not attack. It steps forward and sniffs the air around me. I stay frozen and holding my breath, I have no idea what has just happened but I say a silent prayer to Datriminish for whatever he is doing.

It moves closer again, sniffing harder, trying to find me. It has my scent now, surely it will not take much longer—and then I hear a gritted yelp from behind the beast. Wes has fallen and it does not look like he can get back up, no, he starts to crawl. But, as he does, each wound would scrape against the stone, his muffled cries reach the beast. At the new scent of blood, it turns around and rushes to him. It launches its tail straight at him, impaling his torso.

Though the beast covers my view, I can still hear the wet sound of flesh being torn and bones crunching under its powerful jaw, almost makes me lose my breakfast. I stand as quietly as I can, when it does not move, I start to search for an exit.

Just then, the wall to my left moves, and I know it will be my only escape. I start to slip but catch myself on the wall. I look over my shoulder to see the beast lifting its head from its lunch. As it listens, its mouth drips blood and has Wes's amputated foot hanging from between its teeth. Just before the wall closes over, I run.

CHAPTER 38

JUST PLAYING

Searaphina

DAY TWO, TRIAL TWO

Unable to tear my eyes from the gruesome scene that is Wes's mangled body, I do not notice as Arekin makes a run for it. The Zypalimore rears its bloody maw before taking off after him. Luckily, he reaches the walls just as it closes over, almost taking the creature's paw off as it swipes at him. Realising I was tensing, I let my shoulders relax for a moment.

Just then, my gaze catches on a dark shadow. Is the heat making me see things? No, after a moment the shadow becomes a male... Kadance? As he nears the centre, he walks without hesitation—come to think of it I have not really seen him this entire trial.

With only a few feet before he reaches the centre, he stops. Reaching up, he takes his gorgeous hair and ties it into a messy bun atop his head. Then he takes a single dagger from his thigh holster, flips it in the air, and steps forward before catching it.

The sound of metal clanging breaks me from my trance, just as the floor drops to his left. When it rises once more, it has a Zypal-imore on it. Staring straight at us, he smirks before taking off in the other direction.

The creature instantly gives chase, snapping its giant jaw at him. Tilting his head back, Kadance bellows a laugh before he seems to speed up. Losing its patience, the beast leaps through the air and lands on the other side of the narrow corridor, blocking it. The smirk on Kadance's face is almost aggravating, as it seems he is only playing with us. If only he were not so attractive at the same time.

Preparing its attack, the Zypalimore raises its barbed tail, waiting for him to be in range. Nearing the beast without faltering, he drops onto his backside, extending one leg, and slides straight towards it. Its tail comes down in a large, sweeping arch, intent on impaling Kadance. As he moves between its paws, the tail comes down. It narrowly misses him, embedding into the stone instead.

As he continues to slide under the beast's belly, Kadance must do something to cause it harm, as the creature cries out in pain. Flowing in his wake is a line of dark blue blood. Is he slicing the creature open?

Kadance finally emerges on the other side of the beast just as it drops to the floor and the blood continues to seep out, staining the once-pristine white fur.

Velasilio and I turn to one another, both of our mouths open. Looking back to the arena, Kadance stands, brushing himself off, but there is no removing the blue that now covers his hands and is splattered over the rest of him.

"I cannot help but feel as though he is just playing with us." My voice is barely above a whisper.

"That looks to be true, I believe he activated that trap on purpose, but how did he know it was there?" Shock and disbelief coat each word as she speaks.

"I am unsure but perhaps we have a traitor in our midst, as it is prohibited for the competitors to have any information prior to the trial." Looking from the gore below to Velasilio, she seems to pale.

"What is the matter, Silio? I know you have a soft spot for the beast but you know as well as I that their instincts are to hunt and kill, there is no escaping them." I reach for her hand.

Jumping at the sudden contact, she looks as though she may be sick. "I understand this, I just do not enjoy watching them being gutted for fun." I pull my hand back at the sudden change in her tone. Is she mad at me?

Straightening in my seat, I face the arena again. "If you need to take a moment to *compose* yourself Silio, I suggest you do so in the bathing chambers. Go and splash some water on your face." I cannot keep the annoyance from my tone.

Velasilio

DAY TWO, TRIAL TWO

I almost *run* into the bathing chambers. I need to compose myself. No one knows what I have done, Searaphina does not suspect I have a hand in this, her question about the kiss was about Sobia not Arekin, she does not know what I have done. I repeat those words over and over in my mind. Taking a few deep breaths, I splash some water onto my face. Arekin has proven himself in this trial, I do not know what to do. Should I continue to assist him, or should I end it now before I am found out. I am going to need to get creative if I wish to continue this path. I cannot be seen with Arekin or around his chambers, though I could always pretend to be enjoying his company in a sexual manner.

No, Searaphina would see through this as I have set my boundaries. Why would I break them now? I have already told her I believe Arekin to be a good match, and he just put himself in danger to help

Wes, the male who tried to kill him then ran and left him alone with that beast.

Her tone said that she took my comment about the creatures being killed for fun was taken personally. I mean, how could it not be as these are her trials; she is the one who planned them with minimal assistance, so anything negative I say about them refers to her indirectly. I do not understand why she used to hate such gore and bloodshed and now she almost looks like she enjoys it, craves it. But why?

Splashing some water on my face, I quickly dry it before exiting the bathing chambers once more, taking a deep breath in preparation to speak with her. She walks over to me and takes both my hands in hers.

"I apologise for speaking so harshly just now. Your words made it seem that I enjoy hurting these beings." She sounds sinister, but I can hear something else, maybe hesitation or worry about whether or not I believe her. Her eyes roam my face before she speaks again.

"You do look better, some colour has returned." Patting my hand she lets them go and returns to her seat.

"Thank you Phina, I did not mean to offend you, it is just that such violence is not something I can stomach." I stand at the back of the royal box to give myself a little space to sort out my feelings.

"It is quite alright, apology accepted. Now, we should see the competitors reaching the centre soon, could you bring me a plate of food?"

"Of course." Strolling to the back table, I pick up two plates choosing an assortment of cured meat and fresh fruit for Searaphina and only fruit for myself.

"Would you like a chalice of wine?"

"Yes, a sweet wine." With two plates balanced in one hand and the empty cups and bottle of wine in the other, I make my way to our seats. Place everything down on the small table between us.

"Silio, are you still feeling ill? Your plate is looking rather empty." Casting my gaze briefly to my plate, I swallow.

"The meat reminds me of the beast devouring Wes. The fresh fruit will be enough to sate my hunger." With a nod we both return to the trial below, waiting to see who will or what will die next. My stomach turns at the thought.

CHAPTER 40

RIDDLES

Searaphina

DAY TWO, TRIAL TWO

The trial continues with more near misses as the competitors near the centre. Out of the corner of my eye, I watch as Velasilio raises a single berry to her lips, but she does not eat it. She seems to be searching for one male in particular. I knew there would come a male she would give in to and forget all about her silly 'rule.'

Without taking my eyes off Kadance as he casually walks to the centre, I ask, "So who is the lucky competitor you wish to see survive?"

She jolts at my question. "I, what? You are mistaken, my Queen. I wish them all to survive." Toying with the fabric of her gown, she laughs nervously. I stare at her, waiting for her to look my way; when she does it is with an uneasy smile.

"Silio, you are my closest friend and as you very well know, you cannot lie to me." Keeping my eyes firmly on hers, I wait for her to

203

respond. Reaching for her chalice, she drinks a hearty amount before she places it back down and speaks.

"I may be searching for Arekin, he seems to be–"

"A fine choice, he seems to be one of the less brutish competitors in the tournament, though Sobia would also be an excellent choice." My smile only grows as I watch her eyes go wide.

Holding up her hand she shakes her head at me. "Oh you misunderstand me, I wish for him to succeed so that he can be your husband. He has proven to be merciful and patient. If he passes this trial, he will show his intelligence and cunning and Sobia, I, ah, I do not know why I kissed her back, I must have had too many wines."

"Yes *if* he succeeds today, he will show these traits, but so will any others that complete it. He may have shown mercy in the first battle, but I wonder if that will change in time. You kissed her back because she is beautifully strong, kind and interested in you, too."

The third and fourth trial we will not witness as we do not have the means to do so: the only way to know how they fair is if they return or not.

"He will not become a monster, his heart is pure and he is kind. I am unsure of my feelings for Sobia, lately my body seems to have a mind of its own."

There is confidence to her statement that has me believing that Arekin will prove himself to be the male she thinks he is. But when she speaks of Sobia she is more unsure then I have ever heard her, she has never had a strong interest in other females, but maybe she is not as set in her ways as I thought. I will support any decision she makes.

"I pray to Datriminish that you are correct about him. What do you mean that your body has a mind of its own?"

Her reply shocks me.

"I do not wish to discuss this now." She looks over her shoulder to where Dezmond stands. He looks forward, not showing any signs that he is listening in.

She pulls my focus back when she speaks. "Let us focus on the trial. They will be reaching the centre soon." With our gazes still locked, I notice a shy smile on her lips.

The moment is broken as the crowd surges. Whipping my head forward, I see that Kadance now stands at the entrance of the centre of the maze. In front of him is a large lake set in an arch, with only a thin pathway lining it. His stare is set on the high stone wall at the base of the pool. With no exit in sight, he kneels down beside the water. He dips his fingers in as if to test the temperature, causing a ripple to move along the surface. A thunderous crash sounds and the furthest wall from him cracks and crumbles, falling into the pool below and causing waves to breach the stone edging. Instantly, Kadance is on his feet again with his hand resting on the dagger strapped to his side.

As the dust clears, the only sound to be heard is a low hiss. Peering into the darkness, he relaxes and his hand falls from the weapon.

From the rubble, a large nose appears, followed by the enormous head of the serpent-like creature. Its dark blue scales reflect the light as its head sways gently from side to side. A thin, purple tongue darts out to taste the air. Once it gets Kadance's scent, it swings its head in his direction. All four of its eyes are locked onto him as he stands perfectly still; his shoulders are dropped and he seems almost relaxed. The Ridlemensira studies him for a moment before opening its jaw, showing off the two, long fangs that hang down and the many rows of razor sharp teeth lining the inside of its mouth.

I am not sure if I am breathing. When it speaks, it sounds as though a hundred different people speak at once in the same tone.

"A rhythm so neat, but when it stops, there is no pain. Vital and strong and yet weak. What am I?" Swaying back and forth, the Ridlemensira waits.

Kadance looks from the beast, to me. His stare seems to burn through me as an arrogant smirk tilts at his lips.

"That would be the item which I seek. A heart." Only after that does he turn back to the deadly creature.

Hissing with disappointment, the Ridlemensira lays flat over the pool, creating a bridge with its long body. Kadance does not waste a moment stepping onto its snout and strolling towards the hole in the wall as though he has not a single care in the world.

Just as he begins to disappear into the darkness, Arekin runs into the centre, his gaze locking on to Kadance who, without looking, flips his rude finger and disappears into the darkness. It is hard to see but I swear that Arekin rolls his eyes.

Moving back into place, the Ridlemensira stares at him. Its eerie voices fill the air again.

"What can be heard but not touched, can tell a story without words, and can hide truth or lies in plain sight?"

He seems to be thinking deeply. It feels as though it takes an age before he answers; so long that Buvariris arrives.

Looking into the creature's eyes, Arekin goes to answer. "Hea—" Stopping and dropping his head once more, he begins to mumble to himself.

"Hurry before I am forced to slit your throat." Holding up his blade, Buvariris is growing agitated.

Ignoring him, Arekin looks to the beast once more, with confidence in his voice he answers, "A song."

Laying flat, it allows him to cross. Stopping just before he leaves, Arekin looks back as more competitors begin to file in. Seven more succeed and the serpent's rage at so many tasty snacks missed seems to be hitting a peak. The eighth arrives, Phetire, an orange coloured fae, whose intelligence may be lacking. But his strength more than makes up for it. Raising its head, ready to give the riddle, the entire colosseum is silent as no fae dares to move a muscle.

"I can tell you a secret, even though I'm not alive, in the hands of one with the darkness I provide them with power."

Huffing out a laugh as if this is easy, he answers with too much conviction.

"What a stupid creature you must be, with such an easy riddle. Magic." Stepping forward he waits for the serpent to drop its head. When it does not, he looks up into its eyes. There is a predatory grin across its face, its hiss is one of delight.

The once tone voices sing out. "Your arrogance will be your death, the correct answer was a grimoire."

It strikes, its mouth open wide as it tries to consume the male whole. Instead of standing tall and accepting his failure, Phetire runs, narrowly avoiding the beast's sharp teeth; he does not make it far before its long tongue coils around his legs, tripping him and sending him to the stone floor. Slowly, it drags him back and straight into its gaping maw. Screaming his pleas of mercy, Phetire is quickly devoured whole. The solid lump in the serpent's throat thrashes at first before it stops and begins to travel down and into the creature's stomach.

"Hmmmm, delicious." From the corner of my eye, I see Velasilio covering her face.

After this, things move rather quickly: the last three contestants make their way to the centre and answer their riddles without any further failures. The Ridlemensira is not pleased with its lackluster meal, deciding to move through the labyrinth in search of the blood it can scent from the dead Zypalimore.

I address the crowd. "What a show! Congratulations to the remaining twelve competitors!" We lost more than I thought we would in the trial.

The crowd cheers for the winners as Velasilio and I leave.

With a quick journey back to the castle, I go through my evening routine, a bath before dinner and then to sleep early. Tomorrow is sure to be a long day, I will need to finish planning the feast now that we know how many competitors to feed.

Velasilio leaves me to go and refresh herself, she will meet me at dinner. As I bathe, I am unable to stop thinking about what she said about Arekin.

I can tell from the way that Kadance handles himself that he knows exactly how to take a female, how to give her a night of pleasure she has never experienced before. I find my hands beginning to dip under the water at the thought of his muscular arms wrapping around me, as he tosses me over his shoulder before throwing me onto the bed. Getting onto his knees and... Ahh Arekin may be the smarter choice as for the fae of my lands, though I do wonder, I have seen a few things to make me believe that Kadance may be more than he seems.

Thinking about both males has me feeling rather lonely this evening. Perhaps I will see if one of the ladies is in the mood after dinner. With the plan in my mind, I dry and dress for the night. Now, which lucky female of the court will keep my bed warm tonight?

CHAPTER 41

TO SURVIVE ANOTHER DAY

Arekin

DAY TWO, TRIAL TWO

Stepping into darkness, my eyes take some time to adjust to the dark lighting. The silhouette of Kadance comes into view, before I am able to see again. Leaning against the wall with a dagger in hand, he's picking at his nails.

I rest my hand over my axe just in case he tries to attack, I would not put it past him to ignore all rules set forth. Keeping my distance, I lean against the wall opposite him. I do not trust this male, but as the awkwardness in the air thickens I find myself speaking.

"Had a run in with a Zypalimore?" I look him up and down, taking in the blue blood that coats him.

With a huff, he resumes his task; I take it he is not interested in conversations of any kind.

It does not take long before more of the competitors join us. With each new face, we discuss their riddle and what it may mean.

Sobia speaks up. "Is it possible that we will use these in the third trial?"

Fenterison scoffs, "Are you stupid? Of course they have something to do with the third trial!" Sobia moves into Fenterison's face, causing one of the guards to step between them. A bloodchilling scream makes us all stop and every head turns towards the entrance to the labyrinth.

The scream is followed by pleas of mercy and we know that some fae has failed and is going to become a meal. Looking around, I count how many of us are here, nine in total.

Not long after, three more competitors join us. We are just able to hear the closing remarks from Searaphina before we are all led out of the labyrinth and back to our accommodations, passing through town again. We receive many prayers, favours and notes enquiring for a private meeting. A few of the competitors have spoken about the pleasure they have found within the comfort of those who offer themselves. I have not followed such basic urges, but I did make a fool of myself with the Queen's maid, Velasilio.

Tonight, the local tavern will hold a feast in honour of the surviving competitors. Pulling my cloak tighter to keep the night's chill at bay, I stroll down the cobblestone roads. Darkness has descended for the night and the streets are only lit by a few torches.

As the large tavern comes into view, the sounds of its noisy patrons reaches me. Who are spilling out of the open doors and onto the street. Ducking past one of the many females who wish to catch my attention, I move inside.

The tavern is full this evening; the murmur of conversation washes over me, chairs scrape on the wooden floors while goblets are clinked together in cheers. A small trio is set in the back left corner playing instruments filling the air with their music, singing tales of scorned lovers and battles won.

A long bar is set to the right of the musicians where fae queue to collect their drinks, then return to their seats at one of the many tables in the centre or one of the cosy booths lining the walls. I find Fenterison sitting in one of these booths, shuffling a deck of cards. As I stroll towards him, I pass many of the competitors. I slide in across from him, and he pushes over an ale.

I down half of it before I speak. "Full house this evening."

"We are celebrating!" He raises his own goblet to me before he drinks it all.

We all know there is no point in making friends, not when there is a good chance they might stab you in the back tomorrow, but, after today, I thought I should at least try.

We try to keep things in good spirits between all the killing. Looking over my shoulder, I see that Kadance is the only competitor not here, I wonder where he eats? There are not many places to get food even this close to the castle. Fenterison is insufferable but honest so I know what to expect from him. He is after the crown more than the Queen herself, he has made it clear that she is simply a benefit of winning. Me, on the other hand, I don't care for the crown, I only want to see if she is my twin flame. I often wonder if she has felt the same tug towards me as I have her. It is not unusual for the male to feel the allure first and for the female to need a little more physical touch before she feels even the slightest twinge.

"Look at all these fine females, flaunting themselves to us. Easy pickings, am I right?" Leering at the table closest to us, he winks to the females as they giggle and coax his sight to the swell of their breasts.

Rolling my eyes, I brush off his comment; there is more than one reason I do not plan on making friends with him. His words make me think back to last evening when I saw Velasilio and my young crush on her came back. I gave into my urge to taste her. I blamed it on the ale but I know better and it was wrong for me to take her in such a way.

Unfortunately, I had agreed to play a card game with Fen, which is a mistake I won't make again.

There was no excuse to kiss her without her permission, even if her scent was alluring, delicious, and reminded me of home. I am lucky she only slapped me; she has the ear of the Queen and could have had me expelled from the tournament, or worse, had me killed.

I have heard many rumours about their kinship. I understand it is common for a Queen to have many servants attend to her. But our fair Queen only has one and they are constantly in each other's company. It is possible the alluring scent was not hers but Searaphina's and that is why my foolish heart thought that there was a spark towards her. Velasilio is beautiful and her short stature would prove an advantage in the bed chambers; from that slap I can see she still hides her strength and sass, which she used to let out around her brothers but never any others. I wonder if it would come out in a heated moment of passion? Would a fire ignite between us? If the option presented itself, I would not turn it down.

While my mind begins to swim with depraved thoughts of her body, a small hand lands on my own. The sudden contact is jarring, and I turn towards the cloaked figure kneeling on the floor beside me. Lifting their head slightly, I can just make out tips of silver hair.

"My apologies sir, I seem to have had one too many wines this evening, please excuse me." Even with the hood pulled over her head, it's that same scent she has always had.

"That is quite alright, maybe I should..." Moving to stand as I speak, I don't finish my sentences before she stands and rushes out of the front door.

"Well that was odd." Fenterison also watches her retreating form before going back to his cards.

"Yes it was." Getting comfortable again, I notice a note under my hand.

I tuck it into my pocket. "I am going to use the restroom."

"Ahh shaking the snake, well, enjoy it." Fenterison holds up his goblet in cheers to me. What an odd male.

With my hand in my pocket to keep the note safe, I move to the back of the tavern, hiding myself in the dark before I unfold the parchment and read.

CHAPTER 42

A MEETING

Arekin

NIGHT TWO, TRIAL TWO

I will need a clear head for the meeting tonight, I cannot make the same mistake as last evening. Stopping at the bar I order a meal and a small goblet of ale. The moon has only just risen, I have time before I need to return.

My eyes on the moon goes unnoticed by Fenterison as he recites the same few stories about some of the best sex he has ever had, so time has never moved slower.

Finally, the moon nears its apex. Sliding from the booth, I salute Fenterison. "Well, I am going to return, I would hate to fail tomorrow over lack of sleep."

Laughing at me for being weak, Fenterison stands as well, only he moves back to the bar for another drink. There are only a few hours left until our curfew, most of the others will stay here until the last second.

Leaving the warmth of the tavern, I wrap my cloak tight as I begin the short journey back.

Darkness and silence surround me. I feel a creeping sensation over my skin as the shadows seem to be watching me. I shake it off. I come back to Velasilio and the danger we are both in if our deal is ever discovered.

A glowing torch light ahead shows me the entrance to the courtyard. I begin down the line of rooms until my own comes into view.

Standing in front of my door, with her hand raised to knock, is Velasilio. My lips tilt into a smile at seeing her and my chest fills with anticipation. Her hand falls to her side as she waits. When the door does not open she quickly turns on her heel and goes to leave. I begin to chase after her.

Cursing under my breath, I call out, "Wait!"

As I catch up to her. She whirls around. Pushing me against the wall.

"Shhh! Do you want someone to hear us?" she growls.

"Don't worry, they are still out drinking and fuc—" I stop myself just in time before offending her with vulgar words. I go to speak again, but she interrupts me.

"Even the walls have eyes and ears," she hisses. Looking down she seems to realise that we are currently pressed right up against one another, her hands against my chest. Lowering my gaze, I notice that, from this position I can see straight down her corset. Averting my gaze, I resist the temptation to stare.

"Well, right now we look like a pair of lovers." Reaching up, I take her hands in my own, trailing my thumb over her smooth skin. Her eyes track the movement before her gaze collides with mine once more.

Her long lashes half close as she licks her lips, and I absentmindedly mimic the action. I think of how sweet her lips were and how the taste of them lingered. The image of them wrapped around me enters my mind. I move closer until I can feel the warmth of her breath over my lips.

Her voice is a mere whisper as she leans in as well, almost closing the gap. "What are you doing?"

As our lips brush, she steps back, shaking her head. "We cannot."

I stand straight and fix my cloak before reaching into my pocket and pulling out my keys. "You'er right."

I turn and unlock the door. Pushing it open, I step to the side to allow Velasilio to enter first. She hesitates. "We will be warmer and safer speaking in my chambers."

When she still doesn't move, I try to make her comfortable with a joke. "I will not bite and I swear I will not kiss you again... Unless you ask me to." The corner of her lip tilts upwards, but she makes sure to provide ample space when she passes me.

Closing the door softly, I then approach her from behind and lift her cloak off. She smiles and nods her thanks before rubbing her hands over her arms.

"Take a seat next to the fire, it will warm you up." I gesture to the two armchairs sitting opposite one another, angled towards the fireplace.

"Thank you." Taking the seat on the left, she sits straight up, the fire casting a warm glow on her skin.

Turning to face me once more, she says, "It would seem my advice was taken, you did well today."

Realising I am still holding her cloak while I openly stare at her, I shake it out before hanging it up.

I take the seat opposite her. "Yes, thank you for the warning. Even if the riddle was incredibly cryptic." She doesn't hear the humor in my voice as she balls her fist in her gown.

"I cannot give you all of the answers, some things you must do on your own." Irritation coats each word. I need to placate her, otherwise she may change her mind.

"The riddles are no fault of your own. I don't mean you should be telling me all the answers, it is just that I do not understand what it means. How am I to get a song? It would help us both if you could explain it to me?" I try to sound sincere in my words but they seem to only anger her more, as her mouth is set in a hard line now.

"I am not here to be your personal library, maybe you should try opening a book! I have already betrayed our Queen by coming here, I will not allow our next king to be a twatnuckle who thinks they can just be handed anything they ask for!"

Well shit, if looks could kill I would be dead. "No, I do not mean that, I just mean..."

Why the fuck can't I speak all of a sudden.

Just as I think of what to say, she interrupts me. "This was a mistake, I thought you were different, clearly I was wrong! I shall take my leave now, before our little arrangement is found out and we both are tried for treason!" She moves with haste towards the door.

Before I can think about what to do I am also out of my seat. I reach the door at the same time as her. As she pulls it open I press my hand against the top, slamming it shut. Spinning around, her eyes are filled with rage as she steps into me.

"I am sorry, this is not what I meant and my mind seems to be in a haze. I may have had one too many drinks this evening." I know this is not true but it is easier to explain at this time then my attraction towards her. One I know she does not return, if her slap had anything to say about it.

Her gaze burns into me as she watches my face carefully. "I have had far too many fae use me to get to the Queen, I will not allow you to be another. If we are to work together it must be towards the same goal and I will not accept you criticising me." It is as if her whole body is vibrating from her fury.

I feel my own temper rising at the thought of some fae causing her such harm that she does not trust others. "I promise to treat you with the utmost respect, I am only here for the Queen."

I thought it was true that Searaphina was the female for me. But, in this moment, with our bodies against one another's, I watch the swell of her breasts as she takes rapid breaths. Trying to calm herself down, I am in a trance at the movement as I start to think of all the wrong questions. Like what would her skin taste like? Would her nipples respond to a flick or gentle pinch?

Hands cover her breasts as she catches my attention. "Have you had your fill?" There is outrage in her tone but also something more —she sounds flustered.

As all the blood leaves my mind heading elsewhere, my mouth begins to move before I can stop it. "What if I have not?"

Staring at one another, we both refuse to look away. She sweeps her tongue over her top lip before she speaks.

"We should not." Stepping backwards, she bumps into the closed door.

It feels although an invisible leash pulls me forward, until we are once again pressed against each other. Her hands come to rest on my chest, but she does not push me away. Leaning in so that our faces are only inches apart, my left arm comes to rest above her head. My right hand lazily glides over her outer thigh, moving up until it reaches the curve of her waist, and holding her firmly. Her breath hitches as I rub my thumb up and down.

My voice is deep as I inch forward, my lips brushing the shell of her ear, causing her to take a sharp breath. "No fae needs to know." I nibble her earlobe, before I pull back just enough so that I can look into her lust-filled, violet eyes.

Her heated gaze never leaves mine, as she seems to think for a moment before she speaks once more, and her voice oozes with seduction. "One night."

Arekin

NIGHT TWO, TRIAL TWO

I think my heart stops. I didn't expect her to agree.

Leaning forward, I slam my mouth over hers, and she opens for me immediately. Her hands move from my chest to my neck and she pulls me in, deepening the kiss.

Bending down, I move my arms under her ass. She jumps at the same time, wrapping her legs around me as best she can with her dress on. Holding her, I turn and make my way towards the bed. I slide my left hand under her hair, gripping slightly to pull her head back. When we separate her lips are puffy, her eyes heated.

Panting, I watch her pulse race like the wings of a hummingbird. "Why did you stop?"

"Only for a second, so that I can look at your stunning face and do this." Throwing her on to the bed, her delicious tits bounce before she moves to her elbows. The sight has me groaning as I bend down and cover her with my body, one hand resting above her head while the other begins to slowly trace its way up her leg, taking her skirt with it. Throwing her head back, she moans softly and grabs my shirt, ripping it open before pulling me down to kiss me with a crazed need that causes our teeth to clash together as our tongues dance. I continue to move my hand higher and higher, until I reach the silky fabric of her undergarments.

BANG!

She seizes at the sudden sound and pushes me off of her, our lust-filled haze washed away in seconds from the loud sound.

"What was that?" she whispers. The fear in her voice makes me copy her and speak quietly.

"I have absolutely no idea." Surveying the room, nothing seems amiss. Velasilio is straightening her dress as best as she can before, she slips from beside me and goes to get her cloak.

"Damn it!" I follow her to the door, not wanting her to leave. My pants are too tight and all I can think of is the heat of her pussy under my fingers.

The voice inside my head scolds me. *'Pull yourself together and stop thinking with your cock. She is a lady and deserves respect.'*

Tying her cloak quickly, she rushes toward the door as she speaks. "Whatever it was, it has saved us from a grave lapse in judgement."

I reach out, grabbing her shoulder and turning her to face me.

"Wait." Her eyes go wide and the corner of her lip tilts upwards in a small smile.

"What news of the third trial?" Her face drops. "I did not want to upset you..." Before I go on, she holds her hand up to me with a shake of her head.

She steps back again and out of my reach as if my touch burns her. "It is okay, it is why I am here. The riddle in today's trial, do you remember it?"

It takes me a minute to remember amidst the blood and gore. "Something about a song." Saying it outloud has my mind moving, puzzling on what that could be. And then, like a torch being lit, it hits me.

"A Siren's song? I must retrieve a Siren's song? It is impossible." My dick instantly softens and my mind races to remember anything I know about the deadly creature.

There is no way to get a Siren's song. Even if there is a way to steal it, getting anywhere near one would be a death sentence. All it needs to do is to sing and I am tramped. Dead.

"Do not lose hope, there is one way to steal a Siren's song: you will need a babashiney shell." Before I can say anything, Velasilio slips from my room and into the darkness.

Staring out of the open door I wonder if it really is the Queen who calls to me. I had liked Velasilio for many years when I was younger, but that feeling is different from what I feel around the Queen.

I am more confused now than ever and then I thank Datriminish for the interruption between me and Velasilio as Fenterison stumbles in the open door. He looks at me and then to the messy bedding, he laughs and then stumbles over to his own bed and falls flat on his face.

When his loud snoring begins, I know he has passed out and the chance to chase Velasilio and apologise for thinking with my dick is gone. I finally close the door as a guard walks past, telling me that it is curfew. I go to the small writing desk and pick up a quill and parchment to start writing down everything I know about the Sirens and their songs. I will need a plan to survive this one.

CHAPTER 44

HARMLESS FLIRTATION

Searaphina

DAY THREE, TRIAL THREE

In the early hours of the morning, as the sky turns from a dull gray to a stunning yellow and red, ee stand on the Venterial beach dock, a short walk from the south side of the castle. The third trial will not be held in Neraphina, instead the competitors will be heading to the island of Tarpidora, where they have to find their rare objects and creatures.

All twelve competitors stand in a single line waiting to be addressed; most are slouched with weary expressions on their faces. The feast last evening must have carried long into the night. There were many depraved tales sweeping the castle this morning as the servants began to whisper all of the dirty details. Some of them seem to have taken a lover or lovers to relieve some of their extra energy.

Arekin stands tall but his gaze seems to wander past me and to Velasilio, who stands just behind me. I wonder if that is where she got to last evening? I had received a mysterious message last night, alerting me to the fact she had left my chambers and not retired but instead took off towards the competitors' quarters. I wonder if she has finally broken her own rule.

Looking over my shoulder, I see she seems to be avoiding his stare. Interesting. Turning back to the others, I notice Kadance; his arms are crossed over his broad chest, around his neck is a single blue crystal I have not seen before. It is an intriguing choice given his black and red colouring.

His hair is in a bun at the back of his head; he must know that today he will need no distractions. I am curious to see who makes it back, I am yet to invite any of this round of competitors to my chambers. I have felt a slight twinge in my chest towards two of them, so I do not wish to follow that path. Instead I would like to indulge myself, and I think I know who that will be in.

Fenterison stands tall when I turn my attention to him. He does the same. His eyes peruse my body lazily as if he does not care if he gets caught. He is wearing a pair of tight leather pants that outline his length, his loose dark orange top complements his tan skin. His hair is cut short but still shows off its deep auburn colour. His eyes burn with lust as he meets my gaze, and the rich gold of them is inviting.

"Velasilio." I wait for her to step next to me. Strangely, she keeps her head down as she waits for my instructions.

I whisper to her, "I am thinking Fenterison might be the first competitor I invite to my chambers for a private meeting."

Finally, she looks up and follows my line of sight to him. His eyes dart between the two of us, his gaze growing hungrier by the second.

Clearing her throat she looks back to me. "Would you like me to extend the invitation before or after today's trial?" Her voice is serious; does she think I am angry with her?

Changing my tone, I try to add a jest, "ahh that is a tough call, if I invite him now he will have a prize to claim and if he does not return, well, I guess I will need to find a new plaything." I give her a little nudge with my elbow. This does the trick and a small smile tugs at her lips.

Nodding once, she steps forward. All eyes turn to her to see what she will do. Moving towards Fenterison, his smile grows; as she stops just in front of him he bows his head before they begin to converse. I cannot hear what is being said. Once they finish and she leaves him to return to my side, he seems to stand taller, and the smile on his face is pure smugness.

Velasilio whispers, "He said that it would be an honour to join you after this evening's feast and that, if it pleases you, to call him Fen."

"Thank you, Silio."

The sun finally breaches the horizon, signalling the beginning of the third trial. Clearing my throat, I speak clearly so that the contestants and the few fae who have come to see the competitors off can hear me.

"Good morning, and welcome to the beginning of your third trial. Today you will be headed to the island of Tarpidora, where you will each find a rare item and return with it." Since the creatures on Tapidora run wild and have begun to overpopulate, this will help to keep things under control as well as providing the kingdom with some much needed resources.

Each competitor looks at me with a mixture of horror and surprise. All but Kadance who, as usual, seems bored and irritated. I often question why a dark fae wants to be king of our lands. I should definitely meet with him and feel his abs... Intentions. Find out his intentions.

A gentle squeeze of my hand brings me from my thoughts.

"Your surprise does not bode well. In your last trial, the riddles you answered hold the answers for this trial."

Fenterison steps forward. With a small bow, he enquires, "Excuse me, my Queen, but how are we to know what creature the items come from?"

A gentle smile tugs at my lips. A smart male. I gesture to Velasilio, who has retrieved the twelve scrolls from a bag at our feet. "You will each be given a scroll with the creature you seek on it, the rest is up to you." Waving my hand forward, she walks to each male and hands them the sealed scrolls.

Only myself and Velasilio know what beast they each have received. I notice the slight blush on Velasilio's cheeks as she nears Arekin. What has happened here?

The old dock creaks under Velasilio as she walks to stand beside me.

"As you can see," I continue, "a small canoe is here if you would like to use one. Otherwise, you can fly. I do suggest saving your strength as you are entering a feral land where the most deadly creatures roam free. May Datriminish bless you." With a clap of my hands, they all bow their heads and make their way to the boats.

The old dock shakes under the weight of so many moving around. The wind begins to pick up, signalling there may be a storm on the horizon. The small canoes sway on the water's surface, bumping into the dock's edge. Each male steps in and prepares themselves, tucking away their wings so they do not get wet. When our wings are wet they can become heavy and this makes it almost impossible to fly.

Kadance stands at the end of the dock staring down at the little watercraft with a look of disdain, turning he faces us. "Why would I waste my time in this dingy little thing when I can fly?" His wings stretch out, the impressive width and height causing a shadow over the boards in front of him. Shaking out his shoulders, he winks once before he bends at his knees and, with one powerful thrust, he is in the sky before disappearing from sight in a single breath.

A gust of wind that carries his scent towards us; inhaling deeply, I take in his smoky scent, which sends a shiver down my spine. Shaking off the feeling, I turn my attention back to the others who also seem to be watching where Kadance disappeared.

They all begin their journey. Velasilio and I wait, until they have all become specks on the horizon before we take our leave. They should reach the island in a few hours and return in time for the feast tonight.

With the day warming, we take our time strolling back to the castle through the gardens. "So, what was that I saw with Arekin?" Raising my eyebrow at Velasilio, I wait for her reply.

"Ah no, Phina, there is nothing. He is simply very handsome." Her arm is through mine and I feel the moment she tenses. I see a slight blush in her cheeks.

"Come now, you know there is nothing wrong with you having a bit of fun with any of the competitors." I give her arm a slight reassuring squeeze, and I feel her relax.

She smiles at me, though she still seems to have something on her mind. I need to investigate further, but we also have much to do. "Come, Silio, we need to finish the preparations for the feast and I wish to know more of what is going on with you and that handsome blue male."

CHAPTER 45

STALKED BY DEATH

Arekin

DAY THREE, TRIAL THREE

Fog obscures my sight, shadows taunt me, hiding Datriminish knows what horrors. The scent of salt lingers in the air as the water laps against my small boat, causing it to creek and sway. I try to conserve my energy as I row, slowly crossing the narrow channel from Neraphina to the larger island of Tarpidora. This trial is going to be the most violent and deadly, there are no watchful eyes here. Many of the competitors will let their aggression free, this where the true tournament begins.

Stealing a Siren's song is going to be the most difficult challenge I am ever faced with. I was thankful to Velasilio for the information last night even if I could not do anything with it. Fortunately she was able to pass me the additional scroll, when our hands touched I remembered how her soft skin felt under my hands, how her body reacted to mine, smiling to myself. I remove the parchment I start to read.

Arekin.

The Babashiney shell will be found at the bottom of a waterfall, it should be easy enough to find just look for one with purple and black flowers at its base. I wish you luck

V.

As I am reading, a dark shadow is cast over me, I look up to find nothing there. It must have been a cloud. Rolling the scroll, I place it in my rucksack before I begin to row again.

After some time, the fog clears and the shoreline comes into view. I let the waves carry me in the last few feet, and when I am close enough, I jump out and pull the little canoe to shore.

Looking down the white sand beach, I notice that eight other boats dot the shoreline. Just as I get my boat safely up the shore, I hear a slew of angry slurs.

"Ah ya fucking bastard, piece if piss, shit thing!" Turning around, I see Fenterison falling from his boat. Laughing at him, I stand and watch as he struggles against the waves.

When he does finally make it to shore, dragging his own rickety boat behind him. He looks my way, anger etched in his face, but to my surprise he says nothing and keeps moving.

We have an understanding outside of the trials, but make no mistake we both know there will only be one king and when it comes down to it we are all looking out for ourselves. With only two trials left, friends will be hard to find, even outside of the tournament.

Looking forward to the dense forest I assess the area: there are many gnarled trees reaching high towards the sky, and small shrubs that are sure to hide a number of nasty things. I am glad that I have kept my clothing light, my pants and shirt are a loose fit, made from breathable cotton. Reaching over my shoulder, I remove my axe and prepare to find a waterfall with the purple and black flowers.

The position of the sun shows me that my time is limited, and I must return before night falls. My arms are beginning to feel heavy. I have been cutting a path for hours and still no sign of a waterfall. The heat of the sun feels like it's cooking me alive. Wiping the sweat from my brow, I try not to think about it. My stomach rumbles. I find a rock to sit on and remove the small rucksack from my hip to take out a water skin and some dried meat. I down half of the cold water, but I stop myself from drinking it all in one sitting. I will need fresh water throughout my day.

Packing away the items, I stand and continue on. It doesn't take long before the distant sound of moving water reaches me. I follow the sound and eventually find a river.

I cup my hands into the cold water and splash it on my face, then fill my water skin. A waterfall must be close by.

I hear a crashing sound in the distance but still can't see anything; then the river dips off in front of me and I can see a view of the island. I do not remember walking uphill but the terrain here is rocky and uneven so I must have.

I look down at the steep drop. I will need to find a safe way down, I could fly but I would rather conserve my energy. I notice a small path way to the right side of the fall, clearly used by other creatures in the area. Slipping my axe into its holster on my back, I make sure it is in tight before I begin to make my way down.

Then the world seems to stop as the loudest and most inhuman bellow comes from my right.

My whole body freezes. Turning to my left, I search the tree line across the river but I don't see anything. Just as I turn back, a Quartier bursts from the bushes. Its two legs carry it with such speed, its long neck has its head high and it is looking back as if it is trying to escape something. It rushes towards the river, launching over and disappearing into the forest. My confusion only grows, there is no way that it made that sound, it must have been running from something...

Just as the thought clicks into place, the ground starts to shake and the wind changes direction, carrying with it a foul smell. I know what it is before the words leave my mouth in a murmur.

"Deathwhisper."

CHAPTER 46

SEE AN OPPORTUNITY, TAKE IT

Kadance

DAY THREE, TRIAL THREE

Flying over to Tarapidora yet again, I ask myself the same question I continue to ask: why am I wasting time? Why not take my Gem and be finished with these tedious trials? The answer is because this is fun, and I need to bide my time so that my King is satisfied with my work and leaves me the fuck alone.

I am a general by title. My mother always said I had a warrior's heart. I always looked up to her. She was the only fae that I would listen to as a child.

Sadly, we have not seen a war in many years so I have gotten rather bored. There are only so many soldiers who are willing to allow me to 'practice' with them. I am looking forward to this trial; I am keen to see what it will take to kill a Deathwhisper. Will its heart be black, red or blue? Only time will tell.

These majestic beasts have a hide covered in sharp barbs to protect it while it sleeps and hunts, they have four knifelike claws on each paw and their powerful jaws are filled with a single row of jagged teeth, perfect for tearing flesh from bone. Normally black in colour, with near-perfect sense, all of this makes them the perfect killing machines.

They are known to play with their prey, pretending to lose sight of them before returning to slice them open and devour them slowly. Closing my eyes, I laugh at all the weak males who chose to use the flimsy little boats. Letting my instinct guide me, the sun warms my face. Rolling, I allow my wings time to soak in the sun.

Their dark colouring attracts the most delicious warmth. Soaring through the sky I fly higher and higher enjoying the freedom before I dive back down. And of course I spot the unworthy males below. Images of the others trying to woo my Gem and attempt to fuck her flick through my mind. My anger surges at the thought of another tasting what is mine.

White, sandy beaches and crystal clear water come into view. I land on the shore. My rage only seems to grow as I think about another kissing, licking, fucking what is mine. There may be many deadly creatures hunting today but they won't be the worst beast on the prowl today. Once I locate the Deathwhisper, I will be able to play. I have been on my best behaviour while she can see me—I even had to deliberately trigger a trap last trial just for the chance to spill a little blood. But now I am free to do as I please.

I focus on the knowledge I have about my furry little companion. They usually hide in a cave during the day, preferring to hunt at night. This does give me ample time to toy with the others.

I will be the first to return tonight. I want to seek out my Gem and make sure she is behaving before I present with my rare item; I would hate to delay seeing her, I stretch out my wings and take off. Wind from my wings causes sand to enter my boots. "Fuck!"

Flying high above the canopy of trees below. Spotting a large rock formation, I think I have found what I need. A collection of three rocks make up a slightly smaller mountain. Sunlight reflects off something below and straight into my eyes. Once I land, I approach the object. I pick up what looks to be a broken spear. I see no way to know whose it was. Shrugging, I throw the metal behind me. Turning in place, I begin to look for a large cave.

"Now if I were a terrifying deathwhisper, where would I be?" I muse aloud.

With the cliff face in front of me, I look over the empty land.

There is no life here; the trees are all gnarled and dying with deep claw marks in them. I don't see or hear any water, the beast must only use this as a place to sleep and eat. Stepping over a skull, I remove one of my daggers from its holster at my thigh, holding it ready for an attack. I start to whistle while I search out of boredom, the crunch of dirt and rock echo around me. When I stop and listen. I notice there is not a single sound. The wind is still, there are no birds or little creatures scurrying about. The only noise is the eerie echo of the tune I was whistling.

I must be in the right place if no other beast wants to be here. Rounding a corner, I finally see what I wanted. Approaching the cave entrance, the heavy breathing of a sleeping Deathwhisper greets me.

Stepping inside the cavernous space, I move deeper, searching for my new friend. Its black colouring makes it almost invisible but, with just a few feet separating us, I can make out its outline. Its large, round hide is facing the mouth of the cave; knowing that anything that wandered in here would be impaled on its poison barbs means it can sleep soundly. I may know my own strength, however I am not stupid enough to charge in half-cocked against such a magnificent beast.

I could walk over and take its heart in the blink of an eye, but there is no fun in that, I want the thrill of the chase. Besides, there are others who need my attention first. It's time to let my dark side free.

"Stay here beasty, daddy's got things to do."

Exiting the cave, I spread my wings wide and, with all my might, I take off, leaving a cloud of dust and what sounds like a hungry Deathwhisper behind. '*Whoops.*'

No worries, I will find him again. As I soar above the treetops, the shore comes into view. I notice many little boats littering the sand. I get comfortable in a large tree as the last few competitors make their way ashore. I don't care for their names but I know their faces, especially the ones who have received private messages from my Gem.

One of the last ones is that irritating male, Alek or something... It does not matter. This feeble male believes he can lure my Gem in with his phony kindness act. I watched as her eyes lingered on him during the last trial. Her companion seems to believe he would be suited to her needs. I disagree.

As he wanders around on the ground, I watch from the trees, not wanting him to know I am here. I don't know if I should be happy or pissed off that he is making this all too easy for me. His path has taken him close to my little friend. My smile is a rare one that shows off all of my teeth, including my mating canines. This particular asshat has just provided me the perfect opportunity to be rid of him.

Launching from the tree I had settled in, the branch snaps, falling to the floor, narrowly missing dumbass. I head straight to the cave; the ground indents from my landing. Standing to my full height with wings at the ready, I stride to the entrance.

"Dinner time, my furry friend." Clapping my hands together once, it reverberates back to me. Wait, that's not right. Stepping inside the cave, I don't see the creature. As I venture back out, the most delectable scream pulls me in a different direction.

I pick up speed and tuck my wings in to avoid harming them on many trees and bushes that I pass. The sweet smell of blood grows stronger and the crunch of bones as they snap is music to my ears. The Seathwhisper has found its breakfast and from the look of it, it was a fae.

"Ahh good job my hairy friend." Catching the attention of the Deathwhisper, it swings its giant, bloody snout in my direction.

Its jaw opens wide, showing off all of its large teeth; skin and bone are stuck between them. Blood drips onto the forest floor as it releases an ear piercing bellow. Saliva and chunks of face coat my face.

Staring into his beady black eyes, I wipe away the gore. "Well that's disgusting, I thought we were friends?"

Growling, it drops its head before stalking forward slowly. I smile back at the giant death machine.

"You still hungry? Good, follow me for dessert." With a quick nod, I take to the sky, narrowly avoiding the large paw that swings at me.

Weaving through the trees, I make sure to keep the Deathwhisper close to my heels. "That's right you horrendously, stunning creature, follow daddy."

CHAPTER 47

BRUSH WITH DEATH

Arekin

DAY THREE, TRIAL THREE

At well over seven feet tall and with a weight over several tonnes, they are the largest beasts alive. If that was not enough, their extreme sense of smell and near perfect sight makes them the ultimate hunters. Walking on all fours, they have incredible speed. I will be lucky to out run it— Frantically, I search for anything to help me. Nothing—wait, my axe! Reaching over my shoulder I take my axe in hand.

A low growl draws my attention. Slowly, I turn in place, careful not to leave the sanctuary of the brush I am hiding in. Emerging from the shadows is a large head, blood dripping from its mouth. One large paw steps out in the sunlight, each of its talons glisten, coated in dark red blotches. It lifts its head and sniffs the air, and I am thankful that the wind is blowing towards me. It must be following the Quartier's scent.

My axe is looking rather pathetic now as more of the terrifying beast becomes visible. I try to come up with a plan that means I will live, my hearing returns to me as the sound of the rushing water calls to me. With my wings still away, I don't have time to extend them and take off. My heart beats wildly as I watch the deadly creature. Stepping slowly, I try to make my way back to the top of the water's edge. Only a few more steps and I will be able to jump to safety; from what I remember Deathwhispers are not able to swim.

Just then, the wind changes. I feel the moment its eyes lock onto me. Cursing loudly, I run and launch off of the cliff before I plunge towards the unknown depths below. As I hit the surface of the frigid water, I fight my body as it tries to make me suck in a breath. Keeping my head under, I wait, hoping that the beast can't be bothered with me. Only when my lungs begin to scream do I come up. Trying to breathe quietly, I fail immediately and I heave in large amounts of air while trying to keep myself from sinking into the inky darkness. I begin to swim from the middle of the water to the bank.

Reaching the pool's edge, I pull myself up. I lay flat on my back until I finally get my breathing under control. Then I remember why I was under the water. Flipping over, I hurriedly get to my feet. I grab for my axe, but it is gone. I try to listen, but my heart is beating in my ears. When it finally stops, I listen but there is nothing... No birds tweeting, no scurry of smaller creatures as they hunt the insects, not good.

Getting back to my knees, I crawl backwards towards the water, hoping to quietly submerge myself again. I never take my eyes off the shore line; for a large beast they move surprisingly quickly. But I am so consumed watching the forest that I didn't check to see how far the water was. I fall straight in with a loud splash. When I finally stand up again, I hold my breath. The trees creak as the wind rustles through their leaves. The waterfall creates an eerie sensation that trickles down my spine. **Snap.**

My body is still as my eyes search, praying that I didn't just give up my location. I hear something to my left; turning my head slowly, I look over and straight into a pair of large, black eyes.

Exhaling loudly, and chuckle to myself. "Hello there little guy, you scared me half to death." Reaching out, I pat the little Shenariah. More begin to come around the corner and look up to me.

To believe I was scared of these delightful creatures; they are no larger than the palm of my hand, their fur the colours of a fiery sunset, their round bodies and long fluffy tails wrap around one another while they play. Shaking off my fright, I remember why I am here: the shell. Leaving the Shenariah, I swim back to the base of the waterfall to search.

I see the purple flowers climbing the rocks behind the falls just behind the rushing water. Diving under the surface, I blindly reach around. After a few attempts, I can't find anything.

I stand perfectly still and wait for the water to calm down, and then I see a small flash of purple under the water.

With renewed hope, I dive under; lucky the water is clear this time and I am able to find the shell easily. Part one complete.

Swimming to the edge, I climb out and set off to find a black lake, where I will find the horrendous beast known as Siren. I had better hurry, judging by the position the sun is in.

I have not seen any other contestants since the beach. I hope none have the task of finding a Deathwhisper. Luckily I still have a small dagger strapped to my leg, using it I cut a path through the dense foliage. My feet trample the cut offs as I move. I welcome the shade and cool breeze that warns me of the sun's descent. With time slipping away, I begin to fear I will never find the Siren.

Then soft notes call out to me. I pull a dagger from my boot and begin to slice away like a male possessed to reach the alluring sound.

Finally, I make it into the clearing. Sitting in the last stream of sunlight is the most stunning female. Her long, scarlet hair drapes down her back. Gazing over her shoulder, her emerald eyes meet my own and she turns fully, sitting with her tail tucked under her. I don't know where to look first: her ivory skin stands out against the harsh, gray rock; Her perky breasts catch my attention as she sensually runs her hand between them before taking one of her nipples between her fingers and rolling it.

Swallowing, I reach down to adjust my pants as my shaft begins to harden. She beacons me forward. Taking a single step, the desire to reach her overwhelms me as I pick up my pace. Then the world goes sideways.

CHAPTER 48

USELESS

Kadance

DAY THREE, TRIAL THREE

Halfway through our chase, the shortsighted beast got distracted with easier prey: a Quartier. Although the flightless bird definitely has some speed going for it. Heading away from where I last saw A… Whatever his name was, I am now chasing the most deadly creature. When the stupid bird avoids yet another attack from the Deathwhisper, it lets loose a mighty bellow of frustration before it picks up its pace.

Keeping a close eye on my prize, I begin to lose patience. Right before I decide to end its life, we enter into the clearing with a river running through the middle. Ascending into the sky out of the beast's reach, I watch as the Quartier escapes to live another day.

Movement in the brush catches my eye.

"I have to be one lucky fae." Right there, trying to get to safety is *Arekin.*

The Deathwhisper, still searching for that fucking bird, slowly emerges into the clearing. I don't understand how this supposedly perfect hunter can't see what is right in front of it! I clench my fists and my jaw is so tight it's a wonder it does not break. Right at that moment, the wind changes, and the fae's scent reaches the beast. My joy is quickly dashed as Arekin flings himself from the top of the waterfall.

Rushing towards the edge, the Deathwhisper skids to a stop. Clenching my teeth, I whisper-yell, "That's right, just dive in after the worthless fuck."

Sniffing the air, it looks down and then it walks away. Unable to contain my rage any longer, I scream, **"Fucking useless!"**

Flying above the beast, I think about how I am going to kill it.

I land just up the river, and with my wings open wide, I wait for it to see me. When it finally does, it too seems pissed off. Two meals have now escaped it and the fire in its beady, black eyes says a third will not.

Perfect.

Taking my fighting stance, I pull a single dagger from its holster at my chest, and toss it in my hand. It stands on its back legs to make itself tall and it releases a blood chilling roar before dropping back to all fours. The impact shakes the ground beneath my feet. Its claws seem to extend as they dig into the earth, ready to take off. The poisonous barbs on its back glisten in the late-afternoon sunlight; if I am even nicked by one I'm dead.

A sadistic smile spreads across my face as the adrenaline of battle fills me. I call out to the beast, "Now be a good boy and die."

With a final grunt, it takes off. The ground shudders as each enormous paw makes contact, flicking up the earth with each powerful stride. Its maw opens to show off each of its razor sharp incisors, including the four large canines, each one thicker than my arm. Growling as it nears me, I wait, not moving a muscle.

When it reaches me, it leaps forward with its jaw open wide. It aims for my head. The stench of death curls around me, calling my name. Ducking just in time, I run my blade into the beast's gut, slicing as I roll away.

It's hot, black blood coats my right arm. A slight sting comes from my left arm; my sleeve is torn open at my shoulder. I watch as the dark material grows darker and wet. Turning around, the Deathwhisper hisses at me. It's wounded but not dead.

"Come on, you can do better than that." I taunt.

Shaking its head, it rears, showing me my handy work. The gash looks deep but not deep enough to kill.

Landing on all fours, it charges me for a second time. With my wings open wide, I wait till the last minute to fly up. Claws dig into the flesh of my right leg. Frustration begins to seep in at letting this beast get its claws into me twice.

Deciding this is enough, I land not far from it. Standing, I toss a dagger into the air and catch it by the sharpened edge. My reflection stares back at me. I wait for the charge, as the Deathwhisper snarls and snaps its jaw at me. I hold my ground, and, with a flick of my wrist, the deadly weapon sails through the air.

The ground shudders and shakes as the Deathwhisper hits the grass, sliding on its stomach, straight into the toe of my boot. A single line of black blood drips from its skull. Leaning forward, I wrap my hand around the hilt and pull the blade free.

Standing back, I admire my handy work, that is until I realise...

"Fuck that was stupid, how the fuck am I getting to your heart now?"

CHAPTER 49

PREPARATIONS

Searaphina

DAY THREE, TRIAL THREE

I watch her. She seems to be lost in her own mind as she absentmindedly swirls her spoon in the tea, staring at the patch of greenery to my right.

Clearing my throat, I place my biscuit down and take the napkin to dust off my fingers. "What has your mind in such a haze? You do not seem like yourself, Silio." Frustration seeps through as I speak.

Velasilio's head snaps up at my tone. She opens her mouth to speak, only to close it again. Noticing her hesitation, I push on.

"Especially if it has anything to do with a certain tall, blue and handsome male." I attempt to make the conversation light and place my elbows on the table and my hands under my chin, making my face look as innocent as possible while I flutter my lashes.

"You know my rules, I cannot."

I cannot help but roll my eyes at her before I say, "Well if you are not into sharing then I suggest you do not sleep with..." I almost say it, I almost let it slip. She does not sleep with many others and I want her to enjoy this. One white lie will not hurt. Besides, it was one time.

She looks at me, waiting for my answer. "Who? I better not sleep with who?"

Looking back at Dezmond, his face pales. "Cassidie... Do not sleep with Cassidie." Her face drops as she laughs.

Turning to face one another we nod out agreement. "Lets move to our feast, there is still much to prepare."

I move my tea and signal for a maid to bring me parchment and an ink well. Now it is hard to plan a feast when we do not know who will return, so Velasilio and I will plan as if all twelve will. We have the menu set and the chef is already preparing, any leftovers will be given to the local villages. We chose a round table to allow conversation to flow easily and have three caskets of ale and seven bottles of wine brought out of the cellar.

As the sun moves higher in the sky and our tea is gone, we move to sit under the shade of a small tree by a water fountain. Laying back on the thick blanket, I listen to the bird's songs and it makes me think of him again.

I look to Vealsilio, who is flat on her back with her eyes closed. "Do you think Arekin will succeed?"

Her eyes twitch as her body seems to tense. Sounding far calmer than she looks, she speaks. "I do hope so, for the good of the kingdom and for your sake. He seems like the only good male here."

'Ahh, she would like to keep this game going, maybe it's time to play.' As the wicked thought passes my mind, I press on.

"I see what you are saying, he is a good male, but is he too good?" Pausing briefly, I get the exact reaction I want: Velasilio's eyes pop open as she sits up on her elbows.

"I mean he may have a moral way about him, but how would he treat a female in bed? Would he be as kind and gentle, or rough?" I watch as she swallows before answering.

"This is something I would not know and neither would you unless you... tried him." She visibly shudders at the thought, which means she does like him.

"Although Kadance, now there is a male of strength and brutality. I am sure with a male like that on my arm, no other kingdom would try to challenge my rule, even his own."

Sitting upright now, she stares at me with her mouth open. "He could be a trap, or even a spy. We cannot trust him, no matter what we feel."

"No matter what we feel?" I repeat. "Do you feel something towards this male?"

Her gaze shoots my way. "No, absolutely not," she says with passion. "I would never... He is a beast." I certainly do not believe her. Just as I am about to question her, she continues.

"Ahhh we kissed...Twice!" Dropping her head into her hands, she waits for my reply.

Shock overwhelms me and I do not hide it from my voice. "You, kissed Kadance?"

Her eyes look like they may bulge from her head. She all but yells at me: "NO! Arekin."

Realisation dawns on me, she has been worried about my feelings for him because she is developing feelings of her own. If he is her twin flame then she can have him of course, but if he succeeds it will break her heart to see him with me each day.

"I do not wish to see you hurt, could you take the emotion away and just use him for pleasure?" Maybe if they sleep together she will lose the romantic notion and be able to move forward.

"And if he then becomes your king? That would be terribly awkward."

"Not at all. I am under no impression that either he or I do not have any previous lovers and, besides, if you sleep together and there is no spark, he is nothing more to you than a toy for pleasure."

Still seemingly unsure, she smiles at me briefly before we decide it is time to complete final preparations for the feast and head into the castle to do so. When the sun slips away and darkness takes hold, I receive a report they have returned.

CHAPTER 50

SOME FALLS ARE WORTH IT

Velasilio

DAY THREE, TRIAL THREE

I felt like I was sitting atop of a fire as we spoke at tea. Twice now I have almost told her of my treason. I need to be careful. I am only doing it for her, she has been so different as of late, she does not see this tournament for what it is becoming, the competitors that have succeeded do not seem to be here for the right reasons. My mind was in a mess for the rest of the day.

Searaphina will meet the competitors in the throne room this evening to accept their rare treasures. I do not have the stomach for that part of the trial, as far too many innocent creatures were killed in the process.

After the preparations are finished and Searaphina is in her chambers for a moment of respite before this evening's festivities, I find that I need time alone to think, so I decide to go for a stroll through the castle.

There is a strange sinking feeling in my stomach as though a stone has settled in. The sensation has been gnawing at me all day. What is the point of helping Arekin cheat if I am developing feelings for him? I have felt the smallest flicker of something, but even after our kiss and almost more it has not grown. Maybe this is a sign it is not meant to be.

Even if, deep down, I cannot shake the sensation of an unknown pull towards him.

There is something about the way his ocean blue eyes seem to see straight through me. He is patient, strong and kind and yet he accepted my deal, one of dishonour. But even if it is treason, I know my intentions are pure.

Feeling a renewed sense of determination, I know that I cannot lay with Arekin, even with Searaphina's blessing. I need another to enjoy to relieve this pent up sexual energy that he has started within me.

I do my best to think of the competitors, but my mind is determined to come back to Arekin. Yes, Sobina may seem gentle but I *know* Arekin could be, I can see it in his eyes, even if his actions towards me have been forward. Yes, Elanior may seem calm but I *know* that Arekin is. And then there is the way he kissed me. The feeling of his hands on my body.

Moving down the corridor, my mind continues its wayward thoughts until there is no longer any stone beneath my foot.

As I step into thin air, my stomach plummets. A resounding shriek leaves my lips as the air rushes past and I tumble straight down.

I try to catch my fall but my hands are too slow and my skull collides with the first step. My vision blurs slightly, closing my eyes tightly, I feel a tear drip down my cheek. Tucking my body into a protective position, I try to protect anything vital as I continue to roll forward, bracing for the impact of the second step. When no pain comes, I open my eyes. There is something solid wrapped around my stomach, halting me in mid-air. It feels like my heart is beating inside my head as dark spots begin to dance across my vision.

Closing my eyes. I try to take a deep breath but all that does is cause me to feel lightheaded and dizzy. I reach up and feel the strong arm that is currently keeping me suspended. Hoping that it is just a guard, I try to push authority into my tone as I request, "If you do not allow me to stand, I may pass out or, worse, become ill." Taking in shallow breaths, I try to keep the nausea at bay.

A deep chuckle causes me to jostle slightly as my 'saviour' says nothing. I have not realised the position I am in, thrown over his arm. My head is down and my feet do not touch the ground, I am completely at his mercy. Suddenly, he stops laughing and I feel the slight bulge of him resting in the seam of my upper thighs and sending a slight tingling right to my core.

I feel his arm tighten as if he can tell where my thoughts are headed, my traitorous vagina thinks this to be a great experience as moisture begins to pool between my thighs. I begin to squirm in a feeble attempt to remove myself from his grasp.

I realise my mistake too late, hearing the sharp intake of breath before a husky groan leaves his lips. It sounds like he is speaking through clenched teeth, "Oh, you seem to be a bit stuck. Would you like some assistance?"

"Assistance? The only assistance I need is for you to remove yourself from my back, you beast." I can feel the flush working its way to my cheeks, as I try to sound pissed off and not turned on.

I hear the smirk in his voice. "Oh a beast am I, you have no idea. But if I was to remove myself, you would continue to fall and I cannot allow that to happen."

"You can still put me down without harming me!" My frustration grows, outweighing all other emotions.

Clicking his tongue, he seems to think about my request. Then I feel him bending forward as he drops his voice to a sensual whisper. "I could, but having you in this position... It is more fun."

I almost choke as I feel him growing and twitching against me. I am growing slick with anticipation and the sinful promise in his voice.

'*This is so not the time, or the male, you little tramp.*' I scold myself mentally as I begin to recognise who I have been saved by; I am almost suffocated by his arrogance.

Mustering all my remaining strength I demand, "Well, if you will not remove yourself to save me from the fall, at least allow my feet to touch and ground so that I may right myself and all the blood that now rests in my head can return to its rightful place." I can at least blame the position for my reddened cheeks.

Trying to move my head to the side, I can just make out the shadow of bat-like wings, and it is easy to tell that my 'white-knight' is indeed Kadance.

Huffing out like his toy has just been taken from him, he replies; "I will do so slowly, I don't need you to get ill as the blood rushes back to all the areas of your delicious little body."

It feels like he thinks about it once more before he moves his arm ever-so-slowly and slides me down the hard plane of his body. My core flutters at the way he manhandles me; I am smaller, yes but it still takes a lot of strength to hold another in that position.

As my head is slowly brought upright, I feel the blood rush down my body, leaving a hot trail in its wake. I am glad he took his time, because even with the achingly slow movements I still feel lightheaded.

My body sways slightly and I move to steady myself but my foot slips on the step, causing me to backstep quickly and push myself straight back to Kadance's embrace.

I look down the length of the gray stones into the darkness. The colour drains from my face and I tremble slightly. The fall could have ended badly, to swallow feels like sandpaper. I need a glass of water; turning in place, I face Kadance. Because of our height difference, I have to look up and down. How did I forget how tall he is?

I clear my throat. "Thank yoooo..." The word dies on my tongue as two hands wrap around my hips and I am off my feet again.

I am weightless for a moment before my stomach hits something hard. The air is pushed from my lungs as I collide with Kadance's shoulder. His arm wraps around the back of my thighs, just below my ass. Placing both my hands just below his shoulder, I cannot help but stare at his wings, they are tucked in tight but they are right there, I could touch them. I manage to pull my hand back just before I do. This close, I get a good whiff of Kadance's scent, it is an earthy tone with something smoky too.

"Enjoying yourself?" Chuckling to himself, he begins to descend the stairs.

'WHAT ARE YOU DOING! DID YOU REALLY JUST SMELL HIM!' Mentally chastising myself, I try to focus on not headbutting his back as he rapidly moves downwards and out to the garden.

The green grass comes into view and with a few steps I am swiftly placed onto a wrought iron bench lined with several coloured cushions. Looking from the seat, I see no sign of Kadance, he has vanished. The sun has begun to set and I am left to wonder what was he doing here and why did he help me?

CHAPTER 51

A SIREN'S SONG

Arekin

DAY THREE, TRIAL THREE

It feels as though a large rock has just smashed into my side and taken me to the ground. As I fight to right myself, the overwhelming need to reach the beautiful female is all I can think about.

"Stop! You must stop!" Arms cage me in as I try to punch, kick and bite my way out of the intruder's hold.

Finally, he lets go and I am able to get onto my hands and knees; but before I am able to move, something is shoved into my ears. A loud ringing sets off in my mind and I hold my head as the pain intensifies. I move my hands from my eyes and look up to see the positively exquisite beauty is not that at all; instead, I see the most repugnant beast with sharp, pointed teeth and claws for hands. A hateful smile crosses the face as it begins to cackle maniacally at my almost-death.

I look to see who has saved me from my own foolishness. Fenterison grins at me like a mad man. We both move to stand, I watch him with a wariness, why save me? When we are fighting for the same thing?

Fenterison shows me that he is not here to fight by holding both hands in surrender, before he points to his own ears to show the cotton that has been stuffed in. Fen must also be after a Siren's song, I pull my Babashiney shell from my bag and gesture to it as if to say, 'do you have one?'

With a shake of his head, he points above the black lake to an abnormally large nest with an equally sizable mother Quartier. These bird-like creatures are known for their razor sharp feet and sword tails.

I look back at him, puzzled, as he makes a gesture with his hands. An egg, that is what he is after.

We look at each other once more, then we reach out and shake hands before going our separate ways. I will find another way to repay him. With cotton in my ears, I look towards the rocks where, moments ago the siren sat. The large boulder is now empty with nothing more than a wet patch.

"Shit!" I think about what to do next.

Unfortunately for me, they are smart creatures and now she will know her song will not affect me. There is minimal chance she will resurface from the inky depths. Gazing upwards, the sky is now changing to hues of orange and yellow: time is running out. I will have to fly back and leave my boat behind, not ideal as I will be exhausted by the time I return but it will be the only way to get back in time.

With my plan in mind, I drop my pack and remove the large, purple shell. Removing a piece of string from my rucksack, I attach the shell to my waist, in hopes not to lose and that it might catch her song before I am dragged below. Leaving my pack behind, I stride towards the water's edge, not taking my eyes off the water surface for a second.

The forest seems to hold its breath as not even the wind whispers. The dark water seems to mock me in how still it is, matching the world around it; not a single creature makes a sound. The crunch of leaves echo from each step, and my mind screams at me, telling me I am about to die.

As I near the lake, I reach up a shaky hand and remove the cotton from my ears. Exhaling slowly, I kneel, facing the water. My heart is a drum as I feel myself flinching at the sound of my own breath. Cupping my hands, I dip them into the murky water, trying to calmly bring it to my face. Acting as if I want to wash away the dirt and grime from the day.

I feel like a stupid creature preparing myself for slaughter. Watching the water, I catch no movement. I curse under my breath. I know what I need to do.

I sit and turn my back to the lake. I know she is waiting for me to make a mistake. Taking a steadying breath, I wait. When nothing happens, I begin to lose my patience. Frustration creeps into me and I feel like I might explode. If I fail all because of this stupid fish I will be pissed.

I spin in place to face the water once more, and a splash in the distance catches my attention. Without realising it, I am now hovering most of my upper body over the surface. I do not realise my mistake until it is too late.

Two, dark green, clawed hands shoot from the water, grasping my shirt and pulling me into the lake. The icy-cold depths steal my breath away and I fight the urge to draw in air. I can't see anything nor feel anything in the dark, murky water. With a hard kick of my feet, I realise nothing is holding me down. Propelling myself upwards, I can just see the last bit of sunlight. As I breach the surface, gasping for air, I am ripped back under.

A vice-like grip is around my ankle. My screams of agony are muffled by the water as it invades my mouth. It feels as if thousands of sharp needles are piercing my left leg. I look down and into the evil fuck's face as it sinks its teeth further into my flesh.

With all my energy I aim for its face, slamming my boot straight into it. I manage to get it off my leg but it does take a sizable chunk of my calf with it. With all my remaining power, I make a break for it. Breaching the surface and swimming to shore, dirt digs under my nails as I wrench myself from the black lake. Quickly crawling back a few paces, I cough up the disgusting liquid.

Finally getting my breath back, I yell. "SLIMY MOTH-ERFUCKER!"

Splashing catches my attention as the Siren swims towards me, her white skin reflecting in the fading sunlight. With a powerful push from her tail, she all but launches out of the water. Reaching out and using her claw-like nails, she drags herself towards me. That all too friendly smile showing off rows of sharp teeth; some are missing or look to be rotting away.

Her voice echoes as she speaks. "Oh my tasty little treat, it's not nice to kick."

I attempt to scurry backwards but my legs fail me, the blood I am losing can't be good. The wound is sucking the last of my energy in an effort to heal. Suddenly, her song fills my head and my body betrays me: everything feels wrong and I can't move.

"Hmmmm, hm, hmm come to the depths, join me now, hmmmm, hm, hmm." The call is so strong that I begin crawling towards her. Her long, obsidian tail is now out of the water and sways back and forth in an almost hypnotic way.

My voice is foreign as I answer her. "Yes, my mistress."

It feels like I am losing my mind as thoughts invade that are not my own.

'I must go to her and be with her until the end of time. My Siren, her beauty out ways any I have seen before.'

Only inches from her now, her hand comes to rest on my cheek as I lean in. We are so close, soon our lips will meet and we will become one. I am at war within myself, screaming to run, but helpless to do anything. I am hers to control.

CHAPTER 52

SAVED BY THE SHELL

Arekin

DAY THREE, TRIAL THREE

*W*armth begins to spread from my hip, covering me in a violet glow. My body begins to vibrate with new energy as the shell seems to be activated by the Siren's singing, pulling her song into it. The fog on my mind lifts and I am able to wretch myself back from her. An ear-piercing scream has me cowering on the ground, covering my ears. Raising my head, I make eye contact with the horrible creature as a black smoke floats through the air and into the shell at my hip.

Suddenly, the shell stops and the world becomes silent. The only sound is the slap of a large tail hitting the earth as the Siren uses the strong muscles to raise itself high. Towering over me, I quickly right myself, tripping over my own feet.

Fury rolls off the Siren as it screeches. "You little worm! How dare you steal what is mine! Release my song or die!" The venom in each word is enough to scare the strongest of fae, but without her song she is nothing more than an overgrown fish.

Smiling at the stupid beast, I release my wings, spreading them wide. "You will need to catch me first!" With one powerful beat, I am in the air. Reaching out, she tries to catch me but is too slow.

"When I find you, I will carve the flesh from your bones and devour it while you watch!" Pure hatred burns in her eyes as they shine red.

I race out of that death trap of an island. With only hours left until the end of the trial, my wings are going to be working overtime. They are sizable but not by any means the biggest around.

It takes me two hours to fly back. I am exhausted by the time I land and I am thankful I chose to take the boat over there or I might not have been able to fly back.

I land in the courtyard. A few court fae look at me and applaud me. I offer them a quick wave and then continue into the castle and to the throne room. By the time I arrive, only some of the others are here. With maybe half an hour left, I assume I am correct about the Deathwhisper finding a meal. Not a death I'd wish upon any fae... Well, almost any fae.

Looking past the contestants, I spot Kadance leaning against a wall. His wings are sitting half out; he doesn't care about the space he takes up. Typical asshole. In saying that, his wings are unique, specific to the Vixeruas fae. Unlike our more delicate wings, theirs are more leathery and dark in colour and the sharp, pointed ends are always battle-ready. His head is down and his eyes seem closed. Is he sleeping? How long has he been here and where is his item? I start to look for it when a hand clasps my shoulder, prompting me to turn around.

Fenterison smiles wide as he greets me. "Good to see you made it, I was worried for a moment that the siren might have had you for dinner." In his hand is a large, golden egg.

"She just might have if not for you, I owe you a life debt," I say with sincerity.

His voice is full of humour as he laughs at me. "It was nothing. You can repay me by leaving the tournament. What do you say?" I hear a hint of seriousness in his tone.

Little does he know that, if things with Velasilio turn more serious, I might just step back. I would follow my fate and join my twin flame over a crown, if she is my mate that is. My parents were very lucky to have found their fated mates only a town over and my mother always told me that you know instantly; I am two hundred and twenty nine, if I find my twin flame, I should know quickly. The only way I might not is if they have not hit their two hundred and twenty first birthday yet.

The trumpeting of horns pulls me from my thoughts and the others from their conversations, announcing the arrival of our magnificent Queen. We are shuffled into a line by one of the servants, though there are so few of us still here. As we ready for the Queen's entrance, who should be at the front of the line, but Kadance.

Leaning back, I whisper to Fenterison, "I can't stand that male, his ego makes his wings look small." We both snicker, causing us to get suspicious looks from the others in line.

"I couldn't agree more, but he's not the one with a private invitation from the Queen to join her this evening after the feast, is he?" Fenterison winks, and my smile slips.

I had not known the Queen was taking private meetings with contestants. As I look at him, I wonder if it is the same kind of meeting Velasilio and I had the other evening.

"A private invitation, I was not told that would be part of our tournament?" I hope that I did indeed miss some information. He only raises one eyebrow at me as if I am a small child who does not understand an adult joke.

"It is not of any importance to the tourney. Just a bit of stress relief for our fair Queen."

I am unsure if this is a cover or if he is indeed meeting her for some carnal pleasure. If the Queen is allowed to enjoy a romp in the sheets, maybe I too will find someone to lose myself with, and I think I know just the fae.

CHAPTER 53

RARE ITEMS

Searaphina

NIGHT THREE, TRIAL THREE

Standing at the two, white, stone doors, I prepare to see who has survived. Looking to my left, I see Dezmond, standing in his black leathers with silver chainmail hanging from his torso. A long sword is sheathed at his hip. Stepping forward, he knocks three times, alerting the guards on the other side it is time to open the doors. Stepping back, he takes his place beside the three other Queen's guards. When the large doors are pulled inwards, I enter the throne room with elegance. The stench of body odor and dried blood fills the air, the competitors are lined up and waiting for me. Eight out of the twelve have made it back—or eight are all that are left alive.

All eyes are on me as I slowly walk towards my throne. Gregor offers his hand to assist me. Taking it, I gather my dress in the other, and I ascend the three stairs. I take my seat. Gregor stands to my side, while Dezmond, Cassidie and Onree take positions at the base. With my hands in my lap and crown atop my head, I address the males.

"You are the few who have returned. Once your items have been verified, you will be able to return to your new chambers to bathe before the feast later in the evening." With a flourish of my hand, I gesture to the eight stones at the base of my throne. Each one has a glass prison atop it.

Raising my gaze it locks on Kadance who stands front and centre. His eyes seem to be distant and cold. With a single nod, I gesture for him to move forward.

It only takes three steps for him to reach the first prism. As he moves, I take in his powerful strides. His hair is still up but loose strands now hang over his eyes and down his neck; there is dirt and dried blood on his face, and it looks like he may have tried to wipe it away at some point.

His brow is furrowed as he seems to be thinking quite hard and his mouth is set in a firm line, nothing like his usual smirk. His broad shoulders are as desirable as ever but I do notice that on his left there is not much fabric left revealing his thick shoulder and the hint of black ink. There does not seem to be any lingering injury.

Dropping my gaze, I take in his tight leather pants; they, too, are filthy. My gaze lingers for a moment, wondering what hides beneath the taught fabric, before I continue my assessment downwards. The fabric of his right leg is torn and split as if torn into by claws. Again, he seems to have healed already with not even a pink scar to be seen.

With a sensual tone I ask, "And what have you brought me, Kadance?" Biting my lower lip softly, I flutter my lashes as he finally looks at me.

As our eyes meet, I feel the prick of tiny needles along my hair-line, a warning perhaps? Reaching for his belt, he unties a hessian sack with a dark patch at its base.

His voice is gruff as he announces. "One Deathwhisper's heart, as requested." Kadance takes the bag and unties the top, turning it over and allowing the heart to land with a wet splat. The prism closes around it, glowing a soft gold.

"Congratulations, I am sure this was no easy feat even for you." I try to jest, in hopes he may find it amusing. When he does not react, only stands waiting, I continue on.

"You will now be escorted to your new chambers inside the castle walls. Please follow your maid." With a sweep of my hand, a young maid with her head down and her hands clasped together in front of her steps forward. Her brown hair is in a neat bun and her uniform, a cotton black dress with brown apron, is clean and neat.

With a curtsy she requests. "My lord, if you would please follow me." Her quiet voice is only just audible. Looking back at me once, Kadance turns on the spot and strides towards her. She must hear the heavy footsteps as she pivots, leaving through the same doors she entered with Kadance not far behind.

I track each step he takes, the way his muscles move beneath his clothing, causing it to strain against them. My mouth waters at the thought of him pinning me down and taking what he wants.

Shaking off my lust filled thoughts I straighten and call the next male forward.

Sobia kneels in front of me, her voice is sweet as she presents. "My Queen, I have retrieved the left shoe of the Aminaduh."

Choking back my laugh, I try to speak. "Thank you Sobia, this will serve your kingdom well." Placing the shoe in its prism, Sobia bows before following a different maid.

Buvariris is next. He has the tusks of a Xanvitor. Following the others, he places his item in the prism. He does not speak to me and his demeanour tells me he thinks this is a waste of time as he huffs once before moving past me and on his way to a hot bath. As he moved by I could see he was covered in injuries including what looked to be at least one gouged wound.

Elanior offers a collection of violet deaths, a purple flower that, when crushed, can be a powerful sleeping potion. Something that can be used by healers when needed.

I thank her, as these are rare and are in need in the kingdom. She smiles sweetly before following her maid.

Next is Frekily. They, too, seem upset with their task as Buvariris; stepping forward, they drop a bag into the prism. It makes a wet sound as it opens when it hits the podium. The green moss moves around as if it is living, in a way it is. The lycopodium has many healing properties and can be used again by our healers. I thank them for the item before they too leave with a sour look.

Meliena is next. She limps towards me. Her left leg looks mangled as she half-drags it behind herself. When I ask what happened, she tells me that it was the tournament, Then she drops a collection of Quartier feathers into the prism. I thank her and wave her off.

With only two competitors, left I am excited to end this and have a bath of my own; I cannot help but feel like their grime has somehow floated along the air to coat my skin.

Fenterison struts up and goes to stand on the first step, but Cassidie stops him.

Stepping back with hands raised, he jests, "It is okay, lovely, I have no plans to harm our beautiful Queen, unless she asks for it." With a wink in my direction, I roll my eyes. He may not be the smoothest male but from what I have heard he is a good lay.

With a flourish, he bows deeply. "Good morrow, my Queen, you are looking especially ravishing this evening. I have brought the golden egg of the Quatier." Holding out the golden egg, he strides to the prism and places it down.

I begin to toy with Fin. Leaning forward with my ample bosom on display, I pout my lips before addressing him.

"I do hope it was not too much trouble? I would hate for you to lose stamina this close to the end."

His stare bores into me, then he blinks twice and clears his throat before he speaks. "That will not be a problem for me. The mother was away so it was an easy steal."

"That is good, now go bathe and rest. You will be needing that energy." I gesture for him to follow his maid as well. Once Fen has left the room, Arekin steps forward.

"I see that you are the unfortunate soul who had to wait until last."

With a respectable bow he states, "To have but a moment alone with you, no matter how brief, is something I will treasure." My cheeks heat at the unexpected sweetness. I am used to dirty and obvious flirting but this is something new.

Gathering my wits, I inquire, "And what have you brought your Queen?"

Removing the shell from his hip, he holds it out. The large shell is swirled into a point with an open base, its purple colouring almost seems to be glowing. Seeming rather proud he states. "Within this Babashiney shell, I have captured the song of a Siren."

"An extremely rare item indeed, there are not many who know of these shells and their stealing properties. How did you acquire this knowledge?"

I wait a moment to see his reaction. I notice a subtle widening of his eyes, but as quickly as it happens it is gone, his face back to a subtle smile.

"Thank you, Your Majesty. It was my grandmother, she loved all manner of folk tales and I remembered one about the Sirens and a shell. I didn't know if it would work. I only prayed to Datriminish for luck and safety."

With a gentle nod, I continue, "I am sure Velasilio will be pleased to see you back at court."

I watch his expression carefully to see if there are any signs that he may feel something towards her. To my disappointment, he returns with, "I hope you are as well, my Queen."

Trying to sound sweet, I add, "Yes of course, it is my hand you are here for after all." His smile brightens as his maid steps into the hall.

"Please Arekin, go rest before the feast." With another bow he follows and the doors close behind him. Soon after he has left, I hear my name as if a whisper on the wind.

"Searaphina?" Turning in my seat I try to find who has spoken my name. When I cannot see any fae, I stand. Movement catches my eye at the closed door. A mess of silver hair looks to be floating in the entrance. She never did have great patience.

Rolling my eyes, I step down and move towards her. "Yes Velasilio, we are finished. Let us head to my chambers. I feel gross after being around such filth." With her elbow extended, I slip my arm in and we begin our stroll to my rooms.

As we walk, I cannot help but think of Arekin's reaction; he seemed disheartened that Velasilio would be pleased with his return.

'*Is he using her as a means to get closer to me, or is he wishing to bed her before he may marry me? I pray that is not true and he is a good male.*' I will need to see what happens this evening and, if he hurts her, I have many ways to return the favour.

CHAPTER 54

PEP TALK

Searaphina

NIGHT THREE, TRIAL THREE

Sitting at my vanity, I stare at myself. I look like an ogre with this green gunk on my face. Velasilio swears it will make my face smoother than an Antiporse wing, but I am unsure if I believe her.

The evening chill is beginning to set in, so I move towards my bed and away from the window, to take in the warmth of the fire. As I reach my mattress Velasilio sits up, a scream leaves my lips as in horror at the strange creature before me.

"Phina! That's not fun—" She is cut off as Dezmond comes storming in with Cassidie.

It's her turn to scream in horror, as she turns with haste to hide her face. The two of them sweep their gazes over the room before they land on me and they both crinkle their noses at me for a split second before they school their features.

Cassidie speaks quickly "Apologies, my Queen. We heard your

scream and thought you might be in danger." She bows and drags Dezmond back out as he tries to look past me to Velasilio. The resounding thump of the doors closing has her sitting up again.

Searching the space, she toys with the hem of her gown as she asks, "That was embarrassing, do you think he saw?"

Waving it off, I climb onto the bed with her. "Silio, he is not worth your time honestly, not when there are a few incredibly handsome and horny fae waiting for us this evening."

Pursing her lips and squinting her eyes, she judges me for a moment before. "Phina, what are you hiding from me? Dezmond has been flirting with me for months and I had been holding off because I had not felt a flicker towards him. But I was looking to take things further once the craziness of the tournament has finished; my body is craving physical touch lately more than ever and I am so confused but I have had little to no time to explore the reasons. But Dezmond has been sweet and kind to me. He is also here most days and nights so it would be easier to keep a relationship and still be your loyal maid."

It almost sounds as though she is trying to make herself see that Dezmond is the right choice, as if she is avoiding the fact that Arekin may be a better match simply because he is a part of the tournament. I must take too long to answer because she stands and walks back to the vanity, taking a wet cloth and wiping her face.

Releasing a heavy sigh, she continues. "I was not sure if I truly wanted Dezmond, or if it was because he is already close to you and I knew he was genuine in wanting my affection for no reason other than to have me." A small sob leaves her lips as she starts to cry.

I walk over to her and hug her from behind. She looks up at me in the mirror. We stay in the embrace, just listening to the fire crackle, then she shifts, moving out of my arms and turning to face me. "You have slept with him? Have you not? That is why you have not answered me."

I lick my lips, not sure why I am nervous to tell her this. I inhale deeply before I speak. "Yes Silio, he and I shared a night together, but I will tell you it was not very good and you will be thankful that you did not have to endure it yourself." I feel a shudder work through me.

Velasilio looks at me then goes back to her task of cleaning off the rest of the green mask. She does not say anything.

After a while, I open my mouth to speak, but she beats me to it.

"With only eight competitors left, we are close to crowning you a royal consort, and I hope that it will be Arekin. You need to see if there is more there, possibly a flicker. I will see if Sobia is interested in some quality time, she has already shown interest in me" Looking from her hands to me, she smiles weakly.

Reaching out I take her hands in my own, giving them a reassuring squeeze.

"Silio, I understand your concerns, but if you feel this way, is it not better to explore and see if he is your twin flame before the opportunity is gone? If he is your other half I will not begrudge you for it."

Tears begin to pool in her eyes and her mouth is slightly open. Licking her lips she gently shakes her head.

Her voice lacks emotions as she speaks. "I am here to serve you, to ensure you get what you want and need out of life. Not to take from you."

"He has not won yet and, while I feel some attraction towards him, I have many more males and females I wish to try before I settle down. I only have a short window, our fevers will begin soon and then you will sleep with the closest fae."

When a female fae nears her two hundred and twenty first birthday there is a chance she will go into a fever early before her birthday. It can be a hard time if we have not found our twin flame. A female only has four in a year and our first is the most brutal. We struggle to stay away from any males who have a scent that calls to us, this can lead us to our twin flame if we have not already found them. These fevers last from seven to fourteen days.

"That is all true and we may get a fever soon and find our mates that way. But that does not stop my worry for you. What if that does not occur until after the tournament? I just wish to see you happy if not with a twin flame then with a partner who is honest and true."

"You worry too much. I will find someone, I am their Queen and it's time I started to take that role seriously and find a fae to be with, even if that is not Arekin." I truly mean this, I will honor the agreement I am in and if the tournament fails I will accept the fare of their choice. For the kingdom, and to provide a legitimate heir to strengthen my claim to the throne.

"Let us face that problem if it comes, there are still eight competitors waiting for us to entertain them this evening. If the pull leads you to Akrein please, for my sake, follow it." Standing up, I move towards the bathing chambers.

I feel her eyes as they follow me. When I told her about Dezmond, something cracked, something I have not seen from her before. Did she truly like him? I will need to speak with her again this evening and make sure that everything is okay. This is not the first time she has liked a fae that I have slept with, so why does it feel different this time?

Searaphina

NIGHT THREE, TRIAL THREE

Walking into the great hall, I am thankful that the servants have opened the large, arch windows to the left of the room, allowing the cold, night breeze to cool my heated skin. The reason for my raised temperature stands in a neat line to my right; each competitor is dressed in finery that has been provided to them by the crown.

Fenterison wears a pair of black, silk trousers, with a burnt orange blouse. His hair is washed and combed back. My attraction for him only grows at the sight of him looking regal and poised as he stands tall.

Arekin stands beside him, his face is clean shaven and he wears similar black pants and jacket with a royal blue shirt under, his smile is sweet but hides a secret, I want to find out what it is.

Kadance stands at the end of the line, handsome and brooding as usual, in a full black dress suit and has his hair clean and brushed with half of it pulled back. His dark stubble has grown in and I must say I wonder what it may feel like on my thighs. We have had limited interactions, yet he still invades my mind whenever I see him.

Approaching the round table with Velasilio at my side, I feel confident and sexy.

After we are both seated the competitors then follow, chairs scrape against the stone floor as they take their seats. Looking to the right of the room I nod at the musicians to begin, their music sets a calm and relaxed mood to the space. It feels strange to only have the ten of us in such a grand space, though I think of this as an opportunity to get to know them better, as there are only two trials left.

Once we have eaten and the tables are cleared, the members of court will be allowed to join us.

A chalice is raised to my left and I look towards Fenterison; his stubble has grown in it gives him a more roughish look, but his eyes have darkened circles to them. I hope that he will still be available for our rendezvous later, I do hate to find another so last minute even if it is not a challenge. Clearing his throat, he stands.

His voice bounces around the chamber as he speaks. "To our stunning Queen, I look forward to being your husband." He chuckles to himself before he takes a drink and sits back down. I, too, laugh and copy him, but the others do not.

As my gaze wanders over each of them, I can see that today must have been quite the trial: even after cleaning up and given a short time to rest, they each seem weary and look exhausted. Of course, all but Mister Darkside, he sits as if he has all the energy in the world and nothing can bring him down.

Sitting back in my seat, I slowly sip my wine as I watch how each competitor interacts with one another. As usual, Velasilio sits to my right, though when she sat down she moved her chair slightly further away. She has her back turned to me as she speaks with Sobia, who managed to push Arekin out of the way so that she could sit next to her; interesting.

Arekin does not look happy about it but Velasilio is making an effort to speak with both of them; she does try to include Frekily but they do not seem interested and are drinking a large amount of ale instead.

To my left is Fenterison. He wasted no time to make sure he was in that seat, he basically ran to get it. Beside him is Elanior. She listens as he speaks, though, from the look on her face she is not impressed with what she hears. Buvariris and Meliena are deep in a hushed conversation. They have not interacted with many of the others during the tournament, and they are polite with me and have only seemed interested when I have had servants come to speak with me of crowned secrets.

In the last seat across from me is Kadance. He sits, leaning to his left, with his eyes downcast as he toys with the chalice he was given, it does not appear that he has touched it. He just watches the liquid move around.

A servant comes to me and asks if we are ready for the dinner to begin, I nod and they leave to alert the chefs.

Within minutes our first course arrives, a sweet smelling onion soup, the steam still rising high above the dish as it is set before each of us. A salad with mixed greens and small tomatoes is placed beside it.

Two more servants come out and fill the empty chalices offering both wine and ale. Sobia takes both jugs and places them down in front of her. An interesting choice given that there is still a trial to complete tomorrow. I wonder if she has set her sights on a different prize.

When all tasks are complete, the servants line up, bow, and leave.

I gently tap my ring-clad hand against my chalice and all conversations stop, all turning to look at me. "Congratulations to each of you for successfully retrieving your items, I do hope you enjoy this evening and do not overindulge. Tomorrow comes the fourth trial and it will bring a new set of hardships for you all." Raising my chalice, they all follow before drinking deeply.

Then, the meal begins.

I turn to Fenterison. "How did you find the third trial?"

Wiping his arm across his mouth, he says, "The trial was easy for myself, but I can't speak for others. I walked away without a scratch." I can feel the stare of the others watching as he so boldly mocks them.

Leaning in, he whispers, "I trust you don't see this as too forward, but I can't wait for our private movement this evening. This food is only fulfilling one of my hungers, the other you can help me with." His eyes are hard set on my own, I do not know if I should be flattered or unnerved.

Clearing my throat and taking a sip of my wine, keeping my eyes on him. "That may be a bit too far, even if I may enjoy such company later this evening. I must know, if the third trial was so easy, how will you fare tomorrow?"

Sitting back in his chair he raises his ale. "You see that is the secret, I won't be doing it alone. I have made an alliance, saved his life, now he owes me a debt." With a wink, he drinks the contents.

An alliance, one who owes him a life debt, what a stupid deal to enter. These trials only allow one to succeed, this ally could be forced into forfeit if it suits Fen. Unsure of how to respond to him, I smile and begin to sweep my gaze over the others.

Velasilio and Arekin seem deep in discussion, her eyes are wide and she covers her open mouth with one hand, while the other lays pressed to her chest. Sobia interjects into his story, adding in about her own harrowing journey through the third trial. Velasilio's eyes shift between the two, doing her best to give them both her attention.

I hope that she takes a leap this evening and truly enjoys the full pleasure of being the Queen's friend. Sobia has shown no real interest towards me and I wonder, since their first dance and that steamy kiss, if her plans have changed, only staying in the tournament to be closer to Velasilio.

Arekin is trying to keep her attention, only his eyes still dart towards me. I wonder when he will try to gain my attention this evening. I have heard he is searching for his twin flame and that he believes that may be me. I have felt something towards him but also toward Kadance, it is no more than lust as I have not felt it deepen at any time. Fenterison has had me tingling all evening, each touch of his hand on mine sets my skin on fire, is that just lust or something more? Perhaps I will find out tonight?

Our main course is brought to the table on many trays, one with a mixture of roast meats, another with vegetables. There are baskets full of fresh loaves of bread and three flutes of rich, dark brown gravy. My mouth waters at the sight of the glorious meal.

An individual, pre-prepared plate is placed before me.

Should I want more food, the taster will need to try it all first. Looking from my plate, I see all are waiting for me to allow them to eat. With a wave of my hand, the others begin to fill their plates high. Sobia offers Velasilio each tray before she places them on her own plate. A smile tugs at my lips; leaning into her space I nudge Velasilio with my elbow.

Her head turns towards me. "Yes, my Queen?"

"Have you decided which of these fae is strong and brave enough to bed you?" I let the words out as a whisper, even though she is unimpressed with me.

If she is surprised or annoyed at my comment she does not show it, instead her voice is even as she speaks. "Perhaps I have. Though I see you are set on your own choice?" Gazing past me, she eyes Fenterison, I almost feel that she is judging me for my choice.

When I go to speak with her again she has already turned away and is eating her meal while speaking with Sobia.

I refuse to let this get to me. She is acting like a child. Huffing to myself, I eat as music carries around the grand hall.

I think of all my duties as Queen; this is one of the few joyous things I can do, the hosting of feasts and balls that all enjoy and to see my fae engaging in jovial conversation.

My good spirits halt for, when my eyes settle on Kadance, his posture has stiffened and his jaw is set in a hard line as anger and power radiate from him. The servants give him a wide berth, seemingly nervous to set down food near him or fill his goblet, which he has not touched either. I wonder what has put him into this foul mood, when moments ago he did not seem to have a care in this world.

Deciding to try and get him into better spirits, I raise my voice in question. "I do hope this evening's meal is to your liking, Kadance?" I think he might not answer me, but after a second he lifts his sight from the space he was staring into and his eyes lock with my own.

His eyes are filled with the promise of sex and violence, I do not know if I should fear him or want him. Then he speaks in a deep voice and sends a shiver down my spine. "There is a far more tasty meal in this very hall, one I wish to devour but, alas, it does not seem to be in my lap." With that said, he turns back to the table, stabbing a knife into the meat, bringing it to his mouth and eating it in one bite.

When he finishes, he stands from his seat, the quick action causing the chair legs to scratch against the floor. Stepping away from the table, he moves to the arched entry at the end of the hall and disappears into the gardens. I suppose he may be off to find his tasty treat elsewhere; if he had stayed I might have offered one to him. Thoughts of following him into the night and letting him take me against a tree float into my mind. Perhaps Fenterison and I will take our own stroll into the garden.

Once our meal is complete, we stay at the table talking and enjoying platters of sweet fruits and cakes. The windows have long since been closed as the evening chill has set in and I do not need more of the competitors leaving before the evening truly gets started.

CHAPTER 56

A MESS

Searaphina

NIGHT THREE, TRIAL THREE

As the evening wears on and a few other tables are brought in, as the fae of court join us for desserts, music and dancing. I watch as the competitors each stand and mingle with the court. Buvariris, Freckily and Meliena all stand with their families in what looks to be a heated conversation, when they notice me staring for my seat they quickly look away. I have been moving around most of the evening speaking to the members of court and the competitors. Many were very interested in the small secrets that may have left my lips, with a small smirk I lift my wine to my lips, and drink.

Fenterison has been with me each step, only leaving when asked to do so; now he sits with me. His hand moves over my chalice and he slowly gets me to put it down. When my eyes, full of rage, turn on him he winces and then whispers, "Apologies my Queen, but I am afraid you may have had one too many wines this evening, while you were out with the competitors you may have spilled some royal secrets you don't want to get out."

My mouth pops open. I had not expected this. I push the drink away. "Thank you Fenterison, you are a surprising male and not what I had expected."

He leans in further, his voice dropping low. "Oh and what did you expect of me?" There is no missing his intentions with the way he speaks to me. We are interrupted by a girlish giggle.

Turning to look over at Velasilio, I realise that she has again taken her seat—she got up soon after the meals were finished as though she did not want to be near me. She was dancing with Sobia and I took the chance to speak with Arekin and then, when she swapped, I spoke with Sobia. I thought it would be best to do so while she was distracted, I believe that she is now acting out against me.

As my maid, she is to be poised and here to assist me when needed, but, as I look at her now and hear the way she speaks, I know that she has had one to many wines herself. Annoyance simmers just under my skin. I do not wish for drama to develop this evening, she may make a fool of herself tonight and tomorrow I will see that she faces the repercussions of her actions.

Velasilio raises her wine and drinks the last of it. Arekin and Sobia also seem to be inebriated as all three laugh at what I can only assume was a funny quip.

Laughing a little too hard, Velasilio falls off her seat and into Arekin's lap; he made sure to be next to her this time when they sat back down. He does not seem to mind and his hands rest in respectable places. She apologises rather loudly. "WHOOPS! MY APOLOGIES, GOODSIRE."

Her intoxication is obvious as she tries to stand Arekin and Sobia find it incredibly hilarious to watch as she struggles to get to her feet, falling back to Arekin's lap a few times. When she does finally stand, he is quick to follow with a steadying hand.

Trying to seem like a gentle male he asks, "My lady, did do... ya need me to escortes you to ya chambers?" Sobia realises what is about to happen and jumps up as well.

"Mee, I can do too." Oh, she is worse than the two of them. I watch as Velasilio tries to make a choice. At that moment, Dezmond steps forward.

"Vel, would you like it if I were to walk you to your chambers? It is the safest option." Presenting his hand to her, he waits for her answer. I refuse to step into the mess, Velasilio can deal with this on her own and, to my surprise she does so in a truly unbecoming manner.

"VEL? Who you callling Vel. Please only use my name. And NO, I do not need **YOUR** help!" Taken aback by her abrupt reply, he nods once and moves back into his position.

Happy with this outcome, she links her arms with Arekin and Sobia and they make their way to the exit. Before they leave, she stops suddenly. Turning and leaving the others behind, they look at each other, confused.

Staggering over to me, Velasilio requests, "If it pleeeases, Queen. I request leave." Her words are a slur, she is a mess and an embarrassment at this moment.

"That would be for the best, I will see you bright and early in the morning, *Silio.*" I use her nickname to show her that I will not allow this to come between us, though she has angered me this evening for ignoring me.

I do not truly care that she is a mess, the court will laugh about her antics but that is all. We may be known for our finery, but we all understand that sometimes a fae needs to relax, as long as it does not become a consistent occurrence there is no problem.

She staggers back to the pair and the three link arms and walk off, shuffling back and forth. I huff a laugh. Arekin and Sobia will regret their decisions in the morning.

Turning back to Fenterison, he requests,"May I havea moment

of your time my Queen? To enjoy a stroll this evening?" Standing, he presents his hand to me. I smile at him and take it.

Helping to pull my chair out, he waits for my answer. "It would be my pleasure, and please, call me Searaphina." His soft smile shows his straight, white teeth.

Fenterison leads me to the archway that will lead us into the gardens. The harold standing there announces that I am leaving, the court stops and bows, bidding me a good evening, before we turn and begin our stroll. As we exit the hall the ground changes from stone to gravel. The soft chunching underfoot is all to be heard in the otherwise quiet night. My four Queen's guards follow at a respectable distance, allowing for some privacy.

"How was your meal Maj—" He hesitates for a moment before speaking my name, "Searaphina?"

Freezing in place, I cause him to almost mis-step. He turns to me. Biting my bottom lip, I let my gaze roam over his body. "It is not the meal you wish to speak of, ask me what you really wish to know."

CHAPTER 57

TO HELL WITH CHIVALRY

Arekin

NIGHT THREE, TRIAL THREE

This is not exactly how I thought my night would turn out. Velasilio's body keeps bumping against my right hip, my arm currently looped there on her left side and Sobia on her right. We navigate the halls poorly as we sway with each step. I need to find a way to get rid of Sobia.

'I wish for some alone time with Velasilio to discuss the next trial and possibly steal another kiss, or ask her about the Queen and what she would make of our situation. It is her hand and the pull I have felt for some time that drew me here and even if there is a strange sizzle between the two of us, I still want to see what could be between me and Searaphina. Velasilio and I are exploring and having fun, but is it real?'

I realise that I am lost in my own mind as I look past her to where Sobia had been a few seconds ago, but she is no longer there.

Velasilio must notice at the same time as she looks around and asks. "Sobia? Where are you?"

Looking all around, we see nothing so we walk towards a guard standing at their post and ask if they have seen her. He looks at me and then to Velasilio; I can see the judgement in his eyes as well as the lust for her. "No." The one word answer is all we get.

With Sobia missing, I take the opportunity and rush towards her, taking her hand in my own and leaning in to whisper, "We need somewhere private to talk, where can we go?"

Her gaze is stuck on my own as she bites her lower lip, she shakes her head to clear her mind and then she makes an odd squeaking sound before grabbing my hand and leading me towards her chambers, or at least I think that's where we are going. I have never been there before.

Before I know it, we arrive at her door. Stumbling inside in front of me, there is a soft thud as she leans against the door, her eyes never leaving mine as she pulls me closer, our bodies only inches apart.

Then we fall, I wrap my arms around her as we fall towards the ground, I try to flip us so that it is my back that hits the hard, stone floor. With a heavy thud, we hit the ground, the air is knocked out of me.

She begins to giggle and it draws my attention back to her face. A cheeky smile is on her lips as she wets them. "Oh my, I need more assistance?" The lust in her eyes is putting my chivalry to the test.

I try to regain some sense. Her dress does nothing to hide the curve of her body and the heat radiating just beneath the thin fabric. She lays on top of me, making no effort to move.

She leans in to kiss me and I let her. Our lips crash in a heated movement as our tongues tangle. My dick begins to harden as she grinds her body down on top of me.

When she finally pulls back, her cheeks are flushed and her lips have a wet sheen to them.

She chuckles at me before she gets up, then reaches down to help me up as well—it takes her more than one try. When we are both standing, I turn and take in her room as she closes the door. The chamber is moderate in size and decorated with minimal art and only a single dresser and vanity/writing desk. The bed catches my attention next. It is much too large for such a petite female, covered in such a dark purple sheets, they are almost black.

A soft hand caresses my face. Leaning into the touch, I bring my gaze back to hers.

"What is of intresssst, my bed OR what you willll do to me?" The playful smile and desire in her eyes has me groaning again. I am already half-hard from our kiss on the floor, if she continues I don't think I will be able to stop myself.

"We should not, we have both had a lot of wine, thanks to your game. Even though he might know and now kill me." The sobering thought hits me for a second before I start to laugh.

My laugh is deep as the memories dance in my mind. *'We must drink any time a servant looks terrified or as if they wish to climb Kadance.'*

"Do not say that, we have every righttt to enjoy me... us, this." Pouting her lips she tilts her head to the side before she runs her hand up my chest and racks her nails back down. The slight slur in her words beginning to waver.

I suppress a groan as her hands begin to travel south. "You have no idea the control I need to have around such a stunning creature like you, little minx."

I capture both in my own, bringing them to my mouth and kissing them. "But if you want, we can revisit this when our minds aren't clouded by drink." Pulling her hands from my own, she steps back as her lustful gaze leaves a hot trail as it moves down my body.

"I do not wish to wait and I do not need male's help." Slowly, she raises her hands to the ties of her dress. Her gaze moves back to my own as she bites her lower lip. Painfully slowly, she unties it. Her white underdress is also undone and shows the slightest hint of skin.

My mouth waters at the sight and my shaft hardens more at the thought of what is underneath. With the blood leaving my head, I step forward, Velasilio matches me stepping backwards. I raise my eyebrow at her, she shakes her head.

"I thought we are too drunk, now I want to play with myself." Her smile is playful and cheeky as she grasps the neckline of her gown and pulls it down, exposing her breasts.

Her skin looks so smooth and her nipples are hardening under my gaze; they are the colour of rich chocolate and it makes me ache to taste her. Her hand moves to her left breast, cupping it gently, before she moves to her nipple, pinching it between her thumb and forefinger, rolling it and causing her to moan.

Rushing forward, I wrap my arm around her waist and close the gap between us. Lowering my head, our lips crash into a passionate kiss. Running my tongue over the seam of her lips, she opens to me. She tastes like the sweet wine she was drinking, and her lips are soft against mine. Tightening my hold on her hips, I feel as she rubs herself against me without shame.

I push my leg between hers and allow her to use me. She begins to pant, causing us to separate. Looking down at her, straddling my thigh with her breasts out, her chest heaves and she licks her now-puffy lips.

My words come out choppy as I try to breathe and contain my hunger for her. "We should stop before this goes any further."

There is a strange sensation in my chest like the flicker of a flame. Perhaps we are tied as one and this will be the moment we ignite.

'Would we want that to be in a drunken haze?' As the thought crosses my mind, a gentle hand presses to my chest. Our eyes lock onto each other as she begins to slide her hand down my chest.

The heat of her gaze has me pushing my desire against her. "What if this is what we both want? What if we need this?" Each word is slow and deliberate as if she knows I will crack.

She doesn't know how right she is, just as her hand reaches my hardened length. My own hand snaps out, wrapping around her delicate wrists, and she jumps at the sudden moment. Pulling her hand away, her face falls and she drops my gaze. Placing my thumb and forefinger under her chin, I raise her head to look at me again.

"Is this what you truly want? I need you to say it." My eyes search hers.

Her tongue moves slowly as it glides across her top lip before she bites it gently. Her voice is soft and sensual as she whispers, "Yes, this is what I need."

Groaning, my eyes almost roll back in my head as I capture her lips once more. She whimpers into my mouth as I lean forward, wrapping my arms around her legs and lifting her up. With her dress bunching at the front and riding up she is able to wrap each leg around me crossing them at my back. Turning around we cross the distance to the bed. When the tips of my boots hit the hard base I lower Velasilio down and crawl on top of her as we go. In a somewhat awkward shuffle we manage to move onto the bed without breaking our kiss.

Breaking apart, her face is flushed and hair splayed out around her like a silver halo. Her breasts are still out. I reach her exposed nipples. Taking them between my fingers, I gently pull and twist, causing a breathy moan to escape her.

Smiling to myself, I move my body down hers until my head is at her chest. Taking her hardened nipple into my mouth, I swirl my tongue around and tenderly capture it between my teeth. Her hands reach up and intertwine in my hair, holding my head in place.

Looking through my lashes, I take in her expression; her lips are slightly parted as she moans quietly, her eyes are closed tight. I give one last nip to her breast before I move to the other one and give it the same treatment. Once I am satisfied with the attention I have lavished her breasts, I begin to move further down her body. Taking her gown in hand, I pull it upwards until her naked core greets me.

Looking back at her face, I see that she now has lifted onto her elbows and watches me with a devilish smirk. "I see my little minx has been bare all evening, I do hope it was for me?" Laying on my stomach, I trail my fingers slowly up the inside of her right thigh, causing her to squirm.

"You will never know." Her cheeky reply has me wondering if I should toy with her a little longer or remove all thoughts from her mind with my tongue.

Deciding to show her that I am the only male she needs, with a feather light touch I trail my fingers lazily up her thigh. Once I reach her apex, I run one finger through her centre, causing her to jump slightly. My finger comes away glistening with her need. Feeling her eyes on me, I look at her.

Her voice is heavy as she mocks me. "Are you going to continue? Or should I help you?" I cannot help but chuckle at her, knowing she may very well be serious.

Keeping my gaze on her, I reach down, finding her clitoris. Taking it between my fingers, I gently twist causing her to arch her back and moan loudly. I slip two fingers into her wet entrance. Feeling her squeeze me tight, I curl my fingers and begin to move with haste. Her moans are like music to my ears, she is unable to hold back any longer; her hands knot in my hair, pushing my face where she wants it. My tongue moves over her entrance and clitoris, tasting her for the first time and taking the sensitive bud into my mouth. Her thighs clench around my head as she rides me, her moans increase and she begins to shudder under me.

"Ohh, Arkein, hmmmm." The sting from her hands in my hair only spurs me on. Adding another finger as my pace increases, Velasilio moves with me, using me to find her release.

My aching shaft is rock solid and the pressure of the mattress is only a slight relief. I can feel the mess I am making inside my trousers as I ache to bury myself deep inside her. Without removing my mouth, I look up, seeing that Velasilio is beginning to shake and chase the height of her pleasure. Her eyes are shut tightly and her mouth is open as she moans loudly, one of her hands is still tightly wound in my hair and the other has her nipple squeezed between her fingers. Smiling, I suck her clit into my mouth.

With a large gasp Velasilio shouts "OH FUCK... THAT...DO IT AGAIN!"

Her hand in my hair is almost painful now, her breath is short and choppy. I do not stop, increasing my speed again. Her thighs squeeze tightly around my head, her body stiffens and her back bows from the bed.

Coating my hand and face, she slowly comes down from her high. Removing myself from her, I crawl up the bed and lay on my side next to her. I huff out a breath before I say.

"You taste as sweet as you look." A sweet laugh escapes her, before she rolls to her side, pulling a pillow under her head.

With brows raised and a smirk, her eyes track down my body, lingering on the outline of my erection. "Is this the part where you tell me we are not finished yet?"

Leaning forward, she reaches down my pants, taking my hard length in her hand. Groaning at the sensation, I reluctantly remove it and place our joined hands on her hip. "We are for this evening."

Pulling back slightly, her brow furrows as her lips move into a thin line. Not wanting to offend her, I continue to explain myself. "I don't know if it is wise to go further, we have had many drinks this evening." Leaning in, I brush a stand of hair from her face and press a light kiss to her cheek.

Moving out of reach, she looks me up and down, confusion writing across her face. "Are you concerned that I will laugh at the size or shape of your member? If you are half as good with it as you were just now, I am sure it will be a pleasurable experience for us both."

My eyes pop open and I sit up, turning to face her fully. She does the same. "It is nothing like that, I just don't wish to take advantage of you in this state. I worry the drink has given us both a little too much bravery."

My words must ring true as she huffs out in frustration before she lays flat once more, covering her face with her hands.

I almost cannot hear her as her words are muffled. "Do you not wish for release?" Readjusting my stiff shaft, I lean down to her, removing her hands so I can look at her face.

"I am here to give you pleasure, not take it. If, at tomorrow night's ball, we slow our intake of wine, maybe we can try this again." Her face softens at my words and she sits up.

"Perhaps that would be a good idea, it is getting late and you need rest. Tomorrow's trial will be the most brutal." She begins to fix her dress, pulling it down and readjusting her breasts. Once they are away I hope my length will begin to soften.

Standing from the bed, I adjust my own clothing, not wanting any others to get the wrong idea when I leave. When we have both calmed down and are standing, I bow to her and make my way to the door. As my hand touches the handle I stop, turning to face her.

"Is there anything you wish me to know before tomorrow?" With her arms folded over her chest, she steps forward.

"Oh, ah, yes." Rubbing her hands over her arms, she sits on the bed's edge.

"You will be blindfolded to confuse you, but the island is never too far. No more than half a day's journey." Keeping her eyes downcast she takes a pillow and places it on her lap, playing with the frilled edge.

"Velasilio." I take a step towards her. Looking from her lap, she smiles at me.

"All is right Arekin, please go and rest." Taking a breath, she stands.

"For Searaphina's sake, you would make a terrific king." Placing her hand out she gestures for me to leave.

Hearing her say this confuses me, I want to be king. It is Searaphina that I came here for, I feel something for her, but not after spending time with Velasilio. I am thinking that I may be confused, what if it is her I am to be with. Standing there staring at her, she looks sad, almost like she is hoping I will choose her, but I need a chance to explore things with the Queen before I can make any decisions.

With haste, I bow again and leave the room, the whirlwind of emotions is strange and unpredictable. I thought this was only a flirtation and that if anything came of it I might wed her instead. But there has been no further flame and the spark I do feel is less than when I see the Queen. As I close the large door behind myself and begin my walk towards my own chambers I wonder again if I have made the right choice.

CHAPTER 58

AVERAGE

Searaphina

NIGHT THREE, TRIAL THREE

Though he looks to be shocked at my more abrupt words, I know that he has only been acting the gentle male with me. I am hoping his dirtier side might come out to play.

Stepping towards me, Fen places his hand on my hip, before he asks, "Is this okay?" With a smile, I nod to him. His large hand radiates heat that I can feel through my skirt.

Taking his hand from my hip I lead him towards the willow tree, where the hanging leaves will provide some privacy. My Queen's guard stays in formation, two behind and two in front, but ensure they offer a respectful distance and avert their eyes; they are well used to my antics by now. Especially considering many of them have experienced it, Cassidie most recently as this morning. She is a good female and so far has not shown any jealousy. If anything, I believe she would enjoy watching me with another.

Entering the darkness, there is only one lamp lit in the little cove, providing a nice ambiance to the chilled evening. The sound of stones crunching under boots can be heard as the guards take up position standing just outside.

Cassidie stands at the entrance, her eyes never leaving mine as I take one last look at her, they are lust-filled. This will come in handy if Fenterison is unable to satisfy me, she will be ready to step in.

I face him and place both of his hands on my hips. His smile is dazzling as he leans in whispering to me, "You may be a Queen, but if you allow it I will fuck your tight little pussy like I would any other female." He inhales my scent deeply before placing a sloppy kiss to the side of my neck.

Not the most charming words but, as I expected, he only pretends to be a gentle-male. Good. Wrapping my hand around his neck, I turn to his ear, taking the lobe into my mouth and biting softly.

My voice is soft and seductive as I whisper, "Show me."

I do not get the chance to think before he grasps me under my legs and hoists me up. On instinct, I wrap my legs around his torso, thankful that I have a large slit in this skirt allowing me to wrap my legs and lock my ankles together around his large frame. His hands move to my ass, cupping it though the gown, his lips crash into mine and the kiss is harsh and sloppy.

I feel us moving just before the harsh bark of the tree is against my back, scraping into my exposed skin. The sting is painful but also heightens the pleasure of this very dirty encounter. Unable to contain it, I moan into his mouth.

Pulling back, his gaze bores into mine. Smirking, I decide to get this moving along. "If you want to fuck me against this tree, then hurry up and do it." His gaze darkens as a sinful smile crosses his face.

"You asked for this," is all I hear before he shuffles, seeming to hold my entire weight in one hand before he unties his pants and removes his penis.

Reaching under my skirt, he finds the thin fabric I am calling my undergarments; the first tingle spreads across my body as he runs his fingers over my clit. Leaning my head back, I release another moan. His mouth descends over my exposed neck, kissing, licking and biting at my sensitive flesh. All while he moves the garment to the side, sweeping his fingers through my slick folds and plunging one of his thick fingers into me.

"Ahh, your tight little pussy is so ready and needy, I can feel you trying to suck me up and keep me there."

'Okay ew, I need to stop his incessant talking before I am no longer in the mood.' As the thought crosses my mind, I look at his face.

He brings his hand to his mouth, sucking my juices from it and humming along. Dropping my legs, I land on the soft soil, and it sinks slightly beneath my weight. Gripping the neckline of my gown, he pulls down hard, exposing my breasts; taking them in his hands he leans forward and sucks on each nipple before he places both hands on my shoulders and pushes me down to my knees. My shock at this seems to render me useless as he just watches me go. When the cold dirt bites into my knees, I hiss.

Fenterison pauses briefly asking. "What is wrong? I thought if I got to taste you, then you should have the joy of tasting me too."

"I am not used to males who are so forward, they usually ask first." My tone has bite to it as I stare up at him, his semi-erect penis sits at eye level with me. It looks average with a slight curve to the left, his bush is particularly large.

"Well I am not like most others." I admire his bravery and confidence. Deciding to give this a go, taking his penis in my hand I run my tongue from his balls to the head.

He tastes salty and musky, I know he bathed but I do not think he paid close enough attention here. Standing, I place both of my hands on either side of his face and shove my tongue into his mouth so that he can taste himself. When I finally allow him to break the kiss, his eyebrows are raised and his mouth is open in shock. My sly smirk says it all, but he surprises me with what he says and does next.

Pulling me forward, he kisses me again and presses us together tightly. When he stops, he quickly spins me around. My hands shoot out to catch myself on the tree in front of me. My skirt is hiked up and my undergarments pulled down to my feet, and he asks me to step out of them. I do not know what he does with them. One of his hands rests at my hip while the other goes between my shoulder blades, pushing me down and getting me to bend at the hips. I feel his hot breath against me as he seems to take a large breath in with his face right against my vulva.

Rolling my eyes at his actions, I demand, "Fen, if you do not do something soon I will have to call Cassidie in to finish the job you have started." I hear the slight snicker of the Queen's guard; they know I am not telling a lie. There have been occasions that I have gotten their assistance when my lovers fail or if I am just in the mood, as they are usually the closest fae.

Without saying anything, he stands. I feel his hand come down over my backside, the sting is welcomed. The round head of his penis lines up to my entrance, just before he rams into me.

"Fuck! Your pussy is so warm and wet." With this lovely compliment, he starts to thrust. At first he is slow but his speed increases quickly.

His grip on my hips tightens, causing my hands to move and scrape against the bark. As he begins pounding harder, I almost fall forwards, he catches me around the waist and pulls me upright. Needing more to get me over that hill, I reach into the neckline of my gown, taking one of my nipples between my fingers and pinching hard. My other hand moves down, bunching up the front of my dress and moving underneath. Rubbing my fingers in the mess we are making, I bring them to my sensitive bud and start to move in circles. Pressure builds behind my eyes as they begin to roll back, tingling runs though my whole body, Fen continues a punishing pace as he thrusts in and out of me. I can feel his body going rigid as his thrusts become erratic.

"FUCK ME! You're squeezing me so tight."

I am only moments from my own sweet release' speeding up my pace I apply more pressure. Just as I crest the hill for my orgasm, Fenterison stills and spasms behind me.

He pumps lazily as he has found his own release. Removing himself from me, the cold air hits my wet vulva, sending a shiver down my burning body. Swearing to myself, I realise my mistake; I will need to finish myself off. Looking around for my undergarments I spot them in Fen's hand.

I hold out my hand. "I'll take those."

Fen shakes his head and holds them tighter. "A memento of our first time, my goddess, I will return them after we wed."

I stare at Fenterison, folding my arms over my chest. "I see you have great faith in yourself, how do you know that you will win the tournament?" I keep my face masked knowing that he believes that was a successful encounter. Even if he is bad at fucking me, I only need to sleep with him during my fevers and then, when a child is born, never again. And he was honest in telling me I was spilling secrets to the competitors, that loyalty is something I may need.

He smiles at me, as if he knows what I am thinking, and then he lifts the silk to his nose and inhales before he says, "Now that I have a good luck charm, my odds are even greater, I must rest in order to win your hand." With a bow, he pockets them and walks away.

Shaking my head, I call Cassidie in, she takes one look at my frustrated expression and gets on her knees. What a good girl.

CHAPTER 59

TIME'S UP

Kadance

NIGHT THREE, TRIAL THREE

My fingers dent the wooden seat as I watch her with the other males. I have noticed the last few days that one is getting too close to her. If he dares touch her I will enjoy removing his little prick.

Being around her, I have felt something strange, a dark energy that calls to my own. I know that she is in danger here, there is something else clinging to her, stopping her from realising her potential. I have been spending less time watching her and more time searching for the answers I seek. I know that this puts her at risk for the short term, but if I can find out what the darkness is, maybe I can be rid of it.

The sweet sound of her laughter pulls me from my thoughts. I see that the wankstain of a male is speaking with her again. I have to leave this feast before I do something rash like kill him with a spoon.

It can be done all it takes is the right amount of pressure, so perfect to remove the eyes. Standing from the table, I move towards the gardens, and I feel her eyes track my every step. I am finding it harder to be away from her, the strange flicker in my chest only stops when I have her in my sight and if I spend too long away it becomes a searing pain.

I don't shy from pain but this is relentless. I tried using her smell to keep the pain at bay, but the items I had acquired lost their scent and I needed something new. Clothing was not enough. I need her particular sweet scent that can not be tainted by others around her, this is why I have started to take her undergarments. It has become the only thing to calm the beast inside.

It was rather annoying feeling that fog in my mind, I need a clear head if I am going to find this hidden secret. If she does not have the answer, perhaps her companion does.

Hearing voices exiting the feast hall, I find an alcove of sorts and use my shadows to cover myself, though from the sound of their conversation they are greatly distracted. My blood begins to boil as she exits with her arm around that of another.

I know who will be dying next.

They don't talk much at first but then it becomes too sensual too quickly. It takes only a moment for their lips to meet and I have to restrain myself from killing him here and now for touching what is mine.

I step forward, ready to stop this before he can taste any more of her, but I do not. I need to know more about whatever this evil is that follows her and I need to be able to do that in secret. If she knows that I am able to move about the castle freely, I won't be able to anymore.

Within moments, her perky tits are free of their confines, my mouth waters as I think of how her breasts would taste. Her nipples pebble, begging for the pinch of my teeth.

My cock twitches and hardens, I have to bite back a growl after hearing her moan in pleasure. The shadows around me seem to grow in displeasure, odd, as they have not done that before. Knowing that she is not getting the pleasure she seeks, I smile, watching as she takes charge of her own release. The only reason I am able to not slit his throat here and now is for her safety. My plan is almost in place, I have somewhere safe to take her. It will just be getting her out of the castle that will prove to be a challenge.

But that might just work.

With the idea in my head, I know it won't be long until we are together. Remembering his face, I plan something far worse than a quick death, and the next trial will be the perfect cover.

Finally tearing myself away, I struggle making it back to my chambers. My cock is rock hard from her sweet moans and the image of her riding me.

Slamming the door shut, I curse in frustration. "Fuck!" I have never been so hung up on one female before, I can't even think of another without going soft.

The floor groans as I cross the space in a huff. Laying back on the bed, it lets out a mighty squeak under my weight. Rubbing my hands down my face, I try to stop thinking about her perfect body and that scent that drives me wild.

Untying my pants, I free my throbbing cock; spitting onto my hand, I begin to stroke up and down my length. I imagine her straddling me, looking down at me with such lust as she slowly lowers onto my length, taking her time to get used to my size and girth. I mimic her movement and how she would tighten around me with my hand. Groaning at the sensation, I see her fully seated as she starts to move her hips, grinding down against me so that her clit rubs and I hit that perfect spot. Squeezing my hand tightly, she moans loudly at her release; picking up speed, I follow after her. My balls begin to tighten and my spine tingles. Wrapping my hand around her throat, I tell her to come on my cock like a good female.

That is the image that does me in. On a guttural groan, I spill all over my hand and thighs.

I move to the bathing chambers to clean up.

Laying back in bed, I think of her now enjoying another; my blood boils and my hands clench into fists. Sitting up, I move around the room, packing and making a plan. I will not wait any longer, tomorrow I am taking what is mine.

CHAPTER 60

GOSSIP AND DEATH

Searaphina

DAY FOUR, TRIAL FOUR

In the early twilight hours, the sun is still hidden behind the mountains and the clouds sit low, stealing any and all warmth. Wrapping the fur shawl around myself tightly, I stare at the horizon, listening as the waves crash in the distance. A hand grazes my own, snapping me from my own world. Velasilio stands beside me on the weather dock as the eight competitors are led out in a single line. Each one looks at the large ship that is docked behind me, it will be their transport today. The three, large, white sails are being opened as the voices of the captain and his crew ring out.

Casting my gaze over them I take in their weapons of choice, On Eleanor's hip is a scaber housing a long sword.

Strapped across Fenterison's chest and the tip of a large bow over his shoulder.

Buvariris, Frekily and Meliena all have short swords in their hip holsters.

I do not even bother trying to count how many daggers Kadance has on him as I am sure many more would be hidden.

Arekin's axe is missing, lost in the last trial but there is one dagger that hangs at his hip. Last I see Sobia with not a single weapon on her.

From the corner of my eye, I see that Velasilio is taking stock of the competitors as I am; this might very well be the last time we see any of them. They are tasked to show their survival skills and will be dropped at an unknown location needing to find their way back.

They will be just over half a day's boat ride, just too far to fly, though they may try; we had a guard test the flight with a boat below for safety but they were unable to make it after spending a night on the island, trying to survive, as the competitors will be doing. Once they arrive at the island they will be offered the necessary supplies; there are no rules when they are out there, it is every fae for themselves.

My gaze lingers on Arekin, his kindness will do him no favors, the fourth trial will see them all wishing to draw blood. It is the second to last step to winning my hand in marriage.

Velasilio holds out a basket holding fine, black, silk ties.

"Good morning to you all, congratulations on making it this far. Today you will each be blindfolded once upon this ship." I look past my shoulder to the large vessel, just as the sails fly down and are tied. "It will take you to an unknown location and leave you there, your task is to return to me. Prove that no matter the obstacle you will always find your way back to me."

I walk onto the large run leading me to the top of the ship. The dock cracks and whines with the movement of the others as they follow me. Once I reach the middle of the ship, I signal to the competitors where to stand, then, following my direction, they all kneel. "With these I will take your sight from you, but if your intentions are true you will know the way back to me. If we are fated to be together, you will succeed.”

I wrap a silk tie around each of their heads. My hands shake slightly when I reach Kadance; I do not understand why my heart seems to skip a beat around him. Arekin causes a similar reaction, only it is more goosebumps along my skin. Fenterison elicits no reaction after his lackluster performance last evening. When I reach Sobia, she shakes her head.

“My apologies Queen Searaphina, but I must forfeit my place in the tournament.” Her gaze moves past me and to Velasilio.

“It is your right to do so, I only ask that you are certain that this is the right choice for you.” I wait for her to reply.

She nods and her voice is strong and calm, without a sigh of hesitation. “Yes my Queen, I don’t feel that it is right for me to continue when another has stolen my attention and affection.” I hold in my surprise at the statement.

I feel all eyes on me. “If that is what you wish. I, Queen Searaphina, hereby remove you from the Queen’s tournament.” Holding my hand out, I gesture for her to leave. She goes without a word, her eyes linger on Velasilio as she passes; I wonder if she was waiting for her to say something.

After she leaves, I stand back and take one final look at them all before saying what could be my final words to them. “Good luck and, as always, we hope that Datriminish blesses you.”

Turning on my heel, I speak with the captain for a brief moment to give him the directions to their location before I leave the ship and head back to the dock. Velasilio hesitates for a moment before picking up her pace to follow me. She clutches at her fur shawl as if she is in pain.

When she reaches my side again, I speak in a hushed tone to not let others hear. “What is the matter? Are you unwell?”

Her eyes shoot to my own, her brows raised. “I am well. Thank you for your concern." She is still angry and is trying to hide it from me, so I push further.

"Silio, I know that you are upset with me but do not think I am unable to tell."

Even if we had not been friends, the blood tie that binds us makes it impossible for her to lie to my face. Her body seems to sag before she raises one hand to her chest.

"As we left just now, I felt a gentle pain in my chest as if a fire had begun." Rubbing at the centre of her chest, she looks longingly at the ship.

My eyes widen in shock, it is a surprise that she does not realise what this could mean. With both of my hands on her shoulders, I lean in close to her. "Silio, do you think it is your twin flame?"

Velasilio's brows crease as she places her fingers to her temples massaging slowly, as if she has a pain in her mind. "Surely if it was there, I would have felt it by now?"

I take her hands, removing them from her head. "That is possibly true, but have you felt anything towards any of the competitors yet?" Looking from me to the ship she swallows, shaking her head before she turns away from me to face the vessel.

"May we speak of this at tea? After they have departed." Her voice has a shakiness to it that tells me of her uncertainty. I watch her for a moment, not speaking the truth that we both know. If one of the competitors is her twin flame, she may never truly know. And how do I explain that I, too, feel the searing pain?

CHAPTER 61

A PLAN

Arekin

DAY FOUR, TRIAL FOUR

I'm stuck in my own head, cursing at myself for my own stupid actions. The sweet scent of honey and vanilla wraps around me, taunting me. She is so close that I can almost taste her, but her gaze never meets my own. I just need her to understand why I did not go further with her.

I feel like my heart is smouldering and the centre of my chest aches, but I don't allow it to show as I stand tall and just trying to catch her attention. The Queen speaks, giving me all the information I already have, but I don't know if I still want this. If there is a chance that Velasilio and I are fated do I want to pursue things with Searaphina? Just as the thought crosses my mind, we are made to kneel.

Stepping into my space, her delicate hands tie the blindfold around my head; her scent is floral. I had been so wrapped up in this deal, to ensure I had her hand, I haven't tried to get to know her. I know others have had private *meetings*, having the chance to find out if she is their twin flame before pursuing this further. That's what I should have done, that is what I will do when I return. I will fight for time with her and if there is nothing to this pull, I feel only sexual attraction. I will step down and see what may be between myself and Velasilio.

The Queen wishes us luck and both females leave.

We are given no instructions besides sit down and shut up while our hands are tied behind our backs. I am not usually one to get seasick but not being able to see while the boat rocks side to side is extremely unnerving. With no clue how much time has passed, we are finally released from our binds and told to remove our blindfolds and stand.

Black spots dance across my vision as daylight hits me. The sun has risen fully and now sits just before its peak. When my sight does finally return I look around, seeing the others, who also seem disoriented, all but Kadance. He stands toward the front of the boat with his wings open, soaking in the sun. He looks calm and relaxed like he has done this before. I wonder if he has. Thinking about it now he has had an uncanny ability to almost predict everything that has happened within the trials. I have received additional information, and still I feel lost.

The sound of a throat being cleared draws my attention. "Right, I am Captain Dorsin and I will not be docking at that island." Pointing to his left, I follow his finger to see the island that looks harmless.

The captain is short for a male, probably only just hitting six foot. His round belly suggests a comfortable life, with thinning hair and a gray beard, he must be south of his seven hundreds.

Rubbing at his beard, he continues. "Behind you is a collection of provisions to help you on your way, take what you need but you only have thirty minutes to do so. If you are not off my boat by then, you forfeit. If you do not return to the castle by night tomorrow evening then you will be presumed dead, or that you forfeited and returned home. If you wish to give up, say so now."

The air is silent, only the sounds of the birds cawing and the waves lapping at the side of the boat can be heard, as no one moves a muscle... until Buvariris steps forward. Interesting, I have not heard much from him this entire tournament.

His voice is higher than I anticipated as he speaks. "I will not continue in this elaborate charade. Our Queen is nothing but a harlot who whores herself out to anything that moves, she will not take any one husband, she has been spilling secrets to the entire kingdom and now I know." He pauses.

He casually strolls to the Captain's side. "I am only here to help you all see reason. This is nothing but a game to her. She is nothing but an evil, conniving, dirty..." Before he can spew any more lies about Searaphina, Dorsin punches him square in the jaw.

Bone crunches and blood flies from his mouth and nose. He does not land as, before he hits the deck, the captain takes his arm and leg, lifting him high above his head, and steps out, throwing him off the edge of the boat. A resounding whack can be heard as his body hits the water.

Feeling that my mouth is hanging open, I quickly close it. Swiftly, he turns on his heel and marches past us, muttering to himself. "No fae will speak ill of our Queen! What a pathetic excuse for a male."

Entering the Captain's cabin he slams the door behind him.

A hand lands on my shoulder. Fenterison wears a wide smile. "And then there were six. Well, time to get moving I guess." Laughing at his own joke, he moves past me towards the pile of items: food, weapons and other equipment to help us survive are laid out for the taking.

Something beautiful catches my eye: a large, double-ended battle axe with a wood handle wrapped in dark blue leather tied with a purple and green ribbon. My mind drifts back to the two females who have my attention. Knocking his shoulder into mine, Fen passes me a rucksack and a piece of flint.

"Best we take our fill, no telling what's waiting for us out there." Smiling at one another, we continue to take what might be needed. In the end, we walk away with a rucksack each, with enough food to sustain us for a day and a half, water skins, cotton to get a fire started, and string to tie together some kind of raft.

I watch Frekily and Meliena from the corner of my eye. They do not take many rations, options for weapons, or building materials. Their confidence must be high if they think they will be out of here by nightfall. Packing in silence, Frekily turns to us, nodding once before the pair take to the sky. Elanior is similar as she collects what she needs but does not speak before she leaves.

Fenterison watches with me as they land on the beach ahead. Pointing at them, he adds, "They are a bit chatty today." The comment catches me off guard and my laugh is genuine, one I feel like I won't hear for a while.

We leave the relative safety of the boat.

Tightening our bags, we nod at each other before we take flight. While gathering our items we discussed our plan, if all goes accordingly we should be back by early morning tomorrow. Kadance is the only one left as we soar away. He ignores the pile of resources and takes off not far behind us. He is either arrogant or has something up his sleeve.

CHAPTER 62

SURVIVAL

Arekin

DAY FOUR, TRIAL FOUR

The flight was short and we land on the white beach. As my boots touch down, they sink slightly. I snap my wings in to ensure they do not get coated with the sand, as it itches like crazy. The crystal blue water looks so refreshing; the sun has brought with it a mighty punch, so we will need to find water right away.

Strolling up to the tree line, we begin to make our way through the dense foliage. The underbrush is full of brambles that stick to my clothing and prick my skin. The large trees wind high above my head, providing shade to cool us from the sun. With no idea of where we are, I keep my axe ready. The eerie silence is only broken by the snapping of twigs under our feet. I am happy to have someone at my back, there could be any manner of creatures roaming these isolated forests.

After an hour of travel and no fresh water in sight, we take a break. Sitting on a fallen tree, I reach into my pack and remove some dried meat, offering it to Fen. Holding it up, he cheers as we begin to eat.

I ask, "So you were last with the Queen at the feast, what happened?"

Finishing off the food in his mouth, he smiles at me. "A gentle-male never tells."

Scoffing at him I reply, "You are absolutely no gentle-male and have never kept a sex secret from me since we met." Leveling him with a stare, he just rolls his eyes.

Standing abruptly, he wipes his hands down his pants. "Well, that will be a story for this evening, a little incentive for you. That is, if you want to know how sweet our dirty Queen's tight little pussy is." Raising his eyebrows, he pats my shoulder and begins to move through the bushes.

Shaking my head at his vulgar language, I stand and follow him.

It takes us another hour before we finally hear running water. Using my axe, I cut a path to the lake. The clearing almost seems unnatural as it is a semi-circle on this side of the river only.

Strange. Moving to the water, we both dip our waterskins in and fill them before we drink it all and repeat. When we are both satisfied, we start to make camp.

Feeling eyes on me, I hold out a hand to Fen, getting him to halt. Searching the area, I don't see or hear anything, neither does he as he mocks me.

"Aree relax, there is no vicious beast here. We would have run into one by now." Resuming his task to collect firewood, he chuckles at me.

Shaking my head at him, I retort, "I hate that name for one, and two, do you not feel like you are being watched?"

"Nope." Popping the 'P', he just keeps working. He is either stupid or ignoring it.

Deciding to follow his lead, I get on with our plan, as Fen sets up the fire and some sort of beds, with nothing but a thin blanket to lay on. I start to chop down the closest trees to build our raft. It will take us almost the entire night, but, if we take turns, we will be home before lunch is served.

Standing to my left, Fen watches me before he speaks. "If you keep this up, we should be finished by dawn with little sleep lost." Rolling my eyes at his words, I continue my task. When the large tree starts to crack, I step back. Making sure it falls the direction I want it too, I add one final cut. A loud crash echoes as the tree falls to the floor, a plume of dust spanning out in its wake.

This goes on for a few hours. I cut and trim the wood to size and Fen ties the logs together with rope. As the sun begins to set and our bodies heave with exhaustion, we bathe in the river to clean up before bed.

Our little clearing is no larger than a small bedchamber but, with the river at our backs, it does give me some peace of mind. With the last beams of light, we opt to take a break, seeing as we are ahead of schedule. We light the fire with the leftover twigs; the warmth is welcome against the cold darkness that is creeping in on us. It still feels like there are eyes on us, but Fen waves this off again. Sitting on a fallen log, we dig into another ration.

As night settles in, the sounds of nature lull me into a calm state: the fire crackles, crickets play their tune and the river runs in the background. Laying on my back, I watch as the moon rises, full and bright, not a cloud to be seen.

My tranquility is shattered as Fen opens his mouth.

"What does the Queen's handmaid taste like?" This has me sitting up immediately.

Trying to find the right words, he pushes on. "So I am right, how did you get such an innocent girl to agree to such a sordid affair?"

Staring at him, my mind is screaming at me that I need to protect her. I can't let him know that she is helping me, he thinks it's just sex so I need to keep him believing this.

I stumble over the first words before the lie rolls off my tongue.

"She approached me to see if I was her twin flame, as she had felt a pull towards me. I suggested we spend time together outside of the trials to see and, well, there seems to be no flame, that is why I am here. If she were mine we would have realised it by now." It all comes out in a rush of words, but once they are said I see that there is some truth to them.

Fen laughs at me before he replies. "That is understandable, she is such a fine little female. I bet her size makes it easy for you to throw her around. I bet she makes your cock extremely..." Before he can finish talking, a fierce protection takes hold and I find my anger rising at his words. I can't hold it back as I speak.

"I will not speak of her with such vulgar language!"

"Don't be like that!" Fen replies. "There is no one around for miles. I can tell you a fine story all about our fair Queen's dirty mouth and wet snatch if you would like. You should know that Buvariris was wrong, her pussy is well worth it."

I am now sitting completely upright and stiff, only two seconds from punching him. "I do not want to hear anything of the sort."

Waving me off, he goes on. "Do you think, if one was to marry the Queen, that both Her Majesty, and what's her name, Velasira..."

Grinding my teeth together, I correct him. "Her name is Velasilio and..." Before I can go further, Fen rampages on like a Xanvitor who has seen red.

"Ah yes, Velasilio, do you think they have ever been shared? They are so close, surely they would not be opposed to sharing a male, if they have not already. Oh Velasilio is so small I can see her tight little snatch squeezing my cock as I bounce her..." Using his hands to mimic a female straddling him, he acts like he holds her hips as he moves them up and down.

My blood boils at his complete lack of respect. "Shut the fuck up! They are not toys to be shared and if you continue to speak I will cut your tongue from your mouth!"

Fen holds up his hands with a humorless laugh. "Woah, sorry

Aree, didn't know that would be such a sore spot for you." With a wink, he stands.

"Fen that is not, you can't."

Suddenly, pressing his finger to his lips, he signals for me to be silent. Immediately on edge, I stand slowly and creep closer to him.

Waving his hand at me to stop moving he whispers, "Shh, we are being hunted, I feel it watching."

Holding perfectly still, we both scan the forest edge; it is hard to see anything in the dense shrubbery. When nothing can be seen or heard, we both sag and release our breath.

Tapping Fen's shoulder, I suggest, "Why don't I take the first watch, you can sleep and I will get a break from your vulgar mind." A hearty chuckle comes from Fen surprising me that he found that to be a joke. I didn't mean it as one; I need some time before I kill him myself.

Slapping me on the back, he remarks, "Aree your wit knows no bounds, wake me when the moon hits its apex and we can swap. You will need your sleep if you are to keep up with me tomorrow." Walking towards the bush, he calls out, "Gotta shake the snake." He is extremely loud as he crashes through the woodland, twigs snap and he swears to himself as he goes.

When it all stops, I thank Datriminish for the moment of quiet. Tuning my back on him, I move to the fire and place another log down. When he moves again, he sounds louder, more sloppy. Straining my ears, I listen closely; something sounds wrong.

Fen steps into the light, one hand around his throat and the other on his crotch. Seeping between his fingers dark blood runs down his chest and drops to the dirt in thick globs; his face is pale and his eyes wide in horror. Falling to his knees, he tries to speak, but it comes out as a gurgle just as a single line of dark red leaks from the corner of his mouth and down his chin. He sways back and forth before landing face first in the dirt. Frozen in place, I see a dark shadow step forward into the light, a terrifying smirk across his face.

CHAPTER 63

TIME TO KILL

Kadance

DAY FOUR, TRIAL FOUR

The only thing stopping me from ripping his spine out is the fun I will have watching him squirm before I bathe in his blood. Smiling to myself, I stand on the bow, soaking up the warmth of the sun; this is one thing I might actually miss. The sun shines, only for short periods of time in Vixeruas. There is no knowledge as to why this is, my mother told me many tales of the sun and how it used to shine favouring our lands.

Captain Dorsin did as requested and left me unbound; I have paid him handsomely for his assistance. Watching the other islands that pass, I know the exact route I need to take to return to my Gem. I will have my fun and be back to the island of Neraphina after the sun has fallen and the moon is high. There are answers hiding that I need to find before I can take her home.

I have been far too lenient with her and now she has bedded another. He will die for touching and tasting what does not belong to him and she will be punished. Though I have a feeling she will rather enjoy it. I have seen her darkness, it calls to my own. I am seeing now that my obsession might be more long term.

My skin prickles with the sensation of eyes on my back, not bothering to even glance at the others. I continue to relax. I will need all of my energy for the long night ahead. Nothing can disturb me, not even when Dorsin sends one of the males overboard for his wagging tongue.

Glancing over my shoulder I see the others still standing slack-jawed that seven has become six without stepping off the boat. Dorsin returns to his cabin, leaving the others to rummage through what they believe will save their lives. After they are satisfied with their choices, both of the rotters take off. Giving them some space, I wait before following; this will be the last time they see me until I want them too.

Flying into the treetops, I settle into one with thick foliage. Using my shadows, I surround myself in darkness. I stay hidden within the trees, following them. My joy increases as he seems to know I am here, looking over his shoulder multiple times. When they do finally find water and begin to set up camp I make my plan.

I wait until darkness has descended and they are at ease, feeling confident that they will complete their task and be home before the sun fully rises. That won't be happening. These voices carry over to me, grinding my teeth. I almost give into temptation and kill them both where they stand.

"Ah yes Velasilio, do you think they have ever been shared? They are so close, surely they would not be opposed to sharing a male, if they have not already. Oh Velasilio is so small I can see her tight little snatch squeezing my cock as I bounce her..."

The shadows scream out, flying past me and towards their camp, only stopping when the fire's light reaches them. Stepping forward, I remove my dagger, ready to plunge it into his heart and feel the warmth of his blood dripping down my wrist. Fortunately for me, I step on a twig, pulling me from my thoughts but also scaring both of them. Joy fills me as their fear fills the air, mixed with smoke and ash. The night is cooling rapidly, the animals know a predator is near as only the bugs are brave enough to stay and continue their tune, knowing they are far too small for me to think of.

After a moment, they settle back in, but I can see they are not quite as relaxed.

It sounds like he is trying to laugh away the problem. "Gotta shake the snake." I am presented with a perfect opportunity as the lumbering fool has all the grace of a newborn elephant as he crashes his way into the darkness, my home.

In absolute silence, I follow him, until he decides he has found the right spot. Pulling his trousers down past his ass, he removes his worm. Leaning one hand against the tree, he goes to urinate. Not ready to stop my fun just yet, I make sure to step firmly on a twig; the resounding snap echoes in the empty forest. His body stills as he turns his head ever so slowly and his eyes search the darkness for whatever is here. When he is satisfied he has seen nothing, his shoulders drop and he sighs in relief before returning to his business.

I shake my head at this idiot. He has not realised that the forest is now dead silent, not even the crickets play their songs. Palming my dagger I move to stand behind him; the sound of piss hitting the dirt and its stale stench fills the air. Disgust at being so close to such a pig fills me, so much so I have a slight change to my plan. Reaching around him, I place my blade where no male ever wants such a sharp item.

Freezing in place for a second before his shoulders relax, he chuffs to himself, "Aree buddy, I was only jesting."

'He doesn't know it's me, even better.' I am elated with this turn of events.

Leaning in slightly, I press my blade upwards, slicing into the delicate flesh of his balls. There is a sharp intake of a breath, and a line of hot blood drips down my hand.

With a calm voice, I state, "I might just take these as a gift, show the others what happens when they touch what is mine." I slice further with the word *mine.*

A whimper leaves his lips as he stutters, "I did no such thing." With both hands raised, I watch as they start to shake.

"Oh but your words would suggest otherwise. What was it you said you wished to do with her? *Share her.*" With each word I apply more pressure, severing the nerve endings and cutting through the delicate skin. Blood rushes to greet me as he whimpers, trying to muffle his cowardice.

When he does not speak, I take the final step and sever his balls from his body. Taking the chance, he throws his head back, colliding with my nose; the bone crunches as sweet crimson pours into my mouth. The taste of my own blood and pain fuels me. He makes it all in one step before I grasp his hair at the roots, ripping his head back and next to my face.

With our faces inches apart, I can see his wide eyes as they bore into my own, his hands wrap around mine, trying to get me to release him, scratching and breaking the skin, anything to get away.

Laughing at his feeble escape attempt, I smile, feeling the blood coating my teeth. "That was fun, what should we do next?"

I raise my hand holding the blade and tap it against the side of his lips in thought. "Ah, I know."

Moving the dagger so that the tip sits against his chin, I slowly drag it down his body; a thin red line follows in its wake. All the way to his little worm.

He begins to shake his head, pleading with me. "Please no! I won't look at her again, I won't touch her I swear!" His voice cracks as he weeps.

"Shhh, I don't want your friend to know what's coming his way." His eyes dart past me, trying to see the glow of their fire. We are not too far away, but with the help of my shadows his screams will not be heard.

His mouth opens to plead but all that comes out is a gurgled scream as I slice his limp dick from his body. Quickly, I bring the blade back to his throat, slicing across it, not deep enough to kill him straight away but enough that he will not be able to receive help or heal in time. Dragging him along, I set him at the edge of his camp, giving him a little push forward and into the fire's glow.

Lucky he turns in time; his face pales as horror takes over, watching his friend trying to hold the skin together as blood rushes out, coating his body; I don't think he has even noticed that some of it is not from his neck.

Laughing at the sight of the useless pair, I step into the light, my cheeks beginning to hurt. I don't normally smile this often but this has been fun, especially knowing that I am only hours from returning home to my Gem.

His voice is weak as he asks. "What... did you..." Aw no, he is struggling, I think I'll help him out.

"What I did was have some fun." Tilting my head to him, I wink.

Without care, I step towards him; he, in turn, takes one backwards. My face is in mock shock as I raise a blood-stained hand to my chest. "Oh, you wound me."

Turning in place, he rushes to get his axe from where it lays, against a tree. Laughing, I lunge after him.

CHAPTER 64

A NIGHT FOR THE FEMALES

Searaphina

NIGHT FOUR, TRIAL FOUR

For the love of Datriminish, today was boring. After we left the docks, we had tea in the garden and discussed a few final details for the ball, such as numbers, seating charts and a special surprise for Velasilio. My birthday is only eight days away and with it my wedding, whether that be to the winning competitor or some fae of the Council's choosing. I will be a very busy Queen for the next few days, so I want to have a private moment to relax before it all begins.

Standing in my chambers as night begins to fall, my royal guards bring in the large tub I had requested and two maids begin to fill it. The steam rises high above the rose petal water. Velasilio is resting as she mentioned a headache from the day but she will be here soon. I have five bottles of wine ready to go and the cook is preparing an assortment of nibbles for us. I will find out tonight what had happened with Arkein, she has avoided the subject all day.

Just as I wrap a silk robe over my bathing gown, a timid knock sounds. Looking over the rather impressive set up, the large storm bath seems to glow in the candle light as pink and red petals float along its surface; a small table has been set up filled with treats and wine. Satisfied with my hard work, I call out, "Enter." I am pleasantly surprised when Velasilio enters. Turning my back to her, I wave a hand towards our plans for the evening.

"I thought we may have a night to relax and talk about what has been bothering you. I know I have upset you but we must discuss it." When I return my gaze to her, standing just in the doorway, she rubs her hands up and down the sides of her arms. Only wearing a night-gown, she must have been freezing on the walk over.

Stepping towards her, I take her arm in my own and lead her to the fireplace. "Silio, are you cold?" Shaking her head, she looks up at me. It is then that I see her face is blotchy with rose hues, tears line her eyes, just waiting to fall.

Her lower lip trembles as she tries to speak. "What... What if he does not return."

Understanding who and what she means, I wrap her in my embrace, resting my chin atop of her head, rubbing my hand over her back and trying to speak with a calming voice.

"All will be well, do not fret, I did not know you were so close?" Her sniffling stops for the briefest moment as she tenses in my embrace before pulling away.

Crossing her arms, she tries to collect herself before replying. "Oh we are not, I am just emotional, my fever must be coming soon."

Cocking my eyebrow at her, I plant my hands on my hips. "I vow to always be honest and truthful, to never lie or cheat."

Her mouth pops open at my words. Holding my hands up, I retort, "You made me do it, you know our blood tie tells me if you are lying." A cheeky smile crosses my face but this seems to do the trick.

Looking to the closest chair, Velasilio picks up a cushion and hurls it at me all but yelling, "I did no such thing and you absolutely cannot tell if I am lying!" My smile falters for a moment as her words repeat back to me.

"You absolutely cannot tell if I am lying!" She sounds so sure, has she lied to me?

Shaking off the sinking feeling, I decide it is time to move on.

"Well, if it is your fever making you emotional, then it is good timing. If Arekin does return and is your twin flame, there will be no separating you. It will be like two Antiporse to a flame." Unfortunately I realise my mistake too late as her face falls.

On a whisper she says. "If... If he returns." Cursing my choice of words, I try to move the conversation along.

"There is no reason to dwell on things we cannot change, let us forget our troubles and enjoy this warm bath and delicious food and wine." Taking her elbow, I lead her to the steps.

We both disrobe and climb in; our bathing dresses allow some modesty. Reaching over, she takes two chalices and pours some wine. Passing me a glass, she raises her own in cheers. Drinking down the sweet liquid, it is a welcome chill to the heat of the bath. My mind wanders to thoughts of what my governesses used to say of a fever.

'Now Searaphina, child, you must listen. When your fever comes it will be a most joyous day, you will be able to finally produce an heir. If you have not found your fated, it will also be a time to search for them. All of your senses will be heightened and your sexual appetite will take control, it will be made clear that only suitable mates will be presented to you, for, once you lay with them, you may not stop for several hours or days. Your need for satisfaction and a child of your own will consume you. Another will only be able to withstand you for so long, once you reach the apex, around three to four days in, they will be unable to refuse you.'

A shudder works though me at the thought of having no control over my actions. I have been working with powerful healers to create a tea that will prevent a fever, if not fully at least to give me some senses. It is tricky to concoct, as both males and females will need to be able to take it.

Warm water hits my cheek; coming from my daydream, I see Velasilio waving a hand in front of my face.

"My apologies, I was lost in a memory." Plastering a smile on my face, I watch as hers falls, as she can see right through me.

Fiddling with a petal, she asks, "And what memory would this be?"

"Just about our fevers, if yours may be starting soon, mine should not be far behind." Nodding her head, she looks up and smiles at me.

We sit in silence for a time, just enjoying the food and drinking our wine, occasionally speaking of the events to come. Laying my head back and closing my eyes, I let my arms float. A throat clearing catches my attention.

Sitting upright, I look at Velasilio, who stares at me. "Yes?"

Lifting her hands from the water, she faces her palms towards me. "Am I supposed to be impressed by how quickly you are ageing?" Laughing at my own quip, I do not expect the flurry of water that heads my way.

Breathing in a large amount of liquid, I begin to cough and wheeze. Rushing forwards, Velasilio causes water to spill from the tub as she rubs my back and tries to apologise.

"Oh my I am so sorry, I didn't mean to. You will be okay." Her rather loud words must reach into the hallway.

My chamber doors burst open, hitting the walls behind them. Dezmond and Gregor come in with swords drawn. With my coughing under control before they enter, their sudden intrusion frightens us both, causing us to stand from the tub.

Gregor steps forward, his eyes surveying every inch of the room. "Your Majesty, is everything alright?"

After he is sure there are no intruders or would-be assassins his gaze lands on us; keeping his eyes high he does not balk at our near-naked state. Unfortunately, Dezmond does not have the same issue, eagerly pursuing Velasilio's body which, in her wet bathing gown, is almost completely on display. Using my arms to cover my more private areas, I sink back into the warmth of the water.

When Velasilio does not follow, I look up at her. She stands deathly still as her sight is set on Dezmond. Stepping forward, she does not look away, he does the same. Reaching up, I grab ahold of her bicep and pull her down, this seems to break her dream-like state. Gregor clips Dezmond over the back of the head when he does not avert his eyes.

Turning to face away he speaks, "Our apologies, we heard the commotion and wanted to ensure your safety, we will take our leave."

Grabbing Dezmond in a rather rough way, he drags him out, but not before we hear the most hilarious thing.

Trying to whisper, Dezmond leans in. "Sir, may I have a moment alone?"

All that we know is he receives another whack to his head before the door closes behind them. We burst into a fit of laughter, the kind that makes your stomach hurt. After a few hours, we have consumed all of the food and the wine, our bath is now cold but neither of us care as we enjoy the time together. Leaving the tub is a struggle as we almost land on our rear ends a few times but we eventually dress and crawl into my bed. The wolf pelts warm us quickly, as does the fire that is now almost to its embers. The evening is late and we should sleep. The competitors should return home tomorrow after midday.

I think this might be the only time she will be honest with me about Arekin.

Rolling to my side to face her I ask. "What is happening with Arekin?"

Her eyes almost bulge from her head at my question. Sitting up, she starts to toy with the fur.

I try to ease her mind. "Silio, I just wish to know the nature of your relationship. If he returns and chooses to continue the tournament, I do not want to see you hurt."

Her head whips around to mine as she searches my face before she relaxes and slides back down, leaning on her elbow and facing me. "We have not and I do not know if we will. He said we might if he returns but with only one trial left is it worth crossing that final boundary if he may marry you?"

Not wanting to get into the nitty gritty tonight, I opt to only answer part of her reply. With a smile, I slap her wrist and proclaim in mock horror. "Final boundary, what other boundaries have you crossed? Oh no, did he taste your honey pot?"

Her head falls back as she laughs at me. "Odd choice of words but, yes, he did, and nothing more. I only felt him over the top of his clothing." Pouting, she genuinely looks saddened by this; I do not understand that at all.

"Well... Was he at least good?"

"Oh yes, he was quite good."

"Not many males are. So when he returns, fuck him, simple." With that, I roll onto my back. Velasilio also rolls over, pulling the blankets high before she yawns, causing me to do the same.

Her words are tired as she shares her worries. "Phina, if he is my fated, how was he able to stop? With my fever only days away, the call would have been so strong."

Unsure of how to comfort her, I suggest the only thing I can think of. "Tomorrow we will have tea in the library and we can look for answers there."

Doubt and unease fill my head as I fall into a restless slumber. If he were truly her twin flame there is no way he would have been able to resist her. Could it have to do with the spark I have felt towards him?

CHAPTER 65

ENJOY THE SHOW

Kadance

NIGHT FOUR, TRIAL FOUR

With the filth dealt with, I can now return and claim my Gem. The journey back to Neraphina is easy and takes little strength, the moon sits high in the sky when I see the pointed roof of the white stone castle. Beginning my descent I am in a fantastic mood and cannot wait to see her. I do not enter the castle grounds, instead I make my way around the high walls and to her window. What I see has my mouth watering; she lays on her back with water and rose petals drifting around her.

Stepping into the room, I use the small amount of shadow to stay hidden in the far corner. From this angle, I can see that she wears naught but a cotton dress that has soaked through and is clinging to her breasts.

I have to adjust my cock as I take in her form, aching to take her here and now. My thoughts are halted as another voice speaks. Of course her companion is with her. The other female frustrates me so;

I will need a plan on how to rid us of her, unfortunately I cannot just kill her. I will not be the one to cause such pain to my Gem. No, I will need to be smart about how to handle this.

Tonight, I will return to my chambers and collect what little I have left. Take the time to rest as tomorrow is sure to bring its own challenges. Abducting such a well-known female will not go unnoticed, so I must plan it perfectly. I know where I will take her and we will have all the privacy in the world to get to know each other in every respect.

Her scent surrounds me, calling to me like a Siren's song. I need to leave before I do something stupid like take a dagger to her companion's heart and fuck my Gem like an animal while covered in blood. The thought has my cock pressing against my pants. I enjoy the show for just a second longer, before tearing my gaze away. A burning in my chest has me wishing I didn't.

CHAPTER 66

AHHH WINE

Velasilio

DAY FIVE, TRIAL FOUR

"Shut the fuck up!!" The curse spills from my lips as the usually sweet birds' songs cause me great pain instead. Rolling in bed, I pull the silk sheets over my head; the quick movement has my stomach unhappy, sending a thick acid into my throat. Swallowing it back down, I shiver at the feeling.

Laying completely still, I breathe in through my nose and out through my mouth. I count to ten. Once I no longer feel as though my stomach will revolt against me, I slowly move into a sitting position. Blinking my eyes open, the sun streams in, feeling like a thousand tiny daggers stabbing behind my eyes. Reaching up, I massage my temples in hopes it will subside. When it does not, I throw my arms up and finally open my eyes fully.

"Curse that wretched wine!" I must have fallen asleep on Searaphina's bed last evening. I remember we spoke in length about Arekin and her own possible suitor in Fenterison or Elanior; both have kept the secret that she 'spilled' for the fifth trial. A way to ensure that the royal consort will be loyal, even before they are crowned.

Those who have shared the secrets will be eliminated from the tournament. The first competitor to return tomorrow evening will be the new royal consort, only none of them know this. We also spoke of why I was so angry with her and she tried to get me to see reason but I still feel an anger inside of me at her choices.

But with the tournament coming to an end and her marrying, I will be given more freedom as she will spend more time with them, I will use the space to visit my family again. I will sleep in a tent on the grounds and they will have to speak with me. Cupping my face, I wipe the sleep from my eyes and stretch out my muscles in hopes my body will wake; at that moment the door to the bathing chambers opens a delightful scent of roses and lavender float in the air.

"I see you have finally roused from your slumber, it is time we head to the library and see if we can find you the answers you seek." Taking a seat at her vanity she chooses her jewels for the day. She picks a delicate, silver chain necklace with a single emerald hanging in the centre, it is as fine as she.

Frustration wells inside of me at her upbeat mood. "My dislike for you is at its peak this morning; why do you never seem to be affected in the morning from the wine?" Throwing my arm over my face, I shield my eyes.

Her laughter is light and airy. "I would be feeling the same as you, had I also had three bottles, but alas I was smart and only had two!" Peeking under my arm, I see her smile is bright as she stands and makes her way over to me. Our conversation halts as there is a knock on the door.

"Enter."

"My Queen." A maid enters. With a small curtsy, she continues. "Tea is being prepared for your breakfast in the library. When you would like it, just call one of us and we will fetch it."

"Thank you, we will be along shortly." When the doors close, she does not come towards me again, instead she points to the bathing chambers.

Standing, I see that I am in nothing but my nightgown, remembering that I only wore an overcoat here. In turn to Searaphina and explain. "I will need to return to my own chambers, I have no dress with me."

Without looking at me, she takes her seat once more at the vanity and brushes her long, scarlet hair before she commands, "Do not be silly, bathe here. I have a fresh gown for you." I go to interrupt and refuse but she stops me with a hand out.

"No need to thank me, just go and bathe, I want to start the day." Dismissing me, I have no choice but to do as she requests.

When I exit the bathing chambers, I feel somewhat better. My head still pounds, but at least I do not feel like I will throw up. Searaphina stands in front of me in the most dazzling gown.

The gown is emerald, a corset bodice that has a deep V showing almost all the way down to her navel, the sheer fabric holding it together does add some modesty. Thousands of tiny crystals are in intricate patterns covering the corset. Hanging from her shoulders are two loose, tulle sleeves; they looked so delicate. The skirt is thin, with no petticoat and a slit that went from her toe to mid thigh. When she notices me staring, she does a little spin, the skirt looks as though it had been painted onto her bottom.

"Phina, that is the most remarkable gown I have ever seen. You sparkle with each step."

"Thank you Silio, wait until you see *your* gown!" Stepping to the side, I see the dress.

I do not know what to say. Reaching out, I tenderly touch the gown, worried I may damage the sophisticated work. Before I can thank her, she continues.

"It is a thank you for always standing by me and being a true and loyal friend. Besides, I thought it would be good to dress up for the competitors' return." Guilt rises in my throat; I am no such thing. I have betrayed her trust. Before I say anything, she claps her hands and two maids rush into the room.

"It is time that someone helps *you* dress for a change." Taking a seat on the bed's edge, she waits while the maids assist me.

With a flurry of motion and words, I am stepping into the gown as it is pulled up my body and tied tight. My breasts are pushed up more than usual, something cold is pressed against my chest and I jump at the feeling. Reaching up, I feel the necklace that sits against my throat as a choker with a single amethyst hanging in the centre.

Before I know what has happened, they sit me down at the vanity, brushing my hair out. Taking two sections, they pull it back and tie it loosely before pulling out two tendrils to hang down, framing my face. My cheeks are pinched until rosy and black chalk is applied under my eyes. The makeup feels heavy and has me blinking.

With a clap of her hands, Searaphina sends the maid scurrying away. She takes my hand and leads me to the floor-length mirror. I am shocked by what I see. The gown is a lovely periwinkle colour with silver thread throughout.

The bodice is similar to Searaphina's but the V is not as deep, only hitting to the bottom of my breasts, lucky it has a similar sheer fabric. There are crystals on the bodice, though not as many, and the designer has used stitching to provide the intricate pattern. The sleeves are loose and hang from my shoulders, hitting my elbows. The tight skirt has a sparkle to it each time I move, it only allows movement because of the slit in the leg that reaches my knee.

My hands move towards my face but I stop myself, careful not to ruin the maid's beautiful work. "Searaphina... I cannot accept this, it is too much." I know that this is her attempt to make amends between us, and it may have just worked a small amount.

Shaking her head, she asks, "You can and will, now we must go. We are wasting daylight and they could return at a time." My smile is wide as I look down again; when I return my gaze to her she laughs at me.

"Stop grinning like a lunatic, you do not have your canines yet so it is not scary, just creepy."

Our stroll to the library is relaxing;' the darkness is a welcome retreat from the sun in the darkened corridors. I cannot escape the feeling of eyes on me; looking over my shoulder I see not a soul, only the four Queens guards who follow as usual. My eyes meet Dezmond's and I smile. He quickly looks anywhere but at me. Strange.

CHAPTER 67
THE LIBRARY

Searaphina

DAY FIVE, TRIAL FOUR

It has been a few years since I have come to the library. Velasilio visited a few days ago looking for any information regarding the blood tie. It was my father's favourite place and he used to bring me here to read me a bedtime story.

With high, glass ceilings, the sun shines in, and at night the room is perfect to stargaze. Along the left and right walls are mosaic windows, when the sun shines the room is bathed in greens, blues and yellows, making the space feel magical. There are rows upon rows of shelves laden with so many books that they now sit in stacks at the bases. A long ladder is required if you want to reach the top books.

We sit at the front of the library on one of the many reading tables, this one is closest to the fire and atop a skin rug; it was also the same one Velasilio has been using so there were already a few books sitting here waiting for us. Sneezing for the third time in as many minutes, I cannot deal with this any longer, each dusty page only makes it worse.

Standing abruptly, I move towards the windows. "We must open a window or I may lose my mind from all this dust." My shoes clack along the white marble flooring. Unlatching the first three windows closest to us, I smile to myself as the cool fresh air enters.

I look over at Velasilio who still has her nose buried in a book, she has been searching for information on the blood tie and twin flames. I decide to stretch my legs and take a stroll through the shelves. More memories of my father surface.

I often wondered if he loved them more than me. He always said, *"There is never a question that cannot be answered by these books. One day these will be yours and you must treat them with respect."*

The respect I showed was to not have the entire chamber destroyed. I knew I might need them one day but I mostly found answers in other scriptures, ones that we do not keep here.

A loud thump startles me from the memories. Whipping my head around, I see Velasilio throw her hands up in defeat. "Nothing again! They speak of a twin flame bursting when you become intimate, or at least the pull being so strong that you are unable to walk away. But nothing as to why he was able to pull away! Maybe he is not my fated." The next thump is her head hitting the pile of books on the table in front of her.

I decide to send for tea. "Gregor." The large door is pushed open as he steps through.

"How may I assist you, my Queen?" Bowing deeply, he waits.

"You can tell the kitchen we are ready for our tea and to add some chamomile. Oh, and have them bring the sugar snaps coated in that thick, sweet, coating."

Quirking a brow, he looks to Velasilio, whose head is still on the table. With a nod, he strides towards the door. He mumbles something to the others before he closes the door. When I turn around Velasilio is no longer in her seat; I hear a delicate sneeze coming from the shelves. Moving in the direction I heard her, I call out, but she does not answer, so I continue to look. I had not realised these stacks go so far back, I feel like I am in the labyrinth. Stopping to listen for her, my breath hitches and I go still. Did I hear someone?

I do not move a single muscle as I try to listen, when nothing comes I keep going until I hear it—only just, but it sounds like a heavy footstep and then it is followed by a bone-chilling scream. "PHINA!"

My feet move faster than I ever thought possible, a sense of dread washes over me, and I feel as though something or someone is racing me to get to her.

I stop dead in my tracks; our blood tie should lead me to her a fun trick we have learnt over the years. I take a moment to focus on her. There, a faint tug, it is not as strong as a soul bond but it will do. I take off in a sprint. Perspiration has gathered on my brow. I feel a dark presence at my back, gaining on every step, my lungs ache and my heart feels like it will explode. I almost fall as I round a corner, turning down another stack, and that's when I see it...

CHAPTER 68

DARK SECRETS AND MEMORIES

Kadance

DAY FIVE, TRIAL FOUR

Something is not right with the bond my Gem shares with her companion; there is a foul stench that follows the two of them. Something evil, and not the fun kind. It calls to my own power but not the darkness that protects me. No, this is something even I don't often play with.

I have some access to some of the most depraved magic, the kind of spells that void free will and only take, never giving in return. Lucky I am a true born shadow fae, so the connection I have with my shadows and the beast inside are that of family lineage not blood magic.

With everything taken care of, it is time for me to get the answers I need. Flying up to her window, I peek inside, making sure there are no others here. When I am certain, I step though. Her sweet scent calls to me, irritation fills me at not having her here and being able to sink into her. Without thinking, I stride to her bed, flipping the mattress off and sending it across the room. Next, I move to the desk, pulling out the drawers, flipping them upside down and letting the contents fall to the ground.

I shift through the ink pots, pens, parchment and letters, reading through some of them. Nothing but correspondence to balls, feast and love letters from suitors.

Reading the sordid details, my anger only grows. Reaching out and grabbing the edge of the desk, I throw it to the ground. The sound of wood splintering makes my lips twitch in a smile. It was not my intention to destroy all her items but my patience has worn thin, and I can no longer hide my true nature. Besides, she will know all about it soon enough. Running my tongue over my teeth, I nick it on one of my canines, and the metallic taste lingers on my tongue. I think about when I will get to mark her as mine.

I don't know if they do the same here; if they don't, they are really missing out.

The vision sits in the front of my mind: me laying on my back with her straddling me, my cock buried deep inside her. Sitting up, I brush her hair to the side, running my tongue along her delicate skin, causing her to shiver before I sink my fangs into her sensitive flesh. I can almost feel her cunt squeezing me.

My pants have grown tight as I let my desire run wild. Shaking off the new ideas, I smile to myself. My plans will have to wait, I need to return to my task.

"If I were a dirty little secret, where would I be?"

I turn over every item of furniture and still nothing. My irritation doubles. If what I suspect is correct, I don't know what I will do. It will take everything I have to save her. I am sure that her companion knows what is going on.

It is as if the answer has been staring at me this whole time, laughing at me. Her companion must be hiding it. With this thought, I leave the now-upturned chambers. There are no others in the corridor as I enter. Their rooms are only a few steps away from one another's; as I push the door in I hear two voices to my left. Quickly stepping inside, I leave the door slightly ajar. The two young maids casually walk past, their voices carrying over to me.

"They were both in the bath in only their cotton dresses."

"Together?"

"Yes, upon hearing a scream the guards rushed inside the chambers."

"What was the commotion for?"

"I am unaware, but the guard Dezmond asked to be excused after."

"And what did he do?"

"Nothing, the older guard Gregor made him stand in shame at the door."

They squeal and begin to giggle like the children they are.

Adding this Dezmond to my kill list, I close the door and begin my search. This time, I don't care what breaks or who hears me. If what I need is here, I have to find it. Focusing on the mattress first, I pull a blade from my thigh. Striking down, feathers rise into the air as I run my blade through the silk sheets. Once the cut is made, I reach in to see if there is anything inside before it goes flying across the room. Striding across the room, sweeping my arm over the top of the vanity, bottles of perfumes and other various female crap goes flying, most shattering on impact.

Looking down at the mess I have made I laugh to myself. "That felt fan-fucking-tastic."

My head swings to the dresses next. My feet are loud against the stone as I stride over and remove all of the clothing, tossing them to the floor. I reach inside the empty space, trying to see if anything is stuck to the top or sides. When I don't find anything, my frustration boils over.

"Where the fuck is it!" Throwing up my hands, I head into the bathing chambers where I upturn the bath; it fractures, hitting the stone floors. There is not much else in here, so I move back into the main chamber. Going to the vanity again I place my hand at the back of it and push it forward.

I realize too late that there was a mirror inside and as the wood splitters it falls from the frame, landing on the stone. The mirror spiderwebs before it shatters.

My mother always said, *"Never break a mirror, they are a window into our souls, hiding our deepest darkest fears. To shatter one is to ask for these to come true."*

I stare at the mess for a moment before shrugging it off; it is nothing but a superstition my mother always believed in. Though I can't shake the coldness that wraps around me for only a second before it leaves. When there is nothing left to destroy, I turn to leave. Stopping in my tracks, I look down. The floor is covered in glass, yet I don't hear the signature crunch under my boots. Kneeling, I pick up a piece. Looking it over, the edges look sharp but don't cut me. Placing it in my palm I squeeze it; opening my hand I see only a translucent powder.

I pick up the broken vanity, only a small amount if the 'glass' hangs from its framing. Just behind it sits a hidden compartment that has fallen open, hanging from it is an old string. Opening it further, I see the one thing I am terrified of.

"Fuck!" I throw the small book as if it has burned my skin as the memories flood me.

Looking down at my mother, her eyes are filled with tears as she raises a single hand to touch my face. "Mother. Are you okay?"

Her voice catches as she tries to speak. "All will be fine my son, now go and find your father."

When I come back to, I am on my hands and knees, the nasty little book right in front of my face. I cannot stop the snarl that comes from me, the memories causing physical pain. Before I stand, I notice a page seems to have come loose. Picking up the book, I remove the paper to read it.

BLOOD TIES.

Loyalty, Trust, Love and Death. To complete the blood tie, you must cut your palm with the same knife and bleed together, reciting the vow below, only one needs to vow for the two to become one.

I willingly bind my blood to yours, in trust, loyalty and love. I will never harm you through words, action or mind. We will be as one. If you are to lose your life, I will follow you into the dark. None will take your place.

I vow that my life, soul and body are yours to protect and serve you always.

My wings fly out as I roar. "FUCKING BLOOD MAGIC! She has been fooled!" I do what I can to not scrunch the parchment. I might need it for her to see the truth. Shoving both items into the satchel at my hip, I am unable to pull my wings all the way in when in such an agitated state, so I tuck them back as I make my way to the door.

Just then, I see a young maid, who seems paralysed with her mouth hanging open in a silent scream. Quickly closing the distance between us, I clamp my hand across her open mouth.

With my voice quiet, I demand, "Where is she?" Pulling my hand down slightly, I let her speak.

"Sh...Sh...She's in the library." She tries to swallow as tears slowly track down her face.

Nodding at her, I don't move my hand away just in case she does something stupid. "Is she alone?"

Shaking her head, she speaks again. "No, there are four guards with her."

Dropping down, I get closer to her face. "And her companion, is she there as well?"

She takes a moment to speak. Seeming to weigh her options. "Yes, they are always together."

Covering her mouth once more I remove a single dagger bringing it to her face. I gently tap it on her forehead and I threaten, "Speak of this and I will find you. Trust me on this, you don't want that."

As soon as the words leave my mouth, she faints, falling to the side, I watch as she goes. When she is laying there I check that she still breathes before I step over her and close the door behind me. With the answers I need, it's time to find my Gem and take her home.

CHAPTER 69

LIGHT STALKING

Kadance

DAY FIVE, TRIAL FOUR

Standing at the end of the long corridor, I take in the sight before me. Three guards stand by the door. Three new toys.

Taking out a blade, I step to the wall and run it up the stone. I watch as they seem to debate who has to come and investigate.

Finally one of them begins to stroll down.

I use the dim lighting to my advantage, having my shadows hide me from sight. Once they have walked past, I move behind him, raising my blade to his throat. He barely gets out a plea for help before the skin of his neck is split and warm blood soaks into his clothing. Before his body slumps to the floor, I grab the collar of this uniform and lower him slowly.

"Onree? Is everything okay?" A female voice calls out, just before I hear footsteps headed in our direction.

Deciding to have a little more fun, I leave Onree in the middle of the floor. I hide myself again.

She draws her sword at seeing a body on the ground.

"Who goes there?" Her voice seems to shake as she speaks, I wonder if she has ever actually been in battle.

Her steps are slow and deliberate, with her sword ready as she approaches the body. Kneeling next to him she shakes him. When he does not move, she yells.

"Dezmond! Protect the—" She stops mid-sentence and stands quickly when I step up to her. I smile like a predator ready to have some fun.

Tilting my head, I mock her. "Oh no, was he your friend?"

"You! What are you doing here? Did you?" She looks back at the lifeless body. "Did you kill him?"

I look down at the body and then back to her. "Yes I did. If you don't wish to join him, lay down your weapon and leave."

She hesitates. I watch as she adjusts her grip on the sword before her brow sets in a hard line. Standing quickly, she raises her sword. She speaks with confidence as she challenges, "Why would I do that? Scared to hurt a female?" There is a slight huff to her as she readies for attack.

Pulling another blade from my leg, I raise a single brow. "I thought I would at least give you the chance to leave with your life."

"Not interested." With that, she lunges for me.

Her short sword is aimed at my gut, for maximum damage. Dodging the attack, I swipe out with my own blade as she falters. Raising her weapon again, she calls out as she rushes me, slashing through the air. Lifting my blade, I push back; metal slides against metal as the sword is flung behind her. She may have had a large weapon but I have more strength and skill. Her head stays square on me as the blade clatters to the floor.

Another voice calls out. "What is going on down there? Cassidie, do you need me?"

"NO! Protect the Queen." She slightly turns her head to look up the corridor at that male.

With her guard dropped I step forward sinking my dagger into her gut, her hands wrap around the hilt as she screams. Our faces only inches apart now I lean in to whisper. "No one will stand in my way."

Releasing the dagger, I walk away, listening to the sound of her falling to her knees. Her gurgled protest is muffled as I stroll towards the large doors; just as they begin to close, the faint outline of a male can be seen. Picking up my pace, I reach into the small gap, pulling him back out. He tries to call out and warn my Gem of her fate. Wrapping my forearm around his neck, I squeeze. His eyes are wide with fear as he claws at my arm, trying to get me to realise him.

"Shh, time for a little nap." His movements slow as his face turns a pale blue. Dropping him like a sack of potatoes, I leave him outside and step into the space.

Looking at all the grand—if not a bit overflowing—library, I don't see her anywhere. To my left is a desk set up near the fire with books and parchments sprawled out; curiosity gets the better of me so I go over to read what it is they are here for. The books are all read about fevers and twin flames and there are several notes written in her impeccable handwriting, all in regards to a fated being able to leave his mate when she is in a fever. I know that hers will begin within the next few weeks, as will her companion's. They are born so close together, they may even trigger each other to go into their first fevers. If she is close, I need to get her far away from here.

It will make my plan a bit easier; she will not be able to resist the only male in sight. My perusing is halted when I hear a shout in the hall. How many guards was it, three or four? Deciding it's not time just yet to frighten her, I quickly move to the doors and step out. I see a gray haired guard is bent over the two bodies trying to find a pulse. On silent feet I move behind him. He holds Cassidie, who is still breathing, but it's shallow. I guess leaving the dagger in may have stopped the bleeding. Interesting.

Pulling another blade free, her eyes lock onto me and go wide, she tries to call out but can't. With one quick jab, I ram the knife into his neck. Reaching for the blade, he cries out. His hands go to the blade trying to hold it in place. Ripping the blade free, I stand as he falls to his side. He might survive this; it will depend on his healing.

"Best hold pressure you two, if you want to live." Before I leave them, I look down to see a tray with tea and food, knowing this will aid in my plan. I pick it up before turning my back to them and walking to the library, ready to finally take what is mine.

Knowing she is not at her desk, I turn to the long, dark shelving. I wonder if she has found her way into the very depths of the stacks. Stepping forward, her sweet scent reaches me, mixed in with her companion's. Walking in between the shelves, I begin my search, following her scent. I hear footsteps and follow them, but then I smell something else. Something I have not smelt for many years.

Fear grips me as a scream rings out.

"PHINA!"

CHAPTER 70

WHAT IS THAT?

Searaphina

DAY FIVE, TRIAL FOUR

My head pounds with each beat of my heart, bent at the waist. I try to catch my breath. Velasilio sits with her back against a stack and many more books scattered around her as if thrown down with little care. Her legs are crossed and she has her head down, paying me no attention.

Breathing in short, shallow pants, I struggle to speak. "Silio... You... Scream... Like that."

Her head whips to me and away from the odd creature currently nestled in her lap. With a finger pressed to her lips, she whisper-yells at me. "Shhh! You will wake him."

Standing quickly, my hands shoot up in defence as I whisper back, "I did not see..." There is little lighting this deep into the shelves, so it is hard to see at first, but then something moves. "What is it?" I step back, not wanting to be bitten.

Laughing, she reaches between her legs and picks up the thing.

She holds it up for me to see; its mouth is open wide in a yawn as we disturbed its slumber. When it does close its mouth, it stares up at me: two large, red eyes, a button nose and two large ears that have pointed tips. Its face and the scruff of its neck are all a light gray, where the rest of it seems to be black, short fur, its two front paws hanging as Velasilio grips it under them. I see two back legs and what seems to be a long bushy tail tipped in the same gray. Then I catch just a hint of a black and purple wing, only small but there. Wriggling in her grasp, it all but tells her it is finished with this meeting. Bringing it to her chest, she coos at it while it makes an odd chittering as if in answer.

Gently, she places it back in her lap. It does three little circles before lying down with its head resting on her knee, watching me. Velasilio gives it a final pat before looking back at me. I quickly school my features, knowing that I am currently looking at her with my 'did you really scare me half to death over some odd beast' face.

Her smile is wide and her eyes full of joy as she speaks. "Is he not just the most adorable little creature!"

Slowly, I lower myself to sit on my knees in front of her but keep distance between me and the thing, as I do not want to get bitten. My voice is unsure as I question, "Yes it is, but where did it come from and what is it?"

Her eyebrows shoot up and her mouth drops open before she reaches out and covers the thing's ears. Her brow furrows and she purses her lips before she tells me off. "He is not an *it*!"

"Okay then what is... he?" I throw back at her. "And, again, where did he come from?"

Her hands slip from his ears and she begins to slowly stroke him with one; it begins to purr. Her other hand moves to her chin, rubbing at it while she thinks. Suddenly, she turns her head, looking into one of the stacks. Following her eyes, I see what she is looking at.

The beast has created its own little den of sorts. There are many books all torn and shredded, used for bedding, an obvious indent where it must curl up at night.

Looking back at each other, Velasilio only smiles more. "He must have been living here. I assume, as none have entered the library in so long, he must have snuck in. That must be why there are no vermin in here." Continuing to pat him, she praises him for being such a good boy.

Pinching the bridge of my nose, I give my head a slight shake, not sure how to handle this. Pressing on, I ask again, "So what is he?"

Her hand stills as she looks back to me before dropping to the stacks of books around us. "I am not sure but we are in the perfect place to find out. But he does need a name!"

Shaking my head, I try to reason with her. "Silio, you cannot name him, you are already too attached and we do not know what it..." She looks at me with pure fire so I amend my statement. "Agh fine, *he*, we do not know what he is. He could be dangerous."

Leaning forward, she gently places her hands under his chin and brings its face next to her own before adding with a mushy voice, "Look at this face! Does he look dangerous to you?"

Just as I go to agree and add that looks can be deceiving, it yawns again, only this time, two rows of razor sharp teeth descend. The little thing almost looks like it smiles at me before they go back into its gums.

I look from the creature back to Velasilio. Unsure if I am going mad or not, I ask, "Have you seen its teeth?"

Picking it up she turns it to face her as she inquires. "I did not know you had teeth, can you show me?" She speaks to it as if it understands.

Sometimes, I really cannot believe this female. "Silio, put it down before it bites you." She gasps as snuggles it into her chest, eyebrows downturned and lips pursed.

"That is it, he needs a name so you can stop calling him *it*!"

Looking all around, she seems to search for a name. This should be good. I wait patiently.

"That is it! His name is Nook." Her smile is wide. Laughing at her, I know it would be a losing battle, so I just stand.

Offering her my hand, I respond, "Okay fine, you may keep Nook for now. But if he harms any others, we will need to find him a new home." Taking my hand, I pull her and Nook up.

We speak about where he will sleep and what he may eat as we move back to our study table. Our tea sits on the table, hot with fresh sugar snaps, some with a dark sweet coating. Taking our seats, she keeps him on her lap as she breaks off a piece of her biscuit and offers it to him. I say nothing and lift my tea, taking a sip, after Nook sniffs the food, he is careful to take it from her without harming her. Maybe he will be a good pet.

Taking a sip of her own tea, she asks, "Phina did they add something new to our tea, it has a different taste than usual?"

"I had asked for chamomile to help with any symptoms you get from a fever. I have noticed that I have begun to feel some of the effects myself and thought it prudent to get ahead of things.

"Oh, if we get them together, at least we will not be lonely while the other is off enjoying themselves." With a wink, Velasilio raises her tea in cheers.

We both sip our tea. Velasilio goes to speak again but her voice wavers, as she calls out to me, "Phina, who is that?" Nook leaps from her lap onto the table and begins to growl. I try to stand, using the table to hold myself up.

I try to call out, but the words die on my tongue just as the shadows move towards me. My eyes dart back to Velasilio as she tries to stand as well, when suddenly, we both go down. The last thing I hear is a gravelly voice that consumes me, making my skin pebble and my stomach hollow.

"Time to go."

CHAPTER 71

TO TAKE WHAT IS MINE!

Kadance

DAY FIVE, TRIAL FOUR

When I followed the scream, the last thing I had expected to see was a Trelkin. In their youth, they are gentle and loving but as they grow so does their aggression and their taste for flesh. I keep my distance, so I don't know what is said, but they have finally returned to their tea.

I stand in the darkness at the end of a shelf, listening to their conversation. Slowly, they drink but it doesn't take long for the special ingredient to take effect. Just as they raise their cups, I see them fall. They both try to stand. I move forward on silent feet; they must see me from the corner of their eyes as they seem to panic. I can't help but chuckle at the feeble attempt to escape. The Trelkin growls at me but I pay it no mind, all that it could do right now is take a small chunk of flesh.

When I hear the guards called I laugh; no one will be able to stop me now. Moving in, I say. "Time to go."

Just as I reach her, they both fall. I catch my Gem, wrapping one arm around her back and the other under her knees, pulling her close to my chest. I inhale her sweet scent as her companion hits the floor with a thud. I pay her no mind as I turn and stride towards the closest window. Pushing it wide, I unfurl my wings. The sound of a whining comes from behind me. Ignoring it, I take flight. It won't take long to get her home.

CHAPTER 72

WHAT HAPPENED?

Arekin

DAY FIVE, TRIAL FOUR

*E*verything hurts. I lay face down on the ground. I open my eyes and the bright sun feels like it is trying to kill me as pain radiates from behind my eyes to my head. Pushing up on my forearms, something sticky brings dirt and twigs with me. Reaching up, I feel the dried blood that coats half my face, my hair is stiff and unmoving and, just as I reach the right side, agony shoots through me as warm blood leaves my side.

I lift my hand to feel a blade still inside me. Gripping the handle, I breathe in and hold it as I rip the blade free. Placing my hand over the wound, I pull my hand away and instead use it to push myself up and slowly get into a kneeling position.

My body revolts, sending me to my hands and knees and dry reaching as there is nothing in my stomach to come up. Acid burns my throat before I lay flat on my left side, avoiding my sick. Rolling onto my back, I try to breathe through it.

Something wet lands on my face, causing my eyes to shoot open. I must have fallen asleep; looking at the sky I see that the sun is well past noon and starting its descent. When something fluffy touches my face, I sit up; my vision blurs and my head spins at the sudden moment. Closing my eyes tightly, I breathe in through my nose and out through my mouth. When the nausea subsides, I open my eyes to see the small, fluffy Shenairahs sitting on their haunches, trying to get a look at me.

They are such small creatures and yet so long, their red and black fur covers their entire bodies. They are no taller than my ankle but as long as my forearm, their little round ears and pointed noses are made cuter by their large, pure black eyes. I manage a small smile.

"Hey little guys, do you know what..." I don't finish my sentence as an onslaught of memories hits me like a charging Xanvitor. My head whips from side to side as I try to see him.

"FEN!" Screaming his name, I wait for his reply. When I don't hear anything, I stand, looking for him.

'The tree line. He was in the tree line.' Clarity hits with the thought and I swing my gaze to the edge of our camp. There I see him, lying face first with a dark pool of dried blood under him.

I want to move to him but my feet lock in place. I don't understand why until the Shenariah scatter, running in all directions as quickly as they can. The wind stills and not a single sound can be heard, the sun seems to hide away without a cloud in the sky. The temperature drops several degrees and then the wind starts again, only, this time, carrying the most pungent scent of death. My gaze searches the bushes and, just as I think it's all in my head, I see a very large shadow.

My feet finally move in the opposite direction of Fen. I reach a tree, hiding behind it, but I know this is not enough. If it smells the dried blood on my clothing, I am dead; thankfully, when I passed out, the blood clotted and dried, though my shirt is now stuck to my body. I look around for a weapon but can't see anything besides a small dagger. What good is that? Looking up, I see a branch not far from my reach.

The steady thumping of heavy paws surrounds me, causing my heart to beat faster. Before I climb, I peek from around the tree.

The Deathwhisper is on its back legs, sniffing the air. Just then, the breeze changes and I feel it blow past me, carrying my scent to the beast. Dropping onto all fours, it growls before moving towards me again.

"Fuck!" The word leaves my mouth before I have time to stop it.

Reaching on my toes, I try to get a hold of the branch; my fingers just graze it as a twig snaps nearby.

I can't reach it.

Icy dread runs down my spine.

Not daring to look again, I bend at the knee and jump with everything I have. My hand makes contact just as the beast roars. Gripping the branch tightly as the nails on my other hand dig into the bark, I lift with all of my strength.

Finally, I am able to get my elbow and other hand on as well and reach for the next branch. Bringing my legs up next, I continue to climb, refusing to look down. I don't know if it can climb, but I am sure as hell not giving it an easy meal. When I feel that I am high enough, I dare to look, but there is nothing below me. And then I hear it.

Skin tearing and bone crunching. I look to my left and see a grotesque scene below me.

The sharp claws of the beast shred Fen's skin like butter as its snout is covered in his blood, chewing on his leg. Lifting its head, blood drips from its jaw as skin and cloth hang between its jagged teeth. Sniffing the air again, it must feel another coming; not wanting to share its dinner, it goes to drag Fen away by the leg it was eating. Only, the bone snaps in two and the skin tears.

Dropping the lower half of the leg, it steps forward and sinks its teeth into his gut before it carries him away, leaving nothing but the dark red stain and congealed blood.

With the beast satisfied and who knows what is coming, I decide it's time to leave. As I find a suitable branch to launch from I remember the last face I saw. Kadance!

He is after the Queen, he might hurt Velasilio if she tries to protect the Queen. I have to warn them all. I don't know how far the kingdom is, but I will do everything I can, even swim, to get back.

The journey is long and gruelling and I luckily find a few very small islands to rest at only for a few minutes.

My wings ache and struggle to keep me up. I fly low and try to keep a constant speed.

Finally, a blur of land is ahead and I hope it is Neraphina.

My absolute joy at seeing the kingdom is nothing I have ever felt before. Landing in a small village, I have water and the bread the older females demand I eat before I am given directions to the castle. It's still a two hour flight; the sky is now painted in hues of orange and red. Time is running out.

Finally, the castle comes into view. The day has all but faded away, and I curse myself for the many breaks I took. I hear the guards readying their weapons as I approach; I don't try to fly over the walls. I know they have many crossbows and will not be able to recognise me from that height. Landing at the gate, I am rushed by several guards, including the captain.

Her voice bounces around the empty hall. "I am Shenario, Captain of the Queen's guard, are you our champion?"

My mind stops. All is well? The guards don't seem worried, surely if the Queen was missing they would all know by now. Maybe I made it back in time.

Deciding not to waste time, I soldier on. "There is no time for this. Kadance is here and he intends to kidnap or kill the Queen."

The captain huffs a laugh at me. "If the Queen were in danger I would know, I am captain of her guard."

"There is no time for such foolishness, we must check on the Queen immediately!" I move to push past Shenario but she is a wall of solid muscle.

She eyes me. I know she knows who I am even if she does not believe the Queen is in immediate danger. "Fine, we will see to the Queen, but you will follow in a calm manner. We don't need you upsetting the whole castle."

Saying nothing more, I wait for her to move. When we are finally on our way, I lead the charge with Shenario keeping in pace with me. When we do finally reach the Queen's rooms, I am pushed back as she knocks and calls out, "Your Majesty, are you well?" She waits a moment, but when nothing can be heard she turns to the others.

"The Queen may not be in her chambers. You there." Pointing to one of the three guards who came with us she says, "Go and find out if any of the maids know where she is."

With a quick 'yes ma'am' they are off at a brisk jog.

She pushes the door open, still calling out to the Queen as she goes. But her words stop the minute the door reveals the state of the space.

The entire room has been torn to shreds and the furniture destroyed, shards of glass and feathers litter the floor.

"Quickly, check Velasilio's chambers, they may have sought refuge there." Turning, I head towards the familiar chambers, praying that they will be there waiting.

Without knocking, I push both doors wide open, all pleasantries and protocols are finished with. It is the mirror image of the Queen's chambers and they are not here; both rooms are cold, eerie and silent. Only the silence is interrupted by a faint cry. Doing my best to follow the sound, it leads out of the chambers.

After a few steps, the crying grows louder. Looking down the hall, I see a tapestry that hangs on the wall between the two chambers and it seems to be shaking ever so slightly. Shifting forward, I reach out and pull the tapestry from the wall to find a space no larger than a small closet and, inside, sits a weeping maid.

"Shh, you are safe." Crouching down, I place my hand on her shoulder.

Her gaze finds mine. Her face is blotchy, her cheeks are wet. She has been crying for some time.

Trying to hold in a sob, she asks, "Is he gone?"

My hand drops and there is a ringing in my ears. Fear takes hold as the truth hits me: he is already here.

CHAPTER 73

FIND THE QUEEN

Arekin

DAY FIVE, TRIAL FOUR

The young maid will be in shock for some time but she did tell us where the Queen and Velasilio are: the library. Weapons are being taken out and I have my dagger in hand as we round the corner to the library halls. Just as we turn, we all stop, for laying on the floor are three guards, all seemingly dead. Stepping forward, I feel for their pulses.

The young man who seems to have his throat slit is cold to my touch, his eyes are open in a vacant stare, his lips blue. Looking at Shenario, I shake my head. Moving to the next, an older male, he makes a faint groan as I place my hand to his blood-soaked neck.

"He is alive. Quickly, get him to a healer!" Shenario calls out and one of the guards steps forward, lifting him and heading in the opposite direction.

Next I see, just further up, a female guard sitting against the wall, her hands held around the blade in her gut, but she is alive; her eyes meet mine as she opens her mouth in silent plea for help. Moving to her next, I try to calm her.

"It will be okay, you are going to be okay." Looking at her wound, she bats my hands away.

Her voice is croaky as she demands. "Don't worry about us, go to the Queen, she needs help!"

Looking up, I see the large doors ahead still closed, meaning he could be inside. There is one other body laying just outside the doors, a young male. Shaking my head, I go to push the door open. Shenario stops me, placing her hand over mine.

Turning to the two guards left with us, she states, "We move inside in formation, do you understand?"

"Yes ma,am!" Bringing their weapons up, they prepare for the attack.

"Arekin, we push on three." I want to argue. I want to rush in, but I know that is not what is best so I nod, placing my left hand on the door.

"One, two, three." We move at the same time, swinging the two doors in.

We enter quickly and the door shuts behind us. We scan the area but it is silent and there is no sign of any fae here. I look to the left and see a large desk with many books, parchments and ink pots on it, then I notice the tea cups on their sides and the contents spilled.

My voice is a whisper as I speak. "That's not right."

Taking a few steps toward the table I can see it: resting on the floor just behind the table is a pair of dainty feet. It can't be.

Unknown

NIGHT ONE OF MY ABDUCTION

My head aches and my limbs feel heavy. Opening my eyes, only darkness greets me. I am grateful as the room is warm and silent, allowing my fuzzy mind time to calm. All I remember is having tea and a voice but then nothing. What happened? Who brought me to bed? I try to sit up but I am unable to; rotating my wrists I feel soft ropes binding them as one. Using my bound hands, I push against the soft mattress and manage to roll to the side. Lowering my feet to the floor, something is different. My feet are not immediately cold. The ground is wood, not stone.

My voice is croaky as I whisper to myself, "Where am I?"

My eyes begin to adjust to the darkness, crackling draws my attention to the low glow of the fireplace in the corner. Feeling beneath me, I notice that the sheets are silken and much finer than anything we have at the castle. Sitting in silence, I try to listen for a sign that I am not alone. An odd tingling breaks out across my body, from my head to my toes: I feel eyes on me.

"Who is there? Why am I here?" The only answer is a low, gruff laugh that sends shivers over my skin, causing it to break out into goosebumps. Only one male has that effect on me.

I strain my eyes, trying to make out even the slightest movement. It is then that I see a shadow move.

My voice but a whisper. "Kadance, where am I?"

The floorboards creak under his heavy step as he nears me. As the fire illuminates him, I see that he is dripping wet and only has a towel hung low on his hips. I cannot stop my eyes from roaming the expanse of his naked chest, the broad shoulders and that delicious V that leads down. My thoughts are cut off as he leans in, placing an arm on either side of me, and the mattress dips under his weight. His lips brush the shell of my ear. I do my best to contain a moan that tries to slip free.

His scent surrounds me. Smokey yet sweet.

My thighs tremble at his nearness, for all the wrong reasons.

His voice is low and sensual as he whispers, "Where you were always meant to be."

TO BE CONTINUED...

ACKNOWLEDGMENTS

Thank you to everyone who has been supporting me and giving me the confidence to write this book! I hope you enjoy reading as much as I loved writing it.

Special thanks to my fiance Liam, to all the late nights helping me find the perfect words.

Thank you to my alpha readers Sam, Eilis, Maddy & Emma. You all helped make me a better writer.

To Simmone for being my sounding board, listening to me ramble and helping me to kick Bob's ass!

Thank you to my editor Amanda at A Dove Editing, you have helped me achieve my dream.

And there are so many others who have helped me and I just am so grateful to have so many people around me who are just amazing.

Book two
Coming soon!

ABOUT THE AUTHOR

S.Anne is a new Aussie author.

When younger, S.Anne was not a big reader, but at 27 she had FOMO when her friends were talking books, so she picked one up and, well, here we are now.

After having many people telling her that she reads enough books, so why not write her own? She finally decided what the hell.

A long drive, and a mate on the phone later, and The Queen's tournament was born.

More about S.Anne:

She loves riding her motorcycle with her fiance, sunny days at the beach, and board game nights with friends.